A New Lease On Freedom

Chris Oswald

NEWMORE PUBLISHING

First edition published in 2019 by Newmore Publishing.

ISBN 978-1-9160719-2-6

Cover design by Book Beaver.

Book design and layout by Heddon Publishing.

Chris Oswald has lived in America, Scotland and England and is now living in Dorset with his wife, Suzanne, and six children. For many years he was in international business but now has a little more time to follow his love of writing. His books have been described as dystopian but they are more about individual choice, human frailty and how our history influences the decisions we make, also about how quickly things can go so wrong.

Gerry Thwaites

1954 - 2019

For whom life held no boundaries

A New Lease On Freedom

Chapter 1

1680

Thomas replaced the board carefully, put a straw bale in front of it, then clutched two great handfuls of loose straw and masked their footsteps, walking backwards and sprinkling the straw in front of him.

It would not do for Matthew to find their place.

"We'll be late," Elizabeth said, turning Grace around and straightening her severe bonnet, which sat like a sign of purity on her pretty, round face.

"I know a shortcut," Thomas replied.

But the shortcut took them over a stream, and the rain had been heavy. It did not matter for Thomas; his clothes were drab and dark, ideal for concealing mud. His two sisters, however, wore long white matching pinafores over their grey dresses and could not hide where they had been.

And the ribbons that held Grace's bonnet in place had come undone again, as if rebelling against Elizabeth's ministrations in the barn. Thomas noticed several curls of strawberry blonde hair escaping and felt like he should do something in support; some suitable act of defiance.

Instead, he moved down the side aisle under Elizabeth's lead and squeezed into the front row.

He always had to apply his rebellion, whereas with his younger sister it was who she was.

And he loved her all the more for it.

The pastor was bent awkwardly in prayer, his red face straining with concentration. He was with his God, shaking slightly, like the old machinery in Mr Hunt's watermill. But Matthew noticed their late arrival and marked it grimly in his mind.

That meant their father would hear about it after all. Soon he would straighten that contorted body and turn, re-entering their world with new, fresh glares of anger.

Outside, the wind tugged against the cobbles and stones of men and seemed to laugh in its freedom. The wind was made by God; Thomas knew that, but it went where it would. It had become free with time and bent to no god, unlike the humans packing the pews indoors.

If I were the wind, thought Thomas, *I would blow Grace's bonnet clear off her head and send it dancing down the street, never to be seen again.*

If I were the wind.

Luke Davenport was a large man, tall and gaunt. Thomas' wind would find nothing to get hold of with Pastor Davenport, save the round tummy that sat on him like a growth. He preached vehemently against spirits, or alcohol of any kind. He never danced, nor sang; not even telling jokes or stories during the long evenings by the fire, other than the stories held in the Bible. His sole source of release appeared to be his lectern. His life revolved around it, such that there seemed to Thomas to be an invisible chain attaching his father to the lectern in the little place of worship where he spent his days. Thomas imagined breaking that chain, casting the Good Ship Davenport adrift on the open seas to wash up where it would. He envisaged the whole church as an ark, drifting on the high waters, saving the enlightened for when the floods subsided.

But he would strike out on his own. Any piece of furniture or ragged rigging pushed overboard to cling to, it did not matter. He would swim for his freedom.

Thomas imagined at first his father had a round tummy on his narrow frame because he ate each meal as if it was the last the Lord would send his way.

He went on a perpetual triangle between the dining table, his study with the closed door, and the lectern.

But that was before Thomas knew the truth which settled gradually on the Davenport household like dust on unpolished furniture.

Nobody could say Thomas' father's sermons were dull; far from it. They were enthralling. He became a god as he thundered out divine law from the pulpit. His voice was his great aid. It rose between calm and frenzy; often violent, snappy changes that could not be predicted.

He seemed like a god to Thomas for another reason; many people came to his little church, even if they did not always follow his word.

Which is the way of humans the world over.

But today Pastor Davenport had a special announcement; one he hoped would extend his influence amongst the mercantile class of Sturminster Newton. It was a modest town, surrounded by rich estates producing beef, mutton and milk in abundance. He had a good collection of farmers in his congregation. Some were quite well off, as tenants of large holdings.

But he really wanted inroads into the middle class. And this is where Elizabeth would help him. Her good looks had attracted the attention of Simon Taylor, a middle-aged lawyer who had been married before but whose wife had died in a bout of plague that swept over Dorset in 1664. She had left behind an infant child that Simon had no interest in. She was plain and dull and could not help him advance his business interests.

Those interests had grown over the intervening period, but not as much as Simon had hoped. He had a stake in the Bull Tavern down by the river; a similar holding in Dawsons, the agricultural broker; and loans to various farmers, secured against their harvests. But he also had considerable debts himself.

He did not dwell on them for they depressed him.

But now everything was set to change for the better.

Simon had started going to Pastor Davenport's little church when he first took note of the young Elizabeth. She had turned seventeen, as he learned, on September 19th, the week before. It happened to be his own birthday, although he was now forty-four. It was a sign from God that he and Elizabeth shared a birthday; he was sure of it.

There had been no courtship as such, mainly because Elizabeth disliked him immediately.

"His eyes bulge like a frog, Father," she said when he asked innocently what she thought of him.

"He is repulsive. I could never imagine…" she cried when the wedding plans were first aired. "And his daughter is almost as old as me!"

Amelia Taylor was just five months younger than Elizabeth. They had gone to school together and were in the same class. Never friends, they had lost touch when they left at the age of fourteen.

And it is hard to lose touch in a small town where everybody knows everybody.

"People of God, I bring you news of an alliance sprung from our little congregation," Pastor Davenport said, looking down at them, employing his best voice for the occasion. "It gives me great delight to announce the betrothal of Simon Taylor Esq., lawyer and good neighbour that he is, with my dearest daughter, Elizabeth. The marriage will take place in the sight of God, our Lord and Benefactor, who gives and takes all things at his will, on the fourth Saturday from today. God bless these children in God and may they ever walk in the footsteps of our Saviour. I know my dear wife, Rebecca, God rest her soul, will be looking down in joy at this happy scene."

Simon Taylor nodded and smiled as people whispered their congratulations across the small church. He had made a good match with Elizabeth. She would adorn his arm beautifully at functions in and around Sturminster Newton. He could, perhaps, have married higher but was unlikely to find something as pretty.

It was, without doubt, a step up for the pastor's family. What would his father say if he was alive now, instead of lying in his pauper's grave? With some satisfaction, he recalled the drunkard telling him he would never amount to anything in this world. *I've beaten you hollow in this world, Father, and, in all likelihood, will do so in the next.*

"Father! Father!" It was Matthew, talking in his ear again, springing him out of the triumph gained over his own father.

Matthew was spluttering that his other three children had been late to church. He gave his suspicions with fervour; his voice alternating between whisper and squeal. It seemed they had been playing in the stream that wound through the woods beyond the churchyard. He would have to do something about it.

"Elizabeth too, you say?"

"Yes sir," Matthew replied. "Did you not notice her apron? It was covered in mud from the stream. It's not the first time I've noticed them like this. Coming to church like vagabonds, it's a disgrace. I meant also, Father, to discuss with you my proposals for their education if you have a minute after lunch, perhaps?"

Thomas, Elizabeth and Grace had no lunch that day. Instead, they sat at the kitchen table and had to write out the ten commandments ten times each, in their best handwriting. Thomas itched to be free to roam the fields and woods he and Grace loved. It was warm for late September but had rained throughout the harvest period, flattening the wheat before the scythes could get to it. Mr Hunt had said on every occasion he could that it was going to be a long and hard winter. Mrs Hunt could see the signs in the hedgerows and she had never been wrong in forty years of predictions, so she said.

They were released when the afternoon was close to its end, with beautiful sun and shadow making blocks of light and shade across the familiar streets and fields beyond. Elizabeth went straight to see her friend two doors down, seeking the solace that only a friend could give. The prospect of marriage to Mr Taylor took all joy out of her world. And that depression spilled over to her siblings. Even Grace, in her thirteenth year, could feel the weight upon Elizabeth. Would the same fate await her in a handful of years?

Elizabeth was the perfect sister in so many ways. One of those was the ability to look beyond her own concerns and feel for others around her, especially with her younger brother and sister. She took charge of the situation again, despite the weight upon her, and gave a fragile smile.

"I think you just have time," she said, looking at the

grandfather clock that stood ostentatiously in the hall. "Go out the back way, lest Matthew sees you."

Grace looked at Thomas. Thomas confirmed with the slightest nod. If they ran all the way, they could fit in a short visit to Lady Merriman.

She was not a real lady; they were quite certain of that. But she claimed to be. She lived with no husband but two maids who were sisters, in a big square house on a parcel of land that seemed to the youngsters to contain a hundred different habitats all rolled into one. It created a magical place for a twelve- and thirteen-year- old to escape the drudgery of their lives; to escape the ever-watchful and whispering Matthew, the oldest child in the Davenport family.

Lady Merriman was the strangest thing Thomas and Grace had encountered in their short and plain lives. Her voice was quiet and refined; long sentences seemed to dissipate into the air as she wound through them, often seeming to forget the subject matter she had started on. She frowned a lot, as if trying to remember something and not sure whether it was good or bad; the action of frowning seemed the working of a machine to bring her memories into focus. But as Elizabeth pointed out to the youngsters when they took her there one day in June, shortly after they had first met when trespassing on her land, she smiled with her eyes. Those eyes were large and brown, and glossy with moisture, complementing her soft skin. It was like there was something else inside that delicate body; stories of past adventures, Thomas was sure.

"She's what you call an enigma," Elizabeth had advised them. "You can't work her out. She seems one thing but is another. It makes people uneasy as they don't know what they are dealing with."

Matthew had overhead that early summer conversation. He seemed always to be in earshot. When told to whom Elizabeth was referring, he snorted, as he often did when starting to speak, then said, "Oh, the witch of Bagber. You should have nothing to do with that ungodly creature, lest you be tainted by the devil."

It had led, when reported to their father, to a ban on future visits, which only made them more determined to become friends with this strange and beautiful lady.

The only enigma that bothered Thomas and Grace was why Lady Merriman seemed so confused about her past. It seemed like clarity broke in every so often but mostly she was vague, and full of gentle conflicts. As they sat and ate buns and sweetmeats with her, they tried to question her but got a different answer every time. She often said she had grown up in this house but sometimes contradicted this version with a categoric statement that she had arrived with her two maids just months before.

Often, she would forget her thirty-odd years in this world and play catch and hide and seek with them outside, throwing back her hat and giggling like a young girl as she was caught time and time again. Then they would collapse in a heap on the lawn and laugh away the afternoon until it was time to leave for home.

They splashed down over the ford in the Stour, powered by the September sun pulling them forwards like a magnet. They stopped momentarily at the mill, grabbed a bun each from Mrs Hunt, and laughed when their stitches prevented them running any further. They walked a quarter-mile, then returned to a run. They should have half an hour with the old lady before they had to return for Evensong.

They reached the edge of Lady Merriman's property, marked by crossing the Divelish; a tributary of the Stour. They vaulted over the wall and stopped, gasping for breath. Should they go to the house or directly to the summer garden, where they thought their friend would be? They chose the summer garden, skirting past the old greenhouses, tumbled beyond belief, broken panes and pots littering the hard-packed earthen paths. Grace stumbled and flew forward but righted herself before falling, grabbing the corner post of a greenhouse and swinging her body round in a great sweep. As she swung, her face was a picture of joy and freedom from care. Elizabeth's fate seemed centuries away at that moment.

The summer garden was empty, other than a couple of

magpies pecking at the entrails of a dead rabbit; too busy to pay any heed to Grace and Thomas as the children charged through, calling for Lady Merriman.

They slowed down at the edge of the lawn that surrounded three sides of the house. Grace retied her apron and straightened her bonnet. Thomas, seeing this, tried to push his hair into place below his cap. They were both breathless; joyous abandon bubbling just below skin level.

"Let's... try... the... house," Thomas spluttered, bending over at the waist then straightening up to fight the cramps which were creeping in.

They knew something was wrong as they approached the square house. Long before they saw the guard at the front door they felt a coldness descend, like the devil come to visit.

"You're trespassing," he said, bringing his pike into a suitably aggressive position. "Get off with you before I collar you both."

"Where's Lady Merriman?" Grace asked.

"Who?"

"Lady Merriman, the owner of this house. Where is she, my man?"

It was intended to show authority, but the use of 'my man' was a serious mistake by Thomas. Immediately the pike lowered and wavered close to Thomas' chest.

"There's nobody I know by that name," the guard replied gruffly. "I'm here on the orders of Taylor and Johnson, who are acting for their client. Now, hop it before I ruin your day." The pike came even closer, jerked up within an inch of Thomas' chin.

He moved backwards slowly, eyes fixed on the point of the pike. He felt something tug at his side, resisted, then realised it was Grace's hand looking for his.

Together, hand in hand, they stepped backwards across the lawn. Grace turned first, Thomas watching the pikeman a moment longer; trying to stare him down, but the distance was too great. Then they were running back for the safety of the woods. They did not stop until they reached the ford.

Matthew saw them walking up the hill to their home.

"Father wants you in his study," he said smugly, as soon as they were inside the gate. His voice sounded an ounce too shrill, as if he had rehearsed the half-dozen words under his breath to get them perfect; too perfect. "You have been running on the Sabbath," he continued, now adlibbing. "I strongly suggest you tidy yourselves up before seeing Father."

Thomas brushed his hair while Grace changed her apron. Matthew watched grimly before leading them to the study.

"I think we know our way, brother," Thomas made an effort to rid themselves of his presence.

"I am sure you do, brother. Nevertheless, I undertook to Father to deliver you to him and I intend to keep my commitment." He knocked on the door. "Sir, I have Thomas and Grace to see you."

"Children," the pastor started, even more gravely than usual, "I have some exciting news for you. Matthew and I have managed to secure for both of you places at excellent educational establishments, starting tomorrow."

He dealt with Grace first. She was to go all the way to Salisbury to the residence of a distant cousin, Miss White, to learn practical household matters; sewing and such forth, plus a little French and some acquaintance with the classics.

"Thus, to make you a useful wife to some godly person one day. Now," he turned to Thomas, "as befits a second son of a rising family, you must learn a profession to make your own way in the world. A good grounding in Greek, Latin and the divinities, plus a smattering of law and commerce, should set you in good stead. At considerable expense, all coming out of Matthew's inheritance, I might add, I have secured a place for you at Westfields in Dorchester. What say you to that, my son?"

"Sir, do I have to go? I would much prefer to stay here." Westfields' reputation was known to Thomas.

"Silence, ungrateful child. Be thankful that Father and I have given your education so much thought." Matthew moved to centre stage, seemed for a moment as if he might strike his younger brother; a foretaste of Westfields, perhaps?

The moment passed. Father dismissed them. After Evensong they were to pack and retire early to bed. They both had busy days tomorrow.

After Evensong, while the youngsters slept and dreamed of their new lives ahead, Pastor Davenport and Matthew would lock themselves in the study and trace again their achievements that day. A good marriage for Elizabeth and a sound education for the other two.

After the initial congratulations to each other, he knew that he would take the worn key from his pocket and open the cabinet that dominated the room with its mahogany presence.

He would have a tipple to celebrate; then, no doubt, another, before rinsing the glass with water from the jug on his desk and replacing it in the cabinet.

The sins of the father. He opened his bible at Exodus and recapped the sermon he intended to give in a few minutes.

Chapter 2

1685

Pastor Luke Davenport opened the letter with the shiny silver knife that Simon Taylor had given him for his sixtieth birthday, the previous year. It took several attempts to hold the knife steady enough to break the seal.

It was a report from Westfields.

28th January, in the year of Our Lord, 1685.

Dear Sir and Friend,

It gives me no satisfaction or sense of achievement to write to you once again with regard to young Thomas. He has been over four years in my care at Westfields now. I have many successes to my name, but Thomas stands out as, undoubtedly, my greatest failure. To say he has taken nothing from his stay with us would be but a small exaggeration. He has grown firm and strong and excelled at games in the afternoons. Yet he has learned little or nothing, seeming to live apart from us in a world entirely in his head.

The pastor put down the letter pensively. Then he opened his top drawer and pulled out another letter, recently received from Salisbury.

My Dear Cousin Davenport,

It grieves me sorely to write to say that there is little to be done with your daughter you entrusted into my care. She has steadfastly refused to apply herself to our domestic teachings and shown no interest in household management. The only area we can elicit any interest is in needlework, in which she has much natural skill, but prefers mending to working on decorative projects. I employed her for a while on errands to fetch ribbon or cloth from the shops in Salisbury, but even

11

that was beyond her. She would go out on her task with a broad smile and that would be the last we would see of her. Sometimes she would turn up much later, often with a torn dress or muddy apron. Twice we have had to stop work ourselves and arrange searches across the neighbourhood. We have been obliged to increase the level of discipline, also to reduce her diet and cut out all red meat in favour of gruel, fish and bread. Yet it has been to no avail, other than to magnify her temper tantrums, which can be ferocious.

Sir, I hate to bring this conclusion to your attention, but feel on my honour to report that there is nothing else we can do for your daughter and I do not want to risk my other young ladies being exposed to her behaviour. I feel, therefore, that I must reluctantly ask you to find alternative arrangements for Grace Davenport.

The letter had a few words about the harsh winter in Salisbury then ended with the polite endearments of one distant cousin to another.

The pastor rose from his chair, checked the door was locked and reached for the key to his cabinet, clasping it with shaking fingers. He opened a new bottle of brandy, pouring out half a tumbler. It had been a secret gift from Matthew.

He still had to finish the letter from Westfields.

It concluded in remarkably similar manner. Thomas was a bad influence on the other diligent students and he must – respectfully – ask that Thomas be placed elsewhere. Perhaps he could have a tutor at home to cram him for a spell with a view to reading law at Oxford.

The pastor could not afford Oxford. He had to protect Matthew's inheritance. He would talk with Matthew later, see what could be done.

He poured the other half into his tumbler and sat back, wondering what he had done to deserve such problem children. Well, at least the older pair had worked out well.

The back of Simon Taylor's right hand hurt incessantly and increased his rage. Ever practical and creative, he had devised a leather strap he could hold in the grip of his hand. It was strong enough, yet flexible. It was the prefect substitute.

He had learned in the early months of his marriage to Elizabeth that a single slap across the face had limited value. She was spirited and recovered quickly. She had to be ground down with repeated slaps. First the palm went across her left cheek, then the back against her right. Experimenting, he had discovered that six repetitions of the double swing was the most economical number to reduce her spirit from rebellion to subservience.

But because his wife was responsible for the pain in the back of his hand, sometimes he doubled the dose. Then again, with his new leather, an unlimited number could be applied.

He practised also on the two maids he had inherited with the house. The sullenness of the sisters as they went about their work made his temper into a frenzy. He would make two more straps; one for each floor of his new home.

He reflected on such matters as one of the two maids; Sarah or Kitty, laid out his clothes. He never could be sure which one was which. It did not much matter.

It had been a good time since the wedding four years earlier. First the move to this fine house in its own block of land, yet only twenty minutes' ride to his offices in town. Then the lucrative work that had started at the same time; almost like a wedding present from God. He had quadrupled his income over four years. He hoped and planned to do the same again over the next four.

And then there were three children; first twin boys and then a girl, who resembled her Aunt Grace. Not that Simon had anything to do with them but he was glad that it proved his virility amongst those he rubbed shoulders with. For too long he had been a widower, suggesting to people that he had no interest. Well, he had solved that problem by marrying one of the prettier girls in town.

His mind moved on to his personal balance sheet. He had more loans owed to him than ever before, including a reasonable packet out to his father-in-law. He had taken an interest in the fishmonger and the Red Lion pub. In both cases, he had drummed up legal fees they were unable to pay and they were therefore happy to accept his suggestion to convert the debt to a share in the business.

The source of this wealth was a mystery to him. He received instructions from time to time from an agent who visited the area, ostensibly on business, but really in the employ of the man who paid the bills.

And what payment he made! It was always more than Simon would dare charge and always half up front. Either half would have been easily sufficient for the task.

What is more, the tasks were highly enjoyable ones and well within his capability. He had been told to build up substantial loans to the junior branches of the Earl of Sherborne's family. Every time he arranged a new loan, he received two percent in commission; double if it was a member of the Sherborne family. This had developed into a lucrative sideline, for he invented borrowers and collected the commission anyway. At first, he had just peppered the real loan book with invented names. But he had grown bolder more recently so that three of the last five loans were bogus.

Yet the commission still came through on time; every quarter. Two days after he reported them, a different stranger delivered cash to his home.

Cash to home had the added advantage that he did not have to declare the payments to his elderly partner. Joshua Johnson.

In fact, he was wondering why he needed a partner at all.

Grace arrived home first and with her the news of King Charles' apoplectic fit three days earlier. Rumour was it was severe and the playboy king was facing his maker.

"It will be good riddance," said Matthew when Grace related the news. "He was ever the amoral prince and never serious about anything."

"Except his pleasure. He took that seriously," Simon added, as they took their places at the dinner table, invited to welcome back Grace.

Elizabeth was amazed at the change in Grace. She had come back occasionally over the last four years; never at the same time as Thomas, Elizabeth noted, and her brother's visits were even less frequent. Grace was now seventeen and seemed able

14

to mix beauty and elegance with a continuing sense of the impish. It was a delightful combination.

"You've become a young lady," Elizabeth whispered as they sat at the table. Grace was dressed as Elizabeth would never dress. Instead of the grey and white of their childhood, she wore a blue dress, as bright and hard as the January sky overhead. It rustled every time she moved, making Simon take note of her. Elizabeth, in the intervening years, had graduated from grey to brown; buttoned to the neck with a stiff white collar inked with tiny pink wallflowers. She disapproved of Grace's bright blue but would guide her back slowly now she was back with them.

"I can still beat you in a race to the stream and back," Grace replied. "Anyway, you've grown plump as a chicken while I've been away."

"I have not!" Elizabeth managed to pull the strands of Grace's hair that stood outside the pile on her head. In return, she got a sideways kick in the shins.

It was like old times, except that it was not.

"Father, you don't look well at all. Is there something wrong?" Grace noticed immediately his florid skin and sunken eyes.

"Nothing, my child, except concern for the future of both you and your brother Thomas."

This was the lead-in Matthew had needed. The rest of their dinner was taken up by a diatribe from the pastor-in-waiting, condemnations ringing out like spilt wine at a party.

Only there was no wine at this party. Only brandy for one, and much later on.

Thomas came back six days later and, with him, news of the death of King Charles.

"He never recovered from the fit," Thomas had heard at the staging post in Dorchester, waiting for a coach to go north. "They gave him all sorts of vile treatments, leeches and such like, but to no avail. Do you know what, though?"

"What?" said Elizabeth and Grace in unison.

"Apparently, despite the pain, he was joking to the end,

actually apologising for taking four days to die!"

The three of them were in the barn, where their secret den had been. Thomas, now close to six feet tall at eighteen years old and as skinny as could be, pulled away a pile of rusting tools to check. It was still there but full of mice droppings. Thomas climbed in anyway and found it much smaller than he remembered.

"You've grown, silly," Elizabeth said. "Grace has, too. I'm the shortest now."

They sat on bales of straw, eating buns Elizabeth had brought with her.

"What will you two do now?" she asked, declining a bun, thinking they needed it more than she did.

"That's up to Father."

"He's not well at all," Thomas said. He had had his interview with his father directly on arriving; had been shocked by the deterioration. "So really it will be Matthew deciding."

"And my husband will have a say," Elizabeth added. "Those two are as thick as thieves."

"I wonder what they are thieving?" Grace said.

"No, I meant it as a figure of…"

"I know, Lizzie dear. I was joking." She patted her sister's leg affectionately.

But often there is truth in a joke; more so than in serious discourse.

"There is one thing I am going to do, whether approved by 'their majesties' or not," Thomas said into the silence that had descended.

"What's that?" Grace asked, anxious suddenly to wind back the clock; to be carefree, playing truant with the wind in her hair, running, always running.

"I'm going to find out what happened to Lady Merriman."

"Of course!" Grace replied. "She cannot just have disappeared. Lizzie, you must know something of her whereabouts. After all, you are living in her house!"

This was news to Thomas. There had been so little communication allowed from school.

"Simon won't talk about her, just says 'What do you want with that old witch?' when I ask. And the maids, Sarah and Kitty, have been forbidden on pain of a beating from mentioning her."

Silence was upon them again. It seemed to be intervening in their innocence, forcing thoughts that belonged to grown-ups, thoughts that took them away from where they wanted to be.

"Have you tried the gardener?" Grace suddenly asked, standing up excitedly, adding weight to her question.

"He died," Elizabeth answered. "He drowned shortly after we moved in. He left a widow and four children. They had to move away, back to her parents in Shaftesbury, I believe. At least it was somewhere like that."

"Well, we've got time to track the family down," Thomas said, not disheartened by the removal of the family to Shaftesbury, nine miles away. "I expect Father and Matthew will be dithering forever about what to do with us."

But Matthew and Simon were discussing the future of Grace and Thomas at that very moment, in the pastor's study. He was present, but Simon had poured a particularly large glass of his favourite brandy and placed it on an occasional table in the far corner of the room. Luke Davenport was sitting there now, snatching quick glugs when he thought his son and son-in-law were absorbed in their conversation.

Every so often, Matthew, as the dutiful son, would consult his father but often moved on before the pastor could put together his thoughts.

"It is easy with Grace. She must marry someone who can be firm with her." Simon imagined taming her with his leather strap. He heard the sharp crack as leather struck skin; saw the welling of fear in young eyes. He licked his lips, relishing the prospect, despite not being eligible, as a married man.

Then he brought himself sharply back to the study, saw the pastor staring gloomily at his almost empty brandy glass. He also, Simon surmised, had been dreaming. "I suggest a local person, maybe Jarvis the butcher." Jarvis owed him money, could be controlled easily.

"She can marry better than that," Luke spoke with his tongue thick and furry, slurring the words together like a chain.

The chain that would bind Grace, hands and feet, and deliver her to the butcher's shop, to be an ornament on the arm of the big tradesman.

Only this chain had a fatal weakness in the pride of the father. A gallon of pride, and a pint of love, saved the fate of the daughter.

"She can marry better than that," he repeated, eyes firm on his glass.

"It was just a suggestion." Simon stepped back from open confrontation. There was time enough for decisions; the balance of power in the Davenport family shifted daily towards Matthew, hence towards him. He could wait.

Elizabeth pondered something about her younger siblings; something quite substantially different to how she would approach matters.

Thomas and Grace wanted to go to Shaftesbury to seek out the drowned gardener's family. So did she. But there the similarity ended. They had left immediately, not caring whether they would be missed or not. Elizabeth would have waited, bided her time, planned her absence some weeks ahead, with careful explanations.

Grace and Thomas just left, walking with pockets stuffed with bread and cheese. There was no consideration for the consequences whatsoever.

In fact, as Elizabeth mused on the differences, they were already approaching Shaftesbury, having caught a lift with a carrier going all the way. They ate their bread and cheese on the back of the cart, legs swinging; together again after four years apart.

Three hours after leaving Sturminster Newton, just as Matthew was searching for them at home, Thomas knocked on the door of a tiny cottage directly off the street on St John's Hill.

They recognised the gardener's wife immediately, even as she closed the door on Thomas' right foot.

"Mrs Thurloe, please don't slam the door on us."

"I can't talk to you, please go." She sounded scared, renewing their determination to speak with her.

"We just have a few questions," Grace spoke as Thomas strengthened his foot-wedge in the doorway. "We won't take up much of your time. Please, just a moment or two."

The door opened wider. Thomas removed his foot, to let Grace through first. But it was a clever ruse, for as his foot retreated the door slammed shut in Grace's face. A stunned silence was broken by the sound of a key turning in the lock.

But Thomas was a match for this. He left Grace standing outside the front door, jumped a low wall and was around to the back in no time; just to hear the backdoor lock turn there as well. Mrs Thurloe had had the exact same thought.

They were defeated. They sat on a stone wall opposite, ate the remainder of their bread and cheese and drank water, scooping it in their hands from a stream that rushed down the hill beside the street. They watched two boys playing; building a dam across the stream.

Grace had an idea.

"Do you know the Thurloes?" she asked.

"Who wants to know?" came the cheeky reply.

"Thomas and Grace Davenport from Sturminster Newton."

"They live in that cottage." Both boys pointed to the Thurloe home across the narrow St John's Hill.

"I know that," Grace replied with an air of boredom. "Everyone knows that. I wanted real information. I thought perhaps you were spies. I see I was mistaken."

"No, honest, miss, we is spies for sure." Their eyes shone with excitement. This was better than dam-building! "What do you want to know?"

The information cost a penny. They tried not to laugh as the oldest boy put the coin between his teeth to check it was not fake. But the information was worth a shilling or more, in Thomas' opinion, so they got a bargain, even if Grace bit her tongue trying to keep the laughter in.

They had the short afternoon to get ready. The sun sent brittle rays across St John's Hill as they worked their way around to the back of the cottage. There was little warmth, but a brilliance of light that gave elongated shadows from the slant of the sun.

They chose a deep shadow by a clutch of trees. They could see the hen house just across the haphazard yard. The two spy-boys knew Alfred Thurloe well. They often walked to school with the Thurloe children and sometimes played truant with Alfred, although he was two or three years older than they were.

"Alfred will put the chickens to bed, won't he?" they had said, delighting to help Grace and Thomas in their clandestine plans. "He only does this every day afore it gets dark."

"You mark my words, Miss Davenport, he'll be out there 'fore dark. That's a certainty." Later, as they sat in the shadows waiting, Thomas had said the boys were very taken with Grace.

"Nonsense," she said. Thomas let it drop but could see why they would be.

The back door opened as the sun took on that strange translucent glow just before sunset. The wind was still slight but the temperature promised to drop, with a deadening cold working into their bones.

They remembered Alfred. They had played with him in the woods of Lady Merriman's house. It was over four years ago and he had grown; now approaching adolescence from a gangling height. He sang a repetitive tune as he gathered up a bucket of meal, chickens alert to his presence and squawking around his feet in a game of 'trip me if you can'.

But he was too nimble for the chickens, something Thomas noted in case he had to catch the boy and hold him down while Grace worked her magic on him.

There was no cause for concern, however. When they stepped out of the shadows Alfred said 'what ho', as if they had been playing in the woods only yesterday.

"Aren't you surprised to see us?" Grace asked, a little put out at his muted reaction.

"I knew you'd come one day." His accent seemed broader but the underlying voice was the same. "It was just a matter of time."

"Time for what?" Thomas asked, the initiative draining out of him and spilling into this confident youngster. They thought he was thirteen, or maybe still twelve. Thomas wished he could take back control but was too surprised by the boy's calm attitude.

He was even more surprised at Alfred's next words. "Why, to help me find my father's killer, of course."

Chapter 3

The Davenport household had a breakfast rule; it was one rule of many, but one of the best in Matthew's opinion, for it started the day on just the right note.

If you were not down in the dining room by 7am, you went without. At precisely 7.15, the maid entered the room and quietly but efficiently cleared the breakfast away. By 7.25, there was no trace of the meal.

Matthew liked the rule because it started the day on a serious note, setting a frame of discipline to the day.

And it ensured that Grace and Thomas were available early to be assigned duties.

Since their absence for the day in Shaftesbury the previous week, he had managed to keep the pair of truants completely occupied from morning to night. They had turned out cupboards, wiping years of cobwebs and dust with their dusters, sorting through trunks of accumulated articles as if preparing the household for the next world. They had gone into the tall attics, finding old crates left from the previous occupants, building bonfires to light when the incessant rain finally stopped.

Their mother's room had been tackled next. When she had died almost fifteen years earlier, their father had simply left their bedroom, moving to another room. He had never been back; nor had anyone else. The old bedroom was musty, of course, but it was like a semi-lit shrine to the mother they vaguely remembered as soft and warm. They loved her devotedly but illogically, given their flickering memories.

They had tried to talk to Matthew about her but he had shunned every conversation gruffly, pain standing out on his forehead like a full-sailed ship heading for the rocks.

Instead, Elizabeth had heard of the clear-out of their mother's things and had insisted on coming for two full days, staying again in the bedroom she used to share with Grace. She helped as they sorted out the accumulations of a life cut short by a late but vicious bout of the plague. It had fanned out from London and withered its path through Dorset in 1670. Elizabeth was seven-and-a-half years younger than Matthew but old enough to remember her namesake and mother well. Both Thomas and Grace had been toddlers when she died but Elizabeth had been seven and Matthew fifteen.

As they sorted she talked, weaving a magical vision of radiant light that was their mother; bringing warmth of personality to the cold room and lighting up the dark corners with her witty sayings that had teased the youngsters into better and more considerate behaviour.

"She was like a saint," she said frequently but each time it made Matthew, always present in the background, scowl. Saints were superstition; everyone knew that.

They finished the room on the third day, giving it a deep clean to prepare it for a new life. Then Simon claimed his wife back and Elizabeth left with promises to return soon.

They were cleaning the church one morning in late February. The rain that had seemed to fall with no end had frozen to snow for two days, then it had gone away; gone, they supposed, to torment other souls in other areas; bored suddenly of their little town on the hill with the river Stour winding through fields below. The snow had melted slightly under the unreliable February sun, then frozen again, leaving a carpet of slippery ice across streets and paths everywhere.

Matthew had reluctantly paid two pennies each to two itinerant workers to clear the paths around their house. He had wanted to get Thomas to do the heavy work, with Grace pushing the cart of hot coals. But Elizabeth had objected when Simon passed on the news during a visit to arrange a new loan. She had sent a stern message about it and Matthew had, instead, to part with four copper coins.

With the house clean and tidy, he had set his young siblings to work in the church. Matthew appeared frequently and irregularly to inspect their work. Nothing seemed to please him these days.

"You will be thirty next month," Thomas said during one of Matthew's scowling visits, trying to lighten the mood. "What will you do to celebrate?"

"How can you work with dedication to Our Lord, cleaning His house, when your head is full of idle nonsense?" Mention of his approaching thirtieth birthday reminded Matthew that he was still only an assistant pastor, aiding the father who increasingly drank his way through the day. And their finances were precarious, such that if it had not been for the generosity of Simon making loans to them, they would have been sunk a long time ago. He had tried to make economies but the truth was they had little income, just the donations from the congregation, which seemed to be shrinking now, perhaps as the fire in his father's sermons became quenched in brandy.

Against this diminished income was the cost of three servants, the rent on their town house, the brandy, and now three pounds a month to Simon. And on top of all this, he had to find a dowry for Grace, assuming he and Simon found a husband willing to take her on.

If he got the church shining like a new pin, perhaps the Lord would look down favourably on him and send him some relief. Perhaps a rich husband for Grace; someone who was generous with his money, just like Simon. Yes, they needed another Simon.

"You still have to polish the pews, children." Even he sensed his approach to them was wrong; far too condescending. But then he shrugged his shoulders and moved away; he could not waste time working out how to address these work-shies. He had far graver matters to take up his time.

The Lord was smiling on someone that morning, although it was not obvious at the time. Matthew turned out of the church door, intending to return home to go through lists of eligible husbands for Grace. His mind was on his woes as he stepped out of the tiny church and hit someone side-on, sending them straight into the street, sliding over the ice. There was a nasty cracking sound: ice breaking or bones?

"Have a care, sir!" the aristocratic voice said.

"I'm sorry, sir," Matthew replied, shaken back into the here and now. "Can I assist you?"

"Leave me alone, damn you. You will do me more harm, no doubt!" The sandy-haired young man shook off Matthew's approaches and stood up then crumpled back down in the street. "Damn it, man, I think you've broken my leg."

Now Grace and Thomas were outside the church, drawn by the loud voices. Grace knelt in the dirt and examined the young man's leg.

"It's not broken, sir, just sprained at the knee."

"What do you know? Are you a surgeon?"

"No sir, but I know something of these matters. Thomas and I have injured ourselves more times than we've had hot dinners, it's the truth!

The question was, what to do with the sprained-kneed young man? Thomas had the answer. He disappeared a moment, crying "Hold on!" as he left, reappearing with the hand cart they trundled down the street to carry all the brooms, mops and dusters for the church.

Five minutes later a red-faced aristocrat was being carried on a dust cart back to their home. Thomas and Grace chatted as if they did similar every day. Matthew followed at a distance; a stern look to hide his embarrassment.

Once in the kitchen, Grace proved an adept nurse, ordering the man to remove his britches for examination. There was a graze, deep red, on the right knee; threatening to spill blood at any moment. She cleaned it with warm water, then pressed a cold towel against it 'to reduce the swelling', she said.

"Who are you?" Thomas asked.

"Don't you know?" the man asked, appearing surprised.

But Matthew knew. He had recognised the heir to the Earldom of Sherborne while following the hand cart procession along the cobbled streets. *So much for the Lord watching over me.* He had injured the son of the most powerful man in the region.

"Lord Henry, may I introduce myself?" Matthew was determined to build bridges.

For the first time, Lord Henry looked closely at the man who had knocked him over. "You may, sir, provided you give your occupation." It was a barbed reply, for the Sherbornes were staunch Catholics. Lord Henry felt sure he had the measure of

Matthew's occupation. He was one of those Puritan preachers.

Matthew insisted on formal introductions, just as he had been taught years ago by his tutor.

"My name, sir, is Matthew Davenport and I am an assistant to my father, who is a preacher of the Presbyterian persuasion. I was coming out of our church when I most clumsily knocked in to you."

"So, I'm to be knocked down by a Puritan and then set right by one, too?" It came out a little harsher than he intended. "Pray introduce the others."

This gave Matthew a dilemma. He had been taught to give the name followed by one sentence that summarised the person. But what could he say about Thomas and Grace? They were lazy, undisciplined layabouts. He decided in an instant that God favours the bold.

"This is Thomas, my brother, who is lazy, shiftless and disobedient, and my sister is known as Grace. She is just come home from a period of instruction in Salisbury and now we hope to find some poor soul willing to marry her."

"Good God," laughed Lord Henry, forgetting his demeanour. "I never heard the like! The preacher has three children. One follows his very footsteps to the pinnacle of the pulpit. The other two are regular bad sorts, following wilfully a life of debauchery. Tell me, Mr Davenport, does your religion prevent you from a drop of the hard stuff? It is the least you could do after knocking me senseless."

Luke's best brandy was fetched by Matthew immediately, leaving Grace and Thomas alone with the young aristocrat.

"So, you are a lazy, shiftless pair of brats?" He started the conversation, standing to test his knee as he spoke. "I assume you have not quite so much of the Puritan zeal as your brother evidences?"

"We are Godly," Thomas replied hotly, "just not quite so." Take away the fervour from Matthew's religion and you had that of Thomas and Grace.

"There, you see, you agree with me. And you, Miss Davenport, are in search of a husband while the boy needs a useful occupation?"

"No!" they cried in unison. Both were infuriated; Grace at the suggestion that she was looking for a partner, Thomas at being described as a boy. Thomas voiced that indignation first.

"I am not a boy and when I decide what course I want in life I will damn well choose it!" He had never used the word 'damn' before, even in jest. But now it was necessary to add force to his words and put him on the same plane as Lord Henry.

But, far from showing astonishment, the young man gave a secret smile, like he had just proved something to himself.

Two brandies later, Lord Henry made to go. "I dare say I shall survive my day at Sturminster Newton," he said, "provided I do not drown when inspecting the river."

"Why the river?" Grace asked.

"We aim to build a bridge, wide enough for horse and cart. It will span both the river and the low part of the water meadow this side of the river."

"Who will pay for it?" Matthew asked, fearing a local household imposition.

"Why, a consortium led by me, of course. It will cost a farthing to cross with a cart, a ha'penny on fair days and holidays. Those on foot will be able to use it without payment."

"That is very fair," Matthew said, relieved that the town would not be involved. "We have several farmers who walk to church on Sundays and Wednesday evenings. It would be harsh to make them pay, but walkers will go free so that is good."

"Ah, but Puritans shall pay double and regardless of whether they ride, walk or hobble on their knees! Now, I must take leave. Thank you, Miss Davenport, for attending to the wounds imposed by your clumsy brother. And to you, boy, for your enterprising mode of transport back to the hospital."

He was gone, exaggerating his limp and with a peck on the cheek and the slightest of lingering looks for Grace. It was enough to make her blush and examine the stones on the kitchen floor.

As soon as Lord Henry was out of the door, Matthew

retreated to his father's study to return the brandy, muttering, "Impossible man and a Catholic, too!"

But Grace went to the window and watched him walk, very little limp now, down the garden path, whistling some tune as he went. She watched the space where he had passed for some time.

Then Thomas was tugging at his shoulder. "Sister," he whispered, "now is our chance."

"What do you mean?" She turned to him, a wonderful emotion retreating across her face, replaced with confusion.

"I mean to further our discovery. Matthew has forgotten to give us any other tasks today. We are at liberty to please ourselves!"

There was a need for both haste and quiet. Without communication, they grabbed some wrinkled apples from the store off the kitchen and a hunk of bread that the maid had left out. They poured and drank two cups of milk and left through the scullery by the side door, wanting to open their lungs and run but aware of the ice all around them.

Matthew did not think to look for them until much later. He had intended to work on a sermon for Sunday but was distracted by his father, who was asleep against the study wall, the expensive brandy bottle knocked over on the floor and almost empty. He helped the old man into bed and went back to the study. Instead of the sermon, he went through the household account book again, trying to work out where the money had gone.

He put his fingers through his thinning hair and sighed.

Chapter 4

They ran like the old days, down the hill, aiming for the ford in the river. The wind pushed Grace's bonnet back, sending the ribbons streaming out behind her, so she had to run in an awkward lope, one hand clasping the bonnet to keep it on her head.

She stopped suddenly.

"Look, it's Lord Henry," she gasped.

"So if it is? Let's go, I bet I can beat you to the mill even with a head start."

But Grace did not respond. Instead, she tidied her hair, smoothed her dress and retied her bonnet.

"Well, if it is not Nurse Davenport!" Lord Henry was upon them while she was still fumbling with the ribbons. "Out on a sudden mercy dash, I assume?"

"No, Lord Henry, we just thought we would take a look at the site for the bridge." She ignored Thomas tugging at her sleeve; would not look his way, for fear he would expose the lie she had just told.

"Better than that, my dear saviour, why don't I show you the plans? Mr Milligan is the architect and he has just brought them with him. Mr Milligan, these are my new friends, Thomas and Grace Davenport."

"I know of them, sir," Mr Milligan answered, pulling at his grey beard as if it helped him yank the words out of his tiny mouth. "Everybody knows the Davenports of High Hall Lane. I've never been to their church, being a good Anglican, but I hear tell of rousing sermons!"

"Your fame precedes you!" Lord Henry replied with a grin that spoke of extreme good nature. Thomas was immediately suspicious. He had seemed arrogant and demanding before, although, to be fair, with a sense of humour; why such jollity now?

Mr Milligan tugged his beard before spreading the plans across the back of a wagon. "First, a general picture of the finished bridge. You can just see the mill in the background."

He held the sketch up to the mill in the distance, so they could see how the bridge would look.

"Now, we plan seven low arches across a span from about there to there." He swung his arm to indicate the bridge position. "The central arches will be all stone while the outside arches, two on each side, will be wood construction dressed in stone."

"Why not build it all in stone?" Thomas asked.

"Good question, sir. It is principally a matter of weight. If you build entirely in stone there is greater weight, which means a greater chance of the bridge sinking into the ground. I've seen such constructions before and they make a sorry sight."

"I see. And the shape of the arches; why go for that particular shape? And why seven and not six or eight? What stone will you use? I saw a pleasing bridge on the way from Dorchester. It had little pillars above each arch formation. What do you plan for foundations and…"

"Goodness me, young man, what a lot of questions. Let me try to answer them one at a time."

Lord Henry and Grace were not required to participate in the discussion between Thomas and Mr Milligan. They listened for a few moments and then Lord Henry tapped Grace on the shoulder and led her out of earshot.

"It seems they will be a while with a common interest evident. Shall we walk along the bank of the river while your brother is so absorbed? Will you take my arm?"

They walked west, towards Bagber, under willows and chestnuts and oaks; all stripped bare for winter and looking stick-thin, like peasants at the end of the hardest season. The wind came from the east and pushed the two of them along at a pace, freezing them but for the heat from their bodies, which came out as puffs of white smoke in the frostiness around them.

"Take my coat," he said as a particularly sharp blade of wind cut into them, switching its line of attack to take them from the south. "You're shivering." In their rush, both Thomas and she had come away without coats, planning probably to run all the way to Elizabeth's house; running to stay warm.

"Thank you."

"Tell me why you came this way," he said, hoping it was because of him. But instead he heard about Elizabeth and the house that Simon had taken that used to belong to Lady Merriman.

"I did not grow up here," he said in thoughtful reply. "I don't know Lady Merriman."

"You would have liked her. She disappeared, you know. It was about the time Thomas and I were sent away to school. She was always there when we visited and then she was not and nobody knows where she has gone. I believe it caused a great stir but Thomas and I were both sent away at that time so we could not find out about her."

"Oh, you mean the witch of Bagber? I remember now. I heard of her five or so years back but never met her. It was quite a story when she went missing suddenly."

"She is not a witch!" Grace pulled her arm from his.

"Well, how should I know? That was always her name. She lived in that square house in the woods, less than a mile from here."

"That's where my sister lives now."

"As you said. Take my arm now, Miss Davenport. It is cold enough for a little cuddle, especially as I now have no coat!"

They walked a little further then turned around when the path led away from the river for a short spell, Grace declaring she should get back to Thomas.

"Your sister must be married?"

"Yes, she is Mrs Taylor now. They have three children."

"Mrs Simon Taylor?" Lord Henry stopped dead still.

"Yes, that's right. Do you know Mr Taylor?"

"I most certainly do. He heads a rival consortium to build the bridge. He wants to build entirely out of wood and charge double for each crossing; a farthing for those on foot, too. Why are you laughing?

"Because that sounds just like my brother-in-law!"

Grace had no need to worry about getting back to Thomas. He was totally absorbed with the architects, pointing from

31

imagined pillar to imagined arch, throwing arms in long sweeps across the vista, discussing mortar and stone sizes as if born to it.

"What's to do here?" Lord Henry asked, amusement stencilled across his face. Grace noticed for the first time how his right eyebrow rose with humour in the air; a signal to those who knew him. She found it quaint and kept looking to check whether a joke was being made.

She liked looking at him and noted he was often looking at her, too.

"Young Davenport has been helping us out," Mr Milligan replied. "He has some original ideas, that's for certain."

"I dislike to pull you away, brother, but if we are to get to Elizabeth's today we must leave now. We need to be back before it is too dark."

"Come tomorrow, Davenport, if you have a will. I might have an idea to put to you," Mr Milligan said, then looked at his employer for belated approval.

"Away you go, boy. Mr Milligan will expect you in the morning if you desire to spend a day with him." Thomas grinned his thanks, forgetting to take offence at being termed 'boy' again by Lord Henry, who looked at most a year older than him.

Then Thomas and Grace set off at a run; always running rather than walking.

"Lizzie dear," Grace said, "do you think it possible that Lady Merriman left something here; anything that might give us a clue as to what happened? All we have is Alfred Thurloe swearing his father was drowned in the river. And all he has to go on is that his father was an expert swimmer and swam in the river every day. There was a big cut on his head but the coroner decided that he fell on the shore and hit his head on a rock, then fell into the river unconscious and drowned."

"It's not much to go on," Thomas added, really thinking of the bridge design, then feeling guilty and switching back to the present. If they could find and help Lady Merriman it was their duty to do so.

"There is nothing but a trunk of table cloths and napkins," Elizabeth replied. "And I have emptied it numerous times, thinking just as you do."

"Can we see the trunk?" Thomas asked.

Elizabeth led them to the hallway upstairs, explaining that she did not use the contents of the trunk as they were old and musty.

All three examined the trunk from every angle. They emptied it, felt the lining and lid for secret papers. There were none. Thomas opened a pocket knife and slit the maroon lining in several places. There was nothing contained there. He checked the wooden planking, fiddling with the brass pins that studded the surface, hoping for a lever that would suddenly open a secret compartment.

There were no levers.

Then Thomas turned the trunk on end and examined the bottom; smooth wooden planks that offered no way in.

They heard the front door open downstairs; Simon was returning.

"Quick, he will be angry if he finds me looking in this trunk again." Thomas grabbed a leather handle to lower the trunk, while Elizabeth and Grace picked up piles of cloths and napkins ready to slam them back in.

But the handle came away in Thomas' hand. He was holding a leather tube, open at both ends. He stuffed it in his pocket. The trunk was swaying now on one end. It toppled forward and fell back on the floor with a crash.

"What's that?" Simon's heavy voice came up the wide staircase, followed by his footsteps; three steps at a time. They had little time for disguise.

"What's that?" Simon repeated.

"Nothing, dear. Thomas and Grace were just helping me get rid of this old trunk. I am fed up with it and thought it might be better for gardening tools or something like that. I thought the contents could go to the poor of the parish."

"How thoughtful of you, dear. Be sure that they know who has made the donation. Thomas, I will carry it down the stairs with you. Oh, the handle is broken and missing. You are right to get rid of it, dear. It is falling to pieces!"

"Don't mention the bridge," Grace just had time to whisper in Thomas' ear, remembering what Sir Henry had said about the rival plan devised and led by Simon Taylor.

"What did you say, Grace?" Simon asked, always alert for opportunity or, equally, for any subversion.

"I was just thinking that it was time for us to leave. It will take us an hour to walk back and we don't want Father worrying."

"Of course, of course. I will call Sarah and Kitty to take the trunk down and also the contents which we are donating." He was thinking it would be good for the maids to carry the donations to the church hall; suggesting they were wealthy enough to both give away fine, if old, linens, and employ several maids.

For once they started home at a walk, across the back lawns to the woods that bordered the river. They walked because as soon as they had the cover of the trees, Thomas pulled out the broken handle.

"I do believe it was made hollow deliberately," he started, peering under the half moon, light snatched between the heavy clouds that promised more snow. "See, there is a paper inside." He started to take it out, then rammed it firmly back into the handle and the handle into his pocket. "I don't want to lose it," he shouted into the wind. "We'll read it when we get back, after supper."

And then they ran; into the wind but driven to find out what was hidden in the handle of the trunk.

But first they had to deal with Matthew. He was waiting for them in the kitchen, taking a corner of the big table to be his office. He looked up from his bible the moment Thomas walked in, Grace following right behind.

'There you are," he stated the obvious. "Where have you been all day?"

"We didn't do anything we shouldn't have done," Grace said.

"We went to see Lizzie." Thomas was more accommodating.

"I needed you here."

"But you did not say, brother," Thomas replied. "But there is still a little of the day left. What would you have us do?"

"It was not a chore, Thomas. I wanted to speak to you both about your futures. But now I am commenced on the sermon for Sunday so we will speak tomorrow. I have already eaten so you may take some cold meat and bread to your bedrooms and I will say goodnight."

"Goodnight, Matthew." Thomas bowed and Grace gave a little, friendly curtsy. The cook presented them each with a tray and a small candle. They left the kitchen, closing the door quietly behind them.

"Matthew was odd, don't you think?"

"Yes," Grace replied, "for one, he was not angry; more meditative."

They went past Grace's bedroom, set between those of Matthew and their father. Instead, they went up the narrow staircase to the attic rooms. This floor was shared by Thomas and the three maids, plus the two storerooms they had spent the last few weeks sorting through. The four rooms that formed this floor were identical; two looked east and two to the west. Thomas had the west room at the back of the house. From the window of which, he claimed, he could see all the way to Bagber on a clear day. No one had ever challenged him on this but Grace had often tried and failed to spot the roofs of the manor house. The rooms were large, sufficient for three beds in the servants' quarters, with sloping ceilings and sloping floors so that everything seemed to be sliding down into the river at the bottom of the hill. Thomas had a narrow bed, a hard desk and chair and a tall chest for his clothes.

It was bare, uncomfortable; nothing soft like in Grace's room directly below. But it was their space and no one from the family ever came in.

They were ravenous so ate quickly, stuffing alternative bites of cold meat and bread into their mouths, both sets of eyes dancing with anticipation as they chewed.

Then they pushed the trays away to the end of the bed and Thomas pulled out the trunk handle. Inside the leather was a small scroll of paper, yellowed and torn.

"It's in Latin," Thomas said in disappointment.

"Give it to me then." Grace's Latin had always been better. Several minutes passed while she tried to make sense of it.

"What does it say?" Thomas could wait no longer.

"It's nothing," she replied, still reading and mumbling Latin words she struggled with.

"Nothing? It has to be something! Is it not ink on paper? Then it is something!"

"I meant it has no relevance to Lady Merriman. It is a treatise advocating religious toleration. It is scholarly, with lots of references to the bible and saints and things. And someone has written in tiny handwriting in the margins and between the words. I can't make out what they are saying because the writing is so small."

It was enormously disappointing. The trail had been so exciting, so full of promise, and now it was ended in a Latin jumble of scholarly words.

They sat together on the bed, light from the two candles competing with each other, sending shadows and shafts of light like forces of good and evil across their faces and bodies. All around it was very quiet; an owl hooted, probably in the barn where they had made their den as children. There was a clatter as a neighbour closed a window or door; perhaps a husband home from one of the taverns in town, slightly careless of the sleeping neighbourhood, but certainly not rabble-rousing drunk.

The cheap candles wore down, their appointed lifespan inching down the wax. Thomas thought that people and animals grow taller as they get older, yet candles grow shorter with age. Grace reached across and snuffed out her candle. Thomas understood her action; two candles were an unnecessary expense. He thought of Matthew's troubled face as he went through the account books. He was glad that was not his responsibility.

Suddenly, it came to him.

"Lady Merriman has small handwriting," he said into the semi-dark, just enough pale light to see growing understanding on his sister's face.

"She did," she said, leaning back across to light her candle again. "Let's look at the text once more."

They could not make much out of her writing. It was English, not Latin, but the letters were especially small to fit so many words into the spaces on the page.

"She seems to be in agreement with the argument. See, she has underlined the whole of the conclusion. She has written underneath the text, but the words are truly tiny and I can't make them out. Then she runs out of space altogether."

"It's a wonder she did not think to write on the back," Thomas replied. "There will be plenty of space there."

"Goodness, the back!" Grace turned over the document. There, in a different ink, were a few neat lines written in capital letters:

THEY ARE COMING FOR ME. THEY ARGUE I AM NOT COMPLIANT WITH THE LAW BUT THAT IS THE WAY OF MAN, TO FIND SOME HIGHER MOTIVE FOR THEIR BASE ACTIONS. THEY WANT MY RESIDENCE FOR THEMSELVES AND ARGUE I AM WRONG TO COME HERE AT ALL. I AM NOW A WITCH AND NEED TO BE TAKEN FROM HERE.

THEY ARE COMING FOR ME. THEIR AGENT HAS BEEN PROMISED MY HOUSE, I KNOW THIS BECAUSE I OVERHEARD THE CONCORD BEING MADE. HE WILL DELIVER ME TO THEM AND HIS REWARD WILL BE MY HOUSE. AND THEN I WILL NEVER SEE MY HOUSE AGAIN FOR I SHALL DISAPPEAR.

"This is her. I recognise the writing," Grace looked up at her brother sitting by her side. "Thomas, this is what happened to Lady Merriman!"

"Yes," replied Thomas, "and our brother-in-law is right in the middle of this."

"What about Lizzie?"

"She can't be. I am certain she does not know anything about this."

"I agree," Grace said. "But for now, we must not mention anything to her. Let it be our secret until we know more. The question is, what do we do about it?"

"Grace, we must sleep. It is late and we are both tired. Let's discuss it in the morning when, maybe, a course of action will be clear."

"Oh, you want me to go?"

He could see the hurt he was causing.

"Yes, dearest sister. We must both think on it and maybe tomorrow we will put together a plan."

Thomas had the start of an idea. But he desperately needed quiet to think it through. His brain was a muddle of kidnap, murder, bridges, trunks and secret papers. Yet somewhere in all that kaleidoscope were the foundations of a plan.

He would make it up to her in the morning.

Chapter 5

The morning required some delicate diplomacy, particularly as his plan was only half-formed. Thomas decided to meet it head-on.

"Matthew, I am looking forward to our discussion today. Can we start now?" Thomas knew it was not possible at that moment. Matthew would always want their father there, giving false credence to his authority.

"Thomas, we cannot discourse now. Father is with the apothecary and may be there a while. Also, Elizabeth and her husband are coming this afternoon and I know we will benefit from their advice. We will meet at three o'clock in Father's study. Grace, be good enough to attend also."

"A family conference, what a good idea." Thomas hoped he was not layering the cake too thickly. "Matthew, may Grace and I attend Mrs Moreton by the ford this morning? She has not been well since her husband died and did not come to church last Sunday. We thought we would drop in and see if she is well. It is not far and we can easily be back for three o'clock."

It was agreed, Matthew impressed at their thoughtfulness, suggesting they take two jars of honey or some other pleasant thing from the kitchen.

Thomas explained his plan to Grace as they ran down to the ford. It was full light but they caught Mrs Moreton giving breakfast to her five young children, the youngest of whom would never walk due to a twisted spine. Mrs Moreton was overwhelmed by the gifts they brought – not just honey, but also a ham, some oranges from afar, and two pots of jam.

"There is also a little coffee," Grace said, unpacking things from the hamper they had carried down between them. Mrs Moreton had never had coffee before so Grace showed her how it was made while Thomas fixed the front door that would not close fully, then cut half a mountain of wood for the fire.

"We'll leave the hamper with you and pick it up later on if you like," Grace said as they sipped coffee from chipped cups.

Somehow, thought Thomas, it tasted better from broken crockery.

"Not to worry, my dears. Stephen and John are strong enough to carry it when next we come to church."

Mission was accomplished, leaving them several hours at the site where the bridge was to be.

Both Mr Milligan and Lord Henry were there.

"Ah, I thought you might come today, Davenport," Mr Milligan greeted them, hand on beard again.

"Wild horses would not keep my brother away," laughed Grace but looking at Lord Henry.

He returned the look with equal interest.

"Can I have ten minutes with you both?" Thomas asked.

"If you have the time, Lord Henry, we could cross over the ford and examine the site from the other side. That would give Davenport time to address us, I would think."

Thomas started as soon as they were out of earshot of the other architects in the group.

"Sirs, you must know that our brother-in-law is Simon Taylor, your rival for this work."

"I learned this yesterday," said Lord Henry. Mr Milligan had not known.

"I propose a little subterfuge." On hearing this, Mr Milligan stiffened, while Lord Henry looked delighted. Intrigue appealed to his adventurous spirit, just as conservatism appealed to Mr Milligan.

"I'm not sure I can condone..." But when Mr Milligan heard the full plan, he could not refuse. He even made some valid points about risks and, surprisingly, could offer a fair amount of advice on how not to get caught.

But they bought his plan. Thomas sold it even though it was still in its final stages of construction.

Matthew had now had two uncontroversial and civilised conversations with Thomas and Grace in the last twenty-four hours. Not being in his nature to be hopeful, he fully expected the next one to go badly wrong.

And he had good cause to expect the worst. He had scoured

the town and surrounding area for two people. One to be a husband to Grace; the other to be an employer for Thomas. The Davenports had always been reasonably popular; respected by Anglicans and non-conformists alike. He, and his father before him, before the drink had taken over, had often hinted at alliances of such kinds in the past and received comparable hints back.

Had they not just four years ago achieved a union with the Taylor family through Simon's marriage to Elizabeth?

But that had been their father's doing, not his. Was he to fail at the first hurdle, unable to advance his family in the slightest? The prospect of such failure haunted him, stretching the lines on his face and thinning his fine hair almost daily.

He had witnessed many doors closed in his face. They were usually polite, but distant, but an increasing number just declined in perfunctory manner, not caring to be delicate in the slightest.

It had not occurred to him, until Simon had pointed it out, that the death of the King had changed their family circumstances completely.

"As non-conformists, Matthew, you are socially bankrupt under a Catholic-leaning monarch." The sudden death of the fun-loving Charles II had led to the more serious James II taking over. He was serious about religion and outwardly a Catholic. "I will, of course, help you find someone, utilising my skills and reputation in this town." But, in reality, Simon Taylor was distancing himself from the Davenports as quickly as he could, without risking the considerable capital he had in loans with them.

"Thank you, Simon. I would appreciate your help." But Matthew now realised why Simon did not come to their church anymore.

There should have been a little boost to his confidence through the realisation that the decline in numbers attending church was political and nothing to do with his taking over the services and sermons from his drink-befuddled father. But when you lower your gaze to the ground, you fail to see even the silver linings to the clouds above.

He had found one man willing still to talk to them about a family alliance. His greatest hope, wrapped in many fears and uncertainties, was that Jarvis, the butcher, would prove an answer to both his problems.

If Grace was given to Jarvis, he had said he would take on Thomas as an apprentice, provided Grace's dowry was sufficient to settle some debts he had accumulated.

Matthew had sold the prospect to Jarvis, now he had to sell it to his brother and sister. And this was to be done in front of his father and Simon Taylor. He knew where the battle lines would be drawn. He would have to convince everyone in the family, including their father; he just hoped he would have Simon's support in the matter.

Their father started first.

"I'll not have my daughter married to a butcher."

"Needs must, Luke." Simon had taken to using the pastor's first name as a deliberate mark of disrespect. He relished seeing the flinch each time he employed it.

"Grace deserves much better than a butcher's shop." Grace rallied on hearing her father's response, realising that he was on her side. She sent him a warm smile that pushed daggers into his heart; he had ignored his youngest two, concentrating on the first-born of each sex.

"If you want me to stump up the dowry, you need to accept this match," Simon argued. After he arranged the dowry-loan at a handsome profit, Simon would be able to brag in the taverns how he had settled the affairs of this declining family; arranging a match against all the odds. And the men would admire his business acumen, while the ladies would see a kindness done.

But Simon had not counted that there was steel in the Davenports. His five-year acquaintance with the family had not been their best period, but every wheel turns a full revolution.

Matthew heard the opening lines of this play, wondering how he could be the main actor. He needed to be confident and commanding, yet a role like that sat oddly in him. Something was making him hold back. There was something like spring sunshine in that musty, cold study at the end of winter. He had planned to make the best of a sorry situation, explaining the realities gently but firmly to his bewildered family. But suddenly, through the efforts of their sunken father, there was an ounce of hope hanging in the air.

Perhaps, just perhaps, there could be a better outcome than he had planned for.

"If I don't marry, I don't need a dowry," Grace spoke into the heavy winter, throwing in her own brand of spring. "Matthew, you are not married, so why should I?" That was a mistake and Simon jumped on it.

"Every daughter has a duty to marry well, to better the prospects for the family. If you marry Mr Jarvis you…"

"Will never be short of meat!" Grace could not help the interjection.

And it raised a laugh, knifing through the seriousness like cutting cake. Even Simon realised it was best to imitate laughter.

After all, he, as creditor, had the ultimate trump card. They would bend to his will soon enough.

They were at an impasse so Thomas cleared his throat.

"If I may speak a moment?" he asked politely. "As I understand it, only Mr Jarvis will contemplate an alliance with our family due, no doubt, to the change of monarch and a decided move against non-conformism. Quite why Mr Jarvis is willing when no one else is so inclined, I do not know." He looked at Simon, thinking, *He probably knows for he does nothing by chance.* "But we do not need to concern ourselves with why, just to face the facts that we have before us today. Grace is seventeen and I am eighteen. The difference is only a year but it is actually much greater than that. For I am without skills to earn a living, whereas Grace has time to find a husband. We all know that the political situation changes frequently; what was in before is no longer in today."

He noticed as he talked that Matthew was hanging on every word, sitting upright and concentrating completely on Thomas' face, almost as if he were helping to drag out the words and sorting them through his mind to create solutions to the problems he had worried about for months. Moreover, Thomas' words were driving a wedge between Matthew and Simon and that could only be a good thing.

At least in the long run.

But Thomas was risking his plan, for that involved ingratiating himself with Simon. Diplomacy was tricky stuff! It was time to get to the point.

"What I am saying is that the urgency to the family of sorting out my situation is far greater than with Grace. She has time on her side, whereas I do not. Let us concentrate on my predicament, therefore, and put Grace's future to one side because we never know when things might change."

Thomas looked around. Everyone was nodding, even his father; only Simon looked pensive, wondering, no doubt, how to twist matters to his favour. It was time for Thomas to play his ace.

"We all know how indebted this family is to Simon. Not only did he marry into the family but he has also stood by us through thick and thin as adviser and benefactor. I am going to propose two further requests of Simon tonight, to add to the many the Davenports have put his way in recent years."

He looked around the room, trying to build suspense, but his confidence was not all there. He had to get this done while he was ahead. He looked at Grace, saw her wink at him; he was doing alright.

"First, I accept that Mr Jarvis is a strong contender for the hand of my sister. No, please Grace, wait a moment and hear me out." They had rehearsed this scene several times that morning. Now it seemed to have played out well. "But I think we need to wait a little longer to see if things settle down on the political front and perhaps then Simon can secure an even better match for Grace. My first request, therefore, is that Simon keeps Mr Jarvis warm but not hot; we remain interested but not committed. It is a tricky situation and I can think of none better to handle such delicate matters than Simon Taylor."

They discussed this for twenty minutes, gradually swinging their father around to the idea of matrimonial plans with the butcher, but on hold for the time being. Matthew spoke in favour, sensing a middle path being forged by his younger brother. He spoke with a lightness he had not felt before; relief was dancing in his eyes and lighting up his face.

Especially if it meant no dowry to raise, hence no increased loan payments to Simon.

Elizabeth was fully in favour. She knew Grace needed a husband yet thought a delay to find a better one was the perfect solution. She did not know Mr Jarvis well, but had an image in her mind of her own husband attacking her not with a leather strap but several gleaming meat-knifes to choose from.

Grace, for her part, feigned surprise at Thomas' idea, then sat back and awaited the second act.

Simon said little in this period, preferring to think rapidly. It was not a bad course of action; wait and see. What would be the effect on him, for instance, if non-conformists were suddenly back in favour and the Davenports rose back to the higher echelons of Sturminster Newton society? Perhaps Thomas was not a stupid boy at all, but rather a bright young body who could be useful to him.

It was perfect timing, for just then Grace, watching Simon very carefully, asked Thomas what his second request was.

"Simply that Simon holds a place for me as an apprentice in his office. There is nothing more I would like than to be a student under him, learning the law from an expert."

And that sealed the deal.

It also set Thomas' plan off to a perfect start.

"Come to my office for eight o'clock tomorrow morning and we will set you to work, Thomas."

"Yes, sir."

As the family filed out of the study, their business concluded, Matthew came and stood by Thomas, his right hand resting on Thomas' shoulder. There were no words spoken, none were needed, for gratitude and respect wetted Matthew's eyes like a favoured dog looking at his master.

Chapter 6

Grace insisted on passing on the news to Lord Henry the next morning.

"You've got to start work at Simon's office in a few minutes. I will go down to the ford and tell him."

"How do you know he will still be there?" Thomas asked, rather wanting to give the good news himself.

"Oh, he told me. Now, I must get ready." She left the breakfast table and went back upstairs. Thomas noticed that she had not touched her food. He continued eating, wondering how much energy he would need for filing and copying out letters, assuming he was trusted with such elevated duties.

Twenty minutes later he was putting his coat on, ready to go out in the gloomy half-light, when Grace came down the stairs. Her hair was piled up high under a hat instead of a bonnet and she was wearing a beautiful dress that had belonged to their mother.

"Goodness, where did you get the hat from?"

"Matthew gave me three shillings from housekeeping." She looked embarrassed to see Thomas at the door, knowing he would work out why she was dressed up. "You should go, Thomas, you don't want to be late on your first day." She tried to say it with authority, but it sounded more like a plea.

Thomas looked at the grandfather clock in the hall and said 'damn' for the second time in his life, kissed Grace with the light brush that brothers use and charged out of the door, coat still undone, door left wide open to the drifting snowflakes outside.

It was the first day of March and the first day she and Henry kissed. They walked, as had become their habit, along the north bank of the river in a westerly direction, as if climbing the rushing water rather than riding along with it. The snow was not settling, rather swirling, like skirts on the dance floor. The ground was crunchy underneath from frost, making a delicious sound with each step.

And Grace considered that each of those steps was taking her deeper into an adventure with the man she clung to for steadiness.

She told him the news, starting with Thomas' employment, then working back to the awkward part.

"Simon Taylor wanted me betrothed to Mr Jarvis, the butcher."

"That hairy brute? Surely not! And are you betrothed?"

"No, it was part of Thomas' plan to use this idea of marriage to the butcher to ingratiate himself with Simon and thus get employment at his office. He thought the main opposition would be our brother, Matthew; the one who knocked you down in the street. But he was not an issue at all. It was scary because Simon, not Matthew, was insisting on my marriage and Thomas had to weave the argument in a different way. It is strange that Simon should feel so strongly about the matter of my marriage. I don't know why he would care. But that is by the by, for Thomas did so well in his arguing, convincing Simon to hold on a while, thus giving me a little lease on freedom!"

"Your brother is a remarkable man, Miss Davenport. I think he will be wasted in that law office. As for you having a lease on freedom, I sincerely hope it is a long lease."

"Yes, but the sooner he gets the information about the bridge, the sooner he can declare his mistake and say lawyering was not for him. I hate to think of him stuffed up in that office when he should be outside." Lord Henry's observation about lease lengths passed over Grace, concentrated as she was on Thomas' plan, risks and all.

She did not add his second task whilst in Simon's office, for that was their secret. The declared object was to take note of the bridge design and true costs, to expose the inordinate profit the rival party planned to make at the expense of safety; for Mr Milligan was convinced that their design would lead to disaster.

But the main purpose was to find trace of Lady Merriman.

"Well, Mr Milligan will offer him training as soon as he is available," Lord Henry said, noticing Grace's distracted mood but putting it down to concern for her brother.

"I think he was meant to be a builder, Lord Henry. You can see it in his expression when he was down here by the ford, going over the plans. Two days ago he had no idea what he wanted to do with his life. Now, I think, he knows only too well, Lord Henry."

"Please call me plain Henry."

"If you wish, *plain Henry!*" They laughed at her joke, then they kissed amongst the snowflakes that had changed their minds and were settling their whiteness upon the world.

Within an hour of their first kiss, they had their first argument. True to their times, it was about religion and politics; both interweaved like ivy clambering up the oaks and maples around them. But true, also, to their mood, it was mild, hardly damaging at all; more like stall holders setting out their competing wares.

It started when Henry commented casually that the new King would change a lot, probably for the good.

"I do not believe any good will come of a Catholic on the throne," she replied without thinking. "Oh, Henry, I didn't mean..."

"But you did, Grace. Let's always be honest with each other. I am a Catholic and you a Presbyterian. On the face of it that is a huge gap to breach."

"I'm not the greatest Puritan," Grace added.

"Nor I as a Catholic, so we are half-way there already!"

"Only I cannot hold with transubstantiation. It is quite a ridiculous idea!"

"Well, I can't abide the lack of joy in your religion. There are too many rules and too many proscribed activities."

"Such as?"

"Such as dancing..."

"I dance when I want to. I danced the other day with Thomas. We are not all killjoys."

"Dance with me now."

"Here?"

"Yes, right here. This clearing can be our ball room."

"But... well... there's no music." Grace was suddenly

terrified that he meant to dance with her.

And that is exactly what he meant to do. He cleared a few dead twigs with his foot. "My dearest Lady Grace, will you 'grace' me with your presence on the dance floor? You will note I have arranged a white carpet for you. It signifies your purity and the purity of my attentions."

Henry whistled a tune's opening bars and swept Grace into his arms. A minute later, he stopped.

"Are you sure you have danced before?"

"Certainly I have," Grace replied, thinking of the one time she had tried it with Thomas.

"It's just that you are dreadful!" he laughed. "So, madam, where did you have lessons? I need to recommend a dance tutor for my pet tortoise!"

She confessed then, in his arms, while staggering over the roots and ruts that lay below her perfect white carpet. "I danced once last week with Thomas, but we did not know what to do and felt rather foolish. In the end, we gave it up and went fishing instead."

"Did you catch anything?"

"What do you mean?"

"Fishing, you went fishing."

"No, we did not." As she said each word she beat her fists on his chest. "You are an outrageous person, plain Henry!" Still beating those fists.

Thomas' day was full of tedium. He had arrived at two minutes past eight and was berated for being late. Then he was told to stand in the foyer until the supervisor arrived. He was still there at a quarter to nine. In that time, he had traced a path up the mortar between the stones from floor to ceiling and back again; then all over again, trying not to use the route he had used before.

But for the first time he noted the type of stone and the bond pattern. Then he looked at the roof; large beams crossed the narrow hall in a mess of complication. He tried, head up to the rafters, to trace the stresses the roof must be placing on the wall. How would he simplify the structure to make it more appealing, yet retain or even increase the strength? Could you expand the span of the roof indefinitely or was there a natural limit? There were so many variables; the type and size of wood used, the weight of the roof; indeed, the dimensions and slope of the roof would both be critical. There had to be rules governing such matters and he dearly wanted to know them.

Then he looked at the ground, noticing the gaps between floor and wall; presumably, the floor had slipped since original construction. His mind raced on what would cause that.

"Ah, there you are, boy." It seemed he was fated to be termed a juvenile. "Take my bag and follow me."

He spent the rest of the morning lifting musty files off overladen shelves and dusting them. The supervisor returned irregularly and heavily criticised his efforts.

The afternoon was no different, nor the next day, or the day after that. The only relief was copying text; writing out endless court rulings and case law. He never understood the purpose of all that copying, nor of all that legal speak that tired his brain in no time.

The records store room was entirely constructed of a set of timber frames that were filled with a soft material his boot could leave an impression on. Once it had been whitewashed but now it had slid into an easy grey; nothing to distinguish it. Buildings should be maintained, he decided; it was criminal neglect to leave them to deteriorate.

He decided the filling material was wattle and daub; many houses in Sturminster Newton were built this way, although their own home was stone. He tried to recall the larger buildings he had seen in Dorchester, but he had paid little attention at the time.

The walls of the storeroom were thicker up to chest height, creating a ledge half-way up the room, which ran around all four walls. He thought that must be a cost-saving exercise; using less material as you went higher so the building weighed less in total. He loved the variations and complexities that fed on each other. He imagined the extremes; first, a building so heavy it sank into the ground; then a house built of skinny timbers with its upper walls as skinny as a street urchin. Which would be better? What were the strengths and weaknesses of each? Was there a mathematical formula that gave a perfect middle way?

When he made his way home each evening, walking the dark and snowy streets, his young body ached as if he had exchanged it for a much older one. But his spirit suffered even more, for it was weighed down with the fact that he had not once, not even for half a moment, had a chance to get into the inner sanctuary and look through the records there. It was deeply depressing to think it could be weeks or months before he had the slightest chance of locating the information he sought.

It was even too dark, morning and night, to take note of the architecture of the town. He was enclosed all the daylight hours in a chamber while all around were fascinating architectural secrets waiting to be discovered.

Oh, for the freedom to roam and discover.

When he arrived home on the ninth day without results, kicking off the snow and his frustration in the doorway, Grace greeted him with a hug and a kiss.

"I've got some hot chocolate for you in the parlour," she said, taking him by the hand as if he was a stranger and did not know the way.

When she had him settled down, a steaming dish of chocolate on the table in front of him, she broke her news.

"Thomas, I love him."

"Who?" He had a headache, perhaps a temperature. He felt his brow; yes, a temperature, too. He was not in the mood for a guessing game. "You mean Jarvis?" It came to him in a flash and he sat upright, a circle of chocolate around his mouth.

Was he to lose his sister to wedlock?

"No, silly!" Grace stood, walked around the room, first clockwise then about turn to reverse direction. "Henry, of course."

"Henry?" Thomas' tired mind searched for any Henrys they knew. There were only two. Henry Thurloe was Alfred's younger brother. Then he was certain that one of Mrs

Moreton's sons was a Henry. But both were far too young to engage Grace's attention.

"Lord Henry," she replied. Now he stood up and the dish of chocolate tipped onto the floor, the dish wobbling in skewed circles before coming to a rest, unbroken.

"You can't! I mean, it's just not possible. He's an aristocrat and a Catholic. Goodness me, Grace, he is going to be the next Earl of Sherborne!"

"Still, I love him." She thought there must be something in scriptures, or perhaps even the forbidden but secretly read Shakespeare, to quote now; something along the lines of 'you don't get to choose who you love'. But it escaped her so she repeated, "I love him."

"I just can't believe this." Thomas held his aching head in his hands, slumped back in a chair. "I mean, of course it is wonderful news, but it can never lead to anything. You, I mean our family, are pretty well the opposite of what the Sherbornes require in a wife."

"I can't help that."

"Have you told him?"

"Yes, but only after he told me the same. He wants us to elope, but I can't leave you and Lady Merriman."

Matthew put his head around the door at that moment.

"Supper time," he said. "I couldn't think where you were. You don't often come in here to talk."

"I felt like a change," Grace replied, rising quickly to cut off the previous conversation. "Don't mention this to anyone," she whispered to Thomas as they made their way to the dining room.

"I won't, but we must talk later."

They did not manage to talk later for Thomas was feeling increasingly unwell as supper progressed. His head was a clamour of pain and his balance and eyesight were shaky. As the mutton was served, their father carving and putting his full concentration into making a particularly bad job of it, Thomas tried to rise and excuse himself but fell back, half hitting the chair and falling to the floor.

When he woke, it was pitch-black. He was in a strange room but felt a presence. He reached out with his hand and touched the skirt of a woman's dress; it was finest silk.

"You are awake, Thomas." For a moment he thought it was Lady Merriman, come back to him in his distress. But the voice was plainer than her aristocratic tone; younger, also, and very familiar.

"Just about, Grace," he replied, his throat feeling like someone had rubbed at it with grit. Then he slept again. Each time he woke she was there. But he saw others. He saw Lady Merriman several times. Once, he called out to his mother who was there, tending him at the bedside.

"It's just me, Thomas. I'm wearing one of Mama's dresses."

"Grace," he said, before closing his eyes yet again.

Afterwards, she told him that he had slept for four days while outside the snow fell, making March the coldest month of the winter. But when he sat up in bed on the fifth day, realising that he was in his mother's old bedroom, the sun was shining with a new warmth that streamed through the window.

"The snow is melting rapidly," Luke said, coming into his old bedroom for the first time since his wife had died. 'We were worried about you, son."

"Father, the doctor said the dust at Thomas' workplace greatly aggravated matters. I've spoken to Simon and he has agreed to move him to the main office, where the air is much better."

"That is good news, my dear. What are you staring at, son?"

"You look so well, Father."

"I've been taking a greater interest in the church," Pastor Davenport replied. "I'll let you catch up with Grace and come back later. Matthew and Elizabeth have been asking about you. I'll pass on the good news." Luke left quickly, slightly embarrassed at the observation Thomas had made.

"He's been off the drink since you became ill," Grace explained. "He just stopped the night you fainted. He has come out of his study and is everywhere now, getting involved with everything. I missed church on Sunday, I was here watching you, but according to Matthew he gave a rousing sermon. As a result, the church was packed on Wednesday. Again, I was here rather than in church but the word is that Father is back in the thick of it!"

A little later, Thomas asked Grace why she was wearing their mother's old dresses and, he noticed, some of her jewellery, too.

"Father suggested it. He said they were going to waste and she was about my size. I've had my sewing box out, adjusting them a little while sitting by your bed." She rose and gave a twirl beside the bed. "What do you think, brother? Am I not quite fine these days?"

"Very fine indeed, Grace." He closed his eyes again. She had always been expert with needle and thread, often mending tears in their clothes before they were discovered. He liked the thought of his sister bent over sewing at his side while he slept. However rebellious they were, the Presbyterian ways of hard work were deeply ingrained and it seemed a waste to Thomas for her just to sit there.

Far better to be doing something useful; turning something old into something new.

It was well into the second half of March before Thomas was well enough to return to work. The snow had gone, replaced with blustery winds and light, floating showers of rain that soaked the unprepared before they knew it. It had been a winter of hard ground and frost, then piled high with snow at the end. Now there was a fresh optimism in the warmer air.

Simon was waiting for him in the main office; a little sheepish, perhaps, certainly effusive in welcoming his brother-in-law back.

Thomas arrived a few minutes before eight. By five-past he was sitting at a small desk on his own, tasked with sorting through letters and filing them in the chests against the wall. The room was spacious and well lit. His chair was comfortable and two open windows pushed through enough fresh, warm air to make it almost balmy.

Most importantly, having been set his tasks, he was left entirely alone.

54

He found the chest with the bridge designs just before nine. Nobody disturbed him as he pored over them, taking in every detail. He could see straight away that it was an outrageous design; no calculations on stresses at all.

Thomas took out a pencil and notebook and made entry after entry covering the true costs of the bridge. There were two separate calculations. The first was for public display, giving hugely inflated costs for timber and what little stone they were planning to use. The second calculation was the actual cost they would incur, for the actual timber sizes.

Then he stuffed his notebook away and looked through the remaining chests for any reference to Lady Merriman. By half past ten he abandoned any pretence of filing and just searched the chests set around the four walls.

He searched the rest of the morning and found only one slight reference to their old friend. There was a receipt for cash expenditure of eight pounds for a quarter-year of lodging. It gave an address in Lyme Regis.

Thomas would have passed it over, only someone had annotated it with a clear 'LM' across the receipt so that it was hard to read the address. He could see the road name started with 'R', or perhaps 'P', but the rest of the name was obscured.

But just below the words of the town, 'Lyme Regis', was a signature, as clear as day. Thomas folded the receipt carefully and placed it in an inner pocket, closing the chest lid just as the door opened.

"And how is our recovering invalid doing?" Simon Taylor stood in the doorway, a false smile pasted like a disguise on his hard, angular face.

"I must confess that I am not feeling too strong at the moment."

"You have overdone it, my boy. I said to Elizabeth this morning that you should take it easy on your first day back. If you like, I will stand you a lunch in the White Hart. A few slices of roast beef will set you up for the afternoon."

"Sir, I fear I could not hold down food at the moment. You are right, I have overdone it. Could I be excused the rest of the day in order to rest?"

"Of course, my boy. Shall I walk you home?"

"No sir, go to your lunch. It is only a few hundred yards and the walk and solitude will do me good."

"Be off with you, then. Get some rest and I'll see you tomorrow."

Simon did not see Thomas tomorrow, nor the next day. For Thomas left that day and never came back; not as Simon's employee, at least.

He was a little tired, but nothing could hold back his joy as the last that March could offer bounced a gentle sunshine of the cobbles that warmed him to his bones. It was only dampened by the news, on arriving home, that Miss Grace was out somewhere; the maid confirmed she had left early that morning and did not know where she had gone.

So, Thomas went up to his mother's old room; his now, as if his illness had made an awareness amongst his family and promoted him to the main floor of their minds. He checked the receipt in his pocket again, then looked over the notes in his book. Then he lay on the bed and slept, not waking when Grace entered a little after five in the afternoon; nor when the maid, on Grace's instructions, came to light the fire at a quarter to six, to keep at bay the slight evening chill.

He woke an hour later with Grace by his side and a stomach that rumbled with hunger. She arranged trays for them both. Then, over chicken stew and large glasses of apple juice, he told her of her day, showing her first the notes and then the receipt.

And he was rewarded with her cries of joy and a kiss on his forehead.

Chapter 7

Thomas had a relapse that evening, leading to another ten days in bed. His fever returned with a vengeance; the last throw of the dice from a desperate gambler. During these long days and nights, he ranted, often mentioning bridges and Lyme Regis, so Grace deemed it best to be his sole nurse, inventing a little tale about contagion to keep the others away.

She did not succeed entirely, for Elizabeth came when she could and her father insisted on taking the long, lonely night watch so that Grace could get some sleep.

Luke Davenport used the time for reflection. He could divide his sixty-odd years into four, roughly even, quarters. The first quarter, his childhood, he had left far behind. His own father had been a drunkard and remained workshy and destitute until he had died, when Luke was seventeen, on the eve of the civil war.

The second quarter had both made him and broken him, setting the pattern for the rest of his life. He had gone to war; fighting, at first, for the King but switching sides just before Naseby and bringing a troop of gentlemen soldiers with him. It was not a large force, just eighteen men, but somehow, no gentleman himself, he had become their leader.

It was when Cromwell came to visit him after the battle, promoting him to colonel in the temporary hospital where he lay with a livid sword-wound almost dividing him in two, that Luke realised he could achieve great things, despite his very low birth.

But his fighting days were over. Instead, Cromwell and others used him in a variety of roles, as a recruiter, bodyguard, diplomat and spy. As his twenties ran through he was in Ireland, Holland, France and the West Indies; the adventures he had experienced as a young man could fill several volumes.

It was, strangely for such a Catholic country, in Ireland that he found Presbyterianism and converted. He was busy infiltrating royalist organisations, pretending to be a west country gentleman with loyalist leanings, who had been cruelly handled by a bunch of parliamentarians, thus out for revenge as well.

The subterfuge worked well until his own infiltration was infiltrated. Then it became a desperate effort to escape. He was passed from house to house at dead of night; dark cloaks and muffled boots. He was never told where he was or where he was going next, in case he was caught.

"You must have faith in us," an elderly priest had said when harbouring him close to the south coast.

"Why do you do this?" Luke had asked in reply. "Why do you risk everything and go against your own people?"

"All is not as it seems," the priest had replied.

On further questioning, the priest was no priest but a fervent Irish Puritan planted into Ireland, partly to aid the escape route for spies like Luke. But his principal role was to recruit more spies, turning the Irish upon the Irish in the name of true religion.

They stayed up all night, the 'priest' decrying the old religion and setting a fire within Luke that was never quite put out.

The second quarter of Luke's life was coming to a close, although he did not know it at the time. Dividing up one's life happens in retrospect; there is simply no time for it in the present.

But there was one more event before the half-way mark. He met Rebecca on the ship back to England. She was with her parents, coming to England to start again. Her father was a printer, who saw great opportunities in England at the centre of things. Her mother was a patient soul; kind and selfless, wanting the best for her only child, trusting that the Lord would provide it.

Both parents were horribly seasick on the three-day journey to Bristol. It was winter and cold winds threw them violently about the sea. Luke was the only other passenger, other than the pigs in the hold, who had no say in the matter.

Afterwards, they both declared it was love at first sight. It was a beautiful thought, more so because it was true. It was one of those strange, intense times where so much is crammed into so short a period of time; it was as if time ran on its own variable schedule, speeding up and slowing down to suit its customers.

They only met on the second day, for Luke was queasy himself and kept to his cabin for twenty-four hours. But, if there are only four passengers on a little ship and two of those are confined for the duration, the other two are, sooner or later, thrown together. They met in the makeshift dining area, served by a steward who talked as if words alone could save his soul. They laughed together when they finally escaped on deck, relishing that they only had themselves to listen to.

And the wind and the rain and the sea thrashing against the sides of their little ship.

It was a perfect romance, made more so because the day they met was March 9th 1654 and it was Luke's thirtieth birthday.

Luke slipped into the third quarter in a blur of happiness. They became betrothed in a tavern in Bristol, where Rebecca's parents were staying while deciding where to set up their print shop. Rebecca's father, Patrick, took Luke to one side, embarrassed that he had so little to offer by way of dowry.

"Luke, we have so little capital and we need it for the printing press. I can spare just fifty pounds."

"Sir, I have no need of your funds. I would much rather you kept it in reserve for future requirements or to expand your enterprise once it is established."

But Patrick insisted on something, more so when he learned of Luke's plans to open a ministry in his home town.

"I assumed you were Catholic," Luke said, startled by the revelation that the family was firmly Protestant.

"We are not really Irish in the true sense. My ancestors came from London or the area around it in the time of Queen Elizabeth. We have always been Protestants in a sea of Romans, but we have always managed to get on with them very well. I don't wear my religion on my sleeve. I believe it is a private matter for my conscience."

They settled on thirty pounds, because Luke felt he had to take something. Added to his savings and to a generous pay-off from the commonwealth for services rendered, he had sufficient capital to set up his church in Sturminster Newton.

There had followed a glorious period of hope and love;

creating their church and creating a family together. Rebecca proved every bit as able as Luke. She was less serious and loved her pretty clothes. But she brought in to the church many who would never have considered Puritanism as their religion. The church was packed each Sunday and they were blessed with four beautiful children.

But the plague had come to rob them of all happiness. First, it took Rebecca's parents in London, where they had set up shop. Then three years later it came to Dorset, ranging wide but, in Luke's opinion, picking only the best to take to the next world. Rebecca's death had been long and slow; pain racked her and withered her so that the thirty-eight-year-old on her deathbed looked a full generation older.

Luke was relieved when she was finally pronounced dead. No one can love another and want such pain to continue.

But it left a huge hole in his life. He turned to God. He turned to his children. He turned to his congregation. Yet no one could fill it. In the end, he turned to brandy; not beer, nor gin, for brandy alone filled his need.

And emptied his purse.

It was slow, but relentless, this drain upon his wealth. And it happened from top and bottom. The purse leaked coins to buy ever-increasing quantities of brandy, while a corresponding disregard for his congregation meant an inevitable drying-up of Sunday plate donations.

Matthew had borne the brunt of these worries while the others, much younger, had played and run about. He had tried everything to tame them.

Everything, that is, except love.

He saw that now as the fourth quarter of his life drew to a close.

"Dear Lord," he prayed out loud, "let me have a fifth quarter to my life, so I might be able to redeem myself."

"You can't have a fifth quarter. Even I know that quarter means four parts!"

Luke's eyes jerked open, ready to meet his maker.

But it was Thomas who had spoken, awaking from his fever-induced sleep; himself again, although weakened by the illness.

"Thank the Lord that you are saved." This was said by the father about his son, but it could equally have been the son about his father.

By the second week of April, Thomas was completely better. The news that the town council had selected the Sherborne-Milligan consortium over the Taylor option boosted his morale enormously, sealing the rebound to health. Both the apothecary and a surgeon they brought in from Blandford Forum declared that Thomas' lungs could not take the dust associated with indoor clerical work and recommended outdoor work as a farmer or some such. They believed building work, when consulted as to its suitability, would be ideal.

Building, to Thomas, seemed the only valid occupation. The logics of it made innate sense to him; structures and stresses fitted into his mind like sermons and morals to his father.

"He has a lot to learn," Mr Milligan reported to Lord Henry after Thomas' first fortnight on the job, "but he has a natural grip of the basics and will go far." Henry passed this on to Grace, but suggested she keep it to herself for the time being, explaining that excessive pride can taint the judgement of a young man.

But Thomas was so absorbed in the work on site that they need not have worried about it. He was first on site every morning and last to leave at night. On Sundays, after church, he would walk down with Grace to the ford and explain in detail what was going on.

"Dear Thomas," she laughed one Sunday in early May," I know so much about bridge building from you I could manage to build one myself."

"But where would you start, Grace? With the site or the plans? Oh, I see, you are making fun of me. I am become a bridge bore!"

"You said it, not me." She skipped away before he could pummel her with his fists. "But seriously, Thomas," she had collapsed in a heap, caught by her brother, "when do you think we might go to Lyme Regis to look for Lady Merriman?"

"There is a very interesting bridge in Lyme Regis." It was

Thomas' turn to tease.

"Thomas!"

"Seriously, there is. It is the Buddle Bridge and is part of the High Street. It was built over 300 years ago and I have permission from Mr Milligan to visit it and examine it. He is interested to know how it has lasted so long. He wants his bridge to survive at least the same period, if not double."

"No doubt with you involved it will be the bridge the angels come over from Heaven to earth on Doomsday!"

"No doubt, sister dear! But it would be a pity to travel all the way to Lyme Regis and not stop to see an old friend."

"I see," she poked her tongue at him, "when will you go?"

"As soon as you are free to travel."

"Me? You want me to come with you? That is wonderful." She leant up and kissed her brother on the cheek. "But how will we get there?"

"We will walk. It will take four days there and four days back."

But Grace had a better idea. "We shall not walk. Henry will, I am sure, provide two horses. He has many."

"Will he? That is good news. It will cut our journey time in half."

But Lord Henry went one step further, smitten as he was. He arranged for Mr Milligan to bring Thomas and Grace to Sherborne Hall in Lillington for a meeting to discuss progress on the bridge. "My grandparents are away visiting our estates in Oxfordshire so we will be undisturbed. We will stay the night at home and then in the morning, when Mr Milligan departs, we will go on three fast horses to Lyme Regis. If we start early in the morning, we will be there by nightfall and can stay with my friend near the town."

"You will come with us? Are you not too busy?" He was not, would not be persuaded otherwise. It would be his pleasure.

When she was over the surprise and rush of pleasure at his insistence on accompanying them, she wondered if it was such a good idea. How would they get away to track down Lady Merriman? Henry would have no time for the witch of Bagber.

She spoke to Henry, next time she was with him, walking in the spring as they had walked through the winter. She tried to persuade him he was too busy; someone had to watch over the bridge project if both Mr Milligan and Thomas were away. And then what if his grandparents returned suddenly and found him arm-in- arm with the middling classes?

"It sounds like you don't want me, Grace." His voice was on a knife edge. To one side was humour, on the other sat despair.

"Of course I want you to come, Henry dearest." She gave him a long kiss behind a large rhododendron bush; thinking as she always did, is this how a Puritan girl goes on?

It was settled, they would come with Mr Milligan to Sherborne Hall, then on together to Lyme Regis.

They travelled by horseback six days later, eating lunch from their saddlebags at a small stream just over halfway there. They were already on Sherborne land, so Mr Milligan informed them, adding that their estates stretched across much of north Dorset.

They were welcomed at Sherborne Hall by Henry, on the broad steps leading up to the front door. Footmen took their saddlebags up to spacious first-floor rooms. Mr Milligan had a quiet room at the back of the house, where he had stayed several times before, while working on Sherborne business, including building a new wing to the hall. Grace and Thomas had principal rooms overlooking the park and grand entrance.

There was still just enough light for a tour of the grounds. They split up. Mr Milligan took Thomas to survey the architecture of this magnificent collection of buildings; everything from medieval to that built by Mr Milligan ten years earlier; the modern complementing the ancient; generations of building styles living in happy concord, like ghosts from all times come together in a commune. Mr Milligan was impressed with Thomas' understanding of key concepts; how different styles fitted together and why stone on stone could soar up to the sky to touch the angels as they sang.

Henry took Grace in a different direction. They went beyond the formal gardens into the park, where small deer pulled at tufts of fresh spring grass. He led her, her hand in his, up a gentle slope to a beech wood that covered the whole top of the hill.

"In feudal times, anyone caught taking firewood from the wood was fined two weeks of extra time working in the manor fields." It seemed to Grace that the trees were all old, gnarled men. Each one would have a more sombre, more fantastic, sadder tale to tell of the old days. But now they were silent, for this was the modern world, where people were free to work and play as they wanted. These old gnarled men were not gathering new stories, simply relating the same ones from long ago.

Everything looked bright and hopeful to Grace and Henry; two people in love in a beech wood, with a breeze rustling the new leaves and gentle sunshine edging through the gaps above their heads.

Supper was done in style; five courses carried in and carried out by an army of footmen, silently directed by a butler-type figure who barely moved. Grace drank a little wine for the first time. Thomas had had it before. He told a funny story of sneaking four bottles of claret into his dormitory at Westfields. All the boys had got slightly tipsy and began making silly jokes and climbing on the outside wall from one window to the next. Then Thomas had thrown four empty claret bottles into the courtyard below.

The next morning, they were still there and, magically, the four bottles had landed in a W shape for Westfields.

"We were kept in school for two whole weeks, writing extra essays on the classics, but it was worth it!"

"Lord Henry, look what you have foisted on me, sir!" Mr Milligan's joke rounded off the evening.

"We have an early start in the morning. Parker, please have breakfast ready at 6am. We will go directly after eating."

"Very good, My Lord."

Chapter 8

Lyme Regis had a parliamentary air about it. It always had, and looked as if it always would. It was the political version of the self-made man; a confidence born of success in the streets and trading posts, translated into everyday life.

The heir to the Earldom of Sherborne did not shine in Lyme Regis the way he shone in other parts of Dorset. Henry appeared stunted to Thomas and Grace; reduced in size to an ordinary person. He seemed uncomfortable in the streets, as if his figure was cut out of one painting and inserted, haphazardly, into another.

They stopped for refreshments in a coffee house. It was mid-morning, lots of people about. In any other town people would make way for Lord Henry but here they did not seem to notice him.

"Sir, we seek the Buddle Bridge," Thomas asked at the next table in the coffee house.

"Turn left outside and you will cross it in three minutes. It is a part of the High Street."

The only plan Grace and Thomas had come up with was to bore Henry into looking elsewhere, perhaps seeking his friend or some refreshments. Then they would be free to search the town for streets beginning with 'P' and 'R'.

It seemed hopeless at first, for Henry showed almost as much interest as Thomas. Together, they crawled over, under and around the bridge. Grace was sent to buy a tape measure and came back with a dressmaker's measure, which raised a laugh.

"I didn't think to go to an ironmongery," she said.

Then Henry bade her find pencils and paper. This was easier, for she had noticed a shop selling such things further down the High Street.

Henry proved to be an excellent sketcher. In three hours, he had drawn the bridge from every angle, plus some detailed plans of key features. Thomas took each sketch and made his own drawings and notes on each one; long lines and shaded patches to show stress points.

There was nothing now for Grace to do. The two young men were engrossed with their business of mapping the bridge. Grace could not go back to the coffee shop alone. She called down to the stream below that she was going for a walk. There was no answer.

Lyme Regis was about twice the size of Sturminster Newton. She admired the views and the architecture, wondering all the time when she could go back and then how they would tease Henry into some other occupation for a period. At first, she did a loop around to the bridge, but as she was coming back she realised she might have to do this loop twenty times or more before the sun set and put a stop to their bridge inspections for the day. She turned up a side street, planning to lengthen the walk by turning the loop in on itself; walking in decreasing circles. She turned again and then one more time, coming to a dark outdoor passageway with a house above it. She went through the passageway and out to another set of winding streets, up and down a hill, then left because it looked like it might lead back to the High Street. But it did not, leading instead to another alley, even narrower than the one before. She thought of the camel and the eye of the needle. It was time to turn around and retrace her steps. But where was that passage she had just walked through?

She was lost. And there was no one around.

She looked up at a street sign; not that it would help without a map. The street she was on was Peter's Row. Perhaps she was near a church called St Peter's. She could safely ask for directions, maybe even an escort, at a church.

But there was no church; nothing remarkable to distinguish one building from another, and she lacked courage to knock at a stranger's door.

She wandered another twenty minutes, crisscrossing this part of town, trying to get back to Peter's Row, as if it, alone, offered safe-keeping in this maze of treacherous streets.

Then she stopped, said the name of the street again. "Peter's Row. It has a 'P' and an 'R' in its name! What better place could there be to start the search for Lady Merriman?"

She screwed up her courage and knocked on a door.

"Good afternoon, could you please direct me to Peter's Row?"

"This is Peter's Row," the lady answered. "Who are you seeking?"

"Lady Merriman, I mean Lilly, um Lilly Medley." It was silly of her to give Lady Merriman's real name. This lady could be her jailor!

"Well, whether it's Merriman or Medley, I've not heard of them and I know everyone on this street."

"Thank you, madam." As Grace turned to go she stumbled on the step and fell against the lady in the doorway, gasping in her fatigue.

"Careful, my girl. You'll tear that pretty dress if you throw yourself about the street." It was one of Grace's mother's dresses, chosen for Henry; pink overskirt and a cream bodice. She looked down in horror, jerking her skirts to look for rips. But there were none. "Are you alright, my dear? Better come in for a moment, sit a spell and catch your breath."

Sally Baker had lived her whole life in Peter's Row. She explained that it was nothing to do with a church. "My grandfather was born in the reign of Queen Elizabeth and his name was Peter Baker. This whole area was known as Peter's Meadow, to distinguish it from Michael's Meadow, belonging to his brother. My father inherited the meadow and built the houses around the southern stretch of the meadow, closest to the town. This was the house he built for himself and I have lived here every day of my life."

Grace did not want to ask how old she was, but she looked ancient.

"I was born in the year '12, two years after they moved in here." Sally had seen the enquiry on Grace's face and had answered it before the words were formed. "But now tell me about yourself, my dear."

Grace told about the bridge and accompanying her brother down to inspect it.

"But why look for Peter's Row?" the old lady asked.

"Because..." Grace had to think quickly. "Because our old

nanny moved here when I was small. When we came to Lyme Regis, I thought to look her up."

"What was her name?"

"Nanny."

This produced a clang of laughter like church bells. "I meant her full name?"

"Oh, I see. Well it was Nanny... Nanny Medley." Grace remembered the name she had mentioned on the doorstep.

"And I said there was no one here by that name, my dear. I own all the houses in the row and make it my business to know their names and where they came from."

Sally had produced a dish of hot chocolate for Grace, which she drank greedily. Sally laughed at Grace's messy face and sent her to the kitchen to wash the chocolate mixture away. When she came back, Sally took her breath from her body with her next observation.

"There was a woman come here from Sturminster Newton. It must have been four or five years ago. She was very disturbed. I can't imagine she could have been your nanny, not taking responsibility for children in her state. I asked her to leave because the firm who paid her bills never paid on time. She was only here for a little over a year. Her name is on the tip of my tongue. Yes, my dear?"

"The firm? You said the firm. Who did the firm consist of?"

"Why, the legal firm who had responsibility for her. Their name will come to me in half a jiffy or a jiffy and a half."

But Grace did not have a jiffy to spare, not even a half of one. The clock in the hall had just struck six times.

"Can I come back tomorrow, Miss Baker? I must go now or they'll worry about me."

Sally Baker gave Grace precise instructions back to the bridge, watched her leave with her trotting, anxious feet tapping on the stone road, then suddenly wondered who the 'they' was. She had only mentioned her brother.

Perhaps she would find out more in the morning. In the meantime, she had some old records to look up.

They stayed a second night with the friend of Henry's. All three men were full of the bridge, which the friend had come down to see later in the afternoon. "It's strange that I've lived here all my life and never thought about this bridge."

It left Grace plenty of time to think about the day. After supper she insisted they have their coffee and brandy, stating she was tired and would go to bed. But she gave her brother a warning signal not to indulge in drink. Brandy, they knew, was manufactured in the devil's lair.

On leaving them to their bridge-talk, she went downstairs instead of up. She asked for a chair in the kitchen and enjoyed a dish of tea with the housekeeper and cook, while the junior servants cleared up before bed.

"I wondered how well you knew the town," she said after the generalities were exhausted. They had both lived in Lyme Regis all their lives.

She then told a story, not caring whether they believed her or not. She said she was writing a book. Her grandfather had been a printer and she felt it was in her blood to do something with books.

"I decided first of all to do a book about Dorset; an alphabet book."

"You mean to aid in learning your letters?"

"No, not a child's book, but a guide to Dorset using the alphabet. I thought to do one street for each letter of the alphabet. The trouble is I am stuck on streets starting with 'P' and 'R'.

"There's Peter's Row," said the housekeeper at once.

"Thank you. Any others?" Those two ladies ransacked their minds but could not come up with any more.

"Just Peter's Row; sorry, my dear. Now, we must retire or we'll never get up in the morning."

"Goodnight, and thank you."

"Strange girl," said Cook, after Grace had left.

"Not surprising she is strange, coming with that Catholic brat from Sherborne." They laughed as they locked the final door and took the back stairs to bed.

In the morning, Henry wanted to know why she wanted to go back to Lyme Regis.

"I met a nice lady and said I would drop in today before we go back. We have time, don't we?"

"Of course we do," Henry replied. "Actually, it works out well as I have one sketch I would like to do again. Thomas, would you be able to take your sister to see her friend and I'll come on from the bridge as soon as I've finished? Good, that is settled. Only, what address is it?"

Grace did not have the address, just the street. "It's a big red brick house on Peter's Row."

"I'll find it."

"Ah, Miss Davenport, it is so nice to see you again. And this must be your brother?"

"Yes, Miss Baker, this is Thomas."

Soon they were sitting in a long, low room at the back of the house, drinking coffee and eating sweetmeats.

"I've been racking my brains for someone who fits the description of your old nanny" Sally began.

"But we didn't have a nanny..." Thomas started, stopping when kicked sharply on the shin. *I knew as much*, thought Sally but continued with the harmless pretence.

"Oh, I remember now, the nanny who retired to Lyme Regis," Thomas added after working out the meaning of Grace's urgent looks.

"That must be the one." Sally's voice made it clear that she was not being fooled. "Perhaps you can tell me when you think your nanny came first to Lyme Regis."

"Four, almost five years ago. It must have been September of '80." Grace was pleased to have the conversation back on track.

"Well, that fits well with the timeframe, but not the personality. The woman who came from Sturminster Newton about five years ago was called Glenda Arkwright. She was dainty and delicate and not the type I would put down as a nanny. She was almost regal in her mannerisms."

When they heard the last words, both Thomas and Grace knew they had hit lucky. Lady Merriman was somewhat dainty and delicate but if there was one word to describe her it would be regal. They had tracked her down.

Grace came up with a story about their nanny having another name. It was a sad story all about losing her husband when on her honeymoon years ago and never getting over it, using her maiden name when she was forced to earn a living as a nanny because her family had cut her off when she married beneath her.

The story fitted her regal nature. It fitted her delicate temperament, also explaining her educated voice. But it did not fool Sally Baker.

"I've dug out my records. The firm that arranged the lease was also based in Sturminster Newton. They were called," she flipped over a few pages, "yes, Taylor and Johnson."

"I knew it!" Sally burst out. "My father's lawyers," she added.

"Well, young lady, perhaps you can pass on through your father that the firm of Taylor and Johnson still owe me the sum of four pounds and sixteen shillings. And I have the right to apply interest to that. Because they were bad payers I was forced to ask her to leave. She left on October 21st 1681."

"Did she leave a forwarding address?"

"She did, let me see where I put it. I'll be back in a moment." Sally left the room. As soon as the door closed, Thomas and Grace jumped to look at the slender folder Sally had left on the table.

"Goodness me," Thomas spoke, "it says here that her neighbours petitioned Miss Baker for her to leave as well as non-payment of rent causing her to go. Apparently, she plagued them with endless confused stories about her past!"

"It is definitely Lady Merriman."

At that moment, Sally Baker came back with the address, written in a large scrawl on the back of an old rent bill.

"I remember now. She did not leave on October 21st. She disappeared two nights before she was scheduled to leave. All she left was a shilling towards the rent, saying it was all she had to spare. And she left a note. Do you want to read it?"

"Yes please, Miss Baker."

"You mean her no harm? No one has come for her since her scheduled departure date, when several odd-looking thugs turned up to move her and found her gone. I completely put it out of my mind these last four years. I was nursing my sister, who died last winter. The note sort of makes sense now that you are here. Tell me, what was the name of her gardener wherever she lived before?"

"What a strange question, Miss Baker. Why, it was Thurloe. We visited his widow not long ago."

"Did he have any distinguishing features?"

"Only two fingers missing from his right hand. He had been a sailor before and lost his two fingers when some rigging crashed in a storm. He used to scare us when he told us the story," Thomas answered, then added, "That was when we were much younger."

She handed over the note and Thomas and Grace saw immediately the tiny handwriting they remembered as that of Lady Merriman. They sat down to read it, just as the front doorbell rang and Sally left the room again.

Miss Baker, I give you my address on a strict understanding that you give it to no one other than a young girl and her brother, both with sandy hair and fine countenances. Sad to say, I forget their names now in my distress and being so troubled by memories that dance just outside my reach. But they are gentle and loving and they will one day come for me. If you are in doubt, ask them the name of my gardener, which is Thurloe. They will both remember Thurloe for he was good to them. Ask how many fingers he had for two were missing from his right hand. These two children befriended me before I was taken by evil hands.

If ever I can I will repay the rent owed to you, but please know that I was forced to come here by those that took me away from my home. I must go now. I have a friend who has agreed to take me away. My friend awaits me.

I remain your servant

Eliza Merriman (known to you as Glenda Arkwright, a name I detest and always have done.)

It was the Lady Merriman they remembered so clearly; elegant in her language but clearly confused about so much. Thomas and Grace smiled at each other, memories of the lady flooding both their minds.

And it had been remarkably easy to track her down.

Sally Baker came back in the room, followed by Henry, looking hesitant.

"You need to leave," she said.

"Why, when we have just found our old nanny? You have been so helpful to us." Grace stood, amazed and shocked at the sudden change in her kind hostess.

"You did not tell me there was a third person in your party. Any friend of the Sherbornes is an enemy to me. I'll not have that murderous family in my house, nor their acquaintances. Leave now and take your dreadful, sick lies with you."

"Madam, I think you do us an injustice…"

"Just go."

They left, Henry first out of the door, even more shocked than Grace and Thomas. Grace looked back at Sally Baker but the door slammed in her face as she turned.

They did not speak until they were mounted on their horses and Lyme Regis sat like a grey stone slab in the distance, bordered by a bright blue sea and half a hundred small craft upon it.

"What on earth was that about?" Thomas asked, the first to recover from the shock.

"It seems my family are not popular in Lyme Regis."

"But why could that be?" Grace could not understand anyone not liking Henry.

"Damned if I know," Henry replied, but not with force of anger, more the mystery settling on him. "I sensed something as soon as we entered the town yesterday."

He did not know what had caused the reaction but was soon to find out.

Two hours of riding passed, without much more than polite conversation about waypoints and weather. At last, Grace pulled her horse to a stop at a stream.

"Let them drink for a while. I need to stretch my legs." Henry watched her walk a little way up the stream, swishing at nettles with her riding crop.

He wanted her so badly. She was half-Puritan and half-joy; as if innocently indulging in the pleasures of life. He knew she wore her mother's pretty dresses. Her wardrobe had changed progressively as they became acquainted; adding more colour, more style, yet still demure.

She was wearing a pale blue dress, almost exactly the same colour as the sky overhead; as if the sky had sent a bolt of itself down to earth to colonise the land below. The dress was properly modest for a non-conformist yet was somehow so alluring.

On instinct he got off his horse and followed her along the bank. She turned as she heard his footsteps.

"Oh Henry, you surprised me." She climbed, playfully, onto a rotten tree stump to gain an artificial height over him.

"You always surprise me, my dearest Grace."

He felt, in that moment, like a patch of earth and greenery, wonderful in its way but overwhelmed by the sky he was abutting.

They kissed, sky bending neatly at the narrow waist to reach down to earth. And they stayed in union as wisps of her unruly hair broke ranks and tickled the earth beneath her.

Then she told him everything about their second objective in going to Lyme Regis. He listened intently, imagining her lost in the back streets, summoning the courage to knock on a door. It had been any door, the nearest door to knock on. But it had given her the answer she needed.

"But how will we get to Bristol to find her?" she asked.

"Grace, I'll take you to China if you so desire..."

"Bristol will be fine for now, maybe China next month." She jumped from the stump and skipped off into the trees. He tried to chase but was no match for the darting figure slipping through the undergrowth.

He caught her later, when the trees suddenly opened up to a clearing, making escape much harder. She stumbled and fell and he was up to her, laughing as he helped the sky rise again.

"Seriously, Grace, I will take you anywhere you want to go."

"I know you will, Henry. But right now, you need to get me back to Thomas and the horses. I don't have the slightest idea of where we might be. But I do know he will be concerned if we are not back shortly." It was the same mixture of Puritan with joy, caution with abandon, that he found so wonderful in her.

Chapter 9

Luke and Matthew were both nervous, but their anxiety was visible in different ways. Matthew kept smoothing his scant hair, adjusting his neck cloth, looking at himself in the small mirror that had always been on the back of the study door. He braced his shoulders several times before reverting to his natural state; a slight stoop, with rounded shoulders pushing forwards, making a crescent of his upper body.

Luke, on the other hand, had once been a soldier. His back remained straight. It seemed to his family than even when slumped over drink as he had been until recently, his backbone was still on parade.

The study door opened without a knock; it banged open with an air of ownership, catching Matthew who was re-inspecting his posture, hitting him on the nose. He stepped back in reaction and stumbled over a stool, bringing a stack of books on divinity down around him.

Simon stepped over his body, did not offer a hand, simply kicked an ancient interpretation of the book of Genesis with his buckled shoe so it slid across the floorboards and under the table where Luke sat, still ramrod-straight.

"I'm sorry," Matthew blurted. "You caught me by surprise."

"You did not knock," Luke said in an even tone that sounded dangerous.

"I don't need to knock to serve this." Simon waved a legal document in the air before slamming it down on the table in front of Luke.

Dignity dictated that Simon should leave at that exact point. But he stayed; he had to see the damage his actions inflicted. He expected Luke to open the document, eyes widening with fear as he read the contents.

Luke remained stock-still. His eyes never left the bible that was open on the table before him. Only those eyes moved, topped by craggy eyebrows whitened with age; slowly to the right then faster back to the left, to start another line.

"Don't you want to…" Simon started.

But Matthew was on his feet now, reaching out for the document.

"Leave it, son."

"Leave it?"

"Yes, Matthew. Mr Taylor, you may depart and do not return unless you regain your civility in the interval."

It was the prefect dismissal. Luke willed Matthew not to touch the document until they heard the front door slam and footsteps fading on the cobbles. Then Luke abandoned dignity and grabbed the document.

"It is a demand for 514 pounds, ten shillings and eight pence. Payment is to be made by June 19th, exactly thirty days from now. This must be a mistake!"

"It is no mistake, Father." Matthew had known it was this, when Simon had sent a messenger demanding he be seen by both of them at ten o'clock. The relationship between the two families had broken down utterly but inexplicably. Suddenly, they saw little of Elizabeth, usually a frequent visitor. Could Simon be so incensed at Thomas deciding against a career in the law?

Neither Luke nor Matthew made any connection with Simon's loss of the bridge contract. They knew he had failed in this endeavour and it had gone to the builder Thomas now worked for, but that was the extent of the matter and anything more did not enter their heads.

Nor did it occur to either father or son that the man they had chosen as a partner for Elizabeth could be so fickle as to turn against them because the country was turning away from non-conformance. To them, the rejoicing that spread from Westminster Abbey following James II's coronation ceremony on St George's Day was just national joy and nothing more sinister. James had promised religious toleration and that worked both ways; for his beloved Catholics and for the non-conformists. He had declared that very same intention and that had flowed down throughout the nation as well.

"But how can it be?" Luke looked again at the figure on the demand. It was an incredible amount of money.

"I had to borrow."

"Yes, I know we borrowed a bit, but this is an enormous sum. How could it be?"

There was worse to come, for the Davenports' one asset was at stake as security for the loan.

"You gave him the deeds for the church?" Luke was astounded. "What possessed you to do that?"

When Luke had set up the church in the summer of 1654 he had done something rather unusual. Most people would have put their capital into a home for the family and rented space to make into a church. Instead, Luke, in his fervour, had decided that God needed the best his capital could manage. He had commissioned the building of the little church at the top of Market Street and spent the best part of his savings on it. They had rented the family home, there not being enough money left for both.

And now the foolishness of his son had put their only asset on the line and, with it, their only source of income.

Luke was working himself up into a rage, then Matthew said something amongst his mumbled but earnest apologies that stopped Luke dead in the middle of a diatribe against irresponsibility in financial affairs.

"I'm sorry, Father, it was just the cost of the brandy. And then there was Elizabeth's dowry and the fees for Thomas and Grace. The income was dwindling and I did not know what else to do."

"How much money have we got, Matthew? How much can we call on?"

"Fourteen pounds and eight shillings, but we owe household bills of…" He scrabbled amongst some papers on the desk, "Ten shillings and fourpence."

"So, in round terms we have the fourteen pounds and lack the 500?"

"Yes, Father. What are we to do? I'm sorry to have brought you to this through my mismanagement."

Luke took a large intake of breath. Was he now truly entering the fifth quarter of his life?

"We will pray, my son. But before we pray, you will do one

thing for me?"

"Anything in my power, Father."

"You will stop apologising and give me space to apologise to you. It was my dependence on drink that caused this, just as it ruined my father. I am fighting it now and with the Lord's blessing it will not be too late but, if it is, it is entirely my own fault."

They prayed then, the old pastor thumbing through the bible, seeking relevance in the words. But this was real-life praying, not carefully extracted texts for rousing sermons. In the end, he closed his bible and spoke from the heart, asking God to give him a second chance.

Which is exactly what God did.

Just not in the way he expected.

Matthew went to each of them in turn. He wrung his hands and stepped from one foot to another, apologising even before the requests were made. He did not realise that one had to inspire confidence to borrow money. Very few would lend to someone so nervous, especially to a non-conformist family in an increasingly Catholic land.

He did get pity-money, but even this came to a tiny proportion of what was owed. Surprisingly, Mr Jarvis, perhaps ever hopeful of securing Grace as a bride, gave a gift of two pounds, saying, "Pay me back one day if you can."

Matthew spent a week getting a total of eighteen pounds and a few shillings.

But this was not his only action. He had already written to lawyers in London, asking them, with Luke's blessing, to sell Patrick's print shop. The press had long since been sold and the shop let out to a dress-maker. The lawyer wrote back straight away, saying he would advance eighty-five pounds against it, if they shared, half and half, in the proceeds above that figure when it sold. It was a good deal for the lawyers and a pitiful one for the Davenports, but needs must. The final letter came on June 14th, five days before the loan deadline, enclosing a promise to pay 115 pounds. Apparently, the dress maker had wanted the premises for some time and had jumped at the discounted price for four storeys of good real estate with a spacious yard at the back.

Within a few days of the demand being delivered, Grace and Thomas were back from Lyme Regis, their secret triumph wiped from their minds. Thomas swore he would go to the law office and shake Simon Taylor thoroughly but Luke would not hear of it. Instead, Thomas was despatched to see Mr Milligan, who advanced a portion of Thomas' salary for the next two years, then made a mistake with the calculations and handed over ten guineas with a wink.

"That is too much, sir."

"Don't look a gift horse in the mouth, lad. Besides, without your initiative, we would not have this contract. Perhaps we should treat it as a bonus." He had already earmarked Thomas for partnership one day so he saw it as a small investment in his own future.

Thomas and Grace then did the rounds that Matthew had done. They raised a little more than Matthew had managed, which made the older brother blush when they put it in the pot.

Grace had a further idea. She went one day on her own to Elizabeth's house. She selected a day when she knew Simon was away. She found her sister very subdued and tearful.

"I've been forbidden to talk to you," she said at the door, fear overwhelming love.

"Then don't talk, just let me in and listen to what I have to say." This caused a small smile on her sister's anguished face; a new sunrise after a stormy night.

After listening, without saying a word, Elizabeth went to the study where she kept her household accounts and took the cashbox back to the drawing room. She tipped it out on a side table, shaking the jar to ensure every penny was out. Then she rang the bell and Kitty came. It was allowed, of course, to talk to the maids.

"Kitty, be so kind as to fetch me a little purse."

"Yes, ma'am." Said with a little drop of a curtsy that spoke volumes about the respect she had for her mistress. It was something, Elizabeth reflected, that Simon would never understand. Treat those serving you with contempt and contempt came flying right back. But the thought of Simon sent a shudder through her body.

"Are you alright, Lizzie?"

Elizabeth smiled and nodded as she handed over the purse. She would pay the price later when Simon found there was no housekeeping money for the remainder of the month.

But at least she could look him in the eye, knowing that she had not disobeyed his instructions.

Luke took a different approach to the problem, relying innately on his strengths. In doing this, he displayed the wisdom of his years and raised the most cash of anyone in the family.

He wrote a series of sermons and sent a general invitation to the town. Each Sunday morning and each Wednesday evening for the thirty days he railed against the sins of man, dwelling particularly on greed. By the third week the little church was packed and Luke opened the doors and stood in the doorway to give his sermon, shouting up and down the street and into the church behind him.

And he was glorying in his return to his chosen occupation; the vocation he had discovered when fleeing all those years ago on the rocky coast of Ireland.

Something made him abandon all caution in the composition of these sermons. He aimed to entwine theology with humanity, expounding on the goodness that came from God and the evil that came from the devil.

And how both were played out through mankind; the battle of good and evil, fought amongst the kingdoms of man.

They became known far and wide as the 'Man Against Man' series, for they focused on the lives of two men; one was self-centred, the other selfless. When these sermons were later published, wise people spent hours in interpretation but everyone in the locality where they were written had no need for such analysis. They all knew; even Simon Taylor knew.

The only person who did not guess was Luke's model for his second man, the selfless one. Matthew was too tense with worry and had too low opinion of himself to ever think he could be the hero of the series.

The plate collections doubled over the first two weeks, then doubled again.

"If we only had a few more weeks we could manage the whole debt," Luke sighed on the last Wednesday before the deadline.

The only contributor who had not yet made a donation was the Lord God himself. He stepped in at the last moment, as if teasing out the last vestiges of strength and loyalty in the Davenport family.

He did not send a tree bearing silver fruit, nor a rainbow to follow for a pot of gold. He sent something entirely different.

The news of the landing by James, Duke of Monmouth, in Lyme Regis, where Thomas, Grace and Henry had so recently been, spread like wildfire through Dorset. The illegitimate son of the old King came with a tiny force, in three small ships from Holland. He came with his pitiful handful of followers in order to light again the Protestant fire in England.

Within a few days he had three thousand volunteers and started marching towards London.

Nothing would ever be the same in Dorset again.

Simon had made it his habit to visit the Davenport home at regular intervals over the thirty-day period. Luke had challenged him the first time, only to have Simon point out the clause in the multiple loan contracts that gave him the absolute right to enter their home at any time to determine their ability to meet the prescribed repayments. Matthew in his trust had not read the minutiae.

It was with dread for their future but no surprise that Simon's cocky smile entered the study on June 18th, the day before the deadline.

"How much have you raised?" he asked after an attempt at a genial greeting had failed.

"Just over 300 pounds," Luke replied. "But we still have a day to go."

"I'll take 300 in full and final settlement."

"What?" Just three days ago, with the total at 290 pounds, he had sneered at them, reminding them of the total debt due.

But, of course, the news of Monmouth's landing had not yet reached Sturminster Newton during Simon's last visit. Now it had, although only to a handful, Simon being one of those with advance knowledge.

Matthew was just starting to express his delight when his father cut him short.

"We will pay the full amount or you shall have my church."

"But Father, this is such a generous offer!"

"It is nothing of the kind." Luke thought back to that quarter of his life when espionage and diplomacy had ruled. "Nothing is free in this world. Only in the next world, for those that make it there." This last comment was said with considerable force and directed at Simon, who stood before Luke's desk, not invited to sit down. "So, Mr Taylor, what is it that has changed so suddenly?"

Simon tried to pretend it was all manner of things. Elizabeth had pleaded with him. He had had a turn of conscience. He had only ever meant to frighten them into living within their means. That last one was his best. He saw out of the corner of his eye that Matthew was impressed by the argument.

But Luke would have nothing to do with it. Only the truth would help Simon now.

"I've just heard a rumour, that's all."

"What rumour? Out with it, man."

"The Duke of Monmouth is come to Lyme Regis from exile in Holland. He has an army with him. He means to be King."

"Halleluiah," said Matthew under his breath.

"Halleluiah!" Luke's best sermon voice rose to the heavens in a great cry. "So, now you wish to ingratiate yourselves with us as non-conformity is suddenly popular again?"

"You've always been popular, think of the attendance at your sermons." To Simon, these latest sermons had been doubly painful. He knew Luke had him in mind as the selfish man. It had also greatly increased Simon's anxiety that the old pastor might actually get the money together after all. To prevent this, he had neatly lifted quite a few sovereigns as the plate was taken around the church and street outside.

It was a triumph for the old pastor. But Matthew had the last word. As Simon hastily prepared the release agreement, banished to a corner of the study where the brandy used to be, Matthew crossed the room to talk with his brother-in-law.

"You have the wrong figure in the document, Simon," he said, steeling his nerves as he spoke.

"No, we agreed 300."

"I believe I heard 250. We can ask my father to make judgement if you like."

Simon crossed out the 300 as Matthew counted the 250, selecting the smallest denomination coins possible to weigh down Simon's pockets.

Matthew put the remaining fifty pounds back in their cash box. *Now,* he thought, *I at least have the dowry for Grace.*

Chapter 10

The Earl of Sherborne glared at the stream as if it posed yet another obstacle in his awkward political life. Then he kicked his tired horse and crossed, followed by two-dozen retainers who held back slightly, not wanting to be abreast of the earl in his current frame of mind.

The news of the brat Monmouth's landing was all he needed. He did not want to be in Dorset with its narrow lanes that wound all over the place, up and down the humpback hills. Oxfordshire was far more pleasant; an open countryside of spacious, generous views. Besides, he had had no choice but to leave Maria behind in Oxfordshire. He thought now of her black hair and luscious curved Spanish body. It had only been seventy-two hours but he ached for the companionship of his mistress.

But every cloud has a silver lining, he thought as he reminded himself that war was no place for women. At least his wife, the countess, would not be with him, with her sharp tongue and mean, calculating ways.

His father had chosen this shrew of a woman to be his wife, the decision made when they were both children. The Earl understood why. It added a mercantile interest to their wealth, specifically rich trade in wool, cannon and wine. In turn, he had selected the wife for his son; going, this time, to an old aristocratic family. He considered it rather a coup in gaining the rich Redwood lands outside Oxford, as well as the political influence that came with the connections. Both son and daughter-in-law were dead now, killed in the accident, but the Redwood lands were firmly part of the Sherborne family holdings, centred in dreary Dorset.

But branching out, thanks to his stewardship.

He shuddered to think of a life wholly in Dorset, without the Redwood Estate. It had now become his escape from his wife.

Maria lived in Redwood Castle, waiting for whenever he could get away. It was not a fortified residence but a mansion built on the site of a former castle and retaining the old name.

It was tumbledown since the fire that had taken his son but still pleasant, with pretty gardens over twenty acres and a beautiful parkland beyond for riding.

Maria was the best horsewoman he had ever known. Unlike the countess, who always went by carriage.

Moreover, it was secure; for the countess would never go there, refusing to visit the scene of their son's death, along with his pretty wife. He thought of everything he had strived to pass down to his son. All that ambition, all that effort, and both son and daughter-in-law were suddenly dead, buried under the rubble of the collapsing wing with the flames roaring their determination to devour all around them.

Now, when the Earl went to the next world, it would all pass to his grandson; a joy to him, although he would never let him know it. The Sherbornes were life-tenants only. Yet the old Earl was consumed with an ambition to build it up for generations to come; generations he would never know. And they would know him only as a figure from their family history.

It was a type of immortality; a whole long life led not as an individual but in a relentless drive to increase family wealth and status. And now, approaching seventy, he had to recognise that that ambition would soon end in a stone effigy in Sherborne Chapel, next door to the hall. Or, perhaps, he would defy convention and be buried at Redwood Castle? It would be a fitting way to remind those future generations of what he had brought to the table.

He had, over almost two decades, almost completely put out of his mind the tiny irregularity. It had bothered him at first but now he no longer gave it any thought at all. He had done what had to be done for the Sherborne family; for the future. And when he passed on, that irregularity would be gone forever; buried with him.

But he was losing focus, his mind wandering. He had a daring plan and needed to move quickly if it was to succeed.

It was essential to get to Monmouth before his army gained in numbers to a critical mass.

He would stay the night at Sherborne Hall, leave early and be in Lyme Regis by early afternoon, riding fresh horses hard.

He was annoyed to find candles lit by the dozen when he rode up to Sherborne Hall. The servants had clear instructions not to use expensive candles when the family was not in residence, especially now that the evenings were so light.

"My Lord, we did not expect to see you here."

"Clearly! What is all this waste with lighting up the neighbourhood? Do you think I am made of money, that gold sovereigns spill out of my arse every time I go to the privy?"

"No, Sire, but Lord Henry is here with some friends."

"What? He is supposed to be staying at Sturminster, building some bridge for the locals. I told him... well, never mind what I told him." The Earl barged past the footman and entered the dining room, to hear the words "... and then my grandfather exploded..."

"Too right, I exploded and I'll explode again every day if required." Grace looked up from her soup and had an image of the gnarled old Earl exploding and then being carefully rebuilt in order to explode again.

"Grandfather, I did not know you were coming back so soon."

"Nor did I, my boy. What are you doing here? I told you to stay with that bridge, did I not?" As he asked his questions he looked fondly at his grandson. He was strikingly good looking, not unlike himself at that age. It took the years away, like bark peeling off a silver birch, revealing the sappy growth within.

But this was no time for sentiment. He needed to eat, rest and be off again. He took a glass off a sideboard and poured it full of wine, emptied it and refilled. "What is there to eat tonight?"

"I believe it is carp, duck and mutton, sir," Henry answered. "There is some soup we have just been finishing. If you would like some..."

"Bring me the meat and hang the fish. More wine, also. And some brandy and a loaf of bread."

"Yes, sir," said Henry, as if he were the lowly servant directed in such tasks.

"Yes, My Lord," said the lead of the three footmen as they scuttled out, leaving the empty soup plates in front of Henry and his two guests.

"Well, boy, introduce your guests to me." His gaze went across Thomas, who was amused at Henry being referred to as a boy. Then it rested for a spell on Grace, who was wearing a red and blue gown; another one of her mother's. She had her hair in a delicate bundle on her head, showing her long neck to perfection.

It had been seventy-six hours since he had lain with Maria.

He could see the veins speeding blood just below her skin.

Maria would not care, so long as he brought her a present; always presents.

His gaze was fixed on the slight glow on her neck and face from being close to the fire that burned behind where she sat; another waste of resources but convention in the dining room whatever the weather. Her dress was modest in its neckline but he could imagine what lay below. It was almost better for the fillies to be modest. It left so much to the imagination.

"My lord, your place." The footman had been saying the same four words over and again, finally penetrating the haze of heat and lust.

"Sir," Henry spoke, "these are my good friends from Sturminster Newton, where I have been bridge-building. This is Grace Davenport and her brother Thomas."

"Davenport? Davenport, you say?"

"Yes, sir." Henry looked nervous. He knew this reaction in his grandfather.

"Of Puritan sermon fame? Man Against Man, or some ridiculous notion like that?"

"Their father, sir, is Pastor Luke Davenport. Thomas is helping to build the bridge in Sturminster Newton and we went once before to Lyme Regis to see a remarkable old bridge. Now we plan to go to Bristol tomorrow to see another."

"You will do no such thing! Have you not heard of Monmouth's landing at Lyme Regis? All Catholics in the area will be lynched pretty soon now."

"But sir, surely Bristol will be safer if the Duke is come to Dorset?" Thomas asked, causing the Earl to pause in his slurping of wine.

"And when he marches on Bristol, what then of your safe

hideaway?" The Earl took his seat and grabbed some slices of meat from the plate offered to him, while another footman filled his glass again. "I care not where you go, Master Davenport, but my grandson is not going to Bristol." He turned then to Henry, "Surely you have heard the news?"

"No, sir, perhaps we are too cut off here in Lillington."

The truth was they had not heard this news because they had been cocooned in Sherborne Hall for several days. Grace and Thomas had invented a need to go to an unremarkable bridge in Bristol, but really it was to seek out Lady Merriman. And, for Grace, it was to spend some more time with Henry. In addition, Thomas sought an opportunity to ask his rich friend for a contribution towards the demands from Simon Taylor.

They did not know that that very day, overseen by Matthew, Simon had written out the loan settlement, taking less than half of the claimed amount. Monmouth had saved them, just by his very arrival in Dorset.

News of Monmouth's landing had come all the way to Sturminster Newton but bypassed the youngsters staying at Sherborne Hall, as if leaving the happy bunch to their delusional feast, lit by dozens of candles though it was barely dark.

Between mouthfuls of meat and bread, thrown down with great glugs of wine and brandy, the Earl told what he knew of the Monmouth landings.

It made Henry turn white with fear. Remembering the hostile reception he had received in the home of Sally Baker, he felt compelled to ask for a history of the Sherbornes in Lyme Regis.

But the Earl was loath to go into the past while the enemy, the non-conformists, were in the room.

"Take these two young people upstairs to bed," he ordered a senior servant, hastily called back from his night off because of the Earl's arrival. "I have some matters to discuss with my son."

He left long before dawn the next day, rousing his sleepy guards from the main hall where they lay, kicking those that moved too slowly.

He was away, riding hard, on a mission for glory and wealth against the odds.

He took his only grandson, grim-faced Henry, with him, although they did not speak for the whole long ride.

Thomas and Grace found the house deserted on waking, other than a kitchen maid who gave them a scant breakfast, and a groom who handed them two horses, along with a note from the Earl.

"He says you're to leave the horses at the White Hart in Sturminster Newton until someone comes for them," the groom said, leaving Thomas to haul his sister into the saddle.

They walked their horses to the end of the drive then stopped just outside the stern gates.

"Read the note, Thomas."

"It says we are not to come back here, and to keep away from Lord Henry. Henry is being taken from the bridge project and has gone away with the Earl indefinitely. There is to be no more communication between us."

It was a brutal message, more so because they had no idea what lay behind it.

Monmouth was angry and he let his anger be known; flinging abuse at anyone that came within sight. Most found reason to be away from him but his personal entourage could not avoid their duty.

"Sire, I think it expedient to calm yourself, appear more king-like if you will," Robert Ferguson said in his heavy Scottish accent. It was a dangerous statement to make, risking raising, rather than abating, his anger.

But Ferguson knew something that nobody else seemed to know, or at least would not acknowledge publicly. He knew that James Scott, Duke of Monmouth and eldest illegitimate son of Charles II, would never make a good king. It was a hopeless case, for he lacked even what his father had to offer; good humour, wit and, most importantly, an ability to survive whatever is thrown at you as monarch. Monmouth was superficially popular with the masses but was haughty, whereas his departed father had been self-deprecating. It made a big difference as his popularity would not last.

But he was a lot better than the alternative; a Catholic monarch filled Ferguson with dread, even if the King was of Scottish heritage. Ferguson was a Presbyterian minister, even more firmly fixed in his views than Luke Davenport, who he knew well and admired in a grudging way.

His hope was that Monmouth would last long enough for the Catholic Stuarts to be deposed, then perhaps the nation would turn to a Godly republic; Cromwell come again; with a parliament of sound Presbyterians to advise the ruler.

He thought again about Luke Davenport. Ferguson had read his 'Man against Man' sermons and envied the fellow minister's firm grasp on life. The idea that man is his own worst enemy and the vehicle of all sin pleased him enormously in its neatness

Luke seemed to have combined his religious mission with a happy family life; something denied to Ferguson even though he had tried on seven or eight occasions to convince stoutly Presbyterian lasses that he was good husband material.

"What do you say, man?" Monmouth answered, downing his wine and holding it out for a refill.

"It is the loss of two men, is all," Ferguson said. "Granted, they were useful aides but not essential. I have brought you more recruits through my sermonising than they ever achieved with their parading around. And that is what we need right now; recruits to our cause, who believe in liberty and the true religion. Forget Dare and Fletcher; put them out of your mind." To get his Godly republic, he was going to have to continue to play dirty; isolate Monmouth so he had no friends to rely on. Then he could pounce at his leisure. The broom of Godliness would sweep away all vanities and associated weaknesses. He licked his lips in anticipation.

"But I depended on them for counsel in the ways of war. You do not wield a sword and cannot advise me on such matters. I am inclined to pardon Dare and have use of his counsel once again."

"Sire, I would not recommend that action at all. Dare killed

Fletcher in cold blood and should pay the price of his crime. He should hang as soon as you can try him."

"All over a horse," Monmouth said despairingly. He wanted Fletcher back most of all but Fletcher was dead, on his way to see his maker. Second choice was Dare; still possible, although it would involve a twist or two to get there. The idea that a king should be the source of justice in his kingdom escaped him as he contemplated how to turn justice on its head and get his own way. But, as Ferguson pointed out, it was tricky to achieve it. He disliked such irritations considerably, preferring to dwell on more favourable matters.

And there were other things to drive the despondency away. They had, thanks to Robert Ferguson plus the dashing figure of King Monmouth, recruits flocking to their cause. The small force he had landed a week earlier had grown to over six thousand. At this rate, half the west country would be behind him by the time he reached Bristol.

Fletcher and Dare had been united in most of their advice, just falling out over ownership of a horse, albeit a fine one, and, with Fletcher awaiting burial and Dare to be hung, Monmouth expected he would inherit the attractive mount. That, alone, was a positive thought to wash the despair away.

His two advisors had been united that Monmouth should march his growing army towards Bristol. Capture of a major city would, they had argued, give him credibility amongst the gentry and nobility; key people whose backing he needed for his eventual success.

He would continue with their advice. He already had Axminster secure; the response to his arrival in that town had flattered him enormously. Yet the key figures had held back from his cause.

He would show them who reigned in this country. It did not matter that his pitifully small fleet lying at Lyme Regis was now in his uncle's hands. King James II was a Catholic and not to be trusted; he was no match for King Monmouth.

"Sire," a breathless messenger entered his tent, "I bring news of the enemy."

"Speak, man, and tell all. No, Ferguson, you stay here and listen. I must have advisors around me."

The young solder collected his thoughts while he regained his breath. He had ridden hard and eyed the cool wine with envy. Monmouth saw where his eyes rested and picked the cup up. He held it a moment in his fingers, his intentions unclear; then he drained it lest it be a distraction to the man making report in front of where he sat.

The enemy, he reported, in the form of the Earl of Sherborne with 100 men, was only six miles to the east.

"But, Sire, they do not intend battle."

"How the hell do you know that?" Monmouth sneered, holding out his cup for more. "Did you go up and ask them what they were about?" He expected blushes and denials; a tiny piece of satisfaction in recompense for losing Dare and Fletcher that sun-baked morning.

"Yes, Sire." This answer made Monmouth sit up. "Well not with the Earl himself, Sire, but with his aide, a Captain Hanson."

"What did he say, soldier?"

"He said the Earl would like to meet with you, Sire. He said, before it got too serious, Sire."

Ferguson stepped forward and whispered in Monmouth's ear, all the time keeping his eye fixed on the messenger; it was as if he did not trust the soldier who brought the news.

Monmouth listened and nodded to Ferguson, who then stepped back.

"I am led to believe that Sherborne is a papist," Monmouth said, although it could have been Ferguson talking.

"I understand the same, Sire."

"Ride back immediately and tell our patrol we will let Hanson know before sunset today whether we wish to receive Sherborne or not."

It was high-handed and the messenger had enough common sense to water it down before delivering it to his officer. But, he thought, it was also clever not to agree straight away; keep the other side guessing. He did not know the Duke well, but something made him suspect that the tall and lean Scot had been behind the cleverness.

He saluted and left; he would grab some bread and ale on his way back to his half-winded horse.

It surprised Monmouth greatly that Ferguson argued strongly for treachery; he had not thought a churchman so ready to employ it. Monmouth responded by putting up enough fight and volume to later deny his endorsement should the emerging plan fail.

But secretly, he liked the idea of a pre-emptive strike against a weaker force. For Ferguson, it was all about ridding the country of a few more Catholics. For Monmouth, it was the next step on his path to the coronation throne at Westminster Abbey. He imagined that procession for a moment. He would wear purple as he wore now; reinforcing his kingship in colour, as well as the way he held himself and how he walked and talked.

It was not long to wait. He already had Axminster secure and was on his way to Taunton. His spies told him he could expect an overwhelming reception in Taunton. Perhaps, even, he should declare himself King in Taunton, rather than waiting for Bristol? He would think on it; turned for advice but saw just the tall, thin minister licking his lips as if finishing a sugar banquet.

But, right now, he had a more pressing matter to consider. Should he make a trap for Sherborne or should he meet him as an equal? Well, not an equal but as a king meeting one of his noble subjects? And why not come last week if he meant to parley? Why did the Earl wait until Monmouth had considerably increased the troops at his command? He felt the lack of a confidant keenly, blasting Dare then Fletcher, then Dare again, for letting him down.

Then he made a snap decision. He would break protocol and go and see Dare in his makeshift prison cell.

Chapter 11

There was one single reason why the Earl of Sherborne had not arrived at the Monmouth camp earlier. After the surprise meeting with Henry at Sherborne Hall, he had changed his plans, diverting for two days, dragging his entourage all the way to Wiltshire with a sulky grandson in tow. It was nothing to do with the rebellion, nor the safety of the realm. His motive had no higher cause; there was nothing he could claim afterwards had been a valid distraction.

Except that the Sherborne family had to survive as a dynasty. And simply standing still was actually going backwards. The Earl was driven by the fact that he was near the end of his life. He had one remarkable coup to his tenure as Earl; gaining the Redwood lands. But to mark him out as an exceptional dynastic contributor, he badly wanted a second major achievement. He could do this with his grandson's marriage to a suitable heiress. And by suitable, he meant rich.

The Earl was deeply concerned by Henry's obvious interest in that Puritan woman.

"It's just a passing fancy, my boy," he said as they crossed from Dorset to Wiltshire, riding fast. "You'll forget all about her when you see what I have lined up for you." He added this when Henry did not respond.

He was taking his grandson to meet his future wife. He reasoned if he could make the case that here was a desirable heiress he would drive this infatuation out of Henry's young mind.

Sir John Withers was an obnoxious man in his early sixties. But he was enormously wealthy. He had started life in the slums of London, shovelling shit from the houses of the rich for his idle father, who preferred his children to work while he gambled and spent their hard-earned pennies on whores and drink.

His start was very like a thousand other lives that had begun in 1623, or perhaps it had been 1624, for Sir John did not know his exact date of birth.

But then had come the difference, for John Withers had, by God's grace, a sound business brain and a total lack of compassion for all living creatures, whether human or animal. At the age of twelve he had spotted a business idea and steadily secreted money from his father to form his working capital. It took two long years to hoard sufficient, during which time he honed his idea, hoping no one else got there first.

They did not and in 1637 Withers Fresh started in business, marked by two carts. The first was his father's shit cart, given a good scrubbing by some of his half-siblings. But the second cart was brand new and hung with fresh herbs, to give a welcome fragrance in the hot summer. It was piled high with clean straw, pilfered from the stables of a rich house nearby; or rather, purchased by way of a bribe from a corrupt stable hand who was subsequently hanged for his many crimes. But by then, John Withers was long gone.

His business idea was simple. Rather than just taking away the human and animal waste, why not provide a complete service? He provided fresh, sweet-smelling straw, or rushes for the wealthier. He took subscriptions starting at sixpence a week, for visiting and removing all waste, while replacing the floorcoverings of the houses at the same time. He claimed some early successes, with several aristocratic households paying considerably more than sixpence a week for the finest rushes. He helped himself along the way with a few manufactured statistics concerning much-reduced mortality from disease amongst his customer base, hitting just the right tone with the wealthy.

For money has no currency in Heaven.

By the summer of 1638, he was making a healthy profit and had bought his first tenement building in the East End he knew so well. Within three weeks, it was fully rented out and he was accumulating the capital for his next property. Over the next few decades, he purchased numerous farms on the edge of London, pulling down the buildings and covering the land with cheap housing, plus, in certain places, luxury mansions with fancy names and outrageous prices.

But his next move chronologically was the cleverest and

showed his true business genius. For, when not yet eighteen, he sold the Withers Fresh enterprise for a small fortune. He had seen that there were no barriers to others coming in and that the supply of his unique service would quickly become crowded. He sold to a luckless local businessman who soon after went bankrupt, but only when John Withers had his cash. This was the cash that founded his business empire in property. It was the start of five decades of enterprise that had amassed great riches.

He had married late, when it was hinted that a knighthood might be possible and he had thought it best to have a Lady Withers on his arm. They had one child, Penelope, who had grown up without any fatherly love but with a doting mother who had spoilt her from the beginning.

Now, here came real nobility to visit with Penelope. She brushed again her golden hair and checked her pretty, doll-like face in the mirror. She had cold eyes, she knew that; she had seen the village children shrink back from her stare and rather enjoyed the effect it had on them. She never talked to them; instead the icy stares she had perfected since they had moved to the country six years earlier.

She had all the best. A French governess followed a Swiss nursery maid. Her mother, Lady Withers, had recently tried a series of companions from various European countries, but not one lasted. The only permanent person in her life, other than her parents, was Sally, the black servant her father had brought in for her fourteenth birthday.

"Sally!" she would shout, "Sally, where are you?" And when she came running Penelope would confess she had forgotten what she had called about.

The truth was she was mesmerised by the servant-girl's chocolate-coloured skin. And often, when she closed her eyes at night, she saw Sally's deep brown colouring and wanted, so much, to touch that skin.

Once she had reached out and touched her on the cheek but Sally, usually so breezy and light-natured, had reacted abruptly. She had pulled herself away.

"No, miss, please don't touch."

She had spoken to her mother about it.

"Dearest, it's only natural to want to touch her as she has such strange colouring. But you should not upset her or she might leave."

"I thought she was mine, as a gift," Penelope had replied.

"No, my darling. She is a free woman and can come and go as she pleases. She is not a slave."

And from that moment, Penelope had wanted to own a slave; one, like Sally, with skin the colour that made her dream at night.

Her father had told her to behave for this visit.

"It's important you make a good impression," he said, as if bringing cattle to the market. "Go and change into that red gown you were given recently."

"Yes, Papa." She sounded meek but, secretly, had hoped to be dressed in red; the contrast with her pale, indoor skin was delightful. Going upstairs, she almost skipped along the top landing.

She liked the idea of being a countess but wished she could choose her own husband. She would choose a man tough as nails with others but so tender with her that she could wrap him around anything she desired. Also, she would require him to be handsome so when she hung on his arm he would impress the other ladies.

Perhaps Lord Henry of Sherborne would be such a one. She could but hope.

Sally dressed her in the red, taking several sharp rebukes from Penelope and a few gentler comments from Lady Withers.

"There, miss, you look a real beauty if ever I dare say so." Another thing about Sally was she had the most intriguing sing-song voice. Sometimes, Penelope got her to learn poetry by heart in order to recite it to her.

"Thank you, Sally. Brush my shawl and then you may go. I want my room cleaned while I am with my visitors and the sheets changed. This room is stuffy. Be so good as to open the windows and get some air into it."

"Yes, miss."

Lady Withers added that Sally had done a wonderful job with Miss Penelope's hair and that Sally was a credit to her establishment.

"Thank you, Lady Withers." She curtsied and made to leave. Penelope was looking at herself in the mirror but noticed that her mother reached out and touched Sally on her bare cheek fondly. Sally did not flinch; rather, she smiled warmly and left the room.

Why did the girl flinch when she touched her but not when her mother did?

But there was no time for such contemplation because Sir John was roaring up the stairs for them to come down.

"You've been up there over two hours and I want you in place in the parlour when they arrive."

Penelope's first thought on seeing Henry was, *Yes!* As she curtsied to her future husband, she looked him over carefully. He was handsome and dashing; his hand rested on his sword hilt as if to say 'give me no nonsense'. She liked that in a man. He was two years younger than her; that made it more likely that she could dominate.

It all added up and she gave an admiring glance at her clever father, who had arranged for her to be a countess.

Never mind the mighty falling, how the humble have risen.

The only detrimental feature was the silly scowl Henry, Lord Sherborne wore on his face. She would make it a priority to wipe it completely away. She wanted her husband to look adoringly at her and with haughty pride at the rest of the world.

They were sent to walk in the garden, chaperoned by Lady Withers, while the two men talked business. Her mother knew to keep a discreet distance in order to allow the two youngsters to become acquainted.

Henry would have liked to tell Penelope that he was not interested in marrying her, was sworn to someone else.

But for several minutes he could not get a word in. Penelope did not rush her words out like a babbling girl fresh on the scene. Instead, she spoke at normal speed, but one sentence ran into the next as they worked their way around the pretentious and overplanted rose garden. Several circuits later, she paused long enough to allow him in.

"Well, what do you think, Lord Henry? Surely you have something to say on the subject," she said, as if there had been awkward silences she hoped he would fill.

"Um, yes, well…" He had not been listening; thoughts were concentrated on Grace and his abrupt forced departure from her at the hands of his grandfather.

"You know, don't you, Lord H., that marriage to me will bring a considerable dowry? And then I am sole heir to my father, who is as old as the hills."

In general, he did not mind derivations of his name but hated the particular one she had used. 'Lord H.' had been the favourite term of his much-disliked tutor, who had been liberal with the use of a stick he carried with him at all times. Henry had not been strong on either Greek or Latin and had paid the price in strokes to his legs and hands.

"Madam, you do not have to sell yourself to me." It was a clever comment. Penelope could read it as a compliment, passing over the criticism and missing the insult altogether.

"I know, Lord H., we are a match made in Heaven. You have the pedigree and I have the gold."

In a strange sort of way, Henry warmed suddenly to Penelope. She was direct in the extreme; he liked that. It made him think of Grace, who offered everything a man could want.

But they were so different; his wife-to-be and the love of his young life.

He just could not imagine being married to this woman; shuddered at the thought of it. She held out her arm for him to take. He did not want to yet would, simply because of her directness. She was honest in a deceitful way.

Or was that the other way around?

"Don't they make quite a couple?" The Earl said to a disinterested host, pointing at them through the study window. Sir John had discovered that the Earl had no understanding of business and his ranting about Monmouth bored him; there was no profit to Sir John in rebellion. The other fascination

Sherborne held was for land. Here, Sir John had more interest until he realised that Sherborne was obsessed with ownership of real estate, regardless of how much income it produced.

"They look well enough, I suppose," he replied. "When shall we announce the match?"

"As soon as we've quashed this rebellion."

There he was, off on that damned rebellion again.

If the man were not an earl, he would not give him the time of day.

Chapter 12

She picked up the pails on the cross yoke, knowing that it would cause considerable pain. But, she thought, there is the moment before it starts that is worse than the pain itself.

It was 400 steps back to the kitchen. She counted them every day, dividing the pain into sixteen sections of twenty-five steps each; each time she covered four stages, counting four times to twenty-five, she marked a quarter off in her mind.

It was the way she coped, not just with the aching muscles but also with the drudgery.

Because it was not something Lady Merriman was born to.

Only she was Glenda now, Glenda Arkwright; a bent, yet still young, woman, who did whatever she was told to for a blanket on a pallet and a scrap of food twice a day. Gone was the refined pride of independence. It had been pushed out by the oppression that bore down on her every day for so long now that she could barely remember another life. Sometimes it came in tiny flashes; the smell of some flowers she was arranging or the sound of children squealing with joy; particularly the sound of children. But it was like pulling a heavy cart through a wide, black cave, towards a tiny light in the distance. The floor of the cave was rutted and she had to keep her head bent to face the floor, for fear of tripping or getting a wheel stuck in the crevices that seemed to spring upon her. Somehow, she had also to look up and keep her eyes focused on that distant light, to steer her burden towards it. But she could only glance from time to time and the yellow haven seemed further away with every look.

There was one thing that kept her worn-out body and mind going. She knew there were two people out there somewhere who would, one day, come for her. She felt it in her bones, even deeper than the aches. She could not remember their names; in a way, names were superfluous. It was the heart and soul behind the name that counted.

One day, they would come for her and it would be like the end of the world and an ascension into Heaven. A new beginning.

She clung to that strand as she struggled through her never-ending duties.

Her mistress was her jailer and she ruled every moment of every day with her scorn and ridicule.

"Oh, my lady is a trifle late," she wound on in irritating fashion. "That's extra duties for you, My Lady."

Each 'My Lady' was said with a touch more emphasis than the last utterance of those words; as if her jailor, Mrs Beatrice, broke new records in condescension each time she spoke; as if she needed to top her scorn with a new height.

"Yes, Mrs Beatrice, thank you Mrs Beatrice."

The lower I sink, the higher I have to rise. And that day will come soon.

She could feel it in those tired young-but-old bones.

The problem Thomas and Grace faced was how to get to Bristol. It was several days' ride on horses they did not have. There had been no contact with Henry, not a word from him. Grace was sick with despair and worry.

"We could walk but it would take a week each way," Thomas said gloomily. "And I cannot take much time off work, although Mr Milligan has been very good to me."

"He is a good man, Thomas, but also he sees his future in you."

"What do you mean?"

"I mean that he has no children and he sees your natural talent. He means you to take over his business, to step into his shoes."

"But why on earth would he give me his business?"

"Did I say give?" Grace snapped. "I'm sorry, Thomas, I'm just all in pieces over…" She did not need to say who. "I think he will sell you the business in return for a good pension, to keep him secure."

But Thomas was not thinking of gaining a business, more of losing his sister to despair. He could do nothing about Henry. There was no way to determine where he was, still less to get a message to him. But perhaps if he could find a way to get them to Bristol it would give Grace something else to think about.

But how? That was the question.

The Duke of Monmouth came to their aid, solving the problem for them. Not that he did anything deliberate, just that he marched his growing army towards Bristol.

So, Thomas joined his army, finding a space for Grace amongst the baggage train. Mr Milligan, a pacifist, disapproved but knew better than to attempt to hold on to Thomas. He would be back, God willing. Matthew was not consulted. Luke encountered them slipping out of the house early one morning.

"We're going to join the Duke," Thomas said, preparing to be defiant.

"God go with you, Thomas," their father replied. "It is what I would have done at your age; in fact, I did." The story came out of the start of the second quarter, the adventurous Luke joining the royalist cause and then converting, first to the parliamentary side, then later to Presbyterianism. "If a young man does not go out into the world, he will not find himself. But you, Grace, I cannot let you go."

Grace went anyway, employing a mix of defiance and subterfuge. "I shall just go to Stallbridge to see Thomas on his way." But in Stallbridge she carried on walking. They begged lifts and joined the Duke's army a little further into the day.

The fine summer rain added to Henry's perspiration, amounting to a thorough soaking from both outside and in. He wondered whether this was a turn in the weather or a temporary respite from the intense heat of the last few weeks.

He was a part of the core team that went with the Earl to meet the Duke. They were at Smallridge, a tiny hamlet seven miles north of Lyme Regis and a mile outside Axminster, which now lay in Monmouth's hands.

The Earl was in a foul mood. He had come too late to guarantee success. He had placed family before country and now would pay the price, He would have to rely as much on initiative and diplomacy as relative strength. He had hoped to confront a smaller invading force, explaining that he was the advance party of a much larger army under Churchill. He would offer a deal whereby if the Duke left the country immediately, disbanding his small force and honourably departing England, he would undertake to bring Monmouth's case up with the King. He would use his relationship with his majesty as a fellow Catholic to gain a full pardon for this foolish, youthful act.

And for Monmouth's previous treasonous attempt to kill not only James but his father, the old King, as well. He had fled to Holland after the Rye House plot had failed two years earlier. Now, he was back and his strength was growing.

And the Earl, for this daring and initiative, had hoped to double his land holdings overnight; perhaps even a Dukedom was within reach?

But now Monmouth's scouts had, no doubt, deployed extensively. The Duke would know that there was no big army over the horizon, waiting to pounce. It was several days away, still being formed; still gathering the clutter and baggage that go everywhere with a military force. And even if Churchill's army had been ready, Monmouth's ranks were increasing by the day.

Besides, it was wet, and he was hungry and tired. And his grandson beside him was sullenness itself, like a soggy bag of washing placed in a saddle. He needed all his wits about him to bring this off. Instead, he was being distracted; fighting his heir as well as manoeuvring around the enemy.

"Good God, boy, get a grip on yourself. You are a Sherborne, never forget that." He hissed the words between his teeth. In reply, Henry gave a look of disdain and dropped his horse back several full lengths, to lose himself amongst the pack that followed the Earl.

If he had not been intently interested to see Monmouth, he would have turned his horse and ridden immediately for Sturminster Newton, such was his rage at his grandfather.

And the desire he had to be with Grace, who he assumed to be back at home.

Henry could see straightaway that the Duke, or his advisers, had chosen the meeting place well. To approach, they had to ride up a long open slope, crossing several streams, one of which they had to lead the more nervous horses across. It was not a good place for retreat. Ahead, they could see a small band of richly-dressed nobles. Behind that, further up the hill, was a bank of thick trees; that would be full of firearms and swords, breaking the rules of the truce before the two parties had even met.

Thomas saw the advantages of the site as well. From his station in the woods, heavy pike in hand, he looked down at the small group approaching. There was something familiar about the left-most rider, slumped in his saddle, seeming to not want to be there.

"It's Henry!" he cried. "My friend, Henry."

"Quiet that man or he'll be roasted alive," hissed the sergeant.

But Thomas' voice had sped over the early summer grass, carried on the brisk wind and come to the ears of the Earl and his men.

"There are soldiers in the woods," the Earl cried.

"It's a trap," someone called.

They turned their horses as one and galloped downhill for safety. Several mounts stumbled, throwing their riders sprawling into the tufty grass. They stood, looking behind in panic as their horses cantered away. Monmouth was leading a charge, grinning and waving his sword above his head. What kind of man was he, negotiating with one hand while planning murder with the other?

The Earl stopped, turned on the back of his horse, saw three of his retainers on foot, trying to outrun the pursuing cavalry. Then Henry was galloping past him, back up the hill, drawing his sword as he rode.

"Turn back, boy!" the Earl roared. If his grandson fell, there was nobody left; nobody to build the fortunes for. "Come back this instant," he called but his voice lacked its normal authority and did not cover the growing gap between them.

And Henry was deaf to cries and shouts from behind, hearing only the whimpers of fear from those on the ground.

His sword clashed first with that of the soldier to

Monmouth's right. Henry careered through their ranks, striking left and right in a vicious rhythm. He made blood flow that morning on the slope below the trees in Dorset where he was from.

Thomas was ordered forward, the idea being for the infantry to mop up the residue of the cavalry charge. Thomas moved down the hill in line with his new comrades, seemingly in slow motion. Ahead, Henry had formed a core of a half-dozen soldiers, all now on foot, all now gasping and panting with extreme exertion.

The Earl was thirty yards behind, still mounted, roaring at his grandson to retreat. But Henry stood fast. More joined him, plunging forward from the Earl's position. Henry's bravery was attracting others to his cause.

Thomas was one of them so persuaded. He reached the cluster of the enemy and could not use his pike, nor draw his sword. Henry's mouth fell open when he saw his friend.

"Thomas," he croaked, blood mixed with sweat on his skin. His sword dropped naturally; not offered in combat to a friend.

It was then that Monmouth saw his chance. His sword was more ornate than strictly practical but its blade was still sharp.

"No," cried Thomas, bringing his pike up towards his own commander-in-chief.

The movement with the pike saved Henry's life. The sword blow hit the pike and shattered it but the force was deflected and hit Henry's face, glancing off. His hands raised to clutch at his ragged, torn face, Henry dropped to the ground; new blood, his blood, washing up like a new-found spring, breaking to the surface.

Thomas grabbed Henry's sword and took his place on the battlefield, fighting on Henry's side and against the army he had just enlisted in. Within six strokes of Henry's sword, the Earl was galloping up. He had already sent a lone rider back to his camp for reinforcements.

But the Earl and his contingent did not stay. Two dismounted in a swift moment when they reached Henry. As if long rehearsed to get the manoeuvre perfect, they bent and threw his body over the Earl's horse, while others formed a cordon around the Earl.

The whole operation took seconds to complete. For Thomas, fighting and heaving on the ground, it seemed there were new horses all about then gone again, galloping down the hill to safety.

But they did have the effect of spreading the attacking force. With cries of "There's the Earl!" several horsemen, sensing a more valuable prize, rode around the knot of resistance and charged down the hill after him and the body slung over his saddle. Thomas, in lead position with the defenders, felt a lightening of the ranks against them. Afterwards, Thomas said that this dilution of the attacking force saved them all, allowing them to consolidate their position.

And then suddenly there was no body of soldiers forcing themselves on Thomas and the others; just a blast on a trumpet and a hasty retreat up the hill. The surprise attack had ended. Thomas dared look behind; there was a strong line of the Earl's fresh troops marching in order up the hill.

The skirmish was over. The Earl and Henry were nowhere to be seen. Thomas, panting hard, threw down Henry's sword. It was instantly picked up by another and thrust against Thomas's neck.

"One move and I'll cut your throat," said a triumphant voice. "Sir, I've got one of the bastards here."

Chapter 13

"How is the Earl's grandson?" Thomas asked as soon as the filthy gag was removed from his mouth.

"Shut up and eat, rebel," spat back the guard. "He's alive, which is more than you'll be soon enough!" He chortled over his joke, sitting back on a log while Thomas was allowed to eat.

The last thing Thomas wanted was food, particularly the rancid stew placed before him. His head throbbed. He sensed a wound, raised his hand slowly to feel a livid welt on the very top of his head. The movement of his right hand was painful; he reasoned that was the result of Monmouth's sword blow coming down hard on the pike that had shattered in his hands.

But Henry was alive.

"Where are we?" he asked, forcing a spoon of the revolting stew close to his mouth so that the reek of gone-off meat brought sharpness back to his senses. He had to get out of wherever he was.

"One step away from hell, my boy." His guard clearly liked his own jokes. He chuckled on his log, rolling slightly as it moved backwards so his legs went up in the air to regain balance. Thomas saw his opportunity and lunged forwards, grabbing both ankles and raising them in the air. The guard fell backwards off the log, his laugh turning to a cry of horror as he hit the ground hard.

Then Thomas heard a crack, felt his world closing in as his body crumpled. There had been two guards in the tent.

When he woke next he was not sure if he was awake, or even alive. Wherever he was, there was no light at all.

There were plenty of smells. The first to reach him was damp vegetation. But then he sniffed human sewerage. No, that was not right, it was bad fish; a reek so powerful he started to choke. Then another smell took precedence, the sickly-sweet aroma of flesh left out to rot. It invaded his nostrils, causing him to retch; only his body could not move. Was he just a sad soul condemned in hell? No, he had pain in his body. Therefore, he had a body.

Pleased with his reasoning, he tried to move that body. But no movement was possible. For a second, he panicked; perhaps he was dead and in hell after all, his body rotting on the battlefield above. Perhaps he was smelling his own decay, cloaked in his own filth.

But then rational thought rallied and made a stand against panic. He fought that panic and won.

His body was constrained. He was in some kind of dark place but he was alive and they wanted him alive for some reason.

"Where there is life there is hope," he said into the blackness around him, time and time again.

And presently the blackness lifted with a flood of light like angels standing around him; like the cohort of soldiers brandishing glittering blades on the slope with Monmouth and his lackeys raining down on them.

Grace pulled the hood of her cloak over her face, hiding who she was from the world. They were looking for her everywhere.

"That damned turncoat has a wench he's gone and left," said Thomas' former sergeant. "If'n we can't get to him we can at least get the girl."

She started to move towards the edge of camp, hoping to skip out to freedom beyond the guards and picket line. But the security was too strong. And they were checking every female, looking for her. Groups of soldiers were working through the camp, going in to every possible hiding place. Her heart was beating louder than the regimental drum.

She had to think quickly to avoid capture and all that that involved.

What would Henry do?

She passed a few tents where the soldiers inside had been roused and were formed into long lines stretching across the camp to seek her out. It was only a matter of time until she was discovered.

But the tents were empty. In a flash, she was inside the first one. She saw spare clothes; a rich frock coat and wig, clearly belonging to an officer.

Into the lions' den, she thought as she ripped off her skirts.

Then thought better of it. She needed bulk to appear manlier. She replaced her dress and petticoats and pulled the uniform over her clothes.

"There you are, Ensign. The captain wants to see you." Grace's heart stopped beating. She had worked at the disguise for ten minutes, only to be trapped directly after stepping out of the tent. The whole purpose was to blend into the background, not to promote herself to the captain. She turned slowly in the late dusk, mumbled something and made after the lieutenant.

"What do you make of this wench they're all trying to find? The little vixen has completely disappeared. She belongs to the traitor who broke ranks and struck at the Duke this day. If I find her, I'll throttle her; that's a solemn oath."

"Terrible, for sure... sir." Did an ensign call a lieutenant sir? She had no idea. The lieutenant stopped walking and looked at her a long moment.

"What's up with you, Ensign?" he said gruffly, thinking the voice was unusual.

"Damned hot is all," Grace replied, trying to deepen her voice.

They had to wait a long time for the captain, who came stamping in after midnight. Luckily, the lieutenant had forgotten his concern regarding the young ensign, seeming to prefer to cool himself through swigs from his flask. Grace sweated under her double set of clothes, itching in the heat but not wanting to draw attention to herself.

"Bloody traitor in our midst," the captain said when he finally arrived. It seemed she and Thomas were the talk of the camp.

"Sir, this is Ensign Williams. You wanted a message taken to the burgers at Shepton Mallet."

"Yes, quite right. I had entirely forgotten with this rumpus about the missing girl. We're going to need supplies. Ensign, this is a list of stores we'll need when we next stop." He rummaged around through a temporary desk set up in his tent and found two pieces of paper. "Get this list to Mr Simpson of Shepton Mallet. He apparently has a house on the high street.

It's signed by the Quartermaster so take no nonsense from him about lack of supplies. Bring his reply back to me. We'll be breaking camp as soon as we've found this damn girl so you'll have to track us down on the road."

"Yes, sir."

"What's the matter, Ensign?" The captain looked quizzically at his young officer, peering through the dark, only one lantern giving any type of light.

"Nothing, sir."

"Good, take a fast horse. Here's your chit for the stables. I don't want this messed up." He dismissed both of them with a wave, then called the lieutenant back.

"Price, I want this girl found. Start a new search. I want every single nook and cranny looked into, turned upside down if necessary. It won't go well for me if she is not found. And if that's the case you can damn well be sure it won't go well for you too. You'll wish it was you riding through the night in this heat, taking all the risks of capture, rather than that twelve-year-old ensign. That I can promise you."

"Yes, sir. I understand, sir."

Ensign Williams was mounted six minutes later, turning the horse for the boundary of the camp and trotting out.

"Godspeed," shouted the lieutenant. "At least you don't have to search for this damned girl who is eluding us all!"

As Grace hit the edge of camp, she raised the gait to a canter; she had no intention of heading to Shepton Mallet. Instead, as soon as she was taken up into the blackness of the night, she stopped her horse, dismounted and pulled off her soldier's disguise, dropping the high-quality clothes behind a bush.

It was hard to mount using a regular saddle, with her long dress and petticoats, but she managed, finding the broken stump of a tree and clambering up. She sat with her skirts gathered up, leg down each side like a man, tapped the sides of the horse and moved on through the night.

At the fork in the road, where she should have gone north to Shepton Mallet, she turned east instead, heading straight for where she imagined the enemy camp was.

During the skirmish on the hillside, Grace and a few other women had climbed to the line of trees from where Thomas and the other foot soldiers had advanced. They had seen some of the fight, although the figures were largely too distant for clarity. But she was certain that, one minute, Thomas was advancing with Monmouth's troops, the next he was defending a small knot of rival soldiers, mostly downed cavalry.

Why would he change sides at the last minute?

The other women saw the same. Thomas and Grace were very recent arrivals. There was a lag of time as the women processed events, turning slowly to face her. But she had used this time to melt away, back through the trees to the camp. There she propped herself against a cart and tried to think clearly.

Why had Thomas switched sides? He had not wanted to be involved in fighting; she knew that. But to change from winning side to losing in the heat of battle? It seemed nonsensical.

The women led the charge down the other side of the hill, towards the camp. Perhaps some were wholly justified in their rage. Perhaps they had witnessed their loved ones and protectors hewn down in the conflict. But, Grace was sure, for every woman with justification there was another jumping in for the sake of it.

They were seeking her out. She saw a young boy answer their enquiry with a hand pointed across the camp towards her. Then she saw the soldiers, retreating down the hill. It was not a rout but a co-ordinated withdrawal. Monmouth's troops had been told to expect victory through surprise. Instead, Thomas had robbed them of that feast. Now they needed a route for their vengeance and the obvious path lay through the carts and wagons, to where she sat.

She moved then, hiding here and there, behind stacks of stores or bales of straw, working away from the greatest danger. But she needed a plan. And that plan had come to her when she had dipped inside the tent and seen the coat and wig that now lay, discarded, amongst the bracken and gorse.

It had served its purpose.

She stopped just past the fork in the road. Dismounting, she took off one of her petticoats and tore it into strips, then bound the horse's hooves to mute the sound of him walking. She had to climb on a stile to remount.

The more Simon Taylor employed his sickly-sweet tones by day, the more he ill-treated his wife by night; obsequiousness could be doled out liberally but there was always a price to pay when the sun went down and husbands returned to their wives.

"Your brother disgusts me," he said one evening in late June. She had come to learn that a strong verb like 'disgust' was the precursor to violence; afterwards, he would use words that indicated all passion was spent.

"I'm sorry you feel that way, Simon," she said as neutrally as she could manage.

"It runs in your family, my dear." As he spoke, he turned towards her and stretched his fingers of his right hand. She could feel the leather strap before it was even withdrawn from the curious scabbard he had devised for it, hanging by the fire for all visitors to see.

"Sometimes I have to use it on my wife," he would say when dining with a select group of acquaintances, hoping that if there was a Davenport connection present, they would report it back to the family.

It was a power game but it gave him a sense of control in a rapidly changing world.

He employed isolation to even better effect; Elizabeth saw her family infrequently. Simon became the public face of the Taylor household.

"It's not that I don't like him." Matthew struggled with Christianity on this point; that fight chiselled into his face, carved into wrinkles on his young forehead. "After all, he has always loaned us what we needed, whatever the emergency."

"Neither a borrower nor a lender be," Luke retorted, thanking the Lord for Monmouth's arrival. It had tipped the eternal scales back to non-conformity at just the right moment.

So much of life is timing, he reflected. What if the ship back from Ireland had been delayed and he had never met Rebecca?

"It's just that…" Matthew was trying to be generous but still make his objections known.

"It's just that he is objectionable, without any moral compass whatsoever, and I rue the day I ever allowed him to marry my daughter."

"Well quite, Father, I mean…"

"You mean I am right. Let's call a spade a spade and line up all the angels on one side and all the devils on the other for the last glorious battle."

Luke saw everything in life through the pages of the bible.

A fight between right and wrong.

A strange result of Elizabeth's enforced solitariness was that she was put into the company of the mouse-like Amelia Taylor, her step-daughter, who previously she had had so little to do with. Unmarried at twenty-two, it seemed Amelia would spend her life a quiet spinster, unable to summon enough personality to engage with others.

It happened first when she heard from Sarah, one of the maids, that Thomas and Grace had gone off to join with Monmouth's forces.

"I must go to Father!" she exclaimed, actually thinking more about Matthew, who would worry himself sick about them.

"You shall do no such thing, my dear." More and more 'my dear' was anything but an endearment; instead, it prefixed or suffixed a threat or order, often with mounting rage so that the words hissed out ominously at the end of a sentence.

"But I am worried, Simon. I'm worried for my siblings."

"They made this bed and they must lie in it." Simon was pleased with that comment. It sounded almost biblical in its grandness and solemnity. "If you need company to weep with there is always Sarah and Kitty."

"But they are maids, Simon. Would you honestly want our innermost secrets discussed with the servants?"

"Well then, call in an old matron. No, I know, call Amelia down from wherever she is to sit with you."

"I would sooner the deafest and stupidest old matron."

"That was unkind of you, my dear. No, I have decided that Amelia it shall be."

And, much to Amelia's consternation as well as that of Elizabeth, she was summoned and ordered to sit always in Elizabeth's sitting room from now on. "Bring that god-forsaken tapestry you are still working on with you, for this is the place you shall pick and stitch at now."

"Yes, Father." She scurried out, catching a ribbon of her dress on the doorknob so it held her back a moment while she tried to free it.

"Where are you going, child?"

"To get the tapestry sir."

"Well, get it then and be snappy about it." He had loved his first wife but saw nothing of her in Amelia despite the superficial looks, not realising that everyone is a sum of how they are treated.

The days of high summer were, thus, spent together by two young ladies of similar age, but little else in common. Amelia seemed to want to immerse herself in her lifelong tapestry, while Elizabeth was restlessly pacing, not able to settle at anything. Simon had ordered her to assist Amelia, liking the thought of his second wife playing second fiddle to his pasty-faced daughter.

But Amelia had glanced up from her stitching with a look that told Elizabeth that assistance was not required or wanted. Afterwards, when Simon was gone from the room, she spoke.

"Mother, whatever my father says, I know it is obnoxious to you to assist me in my needlework and I would not wish it upon you." It was another of Simon's insistences that Elizabeth be addressed formally as Amelia's stepmother.

"That is very kind of you, Amelia, but I had not the slightest intention of doing his bidding in this regard. What brings you to laughter?" It was more a stifled giggle. Amelia seemed to Elizabeth like a child told to be quiet but unable to get over what caused the humour, aware that the heavy hand of discipline could be upon her at any moment; laughter and terror lying side by side in the same bed.

"It is the way you voice your defiance, is all… Mother."

"Please don't call me that."

"Then what?"

"Call me Lizzie when he is not here." It was a strange request, for only her family called her by this abbreviation. Perhaps she should not have issued it, but it was done now.

"Yes… Lizzie." She looked up and smiled, her even teeth and pretty red lips in ascendancy over the moon-like features that formed her face.

And Elizabeth stopped her pacing, looked again at the stepdaughter she had despised, and rather liked that tiny spot of spirit that had emerged from the pale girl in a pale dress, fingers endlessly on the never-ending tapestry.

At that very moment, Grace also looked into a face she had not seen before. But it was a hard face; one that expected something for something and no nonsense about it. The face of the farm worker's wife looked over the dirty, tired girl on the big horse, riding like a man, her dress gathered inelegantly about her legs in an attempt at modesty.

"What can you give me?" the woman asked. Grace thought hard. She had nothing but the horse and saddle, an elegant handgun, and the clothes she wore. What would be of greatest value to a poor farm worker? What would give Grace the greatest value in exchange?

For Grace had not eaten for over forty-eight hours. Hunger fought rational thought inside her and hunger was looking victorious.

"Will you trade your horse, lady?"

"For provisions?" But how would she travel further?

"For two loaves and some cheese and a flagon of cider." It was an outrageous price.

But Grace was desperate for food. She was about to accede when the woman noticed something. "What's that you got behind your saddle?"

Grace looked behind her, expecting a purse of coins or the final bend of a rainbow coming to meet the land. "Oh, it's just a shawl," she said in a flat tone.

Then survival kicked in, for she had registered the desirous look on the woman's face.

"It belonged to my mother. It is made from the finest wool. No one who wears if will ever feel the cold again." She drew it down from the back of the saddle and splayed it out so it fell partly over the horse's head, causing the horse to whinny and stamp and the shawl floated in the manufactured breeze.

"She had it made for her," Grace continued, about to weave some story to entice the woman further. But stories were not required. The woman was sold on it.

"How many loaves do you want for it?"

"It's not for sale." Rational thought was back with her again, her spirits lifted; bouncing as they do from low to high.

They settled on a late breakfast of eggs and porridge while the horse rested and grazed in a meadow, then four loaves, a large cheese and the flagon of cider for Grace to take on her continued journey.

Transaction concluded, both sides reasonably content, the woman lost some of her hardness and called her husband into their tiny house as she cooked eggs and ladled out the porridge.

"Ah, Peter, lady here says she's only looking for the army what's been through here yesterday."

"You mean the Earl? He went north, was here last night. They didn't stop. I was that worried that they'd take everything we owned but they trotted right through our village."

"The Earl? Which earl?"

"Sherborne, of course."

Sherborne had taken Henry with him; her heart lifted. In all likelihood, both Thomas and Henry were with the Earl's army, less than a day ahead of her.

"I must go," she cried, rising quickly.

"Finish your breakfast first, dearie. It'll do you no good going off half-cocked. Peter will load your provisions and saddle your horse while you eat.

Grace saw the sense of this and sat down again, plumping back on the seat. She was weary and wanted to lay her head down but would not give in to such weakness. She dug her nails into her wrists to stay awake.

Peter placed her carefully on their one bed. His wife tucked a rug around her and looked down a moment. She was the right age to be her own child, only she had never had any that lived. On instinct she leant over the sleeping body, so calm now, and kissed her on the forehead; much as a mother would do.

"Henry," muttered Grace in her sleep.

"So, she is in love," murmured the woman. "That explains the desperate ride across country, day and night."

When Grace left later that day, the pack the woman's husband had rigged behind her saddle seemed too large. She stopped at a gate and clambered off to check what was inside. The food was wrapped in the shawl that had been her mother's.

"It's a good world we are in," she said as she remounted and rode on in search of the two people she loved most in this world.

Chapter 14

Thomas felt the indignity keenly. But being frogmarched would make anyone feel small. A soldier on each side, grown taller by their ridiculous hats, he felt all eyes on him as he was taken from his prison-tent to another, much larger one. It was the first time he had been outside for several days; he had lost count of how many. He tried, within the constraints of a frogmarch, to flex every muscle; as if limbering up for a dash to freedom.

He was mystified as to why he was under arrest at all. It did not help that no one would answer his questions. Everyone treated him with contempt yet he had changed to their side and saved his friend Henry's life.

He did not know what he was up against. But he was about to find out.

The tent was the largest in the camp. It had a wide entrance, with two guards who seemed almost ceremonial as they stood without any movement at all in that hot morning. It had rained overnight but all that was left was steam rising from the springy grass.

Ahead of the two immobile sentries was the real guard. Headed by an officer who ranged across the broad pathway, the trio asked all comers what their business was and on whose authority they approached. Several were turned away; one was even arrested, taking the limelight briefly from Thomas.

For Thomas was the main attraction, the reason why so many were about headquarters business that morning. Talk had spread across the camp of Thomas' exploits during the skirmish on the slope.

The problem was that they were all malicious lies. He had attacked, not saved, Henry, striking the blow that crumpled him to the floor, rather than taking the main force from Monmouth's mighty sword. He had started in the loyalist army and changed sides to the rebels at the last moment, risking the lives of all involved. There were even a few rumours, discounted by most, that he had evil powers and should not be touched, for touching left an intense burning on the skin. And the scars would never heal.

He was to learn all this over the next half-hour. Then he would understand why they hated him so.

Thomas and his two guards, Private Left and Corporal Right, marched straight towards the entrance to the tent; no questioning was required in their case. Inside it was arranged as a makeshift theatre, or as Thomas imagined one would look, for he had never been to a theatre. There were eight neat rows of wooden chairs and an elevated platform at the front, raised a good two feet off the ground. A

man could just about lie down between the front of the dais and the first row of chairs. On the left-hand side of this gap was a tiny square box marked on the ground with red paint.

The tent was crowded with people. Every chair was taken, with more people lining the back of the tent and around the sides of the chairs. Most were officers but there were a small number of sergeants and even a few of lower rank. Women were there, too, dotted amongst the red and seemingly in their best clothes, if their elaborate hats were anything to go by. Everyone turned as he entered; all chatter dropped away, as if an invisible conductor had indicated silence from the front. That conductor controlled a parody of an orchestra; no music, just the soft rhythm of three pairs of boots on the hard ground.

He was led to that red-painted box and made to stand inside. He spread his feet out and received a sharp nudge from Corporal Right's elbow.

"Keep your feet inside the lines at all times," he hissed.

"Why?" dared Thomas, to which Private Left jammed his musket butt into Thomas' side, in support of his corporal.

The only way to keep his feet wholly inside the red lines was to stand with his feet right together and not move them at all. It was as if someone had taken his shoe size and made the box a perfect fit.

Such details had not been down to the Earl; he had just made known the general tone he wanted at the trial and left it to his subordinates to arrange.

And they were good at granting the Earl's wishes, especially with the purse of gold coins he had left on the table when discussing such matters. A very few of those coins had made it to Corporal Right, who had even given one small one to Private Left.

"All stand." Thomas was already standing.

"Sit." Thomas had no choice but to remain standing. Now the three chairs on the dais were taken; the Earl of Sherborne had the central one, while two young and pasty-faced officers looking nervous and proud at the same time sat on either side.

Just like Thomas, the Earl was flanked in red.

Twenty minutes later, Thomas was led back out of the tent. There had been very little to distinguish his trial from a routine daily order briefing, other than the presence of women. One of those women fainted as the sentence was read out.

You will be hung from the neck until you are dead.

Even the fainting into the arms of a handsome and upright officer seemed to Thomas to be a little contrived.

The Earl had left the tent before the sentence but after the verdict; called away be a convenient emergency delivered into his ear by an aide. The sentence was pronounced by one of the pasty-faced officers, trying to disguise the fact that he had memorised the words the night before.

Thomas was marched back to his prison-tent as if nothing had changed. Corporal Right made a point of handing him over to the tent guards, who looked like they had not moved since Thomas' departure some forty minutes ago. In actual fact, they had been playing cards from the moment of his departure until the cry of the sentence rebounded beyond the trial-tent.

But they appeared not to have moved and that is what mattered.

Private Left made a final strike with his musket, as a fond farewell. Corporal Right, not to be undone, tripped Thomas so he fell into the tent and landed, sprawled on the ground, unable to break his fall with his hands tied behind his back.

They wished him joy in his sentence and left; duty had been done.

The very next day, as if controlled by the new moon with its mysterious force, another trial was taking place. This one was less for show, for Monmouth had no prisoner to exhibit. Indignation was at a similar level, however, and perhaps more justified for Monmouth would have won the skirmish on the slope if it had not been for Thomas' change of sides when he had seen the Earl's grandson in the fore of the tiny defending force. It would have been a decisive first victory, presaging something on a much larger scale that would see him crowned at Westminster, Monmouth's uncle, James II, fleeing for his life.

Like the trial in the Sherborne camp, the direction was led from the top and spilled out like an infection spreading amongst the underlings. They were indignant because their masters were indignant.

But it was more subdued in all regards, if only because they were conducting a trial in absentia. Their hated figure was taken by the enemy, no doubt lauded in triumph and held aloft as the traitor he was.

If they had known the verdict of the previous day, they would have been puzzled in the extreme. But then they did not know that Sherborne, seeing the light in his grandson's eyes, was determined to separate him forever from the Davenports.

And Thomas, more victim than perpetrator, lay bound hand and foot on a rough pallet on the floor; two sentences of execution hovering over his young head.

Chapter 15

"Of course not, Mrs Beatrice, I would not dream of stealing food from you," Lady Merriman lied with as much sincerity as she could summon.

She had dreamt many times of so doing; in fact, had imagined doing far worse in her more lucid moments, when she knew she had had a past and knew that that past had been much better than her present. At such times, thoughts of revenge filtered through her half-crazed mind and devious plans emerged, only to falter and stumble when she forgot them minutes later.

"Nevertheless, Arkwright, I find you guilty. You will go the rest of today and tomorrow without eating. You can work during your mealtimes instead. I despise theft of all types, but in my own household particularly."

"Yes, Mrs Beatrice. Thank you, Mrs Beatrice. I am sorry, Mrs Beatrice."

Then why, if you despise theft in your household, have you harboured me as stolen property for almost four years? You stole me and that is all there is to it. Eye for an eye and tooth for a tooth. There it was again; flickering memories of life before this. She saw in her mind a large square house with big sash windows.

She had been happy there. She felt that deep inside.

And that meant there was something to live for, something to go back to. If she could only work out what it was and then get there.

Later, much later, when Mrs Beatrice was in bed, Lady Merriman pulled an old chamber pot from the cupboard under the stairs. Inside was a loaf of bread, some slices of cold beef and a slab of cheese. She ate exactly one third of it, feeling the rich quality food coursing through her body; sending strength to the near and far points. Then she replaced the chamber pot, hidden under an old rug, walked past her simple pallet on the floor and climbed the stairs silently. She knew which boards creaked and avoided them by a wide margin. Mrs Beatrice slept heavily but her waspish little husband was a remarkably light sleeper. She went past their bedroom and up more stairs to the attic space, where she lay down on a musty feather mattress stored there since the Beatrices' daughter had left home five years earlier.

She would not have dared such actions even a week ago. But something told her change was in the air.

And she would need every ounce of energy and strength if she was to gain something positive from that change.

Amelia had one habit in particular that ground on Elizabeth's nerves. Her sewing was silent in itself. Yet as her hand moved in and out, stretching out the brightly coloured thread to then feed it back through the material, her right foot would start tapping on the polished wooden floor. Her left foot behaved, never moving from its settled position. But the right foot was the rebel; defying the silent order around her; one tiny stand against a world that she sat at odds with.

"I'm sorry, Mother, I mean Lizzie," she would say. And then the foot would behave for a while. But sooner or later it would start again with the constant, rhythmical *tap, tap, tap*.

When Elizabeth went to bed she heard an imaginary tapping in her head; as if Amelia was inside her and trying to chisel her way out; slowly, steadfastly, like a prisoner who has all the time in the world.

But who will become free one day.

"Shall we walk, Amelia?" Lizzie tried on the fourth day, when the tiny taps were making her want to lash out at this girl; this woman who did her patient needlework from dawn to dusk and on into the night.

"If you want, Lizzie," sighed Amelia, gathering up the tapestry into careful folds and placing it close to the fireplace on an occasional table.

If only it were cold and the fire were lit, I would put that Godforsaken tapestry on the fire and be free of it forever.

"I'll just fetch my hat," she said. "Will I meet you by the front door?"

They walked around the grounds. It was too hot for cloaks but they both wore their hats and gloves, as was expected of them. Simon had recently berated Elizabeth for walking in her garden without a hat. "Not only is the fierce sun dangerous, my dear, but think of the lack of decorum."

"Let's go into the woods," said Elizabeth. "It will be cooler there, in all likelihood."

"Should we, Lizzie?" Amelia looked nervous.

When in the woods it was a little cooler with the silver birches and beech trees spattering little specks of shade down upon them. But there was still no movement in the still, heavy air.

"Let's walk to the stream," Elizabeth said, then added, "Yes, I think we should."

They walked down the slope, towards where Thomas and Grace had used to play, when the house had belonged to Lady Merriman. Elizabeth had been several times and knew it quite well.

"Have you never been this far before?" Elizabeth asked.

"No, Mother; I mean, Lizzie. Father always forbade it, said I was not to leave the lawn and flower beds."

"Think what you have missed!"

They had reached the stream now. "See, it is gentle and safe," Elizabeth said. "When it joins the Stour, it gets a little more ferocious. Would you like to see that?"

"No, Lizzie, I think it is time to head back." Amelia turned, but she was faced with two paths and could not remember which they had taken. "Father will be worried."

"Father can worry then," Elizabeth replied, sitting on a stone and undoing her boots. "I'm going to wade in the stream as it is so hot."

Elizabeth hitched her skirts up so that they should not get wet and went out into the dark, still water. It came a little past her shins and cooled her feet, sweeping that coolness up her legs in a delicious sensation. She waded to the centre of the stream, now a little over a foot in and her folded skirts wet at the edges. But she did not care. She turned back to Amelia, her face a picture of delight, to see her companion standing at the fork, unable to decide which way to go back to safety.

Her hesitation was the deciding factor. She did not want to look foolish and ask the way of her stepmother. She was hot and bothered, looked back to Elizabeth and saw her playing with a broken branch, flicking water over herself.

It was so inviting. Would it matter, for the briefest moment?

They soon lost themselves in giggling and splashing each other. Both fell at least twice and were dripping wet when they sat on the bank in a clearing and felt the hot sun warm their backs.

"We ought to be getting back," Elizabeth said eventually, adding, "Come on!" when Amelia lay back on the grass to stare up at the sky above.

"I don't want to," she said.

"Do as your mother tells you!" replied Elizabeth, causing fits of laughter again.

They only moved when the sun went behind the tallest trees around the edge of their clearing, causing a drop in temperature. And then only after Elizabeth had promised to bring Amelia back as soon as they could get away again.

They were lucky, that day, finding their way back into the house before Simon returned from his office. Kitty, the maid, saw two happy girls, bare-headed and gloveless, in place of the two demure ladies who had left for a walk that morning. They laughed and played silly games, their dresses a complete mess.

"Sarah, put some water on to boil. We will need two baths and to do some extra laundry."

Simon arrived home an hour later. He was hot and tired; business was problematic in this time of unrest. Several people had called in loans he owed to them and he lacked the money to repay them. On paper, he had wealth with a healthy loan book of his own, but another sign of the times was that no new loans were being requested. The recent repayment at under half book value of the Davenport loan had left a huge gap in his wealth and income. In addition, the legal work was minimal so no substantial fees came from that. And he was embroiled in a hopeless case against Milligan over the bridge contract. It amounted to a lot of bad news, with nothing good to counter it.

He found the two ladies in their sitting room. Elizabeth was playing the piano, while Amelia worked at her tapestry, right foot tapping in time to the music. They seemed, oddly, too content; his senses told him there was some new communion between them he did not like. He racked his brains to counter it.

"Ah, my dear," he started, the idea forming as he went through the formalities of address. He had forgotten about the tapestry but now it had come back to him. "I have been meaning to speak to you about this. Little Amelia has undertaken such a task with her delightful tapestry. I have asked you nicely and you have ignored my instruction. I now find I must insist that you help her in her labours."

"But, Simon, you know I can't abide needlework."

"Nevertheless, I desire you to be her assistant in this matter."

"Yes, sir."

"You may start now. I am going to change for supper."

He came back twenty minutes later to find them on a long sofa together, the tapestry between them. Both were diligently stitching, heads bowed, in deference to the master of the house.

But Simon felt no satisfaction in this display of man's control over his household, for he sensed he had only increased that new communion between them, not shattered it as he had intended. He saw defiance and it frightened him to the point of rage. But then a calmer voice within said to bide his time and choose his battles carefully, so the fixed smile came back to his face.

"Indeed, it is nice to see the two ladies of my household so happily occupied on such a worthy task. If you both remain diligent, I fully expect to be able to hang the finished work before the month is out. We must consider which room it would suit best."

Amelia looked up at her father but decided to say nothing. Elizabeth was next to useless with a needle and would be minimal help to her. Amelia had been working on this tapestry for three years and it was less than half complete. It would be a long time until the pretty and stylised hunting scenes hung in any room of the house.

Lady Merriman had another secret. This one she barely dared to think about. But she had seen it with her own eyes and it could not be denied.

Unless she was going mad.

It started when someone had come to the Beatrice household. She had been summoned to serve refreshments, so she had seen him in the parlour. He was familiar in a nagging-at-her way, yet her fuddled mind could not place him. He had taken brandy, as he always did. But how did she know he was a brandy drinker?

He had come last week and stayed just under the hour. She had been shut out of the meeting, told not to return until called for and they had not called her.

So, who was he, and why did he look so familiar?

And why did he look at her so strangely? As if she was familiar to him, too.

And why was Mr Beatrice so red-faced when she had brought the drinks into the room, so keen for her to leave that he had said he would pour the drinks himself?

She pondered these things as she went about her housework over the following few days.

She was certain she knew him from a past life; somewhere, and somehow. He was much older now, bunched up with shaggy eyebrows, under which were narrow, cold eyes. She could picture those eyes, watching her with contempt sometime in the deep past. But she just could not place it.

They were evil eyes and she shuddered to think of them.

Then she applied a little of the logic she had obviously once been good at. If he looked much older now then the time she remembered him must have been a while ago. Maybe it was when she was young. She had been young; everyone was young once. But she had no memory of it.

No, that was not right. There was a man, a different man. He had dark brown hair, almost black. And rich clothes, so evidently wealthy and a different class to her.

Or was he? For the briefest moment she recalled a fine dress she wore to a ball, silk and lace in abundance. She danced with this man. She loved to see herself reflected in his warm, brown eyes. They had walked outside together. She felt the cool of the evening air after the stifling ballroom. She was young and in love.

There was something else. Or was it someone else? She could not recall and shook her head as the flashing images deserted her.

"Is there a problem, Arkwright?"

"No, Mrs Beatrice."

"Well get on with your work, then. You've been mopping the same bit of floor for five minutes. Lord knows, I can't afford to keep you in food and comfort if you can't begin to earn your keep."

She would think about it again when she crept up the stairs to the attic and the spare mattress she had taken for her bed.

But by that night she had been worked even harder than usual and collapsed onto the mattress as soon as she was able to sneak up to the attic. The moment she lay down she was asleep, snoring lightly and holding a conversation with herself, muttering as the night wound on.

If only she had been awake to hear herself, she would have been amazed at what she knew.

About her past.

Chapter 16

Grace rode on in strong sunshine; she was riding, she was sure, to both Henry and Thomas. She had food in her saddlebag and her shawl, sold for food but kindly given back to her, against any coolness come the evening. She did not care where or if she stopped for the night. Her focus was on catching Sherborne's forces.

But they found her before she found them. It was late in the evening and her horse was slowing from tiredness. She walked for an hour then rode for an hour, hoping she was moving faster than the Sherborne contingent ahead somewhere. It was as she was dismounting the second time to rest her horse that she heard the voice.

"Don't move, lady. Let go of the reins and step away from the horse." She did exactly as told; just a split-second of hesitation as she registered the situation.

"I'm a friend," she said, not looking around, not moving other than as instructed.

There was no reply, other than a snorted "Yes, a friend indeed. I like my friends young and pretty."

The soldiers moved out into the open. There were four big men and they had a prize to share between them.

"Well, well, well, what have we here, my friends?" came the same voice that had issued the order to her. He seemed to be in charge but Grace did not like the look of his leering face and half smile, as if the right side of his mouth refused to follow suit when the left raised up.

"I think we've stumbled across a damsel in distress," said another, the tallest of the bunch. He was lean, like a willow tree.

"Poor damsel in distress," said the other two, like a chorus in the theatre.

Then a blade pointed at her throat. It was old, it was rusty; uncared for. The eyes that guided it were cruel eyes; the type that light up on inflicting pain. Very slowly, the blade moved up the length of her throat, forcing her head back so she staggered and fell to the ground.

"Looks like this particular damsel wants to lie down for us, my mates." That was the first man, the man in charge of their devilments.

And, being in charge, he claimed first rights, pushing the taller man out of the way.

She closed her eyes as the body descended on top of her. Then opened them again with new determination. She fought her assailant with arms, hands, fingers and nails; battering and scratching.

It worked, for the man rolled over onto his side and lay a while, on the ground, looking up at the darkening sky of mid-summer.

But if it worked, it was a momentary solution, for he scrabbled up on his feet and whispered something to the twosome chorus. They turned together and walked to their horses, returning a half-minute later with two ropes.

"Well don't just stand there, tie the whore up!' the man in charge yelled as if he were a sergeant major chasing the latest recruits around his parade ground. Grace twisted her body to scream, but it seemed they were alone in that patch of wood off the winding road to Bristol and screaming would serve no purpose, other than to give them more delight. "And why you're at it, gag her as well." He had read her thought pattern and was taking no chances.

The soldiers had some discipline. It was not moral discipline, nor the type that stems from order or exercise. It was the discipline of the jungle; the discipline of the strongest.

Grace was raped five times that night as the moon and the breeze pushed out the daylight and with it all hope for Grace.

She was raped five times because they all took turns. First the leader, then the tallest and then the two chorus men, one of whom was the worst with his violent ways. The fifth time was when the leader came back for more; as was his right, he explained to the others.

When they were done they went through her saddle bags and took the food and drink, throwing the old shawl to the ground. Then they left, with Grace still prone on the ground, looking at the stars and wondering how there could be such cruelty in a world that had looked so good that morning.

She had cried while being raped, long moans of anguish. Yet now, with it over, she lay without a tear; just wishing and wishing it had not happened at all.

And thinking of Henry Sherborne and the injury it also did to him. And how much she longed to be in his arms, to feel his presence standing over her.

It was the Earl who found her the next morning. He had met with the royalist army and been despatched back by John Churchill to determine the strength of Monmouth's forces. He rode with a small contingent of minor nobility and a body of soldiers behind them.

The horse's hoof almost sliced her head from her body where she lay, asleep, on the ground. Instead, seeing her at the last minute, it reared up and whinnied.

"Whoa!" shouted the Earl, as Grace woke and panicked, hustling backwards for fear of being attacked again. He dismounted, seeing just a dishevelled girl and no threat in front of him. "What goes on here? Are you mad to sleep alone at night in these woods?"

"Oh, My Lord!" was all she could say, tears returning and multiplying as embarrassment was added to her shock and depression. She tried to pull her torn dress around her half-naked body.

"Don't I know you?" he asked, peering across to where she was bunched up on the ground, back to an old tree stump.

"Yes, My Lord. We met at Sherborne Hall. I'm a friend of your son, Henry."

"Well, you are much changed and that's a fact!" The Earl was relieved that she posed no danger. For a moment he had thought she might be a decoy for an ambush but his soldiers had automatically fanned out across the area and signalled back that all was clear. Then he remembered who she was and how Henry had looked at this girl. But it was too late for that now. The wedding of his grandson to an obscure rich girl had been arranged. He had secured the future of the Sherborne family through his adept negotiating and careful planning. He had surpassed the achievements even of the first Earl.

This girl was no threat to his family now. But he could not just ride on; what would it do for his reputation?

He burst out laughing, suddenly amused by the thought of this Puritan girl lying in her immodest state. Perhaps he should put her in the stocks to exhibit to everyone what she was really like.

But something warned him against abruptness and he cut his laughter as if shutting out the light. Better to tackle this problem with minimal force. A little pretence of kindness would enhance further his reputation; reinforcing the legend he was becoming. "Come, my girl, you need comfort and warmth. And some new clothes." He was almost tender in his concern; gone, certainly, was the gruff masculinity of their first meeting. He shouted a few orders and a small detachment of soldiers drew up behind him.

"Hanson, take this girl back to the camp. Make sure she is looked after, then put her on her way back to wherever she lives." It sounded a little too harsh, so he added a qualifier. "That is my personal instruction, do you hear? This girl has suffered much and I would not have her suffer further." The Earl rode up to the officer and whispered in his ear. "On no account let her see Lord Henry. Do you understand?"

"Yes, My Lord," said Hanson, deciding not to question his commander but wondering why the instruction. He turned in his saddle, looking amongst the half-dozen soldiers in his detachment for the most suitable horse. "Carter, dismount and help the lady up. You can walk beside us and take turns to ride the other horses." He then dismounted himself and walked across the clearing to pick something up. "Here, miss, is this yours?" He held up Grace's mother's old shawl. "It will be useful against the cool morning." But they all knew he meant preserving her modesty, for the morning had started even warmer than the previous day had.

It took two hours to get back to the camp, not because it was that far but because Hanson took every precaution. He doubled back frequently, changed direction often, and once waited for fifteen minutes in a stream under a giant willow that hid the seven horses. He sent one man out on foot to check the approaches to the camp, before he led his charges across the meadow and in to safety.

He rode much of the time beside Grace, chatting easily and lightly but keeping a wary look around. Grace did not want to talk, preferring to withdraw inside herself but Hanson had a cheerful determinedness that brought her out of herself. She found that she could almost imagine the terrible happenings in the deep of the night had been dealt out to someone else rather than her.

Until, on passing the guards, she saw her chief attacker again. He even had her flagon of cider in his hand, swigging as he rolled along. Her face went white, gasping with horror.

"What is it, miss?"

"He… he is the one."

"You mean who attacked you?"

"Yes."

The next few minutes were a whirl of activity. Hanson wheeled away on his horse, calling his men to form a line either side of him, whispering to Carter on foot so that the youngster nodded and slipped back to the guards at the makeshift gate.

"Hold it right there," Hanson's clear voice called out as soon as Carter was talking with the sentries. The drunken man carried on lunging around, drinking from the cider jar. He passed the end man of the rank on the right, who neatly took his foot out of his stirrup and kicked him over. He fell like a skittle in an alley.

"What the hell?" His cider was spilt, trickling a short distance over the dry, compact ground before soaking in as a darker stain.

"You're under arrest for rape," Hanson said, drawing his sword. Leaning over, he placed the tip at the man's throat, causing Grace to shudder; the sword point was just where it had been last night, except then it was pointed towards her.

"The man is called Roakes," Hanson explained when they were seated in his tent. He had posted a guard, sent someone for hot water so that Grace could wash and gone out to seek replacement clothes. "He's a nasty piece of work from somewhere in the north. He squealed straight away, giving the names of the other three. They are being rounded up now."

"What will happen to them?"

"They are subject to martial law. They'll be tried and, if found guilty, they'll hang."

Only it was not as clear-cut as Hanson imagined, for Roakes had friends in high places.

"Mr Hanson, do you know where Henry Sherborne is?" He had found an old dress for her. It fitted her badly, with copious folds and huge skirts, but she felt so much better for being covered from neck to ankle.

"Yes, I do. I heard you tell the Earl that you were friends with his grandson." He closed his sentence with a firmness on his lips. Grace could not mistake his intention; he was reluctant to discuss it further. She was amazed. This kind man had spent two hours attempting to bring her out of herself yet now was shutting down at her simple enquiry.

"Is he alright?"

"You'll have to ask the surgeon." That was a mistake by Hanson, for Grace shot up, a cry of alarm issuing out.

"Is he hurt? Is he okay? Please Mr Hanson, you have to take me to him."

"He is not permitted visitors."

Whatever she said, he would not move on this point. He was a soldier. His job was surely to obey orders? He had been ordered not to visit and that was that. This last point was a stretch. There had been no direct order not to visit. Instead, the surgeon had let it be known that visitors would not be considered welcome for medical reasons that did not seem, to Hanson, to quite add up. And then he had a direct order from the Earl not to let Grace Davenport see Lord Henry, yet, clearly, she knew him and was concerned for him.

At this point, the moral argument weighed in. Can a first party forbid a second party to meet with a third? What if parties two and three want to get together? Then, how did this mixture of motivations work into the debate? Party one might have good reason to forbid a meeting. The other parties may disagree, may want to meet regardless, but they may not know the full story. In this case, the old Earl's motivation was to hide the vivid scar from public gaze so it might recover as best it could without Henry enduring stares and whispers wherever he went.

Hanson has seen the scar or, more accurately, the long, deep and jagged wound that ran across Lord Henry's face. From north of northwest to south of southeast, there was a livid, pulsating course of mashed flesh where once there had been the fine features of a young nobleman with so much to look forward to. Hanson had seen it once and never wanted to see it again.

He was a soldier with a hard stomach but no appetite for such disfigurement. How would this young girl respond to such horror? Yet he sensed that she was not just a friend but something far more.

Grace changed tack, throwing Hanson completely. "What of Thomas Davenport?"

"He is to be executed." He answered without thinking, pleased to be off the subject of Henry. Then his sharp brain caught up. If she knew the name she must know him. More than that; they had the same name. "Miss, are you related…?"

"He's my brother." She was even more agitated now, making for the door of the tent. "Why on earth executed? Where is he?"

"He has been condemned as a rebel. He attacked us."

"And changed to your side. I saw him from the hilltop with my own eyes. That is why I had to disguise myself as a soldier and escape their camp. They were livid with the service Thomas had done your side. And you repay that by killing him?"

"Are you sure of this, Miss Davenport?"

"Of course, I am sure. I will swear to it. Do you have a bible?" Hanson did but did not need to use it; he recognised the honest outrage in her. "Lord Henry will vouch for him."

"Do they know each other?" As soon as he said that, he realised it was a stupid question. He was the brother of Henry's

137

love; they most certainly would be acquainted.

Grace then went back to Hanson, knelt at his feet, looked up earnestly at the soldier.

"Please Mr Hanson, you must help me."

And he knew that he must.

They just needed a plan and plans and strategies were just up Hanson's alley.

The Earl of Sherborne had forgotten all about Grace. It had been a long but successful day, tracking Monmouth's forces to determine their strength. The rebel Duke had over six thousand men but most were ill-equipped farm labourers. He would need double that number, or more, to make headway against the loyalist forces.

It was only a matter of time until defeat was certain. The Earl reported this to Churchill. Actually, it seemed the other way around, for Churchill stood when the old Earl entered his tent and accepted the principal chair. Churchill remained standing; part deference and part nervous energy expended in pounding the ground as his mind worked on tactics and strategies.

Sherborne was impressed by John Churchill. He excused the young general's senior position by stating, repeatedly, that he was too old to command and Churchill, a much younger man, was more suited to be in charge. But he knew the real reason; here was a brilliant military mind at work. If the resistance were to be put down through dynastic manoeuvring, Sherborne would have been the man, but he was no comparison to Churchill as a general.

On returning to his tent, he was faced with the charges against Roakes; these brought Grace Davenport back to mind. He dismissed the case against Roakes quickly; he had known the man a long time and appreciated his usefulness, only wishing he could control his urges and hold back his men as well. Something would have to be done about him, but not now.

"Hanson, bring the girl to me."

"Yes, sir."

He put on his best manner for the ensuing interview. He

could see why his grandson was taken with this young woman; she had beauty but it was mixed with two other qualities. Long a reader of character on slight acquaintance, Sherborne could sense the purity and the spirit that dominated her pretty countenance. He would have her himself, given half a chance.

But she was clearly not wife-material for the next Earl and, anyway, that was now determined with the match with Withers' brat.

"My dear, you have been through quite a trial," he started, hoping the sincerity he added to his tone obliterated the insincerity that dominated his thoughts. "We must, once you have recovered from your ordeal, see that you get safely home."

"Sir, might I see your grandson? We are, as you know, on friendly terms."

"I'm afraid, my dear, that is not possible. You must understand that it would be inappropriate for the Lord Henry to meet with a young unmarried woman at this time."

"Inappropriate, sir?" He had been right about her spirit. But she was playing right into his hands.

"Have you not heard the news? Perhaps you are not such close friends after all."

"No, My Lord, we are very close; very close indeed." Not the wisest thing to say to the Earl, for he enjoyed her discomfort.

"Well, as may be. But the Lord Henry is to be wed next month, as soon as this damnable rebellion is put down." The Earl watched her face; was rewarded with her spirit crumpling.

"No, I mean, that is…" Her voice trailed away. She looked smaller, younger; hopelessly lost in her oversized dress.

"Well, my dear, I must not keep you. You will want to rest a day or two prior to your return to wherever it is you call home." It was a dismissal but Grace was too distracted to notice. "Madam," he tried again, "no doubt you have things to attend to and do not want to be bothered by an old man like me." The next stage would be much more abrupt but it was not required. Grace stood a moment longer in confusion then gathered her voluminous borrowed skirts and curtsied before leaving the Earl's tent.

The Earl would relish the look on her face during the harder days of the campaign to come; it would cheer his weary mind.

Go now and never come back.

He had dealt effectively with Penelope's competition. Now all that was necessary was to mention Miss Davenport to Henry as being a little loose in her ways with men, in his humble opinion.

Humility, in its proper place, had its uses after all.

Chapter 17

She had a name for him. It came to her suddenly when bent over a stack of washing. Mrs Beatrice had obliged her to take in laundry from the hospitals and hospices around; heavily soiled and bloodstained sheets that required scrubbing and soaking until her fingers were worn and aching.

"Parchman," she said, as if holding a conversation with the washtub.

And Lady Merriman suddenly saw a clear picture of Parchman in a study or office, talking with someone else she knew. Only her memory failed her again, for she could not place the second man, just as she had been unable to place Parchman for almost two weeks.

It seemed her memory had been cut up into tiny pieces and thrown into the breeze. Every so often, as she walked through her dowdy life, a shard of remembrance would come to her. Sometimes, they had significance, like the main characters in a painting. But sometimes they were no more vital than the green of a blade of grass or the silver of water bubbling by.

She stopped washing sheets and stood, risking a reprimand from her mistress. There had to be some way to search through her mind and drag to the forefront the relevant information. She concentrated on the image of Parchman again. In this picture he was much younger, had spring in both step and voice.

She thought hard, wrinkling her wrinkled brow, shaking her head, as if the motion would rattle the past back in to the present. She had referred to him walking and talking; that was something. Parchman had been walking up and down the room but was shouting rather than talking. He was shouting in dispute. Now he was slamming his fist down on her father's desk, sending account books thudding to the floor.

They were both arguing; both furious. They had not noticed little Eliza standing by the door, one hand clutching her teddy bear, the other sliding repeatedly over the shiny brass door handle.

It was her…

"Arkwright, why are you standing at the washtub? Did someone whisper in your ear that the sheets would wash themselves?"

"Sorry, Mrs Beatrice."

It was her home, the house she had grown up in.

"Wake up, woman and get to your work."

It was gone. She tried desperately to grab it back but it was gone; evaporated like a steamy mist after a thunder storm. That mist, that fog in her mind, made it hard to think, impossible to concentrate.

Better to follow orders; not to think.

Mrs Beatrice was telling her all this, cutting through the fog with the sharpest of knives, offering relief for her aching mind.

Concentrate on physical activity. Do your duty, dog, and mind for nothing else. Just your duty.

Her mistress offered solace for an aching, troubled mind.

It does not matter what you think so best not to think, just act on my orders. Obedience is all that matters now.

"Yes, Mrs Beatrice, right away, Mrs Beatrice. Sorry, Mrs Beatrice."

But the little pink hand still caressed the doorknob as the young girl watched the furious argument.

Amelia had buried secrets too and they came out over the needlework bit by bit at first, as if she had to sew each revelation into a scene on the tapestry. But soon these secrets trotted out easily, to the rhythm of the needles and her tapping right foot.

"My father has always despised me. No, Mother, do not deny what is evident truth. Why do you think he takes so little interest in your babies? It is not his way to care anything for children and that is all on the subject."

Another time, she told of the affairs he had entered into when her mother was still alive. "He loved her, certainly, but it did not stop him, as it does not now I must add, from sowing his seeds as we sew our tapestry." She looked up eagerly after making her pun, also a little anxious at reference to her father's current infidelity. Elizabeth looked on the beauty struggling to get out and felt enormous tenderness for the school friend who had been no friend; rather a focus for disdain.

But it was only when Amelia delved into his sharp business practices, exhibiting an amazing understanding for the complexities, that Elizabeth came up with her idea; an idea that brightened their days by making needlework something to look forward to.

"These hunting scenes are tedious in the extreme," she said one morning after a long session of deep secrets about Simon.

"I know," Amelia replied. "I wish I had chosen some other subject for my grand work."

"We still can do!" She got on her feet, crouched down and looked up in the face of her new friend. "Let's put your father's peculiar business methods into the tapestry. Then we can tell a story that will never bore!"

When Simon came in a few hours later, he found them stitching away contentedly.

He was intensely annoyed, having never thought that Elizabeth would take to sewing; now he had to find something else to replace it.

Lady Merriman had recurring flashes of memory that ravaged her fragile condition, producing headaches that wore on her nerves.

She had heeded Mrs Beatrice's advice to get on with the laundry but repeated over and over again a name that stuck with her.

"Eliza, Eliza, Eliza." Sounding like a chant all good washerwoman would know and use to speed away the long hours at the tub.

Except the name was too fine for a washerwoman's daughter. It chimed and rang, speaking of quality and taste.

And it opened doors in her mind.

She knew she was Eliza, the little girl by the door. She knew the big square house was her home. She knew the man Parchman regaled with venom was her father.

But as to what they were arguing about, she had no idea.

After a while, she closed her tired mind and sought the solace Mrs Beatrice had promoted so earnestly.

Obedience is all that matters now.

"Let me understand you clearly, Amelia; your father has been paid a secret commission for every loan he makes, plus a bonus if that loan is to anyone connected with the Sherborne family?"

"That's correct, Lizzie," Amelia replied. As she gained in confidence she used 'Mother' less and less. "This is how it works. He persuades someone they have a case to take to law. They ask for his representation and a little later he presents his first bill. That bill is modest and well within the ability of the client to pay."

"What is wrong with that?" Lizzie asked.

"Nothing, only the moral aspect of whether there was a case in the first place. But we can set that aside for now. It is what happens next that gets interesting."

They stitched a few moments in silence; perhaps needing time to process the minor misdemeanour before progressing to the more serious.

"The next bill is a few days late and only a little larger. Even the third month's billing is reasonable, if somewhat complicated to understand. Believe me, I have seen them. But from the fourth month the bills rise sharply higher. Within nine months, the client is bankrupt. Anything worth owning has a charge attached to it. Everything that trader has worked for, sometimes over a lifetime, is in Simon's hands."

"I never knew this, I swear."

"Don't worry, Lizzie, I know that well enough. But do you want to hear the next chapter of this sorry tale?"

To Lizzie's nod, she explained that he then offered to lend his client the required cash. "They invariably take up this generous offer."

Amelia went on to explain the neatness of the set-up. "The banknotes to constitute the loan never leave his chambers for they go straight to repay the debt of fees owed to his firm. Meanwhile, he has collected the commission on the loan, increasing his sordid profit still further."

"Ah, but how does the client then repay the loan?"

"That is the final bit of genius," Amelia replied. "He has the right written into the loan agreement to take a stake in the business if his client defaults on repayments."

"Hence he owns several businesses outright and has part-ownership in others."

"Exactly, Lizzie, and still the loans have to be repaid so he can carry on increasing his wealth ad infinitum."

"Good God!" Lizzie exclaimed. "We have to reverse this evil practice."

"Yes, but how?" Amelia replied thoughtfully then changed the subject, for there were footsteps in the passage outside.

Elizabeth dared raise her eyes once or twice during the following conversation when Simon had entered the room to 'check on his ladies'. She raised them to snatch glances at Amelia and wonder how it was that there was so much to this pale-faced lady she had never seen before.

And all the time during that conversation, two sets of hands never stopped moving; in and out, with a deftness of purpose. That purpose would have made Simon shiver if he had known of it. For the two ladies closest to him in the world were planning his downfall, neat little stitch by neat little stitch.

There was nothing neat in Matthew's world, for envy does not come in tidy packages.

Rather, it floods the mind with switchback currents of choppy waters.

He had hoped to glide into his father's shoes, taking over the job of sermon-writing and delivering naturally. He already did much of the administration of their church. But his father seemed born again with regard to his ability to deliver a stormy lecture from the pulpit. The success of the 'Man against Man' series, delving so expertly into the vices and virtues that made up the moral compass of man, gave new life to him. Gone were the slurred speech and tired clichés of recent years, in favour of new vigour.

Beside this tower of a man, Matthew felt small and inadequate. He had four inches of height on his father yet felt the shorter man.

He had to find a way to shine; to build on his father's great work, to eclipse it with a tower taller and straighter, reaching that bit closer towards Heaven. Each generation had a responsibility to build on the previous one; matching pride and humility like stone and mortar.

"I have one accomplishment to my credit," he said to himself repeatedly, thinking of his trouncing of Simon during the settlement of the debt. He did not count the thousands of times he had checked on the cleaning of the church, or counted out the collection to make ends meet, or managing as surrogate father to his brother and sisters when their own father had been drowning in brandy.

The church collection was growing again, or at least it had been growing rapidly, but over the last two Sundays it had stagnated. But then there were the print sales of the 'Man Against Man' series. All in all, with the loan settlement included, their finances were looking much healthier.

If only the benign monetary situation could spill over to his mood.

Luke sensed his son's despair a little in his quieter moments. His perception of his surroundings had improved now that he was sober. But mostly the aura of success blew with a strong, noisy wind, carrying him forward with little regard for his lost son left behind.

Thus, Matthew struggled while Luke soared and the Davenport household continued to strain at every seam, even with both Grace and Thomas gone to war and not around to add their own elements into the confusion.

Chapter 18

Hanson eased the side of the tent up. The loosened peg allowed movement enough for him to crawl under.

"Who's there?" Thomas asked, too loudly, woken suddenly from his fitful sleep.

"Hush, it's a friend." The next moment, just as the rope binding Thomas' legs was cut, a rough scarf was tied securely over his eyes. "Follow me," the voice said.

It had been agreed between Grace and Hanson that Thomas would not know the identity of his liberator, hence Hanson could not be implicated in any way.

But Thomas seemed reluctant to duck under the tent and to freedom, being led by a man he never met and would have to trust completely.

"Grace is waiting for you," Hanson hissed, trying to sound both reassuring and urgent at the same time.

"What's going on? A guard entered the tent, flashed his lantern around, seeing Thomas asleep on the floor. He held it steady for a moment, trying to make sense of the shadows it created. Thomas had instinctively turned his head away from the lantern, obscuring the blind from the guard's sight.

"You hearing things again, Joe?" called the second guard from outside the tent. "It's your damned turn with the dice."

The inquisitive guard grunted, kicked out at Thomas on the floor and hurried back to his station, knowing his colleague was quite capable of cheating at dice if left alone too long.

After the longest minute of his life, Hanson emerged from the shadowy area behind a pile of broken saddles and straightened his long, lithe body.

"We must go under the tent and across the camp to where Grace has the horses." This time he went right up to Thomas and whispered very quietly in his ear. "I'll guide you."

"Can't you take the blind off?"

"No, Grace will explain, just come with me."

It was a slow business covering the 600 yards from the side of the tent to the boundary where Grace waited with two fast horses. In Hanson's mind he had divided it into three distinct sections.

First was the run from the tent to the sanitation ditch. This involved a zigzag series of sprints at a crouch, taking advantage of the shadows created by the tents they were running past. It was much harder than Hanson had envisaged because Thomas, still blindfolded and bound at the wrists, stumbled on the guy ropes. After a minute or two, he stopped trying to lead the blindfolded man and, instead, propelled him from behind. It was still tricky going but they got on faster.

It was tough to keep Thomas blindfolded but the only way they could keep Hanson's identity secret from Thomas. The idea was that Hanson would bring Thomas to Grace outside the camp and then melt back in, feigning surprise when the guards found Thomas missing in the morning; the morning of his execution.

Thomas was a quick learner. By half-way through the stretch he was responding to a light touch on each arm, changing direction instantly; either to avoid something lying in their way or to dart into a shadowy area to avoid various groups of soldiers.

It was two breathless men that jumped the final barrier; an earthwork put up by the soldiers to make the ditch deeper. They fell into the deep channel below, rolling in excrement but both delighted to have made it. Their panting as they fought to regain their breath for stage two seemed like sirens designed to alert the whole camp.

But nobody stirred. Nobody had noticed Thomas gone and nobody was out looking for them. They just had to evade the perimeter sentries who circled the encampment continuously.

Stage two was easier but far less pleasant. The excrement ditch was deep, up to their knees, with a mixture of human and food waste. The rampart running both sides of the channel gave them thirty inches of cover. To avoid being seen they had to wade the filth, bent over double.

Every time they heard a noise, Hanson tapped Thomas on the

shoulder. Instinctively, Thomas knew to stop dead still; two islands of human flesh in a torrent of human waste. A double tap was the code to move on again; first Thomas then Hanson, guiding him from behind in his blindness.

One time, almost halfway along the length, Thomas received a sharp tap on the shoulder. He stopped immediately. Hanson saw four soldiers lining up along the rampart, the nearest just ten feet ahead. They pissed in unison, almost as if a drill sergeant was behind the exercise. Splashes hit Thomas and a few even reached Hanson behind. Then, almost as one, they turned and walked away.

Thomas remained stock-still, waiting for the double tap to tell him to start moving again. It did not come. He could sense his rescuer standing rigidly still behind him; not a muscle moving, so Thomas copied Hanson and remained rooted to the ground.

Afterwards, Hanson explained that one of the soldiers had stayed behind, waiting for his comrades to leave. When they were gone he pulled out of his haversack a bottle of some spirits, sitting on the edge of the rampart and drinking steadily from his bottle.

Only when it was finished, ten minutes later, did he rise up and slouch away, swallowed into the night and drunken oblivion.

Then, when quiet night reigned again, Thomas got the double tap on the shoulder.

The third stage was the scariest. It was also the shortest; just a thirty-yard crawl across scrubland to the edge of camp. Then down a slope to a cluster of trees less than a hundred yards away. This is where Grace waited with the horses.

But it took almost an hour to do the thirty-yard stretch on their stomachs. Sometimes they lay for five or six minutes without moving; trying, face-down, to estimate the timing of the gaps between the guards who patrolled the perimeter. It did not help when they changed the guard at midnight; new guards meant new patrol habits and they had to wait under some bracken to get the measure of the new movements.

When they reached the edge of the slope, Hanson's instinct

was to run the last hundred yards. But sometimes runners get caught while the stealthy and wily make it. So, after forcing Thomas to roll six feet from the path the guards used, they continued on their stomachs for the entire home stretch.

Tap and double tap. Stop and start again. Tap and double tap.

Once, thirty feet from safety, they heard a shout from the camp. Suddenly, they heard many more shouts from all directions. It was damned bad luck to be caught right in the closing stages of the escape.

And if Hanson was found with Thomas, it would be two people hanging in the morning.

They froze, trying to ascertain where the cries were coming from. Then Thomas started laughing quietly.

"It's echoes is all," he whispered to Hanson. They were in a bowl of land, where one loud call had multiplied from every direction around them, producing a threatening symphony from a single innocent source.

Grace saw them from the copse where she waited. Fearing snorting horses would give her away, she had kept the animals back in another set of trees 50 yards behind her. She was entirely alone, also down flat on her stomach, just like the two figures crawling towards her.

But she had only just made it in time, darting through the trees and falling onto all fours as Thomas and Hanson approached.

She had been busy with her own mission. One that she had not dared tell Hanson about.

She had been to see Henry.

It had been easy in a way. She had hung around the camp for two days, recovering from the ordeal she had been through, if anyone asked. The Earl had been out on another survey of Monmouth's position and strength for much of that time, so there was little pressure on Grace to move on. He had only returned that evening, the evening before Thomas was scheduled to hang.

Hanson had found her a tent, sharing with two widows of the skirmish on the slope who were, similarly, waiting for transport to take them home. They were both wrapped in grief and concern for their future and had shown no interest in Grace, other than an initial and formulaic expression of outrage at what had happened to her.

"Roakes will swing for it, have no fear," one of them said, patting Grace on the head, but illustrating again how little was known of Roakes' connections. At that moment, he was confined in reasonable comfort while the Earl mulled over his future; the principal thought was an occupation for him away from the army so that he could disappear from his accusers.

She had located Henry's tent quite easily. It was one of two that were heavily guarded. Hanson confirmed that the smaller guarded tent was where Thomas was being held but would not say whether Henry occupied the larger one.

But she did not need to ask for she had seen the greasy-haired surgeon going in and out all day long.

She decided on a bold approach. Walking up to the entrance of the tent she declared in a loud voice, "My name is Mrs Merriman. I am here at the request of Lord Henry." Her plan rested on two key factors. First, Henry had to be awake. Second, she hoped he would recognise the name from their trip to Lyme Regis.

He was awake and not only recognised the name but also her voice.

"Do you have a permission chit?" Two guards blocked her way.

"No, I did not realise that I required one. I was given a message by the surgeon to attend as soon as possible."

"I can't let anyone in without..."

"Guard, let the lady in at once. I asked for her to visit and do not want her kept waiting at the entrance a moment longer." It was Henry's voice but flatter; wearier, too.

The guards snapped to attention so that Grace could pass through, the one still mumbling about proper procedure and life being driven by chits for this and chits for that.

She could not help but gasp when she entered the tent. In the lantern light the facial wound appeared terrible; the red tinge of slight infection was exaggerated to glow like the skin of a drunken man. But most noticeable were the livid bruises of all colours and sizes. They crossed his face like outriding hills following a red river that was the wound; giant lumps of misshapen flesh.

Henry lay back on a large bed in the centre of the tent. He was clearly exhausted from his efforts to shout at the guards. He said just two words.

"My Grace."

He shut his fevered eyes and drifted off to another land. Perhaps she went with him to this imaginary world where no damage was done and they walked and frolicked by the river on the way to Bagber.

Grace sat by his side as long as she dared. He woke twice in the hour she spent there. The first time he seemed confused by her presence. The second time he was much calmer. He took her hand and raised it to his ravaged face.

"My Grace," he said again.

"My Henry," she replied, horrified at touching the wound.

Then she did something that defined who she had become; no longer a silly fun girl without a care in the world. She traced her fingers over the wound, scratching and stroking where it obviously itched and irritated him. She found a cloth and soaked it in cold water to alleviate the fever. She spoke so tenderly to the man she loved.

"Henry, most of this will go away," she said, wondering if she was true in this thought. "Most of it is bruising which will moderate daily and one day when you look in a glass you will see nothing but your own sweet face."

He smiled then and kissed her hand. They both knew she had gone too far – there would always be a scar running across his face and it would mark him out wherever he went. But he needed hope; something to cling on to; something to make him believe there was a reason to live.

And, of course, she was the reason he found to stay alive. But then the weight of Penelope Withers came into his mind. In whispered, weak words he narrated that he was spoken for, pledged to another and could never be hers.

In response, Grace took an enormous intake of breath. Her

world was suddenly bereft of joy. She had refused to accept what the Earl had maliciously told her but now heard it from Henry himself. Could he have stood up to the Earl, refused to accept the betrothal? She considered the Earl for a moment. He had manipulated her easily; it was what he did best. She could not blame Henry for being torn away from her.

A little later, she had to leave. She had whispered a few bare facts about the escape plan. He was outraged that Thomas was so accused and remembered his friend coming to his aid, switching sides as the small army bore down on them. He would take it up with his grandfather. But Grace concentrated on soothing him, for she could see he was in no state to do so.

It was then she decided not to go with Thomas. She would see him off safely, let him take the second horse so that he could switch mounts and ride the faster back to Sturminster Newton. But he would go alone with her love and blessings. For Henry needed her and she would stay.

"Are you mad?" Hanson whispered under the shelter of the cluster of trees. Grace had quickly outlined what she had done and the fact that she was staying in the camp. "The guard will recognise you and that will be that."

"No, Mr Hanson, the guard will not recognise me for to do that he will have to admit that he let someone in without one of his precious chits. I'm quite safe on that account."

Thomas and Grace had hugged dearly when Thomas crawled in and the blindfold was removed. Hanson staying on the periphery of the trees, where he could not be seen by Thomas. Now they hugged again; not the joy of joining together but a hug in recognition of imminent parting.

Then Thomas was off again, running through the long grass to the next copse and his waiting horses. But he had no intention of going back to Sturminster Newton. Instead, he would ride to Bristol and track down Lady Merriman. As he swung into the saddle he reflected that he had a side-saddle on the horse meant for Grace. "Prefect for Lady Merriman," he muttered to himself as he broke cover from the trees and cantered towards the hills and flats of Somerset.

"We should get back," Hanson said, still shocked at Grace's decision. "But I have not the slightest idea how we will do it. Getting out of the camp was hard enough but getting in again is going to be a lot harder to manage." He could not take Grace up the excrement ditch.

"Easy," said Grace, linking her arm into his as Thomas disappeared into the gloom. "Don't tell me no soldier has ever taken their sweetheart out for a moonlit walk before." She increased her grip on his arm and leant her bonneted head onto his shoulder. "And this particular sweetheart is exhausted from all that walking and is very much looking forward to her warm bed."

Chapter 19

Grace was arrested at ten o'clock the next morning. It was a beautiful, pleasant morning with sunshine guaranteed by a virtually cloudless sky, tempered by a light, refreshing wind.

There was an appearance of innocence about that pretty summer day that belied the events it contained.

Certainly not a day to be confined, held under dirty-white canvas; unsure of what will happen next.

She had forgotten that she was a Davenport, thus sharing a name with the escaped prisoner, her brother. It was evident from the first examination of the scene that Thomas had gone under the side of the tent; the slightly flapping canvas was traced to a loosened peg. But someone had loosened that peg deliberately and that meant he had an accomplice; who else could have cut the rope that bound his hands and feet?

But outside, the trail grew cold. There was no soft ground to mark footprints; no evidence of which direction he and his accomplice had chosen. They searched the entire encampment, forming into lines; just as Monmouth's army had, looking for Grace. But the consensus was that the bird had flown, or rather ridden away on the back of a stolen horse. That horse had been tethered outside the camp by the same person who had freed him from his binds.

And who was more likely than his sister, recently come to camp in dishevelled state with a preposterous story of gang rape led by Sergeant Roakes, just this morning freed with all charges dismissed and no dishonour to his name?

As a woman, she was not imprisoned with stringency. She was confined to her tent with one of the two lady-wardens instructed to be always in attendance. They did not mind this extra duty for it paid well and both faced uncertain futures with their husbands dead on the battlefield.

The time passed outwardly calmly; the worst moments were telling Grace to sit still and make some use of her time. She took this advice to heart and sat next to them to darn a huge mound of soldiers' socks, for which the two ladies were paid a ha'penny a pair. Grace forced herself to the task and was much quicker than the others, with their stiffer fingers. She placed each darned pair in alternate piles, thus boosting the income of these fragile women a little more.

"You're quite a goldmine," one said. "I hope you are with us for a long time." That was the closest either of her chaperones came to mentioning the inevitable trial coming up.

When the socks were all done, the officers started bringing items for mending; buttons dangling by a thread, loose and tarnished buckles, even boots where the soles were coming away. The army of Churchill had moved with such speed to counter Monmouth that there had been little time to think of cobblers and seamstresses.

And the officers had all heard that there was a pretty girl awaiting trial who was adept with a needle, so the mending pile grew; the stories surrounding her, also. Everyone had to set eyes on this young girl accused of aiding a prisoner escape. As happens when a large number of humans are collected together, more so if they are bored, the story expanded. One minute, Thomas was her brother; the next, her lover. One version was accurate in that she had aided his escape with a horse but then it became a wild adventure across camp; more elaborate each time it was told.

"You must take some of the money you've been earning." Both lady-wardens said several times a day. But Grace would not take a penny, declaring that they were confined here because of her and the least she could do was turn a few coins their way.

But appearances can be misleading. Outwardly calm to the point of seeming unconcerned about her fate, Grace was a raging storm within. She had been so sure the guards would not give her away, for they gave themselves away at the same time. She had been so sure the world was good, had felt the sun on her back and witnessed the tough kindness from those that had so little.

Yet that same day she had been raped violently, discarded; left exposed in the woods to die. She shuddered to think of the penetrating pain, the horror and disgust. She had not told Henry when she tricked her way into his tent the previous night. She had intended to but the sight of him so wounded and feverish had put all thoughts from her mind other than his care, his comfort.

Oh, to be with him now. To take a wet cloth and gently wipe away that fever; to chat and pass the time as the memories and scars fade; to work some magic on his wounds so they melt to nothingness. Just to be with him.

She slept that night but it was fitful and ragged; the sleep of the condemned the night before the gallows. She dreamed that she was accused of being raped. The judge, in bright blood-red topped with a white wig, shook his head and muttered "Preposterous," and phrases like, "Of all the cheek." Roakes was her prosecutor but he jumped from bench to bench in the courtroom, taking the roles of witness, court official and even jury member. His mean, jagged face swung itself into her dream time and time again, causing her to be breathless with fear, shouting out to anyone who would listen:

I cannot be guilty of being raped. I am not at fault, not at fault, at fault, fault, fault... Fault repeated over and again; a drum beat in her head, slewing itself against the sides of her brain, thumping that single word into her conscience.

"Hush, child, you were having a nightmare." Both ladies of her tent were at her side, woken by her cries. "There now," one continued, "everything will work out. You'll see."

"But it is not, Mrs Bradbury, it is far from working out!" Grace tried to rise from her sweaty bed but kind hands pushed her down.

"Tell us," the older one said.

Grace told her story in quavering voice, not thinking it was her own. It was as if these dreadful things had happened to someone else.

Mrs Bradbury and Mrs Bryant, or the two bees, as they jokingly referred to themselves in an attempt to raise a smile from their young charge, listened attentively.

"I know of Roakes," Mrs Bryant said. "He is only a sergeant but he has connections in high places."

"What high places?" Grace had assumed he was confined, awaiting trial for rape.

Mrs Bryant did not want to answer, realising the clumsy move she had made. Mrs Bradbury stepped in.

"He is a henchman of the Earl," she said. "He does his tricky work for him."

It was getting blacker and blacker, like the deeper shadows at the side of the tent, created by the small lanterns they had in the centre by the beds. But those shadows were where Thomas had slipped out to freedom, showing that darkness sometimes leads to light, not just to more darkness.

"I know what you need," Mrs Bradbury said. "A dish of tea." And they set about making one, seeking boiling water from the guard outside. Mrs Bradbury added a little powder from a sachet she kept at her waist.

Grace sipped the tea and fell into a dreamless sleep, reassured that she had new friends by her side who had suffered greatly too and yet stood by her at her time of need.

James Hanson was not under arrest, as they were careful to point out to him. However, there were some questions to be asked.

"Someone saw you coming back into the camp in the early hours of the night of two days ago," the major stated.

"That's correct, sir." He stood to attention in front of the major's makeshift desk; three planks stretched across two barrels of beer. Major Parkhurst was severe in looks, masking his general good nature. He was popular among officers and men, although he would have been surprised to find this out; as far as he was concerned he was just doing his duty efficiently and to the best of his ability.

"You were with a lady, I am informed."

"That's correct, sir."

"Oh, damn it, man, sit down. I can't have with all this officialness. Have a brandy and tell me what has been going on."

What made Hanson tell the truth, he would never know. It was not the brandy, for he had settled on this course before he took his first sip. It was not fear of reprisal for he was a brave and honourable man and would accept the consequences of his actions. Neither was it the decency of the major, for that was known and accepted.

The closest he could come to a reason was the lesson drummed into him since a small child, that the truth always comes out anyway. Why not, therefore, skip the evasiveness and go straight to the truth?

And it worked. The truth worked, pure and simple.

For he wrapped that truth in a package of lies.

The soldiers came for Grace on the third day of her imprisonment. Major Parkhurst led; a stern sergeant-major calling out the step to the platoon that followed.

Left right left right left right left.

The guard outside the tent came to attention and stepped to one side, then drew up the cords so that both flaps of the tent rose up to allow the first two ranks of soldiers to march inside without breaking their step.

Those half-dozen soldiers fanned out, instinctively following a drill manoeuvre they had never rehearsed; it just seemed the right thing to do. They made a curtain of red with bayonets fixed to their muskets, even ranked somehow by size so that the tallest were on the fringes of the line. Over the heads of the smaller men in the centre, Grace could see the deep blue sky outside, almost leaning into their dark tent and taunting her with its freedom.

Major Parkhurst had used every ounce of his soldiery capital to gain this moment. He had gone first to the Earl but had been dismissed with a wave, followed with a threat when he had persisted. Roakes had been in the Earl's tent, sharpening a knife repeatedly. The message had been clear; *trouble me further and my assistant will deal with you.*

He was not to know it but the Earl had more reasons than justice to see the Davenports permanently removed from this world.

Parkhurst remembered his military training; retreat when the odds were against you, regroup, divert, fight again.

He went next to John Churchill, the commander of the loyalist army. Here he got a very different response.

"You mean there has been no trial?" Churchill asked.

"Nothing you or I would consider a trial," Parkhurst replied. "There was the briefest of military tribunals that declared he was a traitor and that was that."

"No representation?"

"None offered and young Davenport was, I am told, barely able to speak in his own defence."

"This is appalling," Churchill agreed. "But what is to be done about it? We are about to move out to chase Monmouth and I hope to do battle with him soon. There is no time to rectify these injustices."

"I think I have an idea, sir." And Parkhurst proceeded to outline Hanson's plan in detail.

Now Parkhurst stood just inside the entrance to the tent; a red figure flanked in red.

"Miss Davenport, will you please come with me?"

"Where to, sir?"

"Yes, where to?" The two bees buzzed, almost in unison.

"I wish to discuss matters surrounding your arrest." He stood aside for Grace to walk out of the tent. "Please do not mind the soldiers," he said in an undertone. "They are here more to impress than for any other purpose. And, yes," he turned to Grace's two companions, "I extend the invitation to Mrs Bradbury and Mrs Bryant. If you would care to follow me to my tent." Grace looked to her two new friends for reassurance, then stepped out of the tent into the sunshine.

They formed the head of the procession; three young women with a snake of soldiers winding behind them. Major Parkhurst took them straight to his tent, where it was evident that some preparations had been made to receive Grace and the two bees. There were several chairs placed around his desk with a decanter of wine and five glasses on the boards that made up the surface.

"Would you like some wine?" Grace decided the moment required it and nodded her head. She had only drunk wine twice before, both times when staying at Sherborne Hall.

"Who else is joining us?" Mrs Bryant asked, indicating the fifth glass.

"Oh, Captain Hanson will be here at any moment. Ah, here he is. You are late, Hanson."

"I'm sorry, sir. The Earl detained me with orders for us moving out."

Then Parkhurst took a large glug of wine, sending it round his mouth and through his teeth while he contemplated exactly how to start.

"Ladies, we have ourselves a quandary. On the one hand, we have an escaped convicted criminal. No, Miss Davenport, please let me finish. I believe you will find it worth your while to hear me out. He escaped with the aid of you, Miss Davenport. This is not a court of law and nothing said here is being written down or will be repeated. Do you deny that you helped your brother to escape?"

"No, Major, I do not deny it."

Parkhurst breathed more freely; the rest would be easier now he had the truth on the table.

"You stole him away from his tent and led him to wherever you secreted a horse for him. I do not need to know the details. We just need to be in general agreement before we move on to the solution. Later that night, Mr Hanson found you wandering about outside the camp and escorted you…"

"No!" Grace rose from her seat; looked at Hanson as if betrayed, saw the honesty of his mistruths written on his face and sat back down again quite suddenly.

"I beg your pardon?"

"Nothing, nothing at all, sir. I was just a little confused that night with my brother riding off and me all alone. It just came back to me, is all."

"Quite so. I am sure you were upset, my dear." His term of address had graduated, moved from formal to avuncular in the space of a minute. "Please bear with me. I certainly mean you no harm.

"Now, onto our quandary. Normally, we would take issue with this escape and send a body of soldiers out to track the escaped prisoner down and bring him to justice. However, we are about to move and hope to do battle within a day, three at most. Hence, we can afford no soldiers for this task."

"Sir, can you dismiss the case then?" Hanson chimed in with his line right on cue.

"Unfortunately not, for the accuser is the Earl and to dismiss a case brought by him would be a grave matter with tricky consequences. However, I should add that Thomas' trial was a travesty of justice. I don't believe anyone should have been convicted on those proceedings."

"What, then?" Mrs Bradbury had picked up where this conversation was headed.

"Well, on to a possible solution. I propose that Grace be liberated on licence and agrees to the condition that she uses her freedom to persuade her brother to turn himself in. I can confirm that John Churchill himself gives his word that your brother will receive a fair trial if he gives himself up. If he does not, however, and is caught, the execution will proceed immediately. There is, however, one condition that might prove problematic." He paused, wondering how best to tackle the condition Churchill had put on the proposal. In the end he decided just to say it as it was.

"Mr Churchill requires a nominee prisoner as guarantee of your word. If you do not return, this person will be prosecuted for aiding your escape, Miss Davenport. Needless to say, it will be the end of my career as well."

"I'll do it," Hanson said immediately. The irony that he was, indeed, guilty of aiding an escape was not lost on him.

"No can do, I'm afraid. It has to be a civilian. Every soldier is needed here."

There was a silence while the three civilians in the tent looked at each other. Then Mrs Bradbury stepped up to the mark with a simple "I'll do it."

"Are you sure, Mrs Bradbury? It is a serious commitment you are making because you will stand in Miss Davenport's place should she not return."

"I'll do it," she said again.

"As will I," added Mrs Bryant.

And in this act of generosity with their very freedom, these two recent widows carved new futures for themselves.

Major Parkhurst was quite prepared to repeat the whole proposition over again and had allocated time for this in his busy schedule. He was surprised when Grace spoke just a moment after thanking the two bees.

"Sir, will John Churchill put his commitment to a fair trial on paper?"

"Yes."

"Will you loan me a horse and saddle?"

"Yes."

"If I am unable to persuade my brother to return, will you accept me back in his place?"

"Yes." That was an easy one, for no honest brother would allow his sister to step into his place and face trial while he remained free.

"And when I return, whether with my brother or alone, will you free these two kind women who have stepped into my shoes while I am gone?"

"Yes."

"I have one more question."

"Yes, my dear?" Parkhurst leant across the table, as if shortening the distance between them would make the question easier to answer.

"Can I see Lord Henry before I depart?"

"I see no reason to deny such a request. I report to Churchill, not the Earl. Churchill has not echoed the Earl's order on this matter. I will take you there now if you like. Hanson will sort out a horse while we are there."

"I know the way, sir."

It hit like a penny falling.

"Of course you do, Mrs Merriman." His severity broke into a mass of smiles.

"Then I accept, Major, on one further condition. I would like Captain Hanson to accompany me to visit Lord Henry, if you do not mind seeing to my horse?"

"I shall manage it immediately!" He smiled, again breaking his normal countenance.

"Now ladies," he turned to the two bees, "I see no reason to hold you captive as I have your word. If Grace does not return within a reasonable period, however, you will be taken into custody. Those are the orders from on high and there is not one thing I can do about it."

Chapter 20

Lady Merriman woke quite suddenly. She was up and off her mattress before the consciousness of a new day bore in. The window in the attic she had illicitly taken over was open for coolness in the hot and stuffy night. She put her head out, long blonde untied hair catching the little breeze.

From the street below came an appreciative whistle and a call that bounded between the houses to reach up to Lady Merriman's ears above.

"Don't get up my darling, I'll come and join you."

"Join me at the washtub if you dare!" Lady Merriman shot back without a thought for who might hear.

The man below made some further limp joke and moved on. But the encounter remained with Lady Merriman all day as she went about her work.

"Arkwright, what are you up to?" shouted Mrs Beatrice, working her way up into one of her cruel tempers. "You've spent half the morning looking at your reflection in anything that shines. Do you think you're something for the men to stare at then, with your straggly hair and aprons askew? Look at you!" Then she realised her mistake and issued a hurried correction. "Don't look at you, look at your work."

"My name is…" It came to her in a flash but withdrew again, retreating as always into the depths of her mind.

"What did you say?"

"I just said my name is Arkwright, Mrs Beatrice."

"Well, your name will be mud if you don't stop daydreaming."

Mrs Beatrice treated Arkwright just exactly as she had been taught. But her training from Parchman had not included how to deal with constant daydreaming. She was paid well to keep Arkwright in her employment and she, like all slaves, could be worked to the bone.

But sometimes, mind you only sometimes, she wondered if it was all worth it.

She also wondered whether Parchman's increasingly frequent visits could be used to her advantage. She tried talking over the opportunities with her husband but he seemed too preoccupied with his cards. Once, when he slept late, she had gone through clothes he had worn the day before and found eight packs of cards in various pockets. She had tried to talk to him about Parchman's visits but instead had got a lecture on man's various and varied strengths compared to the frailer sex.

Well, it was the frailer sex in their household who kept everything together. She managed Arkwright and the laundry business that had developed around her, producing far more income than the pitiful salary Mr Beatrice received as a clerk in the docks. The house had been her parents' before they died. But it had been she who cleverly manoeuvred her brother out of his inheritance, sending him instead to the Americas with a debt over his head so that she received the occasional remittance from that source into the bargain.

That was something she was particularly pleased with; her simpleton brother had contributed magnificently to her security over the years. And, no doubt, it had done him a power of good to start with nothing and have to work with his own hands to create something; as she had done.

And it had been she who had received Parchman the first time, sensing a lucrative deal like a dog sniffs the air for something promising; yes, that was a good way of putting it. Of course, Parchman always addressed Mr Beatrice as the man of the house but even he knew where the real power lay.

But why these increased visits from Parchman? For the first three and a half years there had been just two. Now he had been six times in the last three months. And staying longer each time.

It was a small price to pay for the double bonus of the quarterly payment and the free labour of Arkwright. Plus, the additional pleasure of watching someone so obviously high-born drop so low. She knew nothing of Arkwright except that Arkwright was not her real name. Parchman always said they knew as much as they needed to and she agreed on that point, although she itched to know something of her back story. One day, perhaps.

It was a small price to pay; except that these visits from Parchman seemed to be causing such odd behaviour in Arkwright.

Sometimes she did not know how she was supposed to keep it all together on her own.

But then she was one of the frailer sex.

Parchman's next arrival was too soon and on a weekday rather than the usual Sundays. With Mr Beatrice at work, Mrs Beatrice had to meet him alone.

"Madam," he began, clearly disliking the lack of Mr Beatrice to address, "I feel compelled to warn you that you may very well receive one or two visitors over the next few days."

"Who and why, sir?" She poured his brandy herself, rather than make the mistake of letting Arkwright into the room again; that had caused Parchman a great deal of agitation.

"Two youngsters, brother and sister, very much bad ones, I might add."

"And why should they come here?" But Mrs Beatrice already knew the answer to why; it was something to do with Arkwright.

She had heard the woman mumbling about two youngsters.

It was time for Fortress Beatrice.

She had known it might come to this. And she was ready.

Amelia always rose early, but this day it was especially so. She knocked on Elizabeth's bedroom door, then had to go into the room and wake her; Elizabeth had grown into the habit of sleeping late, with no real duties placed upon her.

"Come on, sleepy-head!" She pinched her stepmother, who came to life with a cry.

"Ow! Leave me alone, you vicious brute." But she was laughing. "It cannot be morning already?"

"It is and we must go quickly if we are to get back in time."

They missed breakfast, were too nervous to eat. They had primed the stable lad to have two horses saddled and ready for 5am.

"Do you have the key?" Elizabeth asked.

"Yes, here it is." She pulled the large key out from a chain attached to the waist of her dress. "I took the whole chain as you never know when we might need other keys of his."

They walked their horses quietly out of the park that surrounded their house, not wanting to make a noise, although no one was there to threaten them. They had chosen a day when Simon was away.

But they still had to get into the office and out again before old Simms came in to open up at 7.45.

"That should give us a clear hour and a half to search the offices."

They needed every moment of that hour and a half.

"I can't believe there are so many files," Elizabeth said as they entered the offices. "How on earth will we cover it all?"

Amelia was not daunted. "We split up," she said. "But first we take a moment to consider what best to do." Elizabeth had already started thumbing through the ledgers nearest the door. "Lizzie, stop a minute. Let's think this through."

"But we have so little time."

"All the more reason to use our heads. Now, what we are seeking is highly unlikely to be in an obvious place because..."

"Because it is underhand business!" Elizabeth completed Amelia's sentence for her.

"Exactly. So, we ignore everything in the general office and concentrate on Father's rooms."

Simon had two adjoining offices. First, they entered an ornately decorated sitting room that stretched from the front to the back of the building, mirroring the general office they had just vacated. To the side was a smaller and plainer office with a desk and heavy bookcases flanking all four walls. There was one small window set high up above the desk; it created the impression of a prison cell.

Amelia delegated the sitting room to Elizabeth and took the study herself.

"Nothing," reported Elizabeth ten minutes later.

"I thought so."

"Then why have me search it, Amelia?"

"Because I needed to be sure." It was a mark of Amelia's growing confidence that she was no longer affronted when Elizabeth was direct with her; a few weeks earlier she would have been mortified to be asked any question in such an abrupt manner. "Now, start at the other end of this big cabinet and remember you are looking for evidence of shady dealings. Flick through, stopping only when something rouses your attention."

They were close to an hour in the inner study, without finding anything. Then they spent twenty minutes in the store room, set beyond the general office. They started with great hope, for the store room had four locked cabinets along the back wall; it seemed like the secrets would be there.

But they found nothing incriminating; there was not the slightest reference to illegality anywhere.

"Well, we've tried pretty well everywhere except the general office. Do you want to look in there?"

"No," Amelia replied. "Let's stop and think a minute." As she spoke, the grandfather clock in the general office struck for half past seven.

They had fifteen minutes left.

"Think, Lizzie, where would he hide stuff he did not want to be found?" Amelia stood up as her legs were stiff from crouching at the cabinets. She walked from the store room back into the general office and across to the far wall, where the window looked onto the street.

Think, think, think, she said to herself, over and over again. As she thought, she paced up and down the length of the general office. It annoyed her that she met the wall with a different foot each time; she could not get into a rhythm.

"Come in here," Elizabeth called her into Simon's reception room. "Don't you think we should check in here again?"

"You do that, I need to think."

Elizabeth did as she was instructed and searched again the small desk at one end. Amelia started pacing this room, just as she had the last.

Suddenly, she stopped dead still. She was halfway through the fourth length of the room. She rushed back to the far wall

169

and started again. Elizabeth thought she had gone crazy; maybe all the pent-up frustrations of her twenty-two-year life were finally spilling out.

"Lizzie, I've got it. This room is fourteen paces long."

"So?"

"The general office is fifteen."

They found the secret cabinet built behind a fake wall. They found it with eight minutes to go. It took another four to work out how to open it; one hand to press a small knob high up on the wall, set like a coat hook but far too high for normal use. Simultaneously, they had to press a wooden panel at floor-level, several feet away. They managed it with Elizabeth reaching up for the knob while Amelia, who was much shorter, kicking the panel by the floor.

"One, two, three, contact," they chanted together. The wall sprang open silently, just a couple of inches; sufficient to get fingers into the gap.

They had four minutes left as they pushed the fake wall, which was set on tiny rails, top and bottom.

They needed one of those four minutes just to take in what they saw. The cavity had been hollowed out into the back wall of the building, creating a space a quarter the width of the room and a little over a foot in depth. There were six shelves running up the wall. The bottom three shelves were stuffed with dust-coated files. The files on the fourth shelf had less dust and stopped a foot short of the end. Simon was filling the secret cupboard from bottom left to top right and was a little over halfway through the exercise.

But it was what lay loosely on the top shelf that took their breath away. The jewellery was quite magnificent, particularly a diamond necklace that twinkled in the morning light, revealing an exquisite centre stone; it was as if it begged to be released back into the world of dinner parties and balls. Next to it lay the most beautiful pearls Elizabeth had ever seen.

On impulse, she picked them up, but did not hold them to her neck. Instead, she placed them on Amelia.

It completed the transformation from dumpy, forgettable girl to elegant woman, beautiful in the sense that both her goodness and her intellect looked outwards through the suffering she had endured, and danced with the pale, slightly pink pearls.

Or was that the morning sun that leant a pink tinge to both pearls and girl?

The front door creaked as it was opened.

"Quick," said Amelia. Elizabeth rushed the pearls back to the top shelf and made to leave. But Amelia was bent to the ground in front of the files.

"What are you doing?"

"Getting what we came for, of course. Take two at random from the top two shelves." She pulled out two from the bottom two shelves, straightened and then bent again, taking a slender file from the very left extreme of the lowest shelf.

The very first file ever placed in there, she assumed.

"Into his study," Amelia whispered as they pushed the wall back along the tracks and heard it click into place. Amelia was totally in charge now; Elizabeth did everything she was told without question.

It made for a good team.

They closed the door to the study a few seconds before Simms opened the door from general office into the study they had just vacated. Simms was old and slow, also partly deaf; not the best to check for burglars as he opened up. He was paid a pittance so only ever went through the motions; thinking more of the dogs he bred at home rather than his duties on opening up the office in the morning.

And that morning he was feeling his old bones. It was twelve minutes to eight. He could sit for a few moments and no one would be any the wiser. He selected the shorter of the two sofas, knowing from long experience it was the more comfortable of the two. His head fell onto his chest as he wondered when Star, his bitch, might give birth and how many puppies this time. Would he turn a fat profit like last time? Lord knew he needed a fat one to supplement his wages.

He had no idea of the almost silent operation taking place in the room next door. Perhaps he would not have cared if he had known.

Amelia directed events in the study. They put the files in a stack on the desk. Then she indicated to Elizabeth to move the desk chair back towards the window. Meanwhile, she slid open the lower casement, very quietly.

"I'll go first, because we need your height to close the window from outside," she whispered.

Amelia climbed on to the chair and slipped out of the window. Then she asked for the files which Elizabeth passed out to her.

Elizabeth caught one of her petticoats on the window latch as she climbed out. It set her off-balance so that she fell out and landed, head first on the grass below the window. Amelia helped her up, her arms handicapped by holding the files. Then they froze as the door to the study opened and Simms' bulk entered the small room.

He sighed, annoyed at his nap being broken early. He crossed to the window, mumbling about idiots who left windows open overnight, meaning his employer but not actually saying his name.

He slammed the window shut; did not look out of the window, therefore did not see the two crouching ladies directly below. Then, still muttering about his grievance against careless locker-uppers, he returned to the sofa.

With any luck, he still had three minutes to go.

They had thought to bring saddle bags and slipped the stolen files into them. Amelia helped Elizabeth mount then led her horse to a low wall, from which she sprang into the saddle with a new vigour.

She is a new person, thought Elizabeth. *If only I had not helped suppress her at school, perhaps she would always have been like this.*

"Amelia, the knob located up high was obvious as soon as we knew there was a false wall. But how did you know to kick the panel below?" They were trotting through the streets of Sturminster Newton, two genteel ladies out for a ride before breakfast.

"That was easy," Amelia replied. "Did you never notice Father kicks panels at home, particularly when he seems agitated? I just guessed from there. It came to me just like that."

"And in the nick of time," laughed Elizabeth as they made their way through the streets then down to the ford and bridge construction site. "Now, I am ravenously hungry and breakfast is waiting for us!"

Chapter 21

Breakfast for Matthew and Luke was long past as Amelia and Elizabeth clattered by the Davenport family home without stopping. They might have seen the two girls if they had not been bent over Luke's latest and radical work. The treatise had no name yet but was otherwise almost complete. They were absorbed in the last details; tiny nuances by which God made his will known to man.

"Shall we say 'we are here to follow God's will' or 'God's will is here for us to follow'?" Luke asked.

Matthew sat back and thought a moment. What were they trying to say? What phrase would capture the popular mood, encapsulating... that was it!

"How about 'God's will comes to the righteous... and... the righteous will follow their Lord... to the end of their days'?" He said it tentatively, phrases rushing out; expecting his contribution to be ridiculed.

There was a long silence as his father stared at him. Matthew felt the scorn rising up through the old man's body; working its way into his lungs. He imagined the brain and vocal chords working frantically together to select the right words, suitable words of derision. He hung his head, waiting for the slam.

"Perfect re-wording, son. We will go with your version." He solidified his approval with a fond pat on the arm. "We are complete now, other than the title which eludes us still."

"Father, let us go about our duties today and see whether anything comes to us. We could meet again after evensong and before supper." There was a twenty-minute period that fitted into this slot. It was perfect and Luke agreed before they parted.

"Pray, son, that the Lord gives us today a title, for this treatise is His work we are doing, following His will." He did not add that something told him it was the last great act he would perform; at least the last great statement of his preaching career.

"Amen," said Matthew, glowing with pride at his father's approval.

Matthew was lost to the world that day, performing all his tedious duties by rote; praying incessantly for a title to adorn the front page of the treatise.

It came to him just before evensong. Luke was absorbed in his sermon notes, standing in the front of the church, while the congregation filed in. When every seat was taken, he closed his notes at the pulpit and stepped down to be in front of everyone. As he did so, everyone stood to signify that the service had begun.

Stand up for the Lord
Stand up and be counted for the Lord
Stand up and be counted.

Pastor Luke Davenport loved his son's suggestion and the treatise was committed to the printers under the title 'Stand Up and Be Counted'.

In their innocence concerning political matters, neither of the joint-authors considered that in troubled tortuous times an essay with this title might be interpreted as a call to arms against the establishment.

Or perhaps they did and did not care and meant it that way.

Elizabeth and Amelia cantered along the river bank, breakfast and discovery luring them on. They clattered in to the cobbles of the stable yard to find Simon waiting for them, horsewhip in hand.

"What is the meaning of this?"

"We went for a morning ride, Simon." Suddenly Elizabeth sensed that, despite Amelia's brilliant initiatives that morning, she needed to take the lead now. "Do you object, husband?"

"Far from it, Elizabeth. Riding is good for one's health and I encourage it wholeheartedly." Were they about to get away with it? She looked at Amelia, whose timid gaze was directed firmly at the ground. She thought Amelia was shaking; yes, she was shivering despite the warm morning. "However, I do not approve of ladies in my household venturing outdoors improperly clad. Amelia, what is wrong with your attire this morning?"

"No hat, sir."

"Precisely. Can you add to this, Elizabeth?"

"No gloves, sir." Now her eyes were downcast as well. Fear is a mighty subduing force, turning the bravest souls into wrecks of humanity.

"You will go to your respective rooms and wait in silent contemplation for me to arrive and deal with this situation." To reinforce his point, he swished with his riding crop at the corner of the stables. It made a cracking sound as it hit the stone, flaking chips and sending them into the air around them. "Boy, take their horses and see to them." It was added humiliation to be so treated in front of the stable lad.

But at least Simon had not asked about their bulky saddle bags.

Simon strode off indoors, blasting weeds and flowers alike with his whip; never imagining that his wife and daughter would disobey him. He was going to enjoy this exercise in male superiority.

Elizabeth took Amelia's arm and tugged at her. "Come with me," she said. Amelia came with her, but it was like dragging a heavy sack of corn. They went around to the kitchen door, Elizabeth leading, Amelia following.

"Kitty, the master has sent us to our rooms for being improperly dressed. If you dare disobey him, can we have some bread and cheese to slink away for the day? And some cider would be nice."

"Better than that, miss. I'll make you up a couple of satchels. Sarah," she turned and spoke to her sister, "run and fetch Miss Amelia's and Mrs Taylor's hats and gloves, there's a dear. We can't have the ladies without their proper stuff, can we?" When Sarah had left, Kitty looked around and behind the two ladies and said, "This isn't right, miss, the way he treats you."

"Kitty, are you on our side?"

"Yes, miss, of course we are, both of us, miss." Kitty's mind was flustered at the turn of questions but her hands moved expertly in putting together ample provisions for a picnic.

"Then tell me about the old mistress, the one who was here

before me."

"Nothing to tell, miss."

"Come, there must be something."

"She was beautiful." Try as Elizabeth did, she could get nothing more out of her. Then Sarah was back with hats and gloves, passing the gloves out, helping arrange the hats, re-tying ribbons and straightening skirts. The moment was gone.

But not the moment for their defiance. Albeit leaving by the kitchen door, they strolled arm in arm, Elizabeth gently propelling Amelia, who was white-faced, grim countenanced. Her father terrified her.

He saw them from the dining room. But they were disappearing from lawn to woods. It was too late to catch them and he would not risk his dignity by shouting or running. He would deal with it another day. He had far more important things to manage.

Today he was finally meeting his business benefactor; the man or woman behind the commission payments over the last five years; the person who had made him wealthy.

He did wonder, however, why Amelia and Elizabeth had both satchels over one shoulder and saddlebags over the other.

"Kitty!" he shouted from the dining room, mouth stuffed with slices of cold beef, "get upstairs and sort out my best clothes."

Best clothes, best hat, best mount and saddle; he hoped he made a good sight as he trotted down the drive and turned left for Sturminster Newton.

In turning left at the gate, he passed within twenty yards of his wife and daughter. They had finished bathing in the stream that led down to the Stour and were sitting on a large overhang, discussing what they now knew about Simon Taylor.

"So, Simon took the house, the whole estate, from someone else," Elizabeth said, summarising what Amelia was piecing together from the oldest file in their collection. Their overhang was almost completely covered with a splendid weeping willow that dipped its branches into the stream as if it, too, wanted to bathe in the growing heat. It made a den for the two ladies; a secret place where someone like Simon could pass within yards and know nothing of their presence so close. Feeling more secure in their bolt hole, Amelia had stopped shaking and was now reading the files with interest, displaying an intellect she had never hinted at during their school days.

It all made sense suddenly to Elizabeth. "That someone was Lady Merriman, she is the good friend of Thomas and Grace."

"You mean the Witch of Bagber?" Amelia looked up from her file to ask the question.

"No, I mean Lady Merriman."

"This document refers repeatedly to 'LM'," Amelia said, growing pensive. "That must be Lady Merriman. She came here for just a few months and then she left suddenly. I suppose that is when we moved in. But Father owns the estate now. Look, here is a deed in his name. It says 'Bagber Manor and its one thousand and forty-two acres'. I never knew the estate was so large."

"For a country town lawyer, your father has done very well for himself."

"I could say the same about your husband!" Amelia replied with a grin. "Look, I am starving to death amidst all this sumptuous food. Why don't you play the mother properly and lay out a picnic for us to enjoy?"

"After I've disciplined my cheeky stepdaughter it will be next on my list!"

But after they had eaten, they grew suddenly serious, putting their mutual teasing to one side. Amelia munched on a piece of cheese as she read the main document in the first folder. Elizabeth watched her as she sat on the overhanging rock, her feet dangling into the cool water below. Outside their willow shade the day was heating up. Amelia had an intelligence that amazed Elizabeth. She thought quickly, good ideas making solutions in her mind, yet also with an honourable side sadly lacking in her father. Perhaps her better qualities came from her mother. She had met Amelia's mother a few times when a young child but remembered only an older version of Amelia, with the same mid-brown hair and rounded yet pretty features. Amelia had been a figure of fun at school because of intense shyness married to a dumpiness that was almost completely gone now. All in all, she was a fun companion and a good friend; something Elizabeth had never had before, other than Grace and Thomas, who always seemed quite a lot younger than her.

"This proves little," Amelia concluded, waving the papers towards where Elizabeth sat. "It is supposition that LM stands for Lady Merriman. And even if that were certain, there is actually nothing that indicates wrongdoing. There is even a bill of sale for the estate. See here," she thrust the document in front of Elizabeth, "on October 13th 1680 Lady Merriman sold Bagber Manor to Simon Taylor. It is the only time Lady Merriman's name is mentioned fully."

"How much did she get for the manor?"

"That's the strange thing. She received no cash at all, just the freehold of a thirty-acre pig farm in Yorkshire. Why would she exchange a thousand-acre estate for a tiny pig farm?"

"It makes no sense, Amelia. But here is her signature in big, bold, looping letters."

They went through the later documents they had grabbed from the shelf. There were a number of very high-interest loans with copies of letters to a number of clients, demanding payment for arrears. There were a few loan settlements, usually giving a share in the client's business for a pitiful reduction in the amount outstanding.

"It's sharp practice but nothing illegal," Amelia concluded.

"But I am not proud to be associated with this man," Elizabeth replied, thinking there must be some way to reveal what he was like in business.

There was one thing of interest. A statement of commission earned for the first quarter of 1684, just over a year earlier.

"It shows clearly that Father receives extra commission on loans made to members of the Sherborne family."

"Does it indicate why?"

"No, it just says what commission is due and has two columns. The first is for general borrowers and the second is for Sherborne – see the word Sherborne at the top of the column? There are six loans to the Sherbornes in this quarter." She turned over the page, then exclaimed, "Ah, now this makes a little more sense. It is not Father's money he is lending out but from whoever is paying the commission. The mystery figure lends the money to Father at twelve percent a year and he is free to lend it at whatever rate he can achieve. The one to Mr Jarvis he made in 1683, I recall from his loan agreement, was for thirty-six percent."

"So, he is more than doubling his money?"

"Trebling it, actually. In fact, even more when the commission is taken into account."

"All these figures are making my head spin. I'm going back into the stream. Are you coming?"

They had taken the precaution this time of removing their petticoats before swimming the first time, in order to have dry clothes when they got out. Now, Elizabeth hitched up the double skirt to her dress and pulled several layers of petticoat down to her ankles, before kicking them in a heap on the rock. A moment later, she was in the water up to her knees. Amelia followed and they kicked and splashed for half an hour, forgetting entirely that they were anything else other than young children at play.

There was time enough later to work out exactly how and where Simon Taylor had broken the law.

Simon Taylor broke a few more laws on his long ride to Somerset that day, but they were the minor ones of trespass, taking a few shortcuts over private land in his hurry to get to his destination. Plus, there was a particular favourite of his; riding up to somebody on foot, he would ask directions, hinting at a reward by jangling his purse. Then, when the directions were committed to memory he would ride off without dropping a coin in the hand of the person who had just helped him.

Why waste good coin earned by the sweat of my brow?

He had been looking forward to meeting his mystery benefactor for a few years now. He had a number of business propositions to put to him; ideas that would increase the flow of funds considerably.

He arrived at the camp after dusk on the second day, having spent the night in a suite of fine rooms at the best inn he could find. There was a lot of activity, despite it being so late in the day. There was a sergeant at the gate who looked familiar to him but it might just be the type of face he had seen; certainly, he could not put a name to it.

"State your business, sir," the sergeant said. He sounded co-operative but there was something in the tone and hard glint of his eyes that warned Simon.

"My name is Simon Taylor and I've come to…" He realised with faltering confidence that he did not have a name to mention. The soldier visiting him at a client's house the previous day had just told him to report to the camp immediately. He should have asked for a name. "I was summoned to meet here with a gentleman of means. I do not recall his name, unfortunately."

"So, you were summoned, sir?

"Yes, sergeant. I just did not ask the name, is all. It seemed urgent and I dropped everything to ride here."

"War is always urgent, sir. Let me check the records of who has left camp today and yesterday to try and track down who summoned you, sir." The man was condescending in the extreme but if it got Simon into the camp he would suffer it.

The sergeant took a list from a guard and seemed to examine it a long time. "That is strange, Mr Taylor. There have been only five exits from the camp over the last two days recorded in our journal. On both days, two patrols have left to scout out the enemy. I doubt very much they would have time to track you down. The only other person is Sergeant Major Harris, who led a recruitment detachment. Ah, that must be it. Have you come to enlist, sir?" the sergeant asked, a mean grin developing on his face. He did not wait for an answer but turned to one of the guards. "Pascoe, escort Private Taylor to the enlistment tent. At the double now! We need all the cannon fodder we can get. That's why we wear red, it hides the blood." He was leering now, his mean mouth curling up at both ends as his face changed shape. The guards were enjoying this also. "That's a fine horse, Private Taylor. The cavalry will be most grateful for its loan but you have just joined the bloody infantry."

"Sergeant, I must protest. I am a man of some means and influence. I am not to be treated in this way."

In response to this, the sergeant changed his attitude, losing all humour. He came up to Simon's horse, held the bridle in his large hands. Something told Simon he would pay dearly before those huge hands loosened their grip, allowing Simon to ride away. When the sergeant next spoke, it was much more quietly but with a force that left Simon in no doubt as to his predicament.

"Well, Mr Taylor, you're a man of means, are you? Any of that means about your person tonight, sir? Shall I have you searched before Pascoe marches you to the enlistment tent? You see, I am a little deaf in my advancing years; too much musket fire and cannon going off all around. I did not hear any denial when I asked you whether you had come here to enlist."

"How much, Sergeant?" Simon knew when he was beaten. Perhaps a small bribe would get his co-operation.

Only Simon most definitely did not have the measure of this man at all.

"Oh, what do you think, boys?" He turned to the soldiers under his command, raising his voice. He sounded so reasonable, as if discussing the price of eggs in the marketplace. "Shall we settle for everything this man of means and influence has got?"

"What? You would leave me in the next county with no coin to pay my way?"

"Beggars go safely, sir. It is only rich folk who tread a dangerous path. We would be doing you a service, sir."

As if instructed without an order leaving the sergeant's mouth, two guards moved forwards.

"Dismount... sir."

The horse was led away.

"Your belongings... sir."

Simon handed over his purse.

"All your belongings... sir. Or shall we strip you, sir? The boys can be a little rough. Your boots too, sir. Remember it is all for the cause of crushing the rebellion in the King's name,

Mr Taylor, sir."

Pascoe brought up a donkey, explaining that it was a long walk to wherever this kind gentleman had come from. Unfortunately, they had no saddle that would fit. Simon was just glad to get away as they launched him onto the bare back of the donkey and slapped its rump with their musket butts.

It was quite a lot later that the sergeant reported to his officer. "Sir, one gentleman arrived tonight, sir. We thought he was come to enlist but he seemed confused and did not know who to ask for. He then made a small donation which I passed straight on to regimental funds, of course, sir. Then he left, sir."

"His name, sergeant?"

The sergeant pretended to consult his list; a list with one name on it. "It was a Mr Taylor, sir. Simon Taylor."

"Idiot!" the officer replied. Sergeant Roakes assumed his officer was referring to Taylor as Roakes was most decidedly not an idiot; he had collected many coins to prove it. "Well, it is too late now to recall him. We are most definitely meeting with the enemy tomorrow. It will have to wait until after we do battle."

Chapter 22

Thomas made good progress away from the camp, riding hard with his second horse trailing behind. He stopped in the early light of the new day and swapped the saddles over, first allowing both horses to graze in a clearing by a stream. Searching the small saddle bag, he found a change of clothing and some food. Estimating it to take at most two days to Bristol, he portioned the food appropriately and put most of it back in the saddle bag. He would not change his clothes yet, would get the journey behind him first.

Would they come after him? He did not know. On the one hand, they seemed to have taken strongly against him; he could not understand why when his actions had saved Henry's life. They would want to track him down and bring him to justice, especially as he had escaped the night before his date with the hangman.

But on the other, he had noticed the increasing signs of activity while he lay in his prison-tent, bound hand and feet. They were preoccupied with some great exercise; perhaps they were preparing to meet Monmouth in force now, rather than the minor skirmish of the previous week. If that were the case, they would not have the spare soldiers to go out after him.

He decided to proceed as if they were following, even though on balance he thought it unlikely. Caution would sit by him, riding on the side saddle of his spare horse like a wife come on a trip with her husband.

With that decision came several consequences. He would have to avoid people. That meant only travelling during the short nights and finding somewhere to hide each day; both him and his horses, which were at risk of being stolen.

Avoiding people also meant he would have to find his own way to Bristol as he dared not risk asking for directions. Then he thought about the food and how it would last over an extended period. Reluctantly, he replaced the half-eaten chunk of bread; he would have to parcel it out much more carefully. He would ride on a little further now for it was still early and not many people would be about. But in an hour, maybe two, he would have to find a secure hiding place, somewhere deep in the woods ahead.

Two days later, a little after noon, he was hidden by a tiny stream that reminded him of the one where they had found the two boys playing in Shaftesbury. Someone had once built a tiny pier of uneven stones that jutted out into the stream, causing the water to rush around it. He dangled his feet in the fast water and felt the cooling sensation penetrate up his legs. It was unbearably hot and humid, indicating a storm was building. The horses were tethered by their reins, taken off the bridles to make halter ropes. Because the reins were so short he had to move them to a new pasture every half an hour. It was so hot that coming away from the cooling waters for even a moment caused the sweat to break out all over him. His clothes stank. The stream was too small to bathe in. He had considered washing his clothes, or at least rinsing them, for he had no soap. But he ruled this out for he would be naked while they dried. The decision stemmed partly from his Puritan upbringing and partly because he was determined to keep the fresh clothes for when he arrived in Bristol.

And for Lady Merriman.

But that assumed he ever got there. The journey seemed to be going on forever; long days in hiding, waiting for the few hours each night when it was safe to travel. His food was getting low, despite rationing in the extreme.

He had tried to keep on the right road but over the last day the heavy clouds and drenching sharp showers had stopped all sight of the sun.

He could be going around in circles; any moment now he might approach the royalist camp from the other side. The thought of recapture and inevitable execution made him shiver in the humid heat. If only the weather would break, everything would be easier.

He did not hear the hooves approach, lost as he was in his gloomy thoughts. He did not even hear the click of the handgun being cocked. But he did hear the laugh Grace gave when she realised that the person she had carefully scouted around and crept up towards was the brother she had been sent to find.

"Thomas," she cried and he turned to see a handgun pointing at him, still cocked, still a danger.

"Grace, put the firearm down," he replied. She had not realised it was between them. She un-cocked it with shaking hands and put it down on a flat stone that began the makeshift pier some children had built one hot summer day, very like the one they were now in.

They embraced warmly, so pleased to see each other again. Grace had been despairing of ever finding Thomas, matching Thomas' own despair. One delightful coincidence changed their situation completely.

And the outlook was suddenly much brighter. They had three horses, a handgun and more food, for Grace had brought a supply with her. She had ridden fast all day long, not caring for pursuers for, with the agreement she had struck, she knew there were none. She had even thought to bring some spare clothes for Thomas, cadged from Captain Hanson. Her horse needed resting so Thomas tethered it with his. He then went behind a big bush and put on Hanson's clothes; too big but the quality was excellent. They washed the filthy clothes he had been wearing and lay them on bracken to dry.

"I believe it is too humid for them to dry," Grace said as, after eating, it was time to be moving on again. Thomas had an answer to this.

"We will tie them to the saddle of the spare horse so they will dry as we move through the sodden air."

It was a strange sight that moved out twenty minutes later. To an observer at some distance it looked like the third horse, the largest of the three, hosted a tiny dwarf, bobbing and weaving as he rode behind the two front riders. To someone watching more closely, it appeared that a young lady and her gentleman were stooped to the lows of taking in washing to supplement their income; yet still had fine horses to ride and fine clothes to wear.

But the biggest change in their fortunes was, undoubtedly,

that they had each other and knew that the other was safe and with them.

With that knowledge, both of them felt they could tackle the world.

Only perhaps not Mrs Beatrice.

They rode fast, but not so fast that Grace could not update Thomas on what had happened. He stopped his horse suddenly as she was explaining the bargain she had struck.

"So, sister, you are sworn to return me to captivity and execution?"

"No, Thomas, I am sworn to return you for a fair trial, guaranteed by Mr Churchill himself, given to me in writing." She produced a letter from her pocket and handed it to Thomas. It was actually from Major Parkhurst but stated above his signature that he had received complete assurance from the commander of their forces, John Churchill, that Thomas Davenport would, provided he gave himself up, receive a scrupulously fair trial in all regards, including the right of appeal to the civilian courts if Thomas deemed it required.

"That is a fair letter," Thomas admitted.

There is one other observation a very close watcher of these two might have made at this point, provided they were near enough to hear the conversation between brother and sister. The observation was a simple one. It did not enter the minds of Thomas or Grace that they would not abide by her promise; Thomas would return to captivity because Grace had said he would.

But there was a nuance to that observation. For Grace then tapped her feet into the side of her horse and moved forwards.

"Come, brother. You are obliged to give yourself in again, but I did not promise that you would do it immediately. If we ride fast we have time enough to get to Bristol and rescue Lady Merriman. Then you can turn yourself in!"

Thomas kicked his horse forward also. They were riding to save Lady Merriman.

Who, at that moment, was very much in need of saving. She had seen Parchman come to visit Mrs Beatrice and it had flooded her mind with conflicting memories. Parchman was older than before. But before when? Before she had been a little girl watching from the doorway.

She was the little girl in the story she kept seeing snatches of! That came to her now with certainty. Her father had argued with Parchman, not once or twice but many times. And sometimes she had sneaked out of bed to watch the arguments, like a play unfolding scene by scene. But often she would stay in her bed and the sound of argument from below would become like a lullaby to drift her into sleep; the irony of bitter discord sowing peace in a little girl was suddenly no longer lost on her.

But now she was remembering a later time. She wore diamonds and other beautiful jewellery. Her hair was elegantly piled on her head. Parchman was leaving as she came down those wide stairs.

Why was he always visiting? Why did she remember so little about her past? She could not just be; she had to come from somewhere.

All my life I have been a stranger to myself

Where did that come from?

She was a washer woman who lived in the Beatrice household. Her name was Arkwright. She had a first name but nobody ever used it; Arkwright would suffice.

They had danced a beautiful dance. She was deeply in love with him.

She had a large pile of washing to do. Mrs Beatrice was expanding the laundry business and that gave her more work. There was no time to idle away with vague memories of an unnecessary past.

But there was time for sweet talk outside in the grounds of the big square house with its large lawns and beech and oak woods around. She loved him so much. They had talked of their future; a future that had not happened.

Because of Parchman.

She plunged the sheets into the tub and scrubbed hard against the wooden rack. Warm grey water slapped over the side and onto her dress. Only hard work would keep her in the present, where it was safe and secure; where she knew who she was.

Or so Mrs Beatrice told her.

She felt tears welling but could not stop work on account of a few tears. There was too much riding on getting the sheets done by midday, including whether she would eat that day. She kept one hand fully in the sink but raised the other rapidly to her face; as if the speed of movement would allow her later to deny it ever happened. But the evidence was planted on her face and head as she brushed the tears away, smearing her face and knocking her cap sideways so that a loose lock of blonde hair escaped and fell to her neck. She knew she had pretty hair but it was kept under the cap, pinned back severely to prevent escape.

Just like the girl that visited in her mind. She too had such pretty hair and it was piled so elegantly, leaving her long slender neck for all to see. Instinctively, she raised her hand to her neck, causing further smudges to her dress and more escaped hair.

But what was she talking about? She could not care about her hair, would cut it short that very moment; well, as soon as she had done the laundry.

Mrs Beatrice would find fault because she always found fault but secretly she would be pleased that Eliza had cut her hair.

She was Eliza! But not Arkwright; that name did not fit with Eliza. So, she was Eliza who? But no time for this now; she had the washing to do.

She thumped sheets for several minutes; fighting memories that reared up in her mind like jigsaw pieces; hinting and teasing as to the picture they were a part of.

All that time, in the room above, she could hear low voices, rumbling like the thunder that rumbled outdoors. It was like an echo game she had played as a child. Someone makes a noise and your job is to imitate it immediately. As the voices above discussed her, so she... But wait a moment, Eliza, pause a second in that scrubbing and rinsing; how do you know they are talking about you with their rumble-rumble game?

You do not, for who in their right mind would talk about the troubles of a scullery maid struggling to fulfil her duties? Struggling to know something of her past, of who she was and how she came there?

They rested only when their horses needed to stop. Even then, with three horses, they worked out a rota to give each horse a rest in turn. They would stop at a stream or pool and Thomas would switch the side saddle if necessary while Grace prepared some food from their supplies.

But even a seventeen- and eighteen-year-old have to rest some time, so they stopped come night time when it was harder to see the way. They camped out in a small but densely packed wood; the perfect hiding place.

"We could light a fire against the rain," Grace suggested. It had started raining mid-afternoon and become steadily heavier from the east, as if the rain was trying to push the sun on westwards and out of the sky.

"No fire," Thomas replied. "We do not want to risk detection, even with that letter in your saddlebag.

They ate the last of the cold meat and drank a little of the cider, looking at each other over the rim of their tin cups as if daring the other to drink a little more.

But then Grace gave a large hiccough and Thomas echoed it with one of his. They laughed long and hard, relieving much tension. Then, Thomas took both cups and tipped out the remaining cider, walked to the stream they had stopped by and filled the cups with rushing water from the rains.

"That's better," said Grace.

"For a moment I thought you were drunk, sister."

"You too, brother!"

Later, when they lay on the ground trying to get to sleep, Thomas asked the question he had been longing to ask since Grace had crept up on him earlier that day; he had expected his sister to bring up the subject so he would not have to raise it himself.

"Have you any news about Henry?" he asked into the silence.

Best to get it out; to tackle the unknown.

"Yes."

"Well, sister, how does he do?" But he had got the tone wrong for there was no humour around Grace at that moment. He realised his mistake halfway through his sentence but too late to retract it; committed already to the form of words.

He realised his mistake because Grace was quietly crying to herself.

It took twenty minutes of gentle persuasion, brother to sister, to get the tears under control so that Grace could talk about it.

"It is all over," she said eventually.

"What?" The question was clumsy but genuine.

"Henry is… betrothed to another."

"How can it be?"

Grace told Thomas about her two meetings with Henry. By the second meeting, he was much recovered physically, although the scar across his face would remain as a cruel reminder of what had happened.

For the tiniest moment, Thomas thought perhaps Grace had walked away from Henry, unable to live with the scar. But then he castigated himself into right-thinking. This was his sister he was talking about; besides, had she not said he was betrothed to another?

On the contrary, Grace would still love Henry if he were cut into a hundred bloody pieces by a human butcher with cleaver in hand.

"His grandfather, the Earl, told me he was to marry an heiress and it was all arranged. He looked down his nose at me and said all the contracts were signed and could not be undone. He feigned sympathy but I could tell he was glad to announce this news to me. I did not believe it but when I met with Henry for a few minutes the first time, he told me about it despite his weakness and his fever; it was very much on dear Henry's mind. That was the night of your escape. He was considerably better when I saw him yesterday, when we spoke of it again. There were great big tears in his eyes but he could not deny it. I said goodbye to him and ran from his tent. I could not bear to me with him and know he is sworn to someone else. I told Captain Hanson I was finished early with my ten minutes and mounted immediately for the ride to find you. And now, a day later, I feel I treated him so badly in running from the tent. Thomas, my brother, the pain is terrible, worse than being raped."

"Raped? What made you say that?"

She had not told him about the rape; there had been no time together until now. So, she told him, opening up completely to the brother she held so dear.

Halfway through the telling, Thomas took Grace in his arms and hugged her like only a brother can do. He did not try words for actions surpass words and his action was only to comfort her. But his mind raced with how and why this could be.

And it still raced on behalf of his little sister, long after sleep had induced the false relief it offers over misery.

But as he sat long into the rain-filled night, Grace asleep in his lap, the most incredible thought came to him. Despite multiple rapes, escape from Monmouth's army and the devastating news about Henry, his little sister had made her brother a priority.

He decided then to tease her without mercy the next day. It was the only way; emotion on the left bank of oars, humour on the right, pulling together as a team.

But there were some people for whom a reckoning was coming.

Vengeance is mine, said the Lord

Thomas gave the horses to the ostler. "Please be so kind as to give them a thumping good rub down, a good portion of oats, and hold them ready for our return. We do not know how long we will be but we may well need to leave quickly when we come back." He handed over several coins, not wanting to stint on the horses' care.

Besides, with the city so full of royalist soldiers, the price of an ostler's services had jumped since the week before.

"You say Fittle Street is close by?" Grace asked.

"It is, Miss. Go up the street and take the left onto Gracewell Road, then Fittle Street is second on the left. It is no more than five minutes from here." He held out his hand and, after a moment of hesitation, Grace fumbled with her purse and put six large pennies in the open hand.

Two of those pennies went straight to a boy who was charged with a message for Mrs Beatrice, that the expected youngsters had arrived and would be knocking on the door soon enough.

The young travellers had paid well and would get their money's worth in good care of their horses. But there was something more than money here; the ostler's wife was Mrs Beatrice's cousin and the ostler had felt both the Beatrices' sharp tongues for quite a few years now. This would buy him a little peace for certain.

Fortress Beatrice was working.

Mrs Beatrice had the neatest idea to hide Arkwright from any that enquired after her. She was chained to the sink in spirits, so why not chain her in person as well?

"I'm fed up of your idleness," she said as soon as the boy came with the message. "Mr Beatrice had these run up at the dockyard." She was carrying a pair of heavy manacles; one for the left wrist, the other for the right ankle. "There," she said with a satisfied sigh, "that should stop you daydreaming. I won't release you until the washing is done. What do you say to that?"

"Yes, Mrs Beatrice."

"And?"

"Thank you, Mrs Beatrice."

If Thomas and Grace had used the front door alone, it might have worked; Thomas' bulk adding force to Grace's sweet voice. But something made Thomas stop twenty yards from the house.

"You go to the front door and knock, Grace. I'm going to go around the back and see what I can find out."

"What shall I say?" Both were dressed in the best clothes they had, to make a good impression. Grace was in a dress given to her by Mrs Bryant, she being the closest in size to Grace but still larger. After leaving Major Parkhurst's tent, the two widows had stitched together like devils possessed, to get the dress adjusted to fit before Grace left the camp on her borrowed horse. They wanted to give something to this girl who had helped with their precarious finances. They had gained over three pounds in mending fees, with more coming in all the time. It was a simple grey dress to which Grace added an oversized starched white apron and a bonnet she had brought with her. All in all, she looked quite the Puritan girl.

That was her intention and also the truth.

And certainly not what Mrs Beatrice was expecting when she opened the door herself, explaining that her staff were ill.

"I'm tending them myself for it seems a highly contagious disease," she added by way of warning, looking at the innocent picture in front of her; taken, it seemed, from a child's picture book.

P is for Puritan.

In truth Mrs Beatrice's staff consisted of one person, Glenda Arkwright, or, more properly, Lady Eliza Merriman. And she was far from ill, chained to the washtub and under strict instructions to be silent.

"Good morning, madam," began Grace, a little hesitantly so that she appeared younger than her seventeen years.

This should be easy, thought Mrs Beatrice. *I'm dealing with an innocent child, and a Puritan to boot.*

"What can I do for you, dear? You must appreciate my circumstances. It would be foolish in the extreme to let you enter when the entire household bar me is down with this debilitating sickness."

"I believe you have a friend of ours... I mean mine." There was no point in reminding the householder that she had someone with her. "I mean that you have a friend of mine living with you."

"And who might that be, dear?"

"Glenda Arkwright, madam. Do you know her?"

"I did," replied Mrs Beatrice, a sudden flash of inspiration coming to her.

"Did?"

"She was one of the first to pass on with this terrible sickness. She was a dear friend of mine and quite frail. She had been sick for a while and I nursed her with a great deal of care. It was a sad day when the sickness came to this household for it took her first. It always chooses the frailest first; picking off the easiest, I suppose."

"Oh dear, when did this happen?" Grace saw that their quest would come to nothing, except the knowledge that Lady Merriman had ended her days, still a fairly young woman, in loneliness and depression, far from her home.

"Oh, about three weeks ago, I believe it was. I grieve for your loss, my dear, just as I grieve for my own. She was a dear friend. I would ask you in but the risk of catching an infection is too high and I would be doing you a great disservice. Now, I must go and tend to the others. Goodbye, my dear."

"Goodbye, madam." Grace turned and walked down the steps. Her search had made its first progress on the steps of Sally Baker's house in Lyme Regis, now it was ended on the steps of 24 Fittle Street in Bristol.

But perhaps, if this lady was to be believed, Lady Merriman had at least not died alone but in the care of a friend.

She walked back to the point where Thomas had left to go around to the rear of the house. Walking away from her sad encounter with Mrs Beatrice, she did not see the figure at the first-floor window. It carried that smirk of victory with it.

But it changed instantly to one of alarm as Grace buried her head in the arms of a young man. How foolish she had been. The messenger said two people would be coming to look for Arkwright. Even Parchman had talked of two youngsters. She had congratulated herself for a triumph over only one half of the invasion. Now she had to cope with both.

And where had that man been to suddenly appear on the street? She could have sworn he was not there a few minutes earlier. She always looked up and down her street each time she opened the door, just as she watched her visitors' departures from an upstairs window all the way to the end of the street. It had started with the debt collectors and bailiffs in the old days, but when the generous payments were established she carried on doing it from habit.

"Oh Thomas, Lady Merriman—"

"Is here, I have seen her."

"What?" Grace jerked back, as if Thomas were not her brother but a would-be lover who had taken a step too far. Mrs Beatrice could see the actions clearly but not hear the words. But she could see the young lady's reaction and guess her ruse had been discovered. That meant the young man had been around the back of the house.

And Fortress Beatrice was breached.

Now they were walking away; down the street, to be lost from Mrs Beatrice's vision. She thought to follow them, then not; wasted time in hesitancy so they were gone before she could decide what best to do.

What would they do next? If the man had seen Arkwright chained to her sink, all her lies to the girl would be exposed. Would they take their tale to a justice of the peace? Her mind ran through the justices they might see. She shuddered at the thought. Only one was connected to her family. He might stand up for her. Or he might not. She remembered an argument at a dinner some years ago. They had not spoken since.

What should she do?

Her father had been a soldier; the type that brought his military thinking home when the wars were over and the swords and pikes hung up for good. His type talked in clipped tones and short, stabbing sentences, as if still practising with their swords and daggers. She tried to think what he would advise.

Do not waste precious resources attempting the defence of a breached wall. Accept reality and stem the damage.

She went downstairs to the scullery at the back of the house.

"Mrs Arkwright," she said, "I see you have done a wonderful job with that linen. Let me free you of these petty restraints and then I thought we could have a nice dish of tea in the parlour upstairs. No, you rest your feet and I will take care of the tea. Perhaps you would care for some cake?"

It was an unusual sight to see Mrs Beatrice struggling with a laden tray while Lady Merriman sat at ease in an armchair, her thin, lithe body looking like an ornament in an upholsterer's shop.

Chapter 23

The rain came from the east on a bitterly cold wind. To Monmouth, it went from high summer to the depths of winter within a few hours. Even the oaks seemed caught out, still dressed in finest green but huddling together against the cold. The wind that brought the rain made the trees moan as they swayed and the thunder rumbled in reply; great echoes staggering across the sky.

It seemed to Monmouth in his gloom that the rain was following him around, driving him here and then driving him there; it was as if King James II had command of the weather.

Or, extraordinarily, God was backing the Catholic.

Looking back over the last week, he could not understand why matters had turned so sour. A week ago, today, he had been proclaimed King at the Market Cross in Taunton. He had not waited until Bristol, favoured by Dare and Fletcher, both now dead and unable to help him further. Perhaps Taunton had been too small a location for such a grand proclamation.

But then he had moved too slowly to seize Bristol and further his cause; he could see that clearly now. News had reached him on the morning of June 20th that Faversham and his cavalry had occupied Bristol the previous day. Should he have taken battle to the Earl of Faversham, knowing that he had little infantry with Churchill elsewhere? He had not; instead, it had prompted his proclamation in Taunton; a shabby place compared to the glories of Bristol.

And then he had started his wanderings. It was still looking strong when he stood in Bridgewater Castle on June 21st, looking over the ramparts on the longest day of the year. Then, like a restless gypsy, it had been Glastonbury, Shepton Mallet and Pensford.

Probably Pensford marked the turning point. The rain had started at Pensford, blanking out the strong sunshine that his army had basked in before. Also, there was the skirmish at Keynsham, where Colonel Oglethorpe should have been thrashed but, instead, had trounced Monmouth's army, forcing him to move on.

The way Churchill shadowed him as he moved about the west country irked the would-be king; especially as Churchill's forces grew while his were falling away rapidly.

He had gone on to Bath, refused entry; far from the triumphant march into Axminster or Taunton. Then on to Norton St Philip, where they were now, seeking a few minutes of peace in order to make critical decisions. Monmouth clicked his fingers for more wine and his servant opened the last case. They would be moving out soon; another attempt to get to Bristol through the Somerset towns. He had time for one more cup before leaving.

The attack came as they were moving out. After the experience at Keynsham, Monmouth was taking no chances and left a heavily fortified barrier across the main entrance to the village; fifty musketeers headed by Vincent, one of the few he could trust. The rain hid the enemy at first, masking both sound and vision. But steadily a group of grenadiers emerged from the gloom, approaching the centre of the village. As this detachment came towards the barricade, Monmouth's heart dropped as he saw who led it.

It was not Oglethorpe come after him again. It was not even Churchill, the man from nowhere, who tracked Monmouth from town to town. Instead, marching at the head of the column, he saw the distinctive features of Henry Fitzroy, the Duke of Grafton.

Monmouth's half-brother.

He had chosen his Catholic uncle over his protestant brother.

But no time for that, for Monmouth saw an opportunity. He sent a regiment to parallel Grafton's forces, making their way around the side of the lane by which his brother approached the barricade.

The idea was to flank Grafton and attack him from the side. It all depended on timing. Monmouth held his breath as his troops made their quiet way into position. Could this be the turning point in his campaign? Could he have a decisive victory here at the Battle of Norton St Philip, balancing out the humiliating defeat at Keynsham three days earlier? Could the rain, for once, work in his favour?

They were in position now, and ready to pounce. Should he give the order now? No, he would wait another two minutes so that Grafton was firmly in his trap. He forced himself to count to sixty, then sixty again. He sensed the strained nerves all around as his subordinates waited for the order. Would this go down in history as the critical juncture? Was this the start of the long, slow walk down the aisle at Westminster Abbey, to sit upon the Stone of Scoun and be crowned as King of England?

Perhaps he had counted too fast. He forced himself to count a further thirty, raising his arm at twenty, flourishing it at twenty-six and plunging it down in a great arc as he came to thirty.

God will lead me by the hand to my throne, for Religion and Liberty are my names.

The clap of muskets was like thunder in the sky. Redcoats staggered, falling on the road, clasping their wounded parts as they slid to the ground.

Monmouth's men were reloading, one rank moving forwards. Muskets raised on order; it was going to be a slaughter. He watched a young soldier crawl across the road, badly wounded; then suddenly still, agony and life leaving his body at the same moment.

Monmouth was going to win the Battle of Norton St Philip. His men were moving forward as they fired. The opposing force was surrounded on three sides, back to a thick hedge against the road. The survivors were scrambling to get through the hedge and to safety. It was the opportunity to turn the whole campaign around. Monmouth felt the excitement rise up his throat, pulsating through his veins.

But he was taking a great risk; if he were captured there would be no more rebellion. No one standing up for Religion and Liberty.

It was his duty not to be caught.

"We'll ride out with the main army," he said, wheeling his horse so that he missed the looks of bewilderment on his aides' faces. "We'll leave two sections behind to mop up the enemy."

"But Sire..." The voice faltered against the noise of Monmouth's trotting horse.

Afterwards, on the road to Frome, the news hit him badly. Churchill had led reinforcements personally into the battle. Those reinforcements had beaten back the rebel forces.

"I believe we won the skirmish, Sire," said one aide. But it did not seem at all like a victory.

Even in victory, Monmouth was smelling of defeat.

And now, the little town of Frome stood before him; another in the chain of towns he visited like he was a small part of a travelling circus. Perhaps he was the clown, dressed in finest purple and not noticing that all around him were sniggering.

He no longer expected a warm welcome at the insignificant towns that broke his march. He kept moving in order to have somewhere to go to; to be in a state of movement masked the fact that he was going nowhere. His army seemed a line of ants, trying to find a way through to their objective: lefts and rights and rights and lefts, turn-about and try again; always with the vain hope of making it through to Bristol.

If he could only make it to Bristol, he could be crowned in that fair city; he need not wait for Westminster. Bristol had merchants; middling men he could rely on. If kingship meant wishing for it then Monmouth became, during those late June days as his dreams evaporated, the best king in living memory.

And so, he wandered in ever-decreasing circles while the net steadily tightened.

But Frome had something else waiting for King Monmouth. It was presented by a round-faced, squat man whose chains of mayoral office seemed made for a much larger man. Ferguson was beside Monmouth again, having magically reappeared as the fighting was concluded.

"Your Grace," the Mayor started, the pomposity in his voice mixing with a nervousness he did not often feel as king in his own tiny world, "I fear I bring information you will not find palatable."

News had reached the town that morning of Argyll's capture at Inchannan, riding to visit a friend; hardly the picture of a leader of rebellion. The parallel revolt in Scotland, seen as such a clever idea at the time, had been a complete flop. According to the leading citizens gathered around Monmouth's entourage like a surrounding army, Argyll was being taken back to Edinburgh Castle, where the executioner awaited him. He already had a death sentence hanging over him.

"I doubt, Your Grace, that he will live out the week."

And where does that leave you, my friend? Roaming slopes and crossing streams with an ever-dwindling army falling further and further behind.

He had never liked Archibald Campbell, the ninth Duke of Argyll. But this was not about liking people; this was about plotting to overthrow an anointed king, a Catholic to boot, and getting it so terribly wrong.

Monmouth returned to his makeshift camp, feeling very alone, despite the dozen who rode with him. He had three cups of wine while his aides argued over what to do next. But he was not listening; he already knew what they would do next.

"Strike camp. We should make Warminster today if we move fast."

Ferguson was used to the rain but usually he was somewhere warm looking out, not trudging through it. He had complained about the heat, now wished for strong sun to dry his clothes, his saddle, his very being.

He was irritated intensely that the Scottish campaign, as he called the open revolt, had failed so miserably and quickly. Now there was just one leg remaining to his plans to vindicate himself as a bringer of the true religion. Wealth and fame had eluded him over the first five decades of his life; he hoped for several far better ones to come.

But now he had one leg left and that leg was looking shaky. He pulled out a stubby pencil and one of his old sermons and wrote his options, as his horse plodded on.

1. Carry on, in the hope of a turnaround of fortunes.

That was the same fortune that favoured the brave. It had certainly been a brave move to come with the fool Monmouth.

2. Leave off from the campaign now, while I can get away.

Hundreds were doing this. Monmouth still had a team around him, meaning Ferguson would not be missed. It was mainly military stuff now and he was not a military man, so what could he offer?

3. Leave off now and turn tail on my colleagues.

This was tempting. He could gain great glory by turning them in, by seeing the light and delivering the main prize to Faversham or Churchill. But, would they forgive him his previous misdemeanours? He was a wanted man. On balance, it was a large risk but tempting all the same. He would need to think on it.

Ferguson was prevented further analysis through a cry from the front. Their scouts had seen a strong force of cavalry two miles ahead, bearing down on them from Trowbridge. They galloped back with the news, only two of the scouts just kept on galloping. They would not stop, in all likelihood, until they got safely home.

Was this the end? Ferguson could not tell. His body was like ice, yet it was not unduly cold. The rain had stopped, the sun trying to re-establish itself but weakened by the clouds that made the rays bounce away to Heaven.

Or down to hell.

Ferguson knew then he had no choice. Whether he lived or died that day, his only option was to persevere. He was so angry with so many people who had let him down. Not just now in filthy Wiltshire and Somerset, with these pathetic lumpy green hills, but throughout his life. Even his parents had shunned him, turning him out and turning away from him; disowning him. There was nobody he liked in this world; nobody but himself.

My God, my God of anger and vengeance, why have you forsaken me, your faithful servant? Why have you led me here to this dirty hilltop to die in the mud when I have preached faithfully of your majesty and power to all and sundry? Why do you turn from me also?

He tapped his heels to make his horse trot to where Monmouth stood, at the epicentre of his aides. He pulled his sword clumsily from his scabbard and offered it upright, like an altar boy holding a cross in a Catholic church.

"Sire, you have my undying loyalty."

"Well, that's all we need," said an indeterminable voice from nine o'clock of the circle.

They survived that day, but only just. Monmouth withdrew after a couple of hours of heavy skirmishing with losses on both sides. He withdrew because it was clear he was not going to get to Warminster and, hence, the Warminster way to Bristol. One more option was cut from him that day near Trowbridge in Wiltshire.

Now he would head west, back into Somerset, in the hope of finding a way to break through the cordon of troops opposing him.

Ferguson was breathless as he heaved his bloodied sword back into its scabbard. He had fought because he was trapped. But he had found it wonderful. He was not particularly good at it and had been saved several times by soldiers around him. He had killed one man. He was lying on the ground, clutching a broken leg, screaming curses in his pain. Ferguson had silenced him, driving his sword tip into the mouth that issued the profanities; going to the heart of the problem, Ferguson considered later.

He had felt no fear, not because he had nothing to lose with despondency's grip tightening its hold. Sheathing his sword at the end of the hostilities, noting the blood of the profane soldier dripping from the mouth of the scabbard to the ground, he felt a different man; possessed again by the God he had briefly despaired of.

The Lord Works in Mysterious Ways.

Chapter 24

Thomas and Grace had enough money for a few nights in the Crown, where their horses were stabled. They started walking to the end of Fittle Street and turned right for the inn. It was an automatic turn; no conscious decision was made, for their minds were full of Lady Merriman.

Grace gabbled through her story, her spirits soaring after being so low.

"But," she concluded, "if she told me such a story about Lady Merriman being dead, she can be no friend of hers or ours."

"Precisely, sister, but there is something I did not mention."

"Is Lady Merriman in good health?" she asked, suddenly anxious.

"I cannot say for certain," he replied. "She looked very tired. She was standing at a big sink, washing what looked like heavy sheets." He stopped talking a moment; his own mind racing ahead with possibilities.

"What was it that you did not mention, Thomas?"

"Just that, well, she seemed chained to the sink she was working at."

"Goodness, you mean like a slave?"

"Yes, like a slave."

"We must go back, Thomas." She turned on the road, causing a cart to swerve behind her.

"Watch where you're going, miss. These damn Puritans think they're protected by their very purity. I reckon I've run down three this month already!" The joke was made for his wife, sitting beside him, but it meant much more to Thomas, who grabbed the reins of the cart. The wife looked down with a startled expression while the husband looked fearful for his wife, his horse and the produce he was transporting. But Thomas spoke quietly to the horse before it could panic in a busy Bristol street. Then he turned his face up to the man, who now had a heavy spanner in his hand; the first thing he could find for protection.

"I didn't mean anything by the joke on Puritans," the cart

driver said, clearly anxious that his jibe should have caused trouble.

"Sir, I mean you no harm and am sorry for startling you. I would beg a moment of your time, please. Perhaps I can buy you a drink at the Crown. And your wife is most welcome, too." His emerging plan might need a feminine touch; somebody more worldly-wise than Grace; also, somebody not known to Thomas' intended victim.

It was just an emerging plan; in fact, it was little more than the barest idea to gain access to the Beatrice household. But in grabbing those reins, Thomas must have been guided by God himself, for he had selected the kindest cart driver in all Bristol.

"Call me Big Jim, everyone does." His preferred choice of drink was beer while Plain Jane, his wife, drank gin. Thomas was pleased, for both were cheap to purchase. He replicated their order for Grace and himself.

Their nicknames were curious for Big Jim was the tiniest man they had ever come across while Plain Jane was, by far, the prettiest, with natural blonde curls and cute, pert features that seemed taken from a childhood doll. She was almost a foot taller than her husband but seemed to look up to him, or so it seemed to Thomas and Grace.

They laughed when Grace took a sip of her gin and went into a fit of choking. Big Jim leant over and slapped her on the back with a force that belied his tiny, wiry body. It was also an act of familiarity that took weeks off the process of making friends.

"You're not a gin drinker, are you, my dear?"

"No sir, but I've twice drunk wine. I found that pleasant."

"Shall I order some wine for you?" Thomas asked anxiously, thinking of the cost.

"No, Thomas. I am not thirsty suddenly. I shall be fine without a drink."

"Do you mind then?" Plain Jane stretched across the table, took the spare gin and drank it in one, her own glass stood empty beside where she slammed the borrowed glass down. "I do like a gin or two," she said, "but can't often enough afford it."

They were down on their luck, as Big Jim explained.

Listening to their story, Grace felt Plain Jane had it the wrong way around. They could not afford gin and beer because they spent all available money on gin and beer. But this pair seemed happy in their togetherness with alcohol. Grace reflected on her father, who had patently been served his brandy by the devil himself. Yet this odd pair seemed so happy in their dependence on drink; bright and positive, just that they would always be down to their last few coppers and not know where their next meal would come from.

"You have the horse and cart," Thomas pointed out, remembering why he had stopped them.

"Yes, but we owe almost ten pounds against it."

"We can give you fifteen shillings," Thomas replied, declaring his total worth at the outset of the negotiations.

"What would you have us do for that sum, Thomas?" The fact that Big Jim refrained from using a term like 'my son' or 'lad' endeared him to Thomas. However, Thomas was concerned that, with his wife, he was drinking in to that fifteen shillings already. He had to get to the point before he had spent all their cash to no purpose.

"Help us extract a lady from captivity."

"You mean from prison?" Big Jim sprung to his feet, wanting no part of a jail-break, wondering whether he had the measure of these two after all. Perhaps their innocence was an alluring front, masking two much more complicated characters within.

"No, not that at all. Sit down and I'll tell you." Thomas waved at the bargirl for more drinks, declining one himself. He had had more than ever before already. Besides, he needed to keep the drinks bill down as much as he could.

Thomas outlined the predicament they faced, with interjections from Grace. It was hard to know who was most affected by Lady Merriman's situation; perhaps best to call it a draw. Thomas had seen her chained and world-weary; a great weight upon someone who they remembered as fun and carefree. But at least he had seen her. Grace had endured the distress of her death, only to then have it reversed; a resurrection, yet she had not seen it and had to go on faith alone.

"Exactly how much money have you got?" Plain Jane asked as they neared the end of the story.

"Sixteen shillings and fourpence," Thomas replied, concerned that the price of their assistance would increase to whatever they had; yet to lie about it never occurred to him.

"Then if you pay us fifteen shillings, how will you pay for beds tonight and to eat? And what will you use for food and tolls on your journey back?" Jim asked.

"I don't know," Thomas admitted, feeling foolish.

"Well, this is our counter-proposal so listen carefully." Plain Jane took over now. "If we can work out a way to help you we will do so for the appropriate remuneration." Here is comes, thought Thomas; here was his first lesson in commerce and he knew he was going to come off worse in the exchange.

"What will that be?" asked Grace, lacking the pride Thomas felt, hence also lacking the insecurity.

"We want you to take us with you."

"Why on earth? You have your business here. Why give all that up?"

The answer was simple. They had debts everywhere and needed a new start.

"If you can take us with you and give us an introduction in Dorset then that will be recompense sufficient for helping to free your friend."

Thomas was about to object, taking exception at them walking away from their debts. He felt sure Grace would back him on this, even if it meant they had to find another way to free Lady Merriman.

"I can't do it," he said into the silence of expectation; the offerors thinking their offer bound to be accepted; barely taking in the rejection. But then, completely on impulse, Thomas qualified his words. "I mean that I can't do it unless you agree to one condition from us."

The deal was sealed on a handshake right then. Big Jim and Plain Jane gave their word that as soon as they were established in Dorset they would start to repay every creditor they had and would not touch a drop more than four drinks a day each until they had repaid every penny.

Now they were free to turn their attention to the question of how to free Lady Merriman.

They painted two sets of signs for the cart, one sign to go on each side. The first set was painted 'Beatrice's Laundry' and they toured around the city under the deception they were employed to gather soiled sheets and bandages from various hospitals. Grace thought Big Jim went too far when he announced in a loud voice that Beatrice's Laundry promised to pick up the dirtiest rags and return them like brand new.

But it worked, for within a morning they had a cart load of the filthiest washing imaginable.

Then a quick sign change and the tradesman became customer. Thomas was particularly proud of the second set of signs, proclaiming that they were part of the Western Constitutional Hospital for the Insane; a glorious, though fictional, institution located somewhere just distant enough for Mrs Beatrice not to have heard of it.

"Good day, my pretty lady," started Big Jim as soon as she opened the door. "My name is James Bigg of the Western Constitutional Hospital for the Insane. Have I the honour of addressing Mrs Beatrice of Beatrice's Laundry fame?" It was remarkable how far flattery could get you. A separate part of his brain considered the benefits of a younger man flattering an older woman and all that that involved and implied, as the larger part developed the flattery further. "Having heard of the reputation of Beatrice's Laundry, I thought to bring a small sample of our dirty articles for a trial wash. Believe me, there will be much more that this paltry amount were we to get established together." He took a deep breath and continued. "We have almost a thousand patients and a considerable amount of washing as a consequence. Madam, might I come in to discuss matters a little more delicate than a doorstep conversation would allow? We pay above the going rate but demand excellent work in return."

The other three all thought he was going too far but afterwards he revealed his concern that he had not been persuasive and effusive enough.

"It hung in the balance when Mrs Beatrice said she had never heard from our hospital with regard to an appointment to visit with her and was it not unusual just to turn up in the hope that she would be able to receive them?" Big Jim offered by way of debrief as they clattered down the cobbles and broken stones of Bristol. This was the point to push so he had carried on.

"Madam, you have heard of our glorious institution, have you not?" There was just an edge of indignation in his tone; more a promise of contempt-to-come if she revealed her ignorance.

"Of course, I have," she lied. "I was planning to visit your august hospital soon to expound upon our capabilities and, hopefully, come away with an instruction from yourselves. And now you are come to me." She seemed genuinely pleased at the potential increase in new business. But her mind was working on several tracks also; one section dwelled on the opportunity and resulting coin that would come her way, while another asked how would she manage the workload having to be nice to Arkwright? But perhaps she was being too cautious? A further part savoured the way she would come down hard on Arkwright the moment these interfering youngsters were gone back to wherever Parchman said they had come from. But then, the final segment asked, could this sudden opportunity be true? "Remind me, please, Mr Bigg, what area you are in so that I might return the laundry once completed?"

"Surely, madam, you would know this if you intended to visit us at work?" This was pushing it too far but Big Jim had a wickedly cheeky way about him that seemed to take people along with him.

"I just do not recall, is all."

"Well, Mrs Beatrice, we are in Poodlebury-under-Charm, midway between Strickington St Mary and West Bygonnington. You know now, of course, to which region I refer?" It was an outrageous list of fictitious names, designed to match the hospital they represented that did not exist either.

"Ah, yes sir. Now I can place it exactly," Mrs Beatrice fibbed again. To Grace and Thomas, so primed to tell the truth, it seemed like a giant house of cards built on fabrication. Yet it worked.

It would come undone in time, but all they needed was a few minutes of distraction.

"Do you all need to come in?" She looked at the four of them, Grace heavily disguised as a bent old woman and instructed not to talk lest her voice be recognised.

"No, dear me not. Just me, madam. I thought the others could go around the back to deliver the laundry."

"How do you know I do it here?" Mrs Beatrice was suddenly quite sharp, her instincts aroused.

But Big Jim was equal to the task.

"Why, madam, you are famous for your laundry, that is how. They say all around the hospitals here 'drop it in Mrs Beatrice's basement stinking like death and it comes out of the front door smelling like roses!'" The professional compliment saw Jim through. Mrs Beatrice opened her front door wide, much wider than the slender Jim needed, such was the confidence he had engendered.

"You three round the back, pronto. Get a portion of the laundry unloaded and meet me at the corner of the street. Make sure it is a goodly-sized amount; there's little point in trying out Beatrice's Laundry with a trifle like we do with the others. Don't hang around the front door when you've finished. Mrs Beatrice doesn't need the likes of you around here spoiling her view." Big Jim was directly in front of Mrs Beatrice in the doorway. He turned back to speak to his lackeys, thus Mrs Beatrice did not see the exaggerated wink he gave them as he issued his orders.

The three of them trudged with the laden cart into the back alley and around to the entrance they wanted. Thomas guided them as to which gate, then they each took a basket of the stinking washing and went down the steps to the kitchen and sculleries located in the basement.

The door was not locked. Thomas balanced his heavy basket on one raised leg so his chin rested on the top of the pile. He turned the door handle. It swung open. It was dark inside; no lamps and no candles. He dropped his basket on the floor and stepped to a window, raising the blind but it made little difference.

Except it disturbed a large rat. It looked directly at Thomas a moment, then ran along a worn skirting board and disappeared into the shadows.

There was nobody in the scullery where Lady Merriman had been chained at the sink yesterday. For six seconds, he doubted whether he had seen her at all; perhaps he had wanted to see her and his want had become a fact in his mind?

But then he shook his head and reality flooded back in, hand in hand with certainty. He had seen her and she had been chained to that very sink. In fact, here were the chains she had been bound by.

Grace, keeping to her disguise, hobbled from scullery to kitchen. She also had dropped her laundry basket at the first opportunity; after all, they were a means to an end, nothing more.

"The kitchen is empty too," she reported, forgetting to use the croaky voice she had rummaged up for this role; a great contradiction of young pure voice coming from a crumpled old body.

"So is the store room," said Plain Jane, also in disguise, but with her it was as a young laundry lad, learning the trade.

"So where is Lady Merriman?"

Big Jim knew the answer to that question, for he was dismayed to see she was sitting in a chair in the parlour, dressed in a fine but ill-fitting and outdated dress, looking dazed. Each hand gripped a knitting needle but the wool never moved on through the process. This was a shawl or a scarf that never would be.

His first thought was to confirm it was her but this was addressed immediately by Mrs Beatrice announcing her very good friend and companion, Mrs Arkwright.

"Poor Mrs Arkwright suffers from seizures and fits of melancholy. She lives with me all the time now, the poor dear. You know she started knitting that scarf two years ago and look how little progress she has made. I take care of her entirely as she would be destitute without me."

His second thought was that the search downstairs was futile. If Lady Merriman was up here she patently could not be down there. But what was best to do now?

He spent a few distracted minutes thinking around the problem, not realising that Mrs Beatrice was talking to him, a mantra repeating itself over and over again.

"Mr Bigg, would you like a glass of wine against the over-hot day? I say, Mr Bigg, would you..., I say, say, say, Mr Bigg, Bigg, Bigg, Bigg..."

He jerked himself awake, nodded to the wine with a murmur of apology, then returned to planning mode. But this time, he put half his mind to treating Mrs Beatrice with obsequious sparks of flattery, such as "A combination of good looks and brains make a great grounding for a business woman," and, "I can see your success is entirely down to the qualities you bring to your ventures."

"Madam, I believe that concludes matters between us most satisfactorily. If you could just return the clean laundry for a final check and approval, little more than a formality, I assure you. I believe we will have a sound working relationship for many years to come. Now, do you mind if I go by the back stairs to ensure the half-wits I have the duty to command have done the right thing? Do you not find, Mrs Beatrice, that having employees is a thankless task that wears on soul and body alike?" This was a master stroke, promoting Mrs Beatrice to an elite body; confiding in her as one of those elites.

"Ah, Mr Bigg, you are indeed so correct in that statement. And now you must go and attend to the never-ending duties to which you refer. It has been a joy to meet a kindred spirit in business; one who sees eye to eye. I do hope we will meet again soon." This last statement, Jim thought, translated as 'you can come and flatter me some more at any time'.

"Well, goodbye then, Mrs Beatrice. It has, indeed, been a rare privilege to meet with you today." In truth, he ached to be away from her.

Thomas came up with the plan they hastily assembled in the gloomy basement.

"With this pile of laundry come in," he started, "she's bound to set Lady Merriman to work again."

"But we will be long gone by then," Jane said.

"You will be but not me," Thomas replied, unable to hide a streak of smugness, for he was sure it was a good plan.

It centred on a rapid transformation from broom in the cupboard to laundry lad on the cart. "This will ensure, if she's watching, that she counts four of us going back down the street again. Hence, her suspicions will be settled."

It was a good plan, with a reasonable chance of succeeding. Thomas would stay behind, hidden in the broom cupboard. The broom, cloaked and padded with laundry items, would sit in the cart as the fourth laundry worker. When Lady Merriman was sent down the stairs to start work on the washing, Thomas would rescue her, guiding her out of the house the back way.

And to a new lease on freedom.

Only it did not work out that way.

Chapter 25

The rat sniffed at his leg, looking for something to eat. Thomas wondered if it was the same rat he had seen before. In the almost pitch-black inside the cupboard it was impossible to tell. The rat moved away, giving up on a search destined to end in failure for Thomas had no food upon him and the cupboard was bare. The sniffing left a trace of feeling on his shin that he desperately wanted to scratch. But he dared not move for in the kitchen, directly outside the cupboard he had chosen for his hiding place, stood Mrs Beatrice. She was addressing Lady Merriman as if she were a child but to Thomas the strained patience was every bit as chilling as naked aggression.

"So, you see, Mrs Arkwright, I have so much on my shoulders with worry for your care and that of my useless husband. I have the business to run that puts the roof over our heads and food on the table. You do like your food, don't you, Mrs Arkwright?"

"Yes, Mrs Beatrice." It was the same voice he remembered from four years ago, yet somehow shredded by suffering. And a paler version, too; more like a memory than the actual voice.

"And who is it working hard to ensure your favourite little food items are secured?"

"You do, Mrs Beatrice."

"And are you not happy that I am here to look after you in every way, large and small?"

"Yes, Mrs Beatrice."

"Then what do you say, my dear?" The 'my dear' struck Thomas as particularly thin.

"Thank you, Mrs Beatrice."

"And all I ask in return is a little bit of help in the laundry that, through my diligent management, provides for us all."

"Yes, Mrs Beatrice."

Her voice wound on, punctuated by the sounds of laundry; slopping water, slabs of sodden sheets hitting surfaces, groans of effort in lifting heavy objects repeatedly.

How long would he have to wait in cramped darkness? He had taken no regard of his stance from a comfort point of view, since he had only expected to be a few minutes in the broom cupboard. But the minutes went on, with Mrs Beatrice still in the kitchen. He heard the sound of a kettle on the stove. Was that hot water for the washing, or was she settling in for the duration?

He tried counting to 600 slowly. Surely in ten minutes she would be gone? Then he counted another 300, forcing himself to slow right down so that the resulting five minutes he ticked off in his head were closer to another ten.

Then he took a deep silent breath and promised himself that after a further 1800 he would be rid of this woman. He had got to 467 when an itch on his back became unbearable. The more he tried to ignore it, the more it came to the centre of his mind. By 585 it consumed him; nothing else mattered except resolving the itch. He wondered if this was not a broom cupboard at all but rather where Mrs Beatrice stored the itches she employed in defence of her home and her wicked, exploitative ways.

Maybe he should fight the itches, thus fight the woman and free their friend. He moved his right arm slowly backwards and up his back. He did it in tiny individual movements, like a mother inching out of the room of her finally sleeping child; praying that a thousand silent and tiny moves would not wake the fractious baby she had finally coaxed to sleep.

He got there and could rub the itch up and down through a two-inch cycle using the nail on his thumb, then pressing hard with his whole hand to ease an ache from standing still so long.

But he forgot about the law of the itch; tackle an itch and it simply reappears in some other place; tackle the second one and they start to multiply. He had successfully eased the one in his back but it seemed magically to jump from back to leg. To reach his lower body he had to do a controlled crouch. He made it but found the itch had moved north and was plaguing his neck. His neck, though, was easy to reach.

Then he made his first mistake. Growing confidence in his ability to move silently in the broom cupboard meant too rapid a movement, or rather two moves in one. He stood from his crouching position while also running his right arm up to his neck. It hit a tin pail hanging on a hook with the dull thud of an out-of-tune drum, followed by the clatter of a mop sliding over from the upright and hitting the door to the cupboard.

"What was that?" Mrs Beatrice asked.

"Probably just rats," Lady Merriman replied.

"Well, if that's all, there's work to be done. I'll be upstairs working on the invoices for this job." Thomas could hear in her voice that she had no desire to be around rats. Perhaps his plan was salvageable after all. Perhaps his mistake in moving too much would turn out to be the key to unlock the problem.

He had to wait five minutes, so reverted to counting to 300 this time. But in his excitement, he forgot where he was and felt sure he had done the run-up to 200 twice. It was time to move. He prised open the door a crack to peer out but found it suddenly opened fully and Lady Merriman standing slightly back from the sink, a mop in her hands that she had used to open the door, bringing it down on the handle and then swinging it open with the mop head.

They looked at each other for a long moment. Thomas looked into her eyes, dulled by long hours of drudgery. But he saw the joy that had marked her out before. It was deep within; had to be searched for. But it was there.

"Thomas," she said.

"Lady Merriman," he replied, almost in a trance.

"You've grown taller," she said. "Why, I do believe you are as tall as my father."

She could picture her father now. Lord Merriman was an upright figure, tall and thin, but neither excessively. He had dark brown hair in abundance and hazel eyes, just like hers. He used to tease her that she was born without eyes so he had lent her his spare ones, "But I might need them back one day!" The twinkle as he had said that came to her now. He had been a generous, warm man from whom love had flowed easily. They had lived together at Bagber Manor; a tall, square house that sat proudly watching the activities on its estate around it.

Her home. Her ancestral home. Why had she left?

Her mind clouded with less happy pictures. Four big men,

cursing as they picked her up and threw her in the back of a cart, fighting and scratching for what was her birth right, her inheritance. A long, bumpy ride to take her somewhere reasonably tolerable. She had her own little house and a kind landlady but was moved on too quickly. No, she moved on her own initiative, with Mrs Beatrice pretending to be her friend but taking her here instead. And then there was Parchman, who had killed her father. Tears came to her eyes.

So many memories triggered by Thomas.

She moved her hand up to wipe away tears and found she could not reach her face. She was chained again; just enough latitude of movement for laundry operations.

"The keys," she said, "they are with Mrs Beatrice."

It was worse than that for the keys were on a bunch tied securely at Mrs Beatrice's waist.

Thomas felt he had come so far and yet had travelled not at all.

He could not leave her, not chained to a sink, not anyway at the mercy of the wicked Mrs Beatrice. And there was Grace to think about; she was depending on Thomas to bring Lady Merriman out of her prison. To think it had been his clever idea in the first place. Now he had to think again and think quickly.

But his mind was a blank. No new ideas entered to sweep away the panic; he went over and over the circumstances but did not move anything forward. Yet there had to be a way.

"Are you well, Lady Merriman?" he asked, more to grasp on to something that might guide him.

"I am Lady Merriman," she replied, shaking her chains. "But now I am reduced to this status. The tide is high and then the tide is low but it is high on the other shore."

"What do you mean, Lady Merriman?"

"I mean, my dear boy, that the tide goes back and forth; first the rain falls and then it rises to the sky again. I am fallen but the fallen can rise again, just as those risen high can fall."

Rejoice not against me, O mine enemy: when I fall, I shall arise; when I sit in darkness, the Lord shall be a light unto me.

At first Thomas thought that their old friend had gone mad;

218

her thoughts seemed rambling, coming from all directions at once.

But then it came to him.

"Just as those risen high can fall in the wheel of life," he cried, then clasped his hand to his mouth; he had been too loud. He moved towards her and gave her a hug. "Lady Merriman, I will make you rise again; please believe me." This was whispered in contrast.

"I always knew it but the question is, how shall it be done?"

"I have a plan," he replied, almost absentmindedly. "Now, please tell me the layout of the rooms upstairs and anything you know of Mrs Beatrice's habits and procedures."

Ten minutes later Thomas, having made a few preparatory arrangements, took the pail he had bumped into while hiding in the cupboard. He handed it over to Lady Merriman and gave her some hurried instructions. He then took his station below the stairs and called back to Lady Merriman to start her racket.

"Help, help, I'm being attacked. Help me."

It took Mrs Beatrice only a moment to come down the stairs to protect her investment. She took the steps two at a time, jumping off the last three with an athletic capability that surprised Thomas, spinning around to face the opposite direction whilst still in mid-air.

She landed right foot-first. It hit the liberal coating of cooking oil spread along the passageway to the back of the house. She skidded, landing on her back with a thud as her head hit the stone floor.

Thomas leapt out and felt for a pulse.

"She's out," he said. "It worked perfectly."

Only, there were no keys around her waist. Thomas searched several times.

"The keys are not here, Lady Merriman," he said. "Where else might they be?"

"They'll either be in her desk in the study or in a drawer of her chest in her bedroom. Hurry, Thomas, she is stirring already."

Thomas took a few vital seconds for the message to sink in, then he was moving, remembering at the last minute to step carefully around the cooking oil. In passing the groaning body of Mrs Beatrice, he tapped her gently on the head with the pail so she sighed and settled back into her unconsciousness. Only then did he charge up the stairs.

He had an imprint of the rooms laid out in his mind but even so had to stop and think at strategic points. The study was ground-floor, at the back of the house. It was late afternoon, just sufficient natural light to see despite it being the height of summer. Outside, it rained with a darkened, end-the-day-early type of gloom. It would make their getaway harder in one respect, for they could not run in such weather, but easier in another for pursuit would be harder.

But why was he thinking of getaways? He had first to concentrate on freeing Lady Merriman, which meant finding the key to the chains around her wrists and ankles.

They were not anywhere in the study. He checked and checked again each drawer to the desk, pulling out laundry records by the dozen; also a number of letters and agreements.

He would have to go upstairs to the bedroom. In going out into the hall he noticed the time. It was ten minutes after six o'clock. Lady Merriman had warned him that Mr Beatrice would be home between twenty- and half-past the hour. He was running out of time.

The keys were on the bed; a great heavy chain still attached to the dress she had been wearing. Lady Merriman's racket had happened just as Mrs Beatrice was changing for the evening. If they had waited another minute she would have attached her keys to her evening dress and they would have been able to leave the house by now, probably walking down the street in the rain to meet the others.

He picked the whole bunch up, then heard the front door open and close again. Mr Beatrice was home. Thomas wished he had thought to ask Lady Merriman for Mr Beatrice's routine, as well as that of his wife. Perhaps he would come upstairs to change himself, find Thomas in his bedroom and raise the alarm by shouting through the window. All the householders around would react despite the downpour, for they would assume Thomas was a burglar.

In a way he was. And he certainly had to think how a burglar would think. With a rush of adrenalin, he opened the bedroom door and went out onto the landing, just as the door to the parlour closed behind Mr Beatrice. Now was the opportunity. He rushed down the stairs, slipped and rolled over himself, landing in a heap at the bottom.

"Is that you, my dear? I'm in here, just having a glass to calm my nerves after a tiresome day," came a voice from the parlour but no movement towards the door. Thomas picked himself up and headed for the basement stairs, passing the study door at the back of the house. He was nearly there.

But what he did next put all that in danger.

He stopped with first foot on the top stair, paused as he struggled with the fear of capture, for it meant not only his hanging as a common thief but would condemn Lady Merriman to a lifetime of continued slavery.

But he had to do it. In going through the desk looking for the keys, he had noticed an agreement folded into three to hide the contents but the words on the outside were clear that it was an agreement concerning Lady Merriman, or Arkwright, as she was known to them.

He went back up that single stair, steeling his nerves with every silent step.

"My dear, please be so kind as to bring some brandy. I see we are all out." The voice sailed out from the parlour door as if it was any other day returning from the office; no drama around him at all.

When there was no response to his second conversation, the man rose from his chair and opened the door with a sigh, just as Thomas closed the study door to conceal himself in the gloom of the study.

With his heart beating too fast to remain long in his body, he moved towards the desk. Some primeval instinct remembered exactly both where he had dropped the agreement in his search for the keys and its exact shape. He found it immediately.

The study door opened and Mr Beatrice swore against the

gloom, left again to fetch a candle. This gave Thomas his chance.

"I say, my dear, this game of cat and mouse is a little tedious after a long day at the office. All I require is a drop of brandy to soothe my shattered nerves. Do I have to go into the kitchen to find it for myself? Then so be it, but it seems all wrong for the breadwinner of the house to be so neglected." Thomas thought it odd how they both claimed to be the breadwinner, carrying the weight of their heavy household on their broad shoulders.

The next problem was that Mr Beatrice was taking his small frame down the stairs to the basement. In a moment he would see his wife, lying on the floor. He would raise the alarm but if Thomas moved with lightning speed he could be away before others came to the scene.

He went straight to the front door and raced up the street.

Lady Merriman stood by the sink she was chained to. In truth, she had little choice; she could not move away, nor even lower herself to sit on the floor. But she was little panicked. With her returning memory, like Samson's hair growing back, came a new type of fortitude; the strength that had got her through the last nineteen years since her child had been born.

Her child! Where was he now? Her memory was not entirely back. It was like reading a novel with many missing pages. She had a picture of a baby being torn from her. Parchman was close by. Parchman was ordering a woman to take the baby. Then there were many missing pages, for her memory was quite blank. The next thing was finding Thomas and Grace – she remembered both names now – playing in her garden. What a summer that had been. Her son would have been about their age; a young man now, then.

It was getting dark outside; much earlier than it should be for this time of year. There was rain pelting down but the semi-underground status of her domain within the house was a partial shelter to the noise of the downpour.

God willing, she would get away now. Thomas would find the key and release her and together they would go far away; back to Bagber and her ragged inheritance.

The house she loved. And the child she loved more than her life itself. Could she find her son again?

There was her jumpy jackpot memory again, springing on her that her chid had been a son.

The basement door opened above her. She heard footsteps coming slowly down. Thomas was come back for her with the keys; treading quietly, no doubt, in order not to disturb Mr Beatrice upstairs.

But then a cry came from the passageway where Mrs Beatrice lay. It was not Thomas' voice at all. Had it all gone wrong? Was Thomas now arrested and held in chains like hers?

The back-scullery door opened a crack, just a crack. Perhaps this was the local constable come for her, to arrest her too. Was she fated to spend the rest of her life at this sink?

"Lady Merriman, are you alright? I have the key ring." Blessed relief swept over her like the breeze over the fields leading down to the Stour at home; her home. Thomas entered the scullery, dripping wet like some youth thrown in the Stour by his friends for a laugh. He held up the large key ring and looked at the two locks; one around her wrist, the other around her leg.

The second and third keys he tried released her.

"Quick," he said, "we must go the back way." There were many more voices in the passage now. It was only a matter of time until someone thought to look for others in the house.

"I'm afraid you are going to get wet, Lady Merriman." But she did not mind, for the heavy rain cleansed her of Fittle Street and Mrs Beatrice, washing it out of her like dye running and channelling in the road behind them as they ran. And there, at the end of the road and around the corner out of sight from the Beatrice line of vision, was the horse and cart belonging to Big Jim and Plain Jane. They and Grace were sheltering in the back but Jim jumped straight into the driving seat while Thomas helped Lady Merriman into the back. Thomas stepped up alongside Jim.

"Don't you want to shelter in the back?"

"No, I like the rain and I want to see us safely away from here."

And that is what they did, only stopping briefly at the Crown for their three horses, which they tied to the back of the cart.

Lady Merriman, after hugging Grace and shaking hands with Jane, took a seat at the back of the cart, where the makeshift cover dipped down and allowed a view of disappearing Bristol behind her.

She had a new lease on freedom and it felt like she was a young girl all over again.

Chapter 26

There were two people who most keenly felt Simon Taylor's rage. And rage borne of humiliation is by far the worst for others to endure, especially given the size of Simon's ego. At least the scene at the camp gate was known only to him but there was no disguising the fact that he turned up at Bagber four days later on a donkey and half-starved, with no money to his name.

He had tried to arrive when nobody would see him; late at night. But even that had not worked. He had lain low in the woods of his estate, waiting for the dead of night and relative safety. But he had been discovered by his gamekeeper, a vicious man called Grimes. Simon had hired him to protect his rights from the common people. For he had felt as if he was rising and needed sharp divisions with his origin.

But when the gamekeeper found a ragged, mumbling fool on a donkey, Simon was quickly made to feel that he had risen nowhere, despite his almost fifty years of striving in this world. And when that mumbling fool claimed that he was the master of the estate, he was met with derision and scorn; his true identity masked by the very night he had planned would shield him from ridicule.

He was held that night in an outhouse. It was an old chicken run, bolted securely against foxes and the only place the gamekeeper could think that was secure. It also delighted the gamekeeper's sadistic nature to bring a low person down lower still; the thought of the old fool bedding down in the filthy straw gave him a warm glow inside.

It also meant he was thrown out of his cottage that morning; bag in each hand, looking for new employment.

If the scene had been kept without an audience, perhaps Simon would have been content with a severe reprimand for his gamekeeper. Perhaps, even ending in a word of praise, for such rough justice administered to real poachers is why he had been employed in the first place. In fact, on second thoughts he sent a man out after Grimes.

It appealed to him to dismiss and then rehire, creating gratitude, hence loyalty; never thinking that pride in someone as contemptuous of fellow humans as the gamekeeper was might build derision rather than lasting loyalty.

The scene of his unmasking did have an audience, for he was ushered into the estate office early the next morning, where Elizabeth and Amelia had been asked to assemble in the master's absence. In his triumph, Grimes had not noticed the sniggers and whispers as he led his prisoner to the estate office. Their master being led to justice by a gamekeeper. The onlookers had no love for Simon and none also for the hard gamekeeper. They would let the scene act out to its natural conclusion.

"Simon, are you alright? Why the disguise?" Elizabeth recognised him immediately, despite the dishevelment.

"I was robbed." It came out before Simon could help it. A better answer would have been to go along with the disguise theory; perhaps even inventing a secret mission he had been assigned. But it was too late for anything but the truth. "I was robbed by the very people I was going to see. Well, the soldiers at the gate, anyway. They would not let me in and suggested I was enlisting."

Elizabeth and Amelia found it hard to conceal their amusement, resorting to staring down at the tapestry to avoid detection. But periodically, as they listened dutifully to Simon's tale of woe, Amelia stole a glance at Elizabeth and a new set of stifled giggles took over.

At the end of the long story, in which he had stood up to a dozen soldiers but had been surprised by a musket in his back, then robbed of his portable wealth, including his horse; given a donkey on which to ride home, Amelia took the liberty of asking a question. She had waited patiently for her father to exhaust his outrage before moving to her preferred subject.

"Sir, might I ask who owned this house before we did?" Nevertheless, the question stuck out like the quiet after the storm.

"Why do you want to know?"

"No particular reason, Father, I just wanted to know a bit of history about our home."

"It is a sad story," he replied, thinking fast; better to give some truthful facts than build a construction of falsehoods that would come tumbling down at some future critical time. "She was a mad woman. I forget her name now." That was two lies in his opening sentence. Elizabeth knew Lady Merriman and she seemed eccentric but by no means mad. And he certainly knew the family name of Merriman; they were local minor nobility.

"Did she live here long, sir?" Elizabeth added to the questions, wanting Simon to talk.

"She was born here, I believe. But I know little of this. She left the house when still young and moved north somewhere. She came back for a few months about five years ago and then sold the house to me for a... fair value." Lie number three, Elizabeth thought. A squalid pig farm was never fair value for Bagber Manor. Yet it was her home now? Did she want to give up the wide lawns and pretty copses that led one from the other? Did she want to move back to Simon's old house in Sturminster Newton and give up these large square rooms with high ceilings and decorated cornicing?

As so often when facing a dilemma, she asked herself what her father would say. Perhaps she should try and see him, if Simon would allow it. On a farthing, therefore, she decided to change tack.

"Oh Amelia, my dear, let us cease these tedious questions that irk your dear father. He has had an ordeal and an adventure rolled into one. Let us welcome the man of our household back with open arms and, if we are to ask questions, I for one would like to know more about how he stood up to those brutish soldiers."

"But..." Amelia looked surprised but settled when she saw the glint in her friend's eyes. "Of course, you are right, Mother. Father, please do tell us exactly how you dealt with those wicked people who robbed you."

Elizabeth, for her display of matrimonial loyalty, was granted a visit to her father the next morning. The price was another rendition of Simon the Bold standing up to bullying, only finally falling due to the weight of numbers bearing down on him.

Because, as he said several times, it is the principle that counts.

Elizabeth took Amelia with her on the trip to visit her father and Matthew. She found her father much changed; charged again with the Lord and doing his work with a boyish enthusiasm. It gave Elizabeth a glimpse of what he must have been like as a young man.

"I understand they are marching on Bristol," he declared as soon as she had offered her cheek for a kiss of welcome.

'They' were the growing numbers following Monmouth, although his information was out of date, as Monmouth's forces were shrinking rapidly as June gave way to July.

"There was a battle, or rather a skirmish," he continued.

"How do you know, Father?"

"I had a letter from Grace. It was hurried and scrawled on the back of a bill of sale for some items for the army but it was from her." To the inevitable cries of enquiry, he continued, building suspense like he did every Sunday in the pulpit. "It was not a long letter but had high significance in the things it said."

"What did it say, Pastor Davenport?" Amelia showed great interest in the war, especially for one so feeble in body and mind, as her father often said when dining out with friends.

"My daughter, Grace, witnessed the fighting. She was situated in the woods behind Monmouth's forces. She wrote that Thomas was involved and struck mighty blows for the force of good. However, he was captured and right now she is on a mission to free him, employing all those that will assist her." It was a grossly sanitised version of events that Grace had scribbled on the back of an invoice she had found in her borrowed saddlebags. She had omitted to tell her father that Thomas had changed sides in order to save the life of someone she loved. There was a need for brevity during her urgent ride north to Bristol, but her omissions had more to do with a desire not to tell her father that she was in love with a Catholic and, moreover, that Thomas Davenport was a hated name in the Monmouth camp.

Elizabeth found the change in her father incredible. He was animated; as if he had charged down that slope next to Thomas and clashed heavy swords with the enemy. His eyes that for years had looked washed out; worn out, even, had a life-of-their-own look about them. That look told her she would not find much clemency if she were standing before him as a felon following some minor malefaction. It was almost other-worldly; divorced from considerations of the body.

He had the look of a fanatic.

The Monmouth Rebellion had brought about this change. It had re-ignited a flame long gone out, doused in brandy and self-pity. Now it was a beacon on the hillside, shining out bravely and assuredly. And, Elizabeth felt, it was a reckless and unnecessary beacon; announcing to all that Pastor Davenport was unequivocally on the side of dissent. No, not dissent, but outright resistance to the establishment. Why, she wondered, would he do that, risking his livelihood, maybe also risking his life?

And then, as her father raged on, building to a crescendo, she realised that she had the answer to this question about him.

He did it because he believed it was right.

And that gave her the answer to her own question, such that she did not even have to ask it of her father.

With regard to her husband Simon and his past misdeeds, she should do what she considered right.

And it was most patently not right to occupy a house and estate that belonged to someone else; which was purloined by trickery or some such evil.

Wherever you find evil, root it out.

After lunch, the pastor went to his study to work on his sermon. In the old days that would signal an indulgence with the bottle and very little, if any, sermon writing. But these days the sermons were trotting out.

"And they are brilliant too," Matthew said, unable to hide his envy. "They are regular firebrands. Do you know, for instance, the "Man Against Man" series has already sold over five thousand copies? The joke at the printers in Shaftesbury is that they cannot produce them fast enough."

It was a remarkable achievement given the book was only three weeks old.

"And "Stand Up and Be Counted" is even more radical" Matthew added, as if throwing fuel on a mighty bonfire of righteousness.

"But I worry that it is too radical," Elizabeth replied. "I know it is right to state your conscience but common sense also dictates a little caution in these uncertain times." But Matthew was a little Luke in this regard and could not be persuaded that caution had any role where the Lord's work was concerned.

"Do you not see the danger to Father?"

"Sister, I see that Father is doing right in a wicked world. He is standing up to be counted. That is all that matters at the end of the day."

"Sir, if I might be permitted to offer my opinion," Amelia said politely. Matthew looked astonished; everything Simon had said about his daughter implied she was a dullard.

"Of course, Miss Taylor," he replied weakly, wishing she would not.

Amelia stood up and moved out into the open area in front of the chairs they were occupying in the parlour. She cleared her throat, scooping up her nerves and managing them somehow.

"I believe that the world is not wicked in whole but only in part. It seems to me that it consists of good and evil in roughly equal proportions but see-sawing through the ages. By that I mean that the sum of evil and the sum of bad fluctuate around a mean. Some people are wholly wicked and some are like the saints but most of us are in between; that is to say, sometimes good and sometimes bad. Civilisation and manners place constraints on naked evil but good people with good intentions can be a force for good and that is our responsibility; to manufacture good from bad through our faith and the example we set."

This speech was met with silence. Even Elizabeth, becoming

more familiar with the hidden treasure that was Amelia, was stunned by her insight. It was exactly as she herself thought but, despite considerably more confidence, she would never have dared voice such opinions in front of a man, even her brother. Elizabeth thought back to the early morning search of Simon's office; how Amelia had taken command so naturally and easily. The girl she and most others had treated with such disdain at school was proving to have remarkable depths.

Matthew, too, was speechless but was saved from examining why for at that moment there was a loud clattering from the street outside, followed by several bangs on the door.

"We're home," Thomas cried, helping first Grace and then Lady Merriman down from the cart.

Elizabeth was first to the front door. There she saw her sister and brother, but also the lady who had exchanged her estate for a pig farm in some other part of the country. The current Lady of Bagber looked at the previous Lady of Bagber.

And the current lady knew her decision to go with the right of the matter was right in itself.

Luke was drawn from his study and embraced his two youngest. He was introduced to Lady Merriman, who curtsied, not from deference but respect.

"I am not of your persuasion, sir," she said, as she knew his occupation from his children. "But I respect your beliefs."

"Are you Roman?" Luke asked, affronted by the prospect of a papist in his home.

"Certainly not!" she replied with the tinkling laughter that had endeared her to Thomas and Grace. "I am not such an exciting character as to be a Catholic. No sir, I am Anglican, pure and simple; one of the multitude that are not fanatical about their religion but, nevertheless, hold their proper beliefs very dear."

"Come now, Father, you can surely tolerate an Anglican in your home, brought by two of your children who probably will never speak to you again should you turn her away!" Elizabeth teased her father with surprising ease. She had never teased him before.

"Hush, Elizabeth," Matthew said. "It does no good to disrespect your father. Besides, you must consider…"

"No, I own my shortcomings," Luke interrupted, silencing Matthew's defence of him before it had moved into full flow. "Now, let us drink tea and hear the adventures these two rascals have been up to."

"First, I have two more people to introduce," Grace said, pushing Thomas back outside the door. "Go and fetch them, Thomas."

"Yes, Your Highness," said with some humour but a good deal of dread.

The cause of that dread was that, during the journey home, Jane had confided that she and her cheeky husband were Catholics.; the disclosure came in nervous stages as they learned of the illustrious Puritan father they were heading towards. Grace and Thomas had discussed this between themselves and had decided to say nothing of it; let it out if it would but they would not mention it deliberately.

But Luke took a shine to the newcomers immediately. There was something about the cocky spirit of them both that appealed to his gravity. It seemed like apple and cheese, or eggs and bacon.

It was aided by Jane, in particular, taking a great interest in his work.

"I'd be happy to show you some of my publications if you have a mind to look them over," he suggested when the tea was drunk. Jane nodded and rose.

"I'd be delighted, sir." And she meant it, nudging her husband to follow them.

"Where will they live?" Matthew asked as the door closed.

"Why here, of course," Grace replied.

"But they cannot. Besides, we have no room."

"You have Thomas' attic and also my room. It will only be while they get themselves established."

"But then where will you sleep?"

"We have to go back to Churchill's army," she replied, then told the full story about the oath she had given to return with

Thomas.

They would need to leave the next day.

There was one other newcomer in their midst. Elizabeth thought to ask about her accommodation but Amelia got there first.

"Lady Merriman, you will, of course, come to stay with us at Bagber Manor?"

The shock was absolute and immediate. Lady Merriman had been chatting with Matthew, thinking he was pleasant but hard-going. She froze mid-sentence, slowly turning her head towards Amelia, as if every degree of turn was racked out by sailors on a heavy capstan. There was instant silence in the parlour; everybody sensed a heavy moment. Finally, Lady Merriman spoke; little more than a hoarse whisper cut, cut and cut again with razor-sharp memories piling up in her mind and hurting her very thought process.

"Did you say Bagber Manor?" Her voice came out in a million broken pieces; the fine stone of resonate sound shattered by impact.

"I did, Lady Merriman. I believe it was your house once, before you moved to a farm somewhere in the north." That was intentionally forward but not at all possessive.

"The pig farm, yes, I recollect now. Thank you, young lady, I would be delighted to stay with you awhile."

Throughout the ride home with Elizabeth and Amelia, along paths Lady Merriman knew so well, her memory of the pig farm haunted her. It had been a squalid place; a stone-built cottage in the wilds of the Yorkshire moors. They had called it 'The Big House' because it had four rooms, but she had known at the time that it had been some form of mockery of her. Parchman had taken her there. Parchman had sneered as he rode away, leaving her in the care of Kitty and Sarah, her only companions for fifteen long years.

She had a modest income from somewhere, which she had not spent, and allowed to accumulate. It was not a matter of principle, simply that there was nothing to spend it on. They bought material twice a year to make new dresses. She went to the library once a month and ate in the little tea shop in town. But all this was paid for by the profits on the tiny piggery run by the only other person she saw regularly; Mr Harding. He was a gentle soul but even after fifteen years she had not penetrated his thick accent sufficiently to hold a proper conversation. He lived in a two-room shack the other side of the bank of pig sties. She could close her eyes and hear the pig noise, smell their bodies and see the mud.

She had known all along that there was something more to her but had been unable to bring it to mind. She knew from the first day that she did not belong; there was a glorious past that had been flattened out of her mind. Somebody had taken away her memory; robbed her of who she was.

There was another person at that time. A vision of a large, bumbling man came before her. He was gruff, but with a kind heart. He had a room she used to visit him in. Even now, with so much come back to her, this part evaded her. She sensed he was the clue to much of it. For fifteen years she had been an exile in Yorkshire then she had come back to Bagber Manor, but how and why? She had been briefly happy again, meeting Thomas and Grace, just the same age as her son; the beloved son who had been torn from her arms and given to another.

But she recalled the summer at Bagber. She had been happy then. It had been a homecoming. It was her childhood home. But then those four men had come for her one day, early in the morning. Kitty and Sarah had screamed and shouted but there was no one to help as she was carted away.

And then the real nightmare had begun.

Amelia kicked her horse and cried, "Race you to the manor!" Elizabeth responded instantly, leaving Lady Merriman behind on her own. In a fit of delight on that muggy July day in 1685, with the world around them in the turmoil of excited rebellion, she urged her horse on and soon was galloping after them. She lost her hat to the wind; that same wind tugged her long, fair hair out of its restraints and sent it streaming backwards as she pounded the woodland and turf beyond. She was determined to catch them.

And she did, pulling up a full length ahead of the others and jumping from the horse in breathless laughter.

"I won, I beat you both," she cried, just as the front door opened and Simon Taylor stood on the broad steps, looking down at the three of them, his features unreadable.

And Lady Merriman's world closed in at the sight of him. She heard Elizabeth and Amelia rushing to break her fall, then the dark despair took over.

Chapter 27

Parchman looked down his long nose, unable to control the face-twitch that hit him at times of stress.

"You allowed her to escape?"

"She was assisted, Mr Parchman. There were six or eight of them, at least. Arkwright cajoled them into helping her escape. She even hit me on the head; see, here is the bump." Mrs Beatrice offered her head for examination but Parchman declined to take her up on it.

"Whatever the circumstances, she is gone," he growled.

"Yes, and I need to know how I am supposed to run the laundry business without her."

"A plague on your laundry business. Do you think I care about your livelihood?"

"You will continue to pay us, of course?" Mr Beatrice saw with a chill the end of the good times; was desperate to hear to the contrary. He owed the next two months' payments in gambling debts, although he had not yet told his wife of this.

"The agreement, Beatrice, was that you would keep her safe and secure, doing what you will with her, and I, in return, would deliver a monthly bonus. You have let the woman go through your carelessness. This will cause my employer considerable aggravation and expense. Tell me, Beatrice, would you pay someone in this situation?"

"No, sir." Then he thought again about his reply. "Although I might under certain circumstances…"

"Quiet, husband, and listen or else I will put you into such an unhappy state you will wish yourself died and gone to hell."

"I was only trying to help the situation, my dear."

"Well, you can help me by keeping your mouth firmly closed. Better still, take your sorry body to the cupboard and bring me a brandy."

Thank the Heavens, thought Parchman, *that matrimony and I took different roads through life*. He shuddered at the sight of Mr Beatrice scurrying to the brandy cupboard, thinking of a lifetime under her thumb. He had no desire to spend any more time with Mrs Beatrice than was absolutely necessary.

He would soon be wishing he had never met the woman.

"Sir," Mrs Beatrice took command of the conversation, "am I to understand that you are intending to desist from our established monthly stipend?" She was a woman of good intelligence, but ill education; seen in her resorting to the most complex phrases her lexicon could manage. She was under stress; loss of the lucrative laundry business based on slave labour was a blow. But far more serious was the stopping of the hush-payments that underlay their whole middle-class existence. She was under stress indeed; visibly and audibly so. Exactly where Parchman liked his underlings to be. But she was fighting her corner and Parchman had to grant her that much, although he detested the woman.

"Your understanding is entirely correct, madam." He was going to enjoy this.

"I would advise you not to take that action, sir." Was there a layer of defiance laid over the top of her voice? He would have to stamp that out.

"I do not believe, woman, that you are in any position to advise me on any subject under the sun. Now, I have wasted enough time today in the common courtesy of bringing you up to date with your changed circumstances." He rose as he finished speaking.

"Sit down!" This was said with such force that, without thinking, he sat down again. Round one was gone to Mrs Beatrice.

"There, that is better. Now we can have a proper chat." She was rubbing it in. "I advise, sir, against any precipitous action, purely in your own interests, of course. I do not seek to advise, other than out of the extension of friendly relations between two colleagues of business." Mrs Beatrice was running out of serious-sounding words. She would need to move on; hurry the process up before she fell apart. "You see, I know who your employer is."

Whichever way one dresses up blackmail, the final demand, the final statement, is always naked in its simple crudity; there is no way to cover it up. Hence it is recognised immediately.

In fact, Parchman, a master at meting out blackmail, had seen it coming right at the beginning of round two. He was ready for this one.

"Tosh," he said, "that is known only to me."

In reply, Mrs Beatrice used no words. She was beyond words, having used up the grandest she had available, with words scattered on the floor like spent bullets. Instead, she remained silent as Parchman counted round two for himself.

Then came the unseen punch. Mrs Beatrice pulled a note from the sleeve of her dress and slid it across the table towards Parchman.

He picked it up, read the single word on the reverse and knew he was beaten. The vixen had totally outmanoeuvred him.

Unless he resorted to his favourite tactic; always a joy to fall back on. Violence beat mind games any day of the week. He loved best of all the snap of broken bones, blood gushing its glorious bright, pulsating red; alarm and pain spreading across faces like the new sun pushing out night.

Timing was a key part of the employment of successful violence. A blow too late or too early lost its effectiveness; that tremendous sensation of dominance built on total surprise. He flexed both muscles and mind, sensing the time approaching.

Acting was equally key. He was good at this. He frowned, looked puzzled a minute, then dejected; all the time keenly watching Mrs Beatrice's reactions. He added a sigh for good measure; she was buying it, he could tell.

Final preparations were important, too. He sensed his dagger by his side; planned the move of his right hand. What could possibly go wrong?

All three components of success in utilising violence were coming together nicely. In just a moment he would spring, dagger drawn with lightning speed.

He sprung, never imagining in his supreme confidence that he had forgotten the one other vital aspect. For as he rose up and pulled his dagger free to plunge it into Mrs Beatrice's round belly and up through her chest so that he could watch her die, Mr Beatrice rose, too. Strong hands; a strength Mr

Beatrice never knew he had, gripped Parchman's and turned the dagger around on itself.

The force he had put into his decisive blow was turned back onto him. The dagger entered his stomach at the exact point where he had planned such for Mrs Beatrice. She sat and watched as he slid very slowly to the floor. Hands clutched the dagger but were too weak to pull it out. Instead, in some sick parody, his hands turned the knife deeper into his belly; twisting the agony around and around and around. Grey came to the edges of his vision as he seemed to retreat from the world. He hit the floor and stared up for a long moment; the eyes of the vanquished rested on the victor. But there was no triumph in her voice when she next spoke.

"You idiot husband! Look at what you have done. Now we will just have to go to the head man himself."

Which is exactly what they did, although it took them into the very centre of danger.

Thomas and Grace were also setting out on an uncertain journey; not knowing whether it would end in a hanging rope for Thomas and maybe transportation to the new world colonies for Grace, as an accomplice to Thomas' escape from custody. But they rode, at least at first, with light hearts, for doing right takes the weight of one's shoulders in a wondrously naive way.

They rode to possible disaster, not seeming to care; they had placed their future in the hands of a young, rising general and the word he had given.

"Let me get this right," Thomas said into the rhythm of hooves striking the ground. "Amelia Taylor is Simon's daughter from his first marriage, so she is Lizzie's stepdaughter?"

"That's right."

"I remember her at school."

"As do I," Grace said. "She was dumpy and shy and everyone made fun of her. It is strange that Simon never brought her with him when he visited us. I always thought she was a simpleton and lacked any confidence because she was so plain and un-shapely."

"Yet she looks quite pleasing now and so obviously intelligent."

"So Lizzie says." Grace gave her brother a sharp look.

They rode hard all day, crossing quickly into Somerset, then asking direction after direction to Churchill's camp near Bridgewater. The rain, so torrential for the last few days, held off but hung in the air, as if sunshine should be all that was needed to lure them to their fate; but the storm was held in reserve, just in case.

The first chill of the evening came not from the sultry, rain-threatening weather but from the camp guard as they finally approached the makeshift gate with evening giving way to night. For Roakes was permanently assigned as Sergeant of the Guard now; a position that had the added bonus of taking him away from the direct fighting; security within security.

Grace had grown quieter all day, as the prospect of arrest mingled with the fact that she was riding ever closer to the man she loved and who she could never be with. Rank and religion were brick and mortar that made a towering wall between them.

Would he recover from his wounds? Physically, he was on the mend already; she had seen that in her last hurried visit, before she had left in search of Thomas; the night of her conditional lease on freedom, payment for which she was now honouring in full.

But quite possibly she was bringing her beloved brother back to his death. She had given her word and Thomas considered himself as beholden to that word as she.

Her thoughts flicked between lover and brother as they rode towards captivity and uncertainty. Henry was certainly mending physically. But it was not physical recovery of Henry that worried Grace. It was his spirit. He had been very low during that last hurried visit in his tent. There had been no jokes, no teasing; nothing to indicate recovery of spirit.

Perhaps he had been persuaded away from her as an unsuitable match. She was not noble and had no fortune; she had nothing to offer a man like the Earl of Sherborne.

Roakes was delighted to see them and sprung a trick immediately. He had known Grace and Thomas would return, precisely because, in their position, he never would. He would be back in his native Yorkshire by now, seeking new opportunity wherever it lay.

"Well I never!" he pretended surprise. "Peters, Grant, take the young 'gentleman' into custody." Two hands grabbed Thomas from the right and hauled him out of the saddle, then marched him away between them. "Smith, Powers, escort the 'lady' into separate custody. You may care to dismount or my fellows will tear you from your horse. It is your choice." Grace dismounted, looking at her two guards. They were the two that had raped her after Roakes. "I'll be along later to check on you," Roakes added with a sneer. Things were certainly working out well for him. The post of Sergeant of the Guard had proved both lucrative and entertaining.

Grace and Thomas had never imagined they would be separated on arrival; thinking they would see this through together. Thomas turned to see his sister being escorted away by two leering guards.

"If they hurt her they will have me to answer to."

"Silence, prisoner." Grant, or maybe it was Peters, gave him a jab in the side with his musket. The other of the pair grinned at Thomas' discomfort.

One bad apple will spoil the barrel.

Grace stepped into the crude hut with trepidation but quickly, a second before she was pushed; hence denying her guards the pleasure of shoving her into the dark. Inside, door bolted, lacking a window but fully dark with heavy clouds now anyway, she felt around to get an idea of the place.

"Ouch," said a voice she knew.

"Mrs Bradbury, is that you?"

"Miss Davenport! You came back?"

"Hello dearie!" Mrs Bryant chimed in from somewhere else in the darkened room.

They had grave news. "Major Parkhurst is dead. He was shot

in a minor skirmish."

"Shot from behind, everyone is saying," Mrs Bryant added with a degree of bitterness.

"The moment his poor body was brought back, we were arrested and thrown in here."

"There are powerful forces working against you, my dear."

And that was the moment when Roakes came back for more. The door swung open wide and he stood there with a drunken grin and unsteady stance.

"Well, if it ain't the little miss come back to see her Sergeant Roakes!" The idea of repeat rape with an audience of two terrified women appealed to him enormously. Life was certainly working out very nicely right now. He moved into the hut, swaying as he walked, stumbling over the door stop so he seemed to rush in like a bull charging a red rag.

Instinctively, Grace went backwards, tripping on a chamber pot but not spilling it. Then Mrs Bryant seized the chamber pot and threw its contents over Roakes.

"What the hell..." But he never finished for Mrs Bradbury stamped on his foot while Mrs Bryant swung the empty chamber pot at his most sensitive part, then continued the upwards thrust so that it crashed into his chin, breaking teeth and shattering the pot in the process. There were shards of tooth-size porcelain spraying all over the place, giving the appearance that the man had lost a hundred teeth with one blow.

Roakes gave a groan and slumped to the ground.

"Is he dead?" Mrs Bradbury asked.

"No, just out cold. What do we do now?"

Grace knew.

"We free Thomas and then find Captain Hanson."

They unclipped Roakes' key chain from his waist and went out into the cloudy, hot night, whispering Thomas' name at each tent. They disturbed a semi-drunken game of cards in one tent; Mrs Bryant abated the inevitable suspicion and opportunity of three women out in the dark at night, by sitting on a soldier's knee and singing a silly song about her love going off to fight.

But he was not fighting an opposing army but the mice who invaded his barn. Armed with sword and shield he swiped and struck at them but to no avail.

Finally, she slipped away and their hunt resumed.

They found Thomas in the hut behind theirs. They had set off to the right and never thought to look for other makeshift prisons nearby.

"Yes, it's me, Grace," he called back in answer to her urgent whisper. "Are you free? Can you get me out of here?"

He was free within the minute. Introductions to the two bees took another half.

"Come this way for Captain Hanson," said Mrs Bryant, indicating some shadows off to the left.

"How do you know?" Grace asked.

"I asked that soldier," she replied, jerking her head back towards the tent that contained the card game. "He charged me a kiss and a grope. I suggested there would be more of the same if he could tell me where Captain Hanson was. He talked readily enough."

They found Captain Hanson a few minutes later. He was asleep but needed only seconds to appreciate the situation.

"You must stay the night here. Thomas and I will sleep in the day quarters. You three girls shall take my cot. In the morning, I will work out what to do. Things will seem clear enough in the morning."

It was a tight squeeze and nobody expected to sleep but they did. Surprisingly, Grace and Thomas both slipped off first. As Grace closed her eyes she thought of Major Parkhurst and the bullet in the back of him. Was it murder? Was the army investigating it, or had they more pressing things to concern themselves with? After all, 'King Monmouth' was very close.

There had been too many lives ruined already. First Lady Merriman's gardener had undoubtedly been slain. Well, before that had not Lady Merriman mentioned that her father had been murdered by a man named Packman or some such? Then Lady Merriman had been the victim of some cruel torture of the mind; designed to eradicate her memory and turn her into a near-slave. There was her rape, of course; something she shuddered to think about. There was dear Henry with a livid gash across his face, and Thomas blighted by this unfair conviction for treason when he had saved Henry's life. And finally, there was Major Parkhurst's suspicious death, shot from behind as he went bravely forward with his troops.

She snuggled closer into the bodies of her older companions; thinking they too had suffered through the loss of their husbands. Then sleep took over.

Mrs Bradbury was last awake. She heard the clatter of two horses arriving in the depth of the night but thought nothing of it.

The morning woke them with two things. First, the cries from the corporals and sergeants rousing the camp. Second, a thunderstorm that seemed like a waterfall the moment one left shelter.

Hanson woke them all, while a servant brought in coffee and bread and cold beef. "It's the best we can do at the moment. We're marching to find the enemy."

"What of our case, sir?" Thomas asked.

It was then Hanson had his idea. "Follow me, Thomas," he said. "You've been a soldier before so this should be easy."

And Thomas went into battle for a second time. He left with Hanson, newly appointed his aide. Most captains would not run to an aide but it served their purpose.

"Besides," said Hanson, somewhat shyly, "with Major Parkhurst dead, I've been made up temporarily to major, with three companies at my command."

The ladies were instructed to stay in the tent. Hanson's servant was going to fight but first he found a couple of loaves of bread and some cheese and more beef, plus a flagon of cider, purchased from the farm they were camping on.

"Just in case it is a long battle, ladies," the servant said with a grin. "Although I expect we'll be back for lunch!"

It is as well that they had these provisions for the Battle of Sedgemoor only began that night and raged on through the dark hours and rain. The three women waited as women do in time of war; holding their nerves like guy ropes tightened too tensely. They created conversation for the sake of it; polite chatter when they already knew each other so well.

For sharing danger, while terrifying, gives a comradeship and knowledge of one's companions second to none.

They kept to their tent as instructed. Hence, they did not see Mr and Mrs Beatrice struggle through the rain to take refuge in an empty tent, leaving their horses, saddled and bridled, in the rain. But at least they were dry; that was what counted. They had no food but Mr Beatrice, full of initiative, had put a bottle of brandy in the hastily packed saddlebags.

And, as luck would have it, the tent they chose for shelter, had a good supply of more and the quality surpassed their every dream.

Chapter 28

"I won't have that woman in my house."

"It's not your house, Father."

"What? How dare…"

"This house and estate belongs to Lady Merriman. We are effectively her guests." Amelia had never interrupted her father before. Her mind was outside her body; sitting high up in the circle, looking down at the stage where her body was acting its role; saying her lines with conviction that surprised her. That same mind, while carefully but decisively controlling her defiance, was also able to range in time, considering the consequences and rehearsing the next part of her argument.

She had caught her father off-guard and had the advantage. She also had reinforcements in Elizabeth, her dear friend, who finished the final stitch in the picture she was working on; a harried and flustered man being turned out of his house. She laid down her needle, looking up at her husband.

"Your daughter is correct, sir." The use of 'sir' instead of his name usually pleased Simon but now it infuriated him because it spoke of lack of respect rather than reinforcing it. "Lady Merriman has no recollection of selling her house to you."

"What nonsense, I have the deed of sale to prove it. She is a muddled lady, for certain. I think she has led you up a false road with her poor memory." He had them now; pushed out his chest like a cock amongst the hens.

"Do you mean this deed of sale?" Elizabeth pulled the document from underneath the tapestry. She noted the neatness of its hiding; positioned directly underneath the stitched house that the stitched man was being evicted from.

"How did you get it?" He took it, looked it over quickly, then stuffed it in his coat pocket. Again, it had been easy to get the better of the two girls. They lacked experience in manipulation.

"It is a copy, sir, drawn up by a clerk at Wrights and Pascoe of Sherborne. They have agreed to represent Lady Merriman. The original is in their safe-keeping."

This was a concerted effort against him by the two people in the whole world who should have been most loyal to him. What was happening? The attack was co-ordinated, thought through; hardly the product of two idle females.

"It is still a deed of sale, establishing the existence of the original." He sounded flustered, nowhere near the control he normally had, especially in his own home and talking the law. But, surely, they would see the futility of their approach; if they had a copy of the bill of sale that must prove that the original existed.

"But a forgery, sir," Amelia added, driving it home hard. Simon jerked his head back so he was staring at the ceiling. There was a line of cracked plaster that ran across from fireplace to window. The plaster bulged like the veins of a sick man.

"Nonsense!"

"Do you care to look, sir, at Lady Merriman's writing in this list? See, she has a tiny hand in writing and delicately formed letters. Her writing is quite impossible to read because of the smallness of it. Now, please look at the bill of sale and you must notice that the handwriting is quite different. See, sir, her signature is in big, looping letters. Wrights and Pascoe have a gentleman experienced in such matters and he has concluded in this report that the signature is undoubtedly a fake one."

"You have been cheated, Father," Amelia added kindly, but with a firmness that was news to Simon.

But they knew. And he knew that they knew. The large, looping letters had been the hand of Parchman five years earlier, when Simon had gained title to Bagber Manor in return for numerous legal services concerning Lady Merriman. It had suited Parchman's sick sense of humour not to do a straight sale but to do an exchange for the pig farm she had tenanted for the previous fifteen years.

"It has a finality and neatness about it, don't you think, Taylor?"

Simon had acquired the pig farm only the previous day. It had cost him just a quarter's commission on his loan business and Parchman had pushed for the purchase, saying he would not be disappointed in it.

247

"But why would I want a smallholding in Yorkshire?" Simon had asked.

"Because, my man, however degraded that farm is, it makes you a man of property. Trust me, Taylor, you will not be disappointed." Simon had trusted the architect of his new wealth and had signed and paid for the pig farm that afternoon. The very next morning it was sold on again, exchanged for the glorious Bagber Manor with a wink from Parchman as he completed his sleight-of-hand.

He had not been there when Lady Merriman was taken away in the back of a covered cart, for Amelia and Simon, on advice from Parchman, had delayed their move into the manor until the following day.

That had been five years ago. But now, the very foundations of his success in life were suddenly exposed; bare to all and patently inadequate. He sat down heavily, seemed suddenly so much smaller, so much older.

"What is to happen to me?" Forgery was a hanging offence. At best, he could hope to rot in prison as an accomplice. He would be fifty at Christmas; too old to survive prison and start again. This was the end. He stared at the empty fireplace that he had so often strutted in front of, laying down the law for the womenfolk. It was not rightly even his fireplace. He was finished.

"Nothing," Elizabeth said, both ladies moved by his deflation. But he did not respond.

"Nothing will happen," she repeated but still no response; no way in to where he was.

Amelia rose from the sofa where they had been working at the tapestry and went to him, knelt by his side. Elizabeth followed suit and knelt at his other side. She had never liked her husband but was shocked by his sudden fall into despair.

"Father, "Amelia picked up his limp hand and held it in hers, "Lady Merriman does not want to go to law over this. You must give up the estate, that is clear, but we will move back into town. We will have our old house again." She did not add that she and Elizabeth planned to be regular visitors at Bagber

Manor; that would have been to twist the knife in further.

There was a moment then that the two young ladies would remember for as long as they lived. It was the briefest of moments, cut short by tragedy of an altogether unexpected kind.

Simon Taylor, once master of Bagber Manor but no longer, raised his head to look at first his daughter and then his wife; the two architects of his fall.

"I am sorry. I have failed you. I have chased things not worth having."

That was the end of the moment for a convulsion took over. As they watched in growing horror, the right side of his face sank below its natural level, as if it were made of clay and had not dried properly. He went bright red, shook several times to the core. He tried to talk but slurred nonsense and spittle came out in equal proportions.

"My God," said Elizabeth, "I believe he is having a stroke."

The stable lad galloped on their fastest horse for the doctor. He came quickly and put Simon to bed. The prognosis was not good.

"He will need constant caring for. Unless he improves, which happens sometimes but not often, he will need washing, dressing, feeding and so on, like the care given for a new-born child."

"We will do it," said Elizabeth, so used to duty.

"Yes," said Amelia, so full of love for the father who had ignored or ridiculed her all her life long.

The two women sat together at first, then realised it was a waste of resource, although each other's company was sweet. Elizabeth put together a rota, allowing some time with them both there together, but mostly on lone sentry-duty.

Kitty and Sarah said they would help, although they both expected that they would be leaving soon, now that Lady Merriman was back. They had overheard little pieces of talk amongst the Taylors that led them to believe that Lady Merriman would be departing Bagber, taking her two servant-girls with her, as if possessions to pack in a trunk. They had never liked Simon Taylor with his commanding and abusive manner, but would do what was required of them as dutiful servants until they departed with Lady M.

This surprised Elizabeth, who thought they would refuse to care for her husband in the slightest way.

But it was Lady Merriman who had the bigger surprise.

"This rota is too demanding on you and Amelia," she said, on looking it over.

"It's as it must be, Lady Merriman," Amelia replied firmly.

"You must add one more name to the rota," Lady Merriman said. "I will gladly take part."

And thus, it happened that, just as the women waited while the men did battle, so five women took full care of a man who had never showed any one of them a kindness; in fact, had worked hard to gain at their expense and caused much misery along the way.

And whether it was the servant or the lady of the house, the wife or the daughter, they all gave without any hesitation.

Let me give without counting the cost

And proving that there is hope in this sordid world after all.

Mr Beatrice had a fine voice and so did his wife. As the first bottle neared empty, he broke into song first. She scorned him to start with but, by the third-gone mark of bottle number two, she added a sweet harmony to his singing sad songs and happy songs; songs about love misplaced and going to war and going to sea; opportunities gained and opportunities lost.

They sang at the top of their voices, howling sometimes in their drunken madness. But the storm outside took their songs and chewed them up, throwing them to the wind which carried them away, lost forever to human ears.

And the only sound in that camp where they all waited was the wind and the rain and the flapping of tents left open to the elements. But then the storm died with the day, leaving just the still night to soak up the cries of anguish from the battlefield nearby.

And the sober shuddered while the drunk sang.

Grace was alone with her two friends; together but apart. Torn by her brother gone suddenly to war. Torn again by the thought of her lover lying in his tent; his beautiful face torn to shreds. For all she knew, he could be in the next tent, close enough, when the storm abated, to hear his fitful breathing while he slept. Was he dreaming of her or was she now a figure in his past; his once was but no longer? She paced the tent; up and down, left and right; had been so doing all the long day since Thomas and Hanson left early that morning.

"Why don't you go and find him?" Mrs Bryant cut into her thoughts like the swords on the battlefield.

"Who?" she asked weakly, shaken by the question.

"Henry Sherborne, of course," came the reply.

"Captain Hanson said to stay here."

"Captain Hanson can pee in the wind for all I care." Mrs Bradbury came to sit with them. "You're pining for him and worried about your brother. Go and find him this very minute and, if nothing else, it will take your mind off Thomas, who will be absolutely fine; I feel it in my bones with that one."

"How do you know?"

"Because they are fighting a rabble of an army. They are peasants and disaffected labourers, not soldiers. Mr Churchill will win a great victory when ever this battle finally starts. He has the makings of a great general, mark my words. Now, go before you dither the night away, as you have the day already." Mrs Bradbury's words were said with more conviction than she felt but she justified the exaggeration with regard to Thomas' chances of survival as a white lie.

"Where do I look?" Grace stood up, as if her body had decided but her mind not yet.

"Who does Captain Hanson report to?" Mrs Bryant asked.

"Why, Major Parkhurst, I believe; or used to."

"I mean further up. Go to the top."

"Well, he was with the Earl of Sherborne when he rescued me so I suppose his commander must be the Earl."

"There you have your answer, my dear." And when Grace looked blank, she added, "I see I need to spell it out for you. This is Captain Hanson's tent. Captain Hanson is a captain in

251

Earl Sherborne's troop. Tents are…"

"Grouped by troop!" Grace cried. "Do you really think I should go?"

"Yes," they replied as one.

In fact, they went a stage further, for they came with her. Three heads; three voices to whisper his name; three pairs of ears to listen for a response. Three friends together.

They found him. But it was the last tent in their section, as hope had passed its zenith and was well into its decline. Grace kept saying to herself, *There are lots more tents to search and he will probably be in this row or the next.* But he was not. Most tents were empty, deserted in the clatter to arms that morning; a morning that seemed a life time ago now. A lifetime of waiting like women do.

But these women had waited enough and they persevered through the night, with cries ringing out from before them and off to the left and right; shouts of agony and triumph from the battlefield close by. It seemed an orchestra of frightful noise; when the strings eventually silenced to their left, so the brass started up on the right. They were listening to a symphony of death; yet had more urgent things to do in finding Henry Sherborne, hence exhibiting the kind wisdom of the two bees, for Grace's thoughts were not on Thomas for most of this time but concentrated on finding Henry.

They came to a large tent, from which fine singing rose. A man on the tune and a woman who harmonised perfectly, making a sweet noise against the cries from afar.

Perhaps this was Henry singing with his bride-to-be, the one chosen for him by his grandfather, the Earl. Perhaps Grace was forgotten to him now; a friend he had once been close to.

She stopped at the entrance to the tent, listening for some sign of it being Henry inside. They were chinking glasses; making merry while others were dying. In outrage, she leaned further into the tent to catch a glimpse of those inside; certain that it was Henry with another.

That was when she tripped on something by the entrance and flew into the tent, banging into a laden dining table and causing the opened bottle of champagne to wobble and tip slowly over the side. Gathering speed as these things do, it crashed against the hard-packed ground and broke with a dull thud you would never expect of champagne.

"Well I never! The wind has only taken our bottle," came a male voice out of the gloom beyond.

"No matter, plenty more where that came from." The female voice was familiar; very familiar. Then it came to her. It was Mrs Beatrice. She was here, in the camp, of all places.

But that meant it was not Henry with his bride-to-be. There was hope after all.

Except they were running out of tents to search.

She was certain the singing Beatrices had not seen her so she kept completely still, forcing her heavy breathing to slow down by degrees until she felt relatively calm. Then she looked at her options. The only viable one was an exit that reversed her entrance. She favoured similar speed on balance; hence, she shifted bit by bit to get into position, tensed her muscles and sprang.

Mr Beatrice saw her that time but it meant nothing to him except a pretty girl leaving the tent they had happened on. He had never met Grace before. He kept quiet this time, planning to find that pretty girl when his wife finally collapsed from drink. On past experience that should be soon and he licked his lips in anticipation.

Outside, Grace forgot the obstacle in the entranceway and fell over it again, banging her shin painfully and hopping away. It was an empty crate that once held quality wine. Whatever those non-combatants were up to in the tent, they had seemingly stumbled on the Earl's personal supply.

There was only one tent left, next to the Earl's but slightly apart, as if rank gave the privilege of space in a crowded camp. The two bees had run out of tents to search and had stopped on the hillside where they could just see Grace in the dark. The tunes sang out from the Earl's private quarters, oblivious to the night, the battle and the searchers outside; oblivious to everything but their drunken state.

Grace went up to the last tent. The two bees waited while she whispered, whispered again. Then, with drooping shoulders, she turned away. Then she turned back by continuing round in the direction she had turned; a full revolution instead of a half.

And she entered the tent with a wave back to her friends on the hillside.

Chapter 29

Thomas' second period as a soldier proved as short as his first; but, also, as slow to start with. He had waited all day in the woods above the slope before descending for the surprise attack on Sherborne's party. Now, he waited all day while nothing much seemed to happen.

Although officially Acting Major Hanson's aide, Hanson advised him to keep a low profile and sent him on an inspection of the two companies he had strung across Sedgemoor. The rain came down all day, creating mini-rivers everywhere and making the royalist soldiers thankful for the large drainage ditches crossing the moor, it seemed in every direction.

Lieutenant Davenport's tour of inspection had the added advantage of keeping Thomas away from the Sherborne command unit for the entire day.

"I want reports back every hour, of what our pickets see and hear; even what they smell."

"Yes sir," said Thomas, saluting his new commander.

"Take Sergeant Powell with you. He is the most experienced NCO I have."

That meant, while Thomas was not idle at all, Sergeant Powell took full responsibility for gathering, checking and then passing back the information to Hanson. Thomas became a kind of apprentice called 'Sir', learning on the job.

Hanson's plan was to keep Thomas away from the Earl at all costs. He wanted to keep him busy so he did not seek out other things to do. Hanson did not think it would come to a fight at all because Monmouth's force had dwindled to such an extent that it was a grossly uneven combat. He expected no battle that day or the next and then an eventual negotiation of terms of surrender by Monmouth.

But should there be a battle, Hanson wanted Thomas away from the fighting. And what better way than to exhaust him, running somewhat pointless errands all day so that he and Sergeant Powell would be stood down when any fighting did occur?

But he was certain there would be no fighting in the next few days.

We will lay down our arms and fight no more.

Hanson's reasoning fell down in one key area. It took no account of how desperation and pride swing a man's mind when he is staring at total loss laid out before him. Monmouth spent the afternoon of July 5th standing in the tower of St Mary's church in Bridgewater. From there, he could see the royalist army camped on the moor at Westonzoyland five miles to the southeast. They seemed well organised, with lines of neat tents and neater still squares of soldiers drilling in the drizzle.

They blocked his way to Bristol; whichever way he turned, it seemed there were troops to bar his way.

"Where are the cannon?" he asked.

"Which cannon, Sire?"

"The only damned cannon we have." The answer was short, exhibiting the tension he felt.

"They are in Minehead, Sire."

"Well, we need them here and not in Minehead." After some discussion, it was decided that a detachment of cavalry would fetch them. Grey was told to organise it as quickly as possible. Grey left the church tower, thinking this should have been done two days earlier, when they were on their way back to Bridgewater. But at least it was being attended to now.

Grey returned thirty minutes later, just as the evening sky broke away from the heavy cloud base and a light wind pushed those clouds away to trouble someone else with their incessant drizzle.

"Sire, the cannon will be with us by morning. What do you propose to do with them?" Grey envisaged a battle on a bright day with artillery, infantry and cavalry playing games with clever manoeuvres.

"Nothing," Ferguson spoke up.

"Then why go to all the trouble to bring them up to us? We could have left them in Minehead."

"Subterfuge, my boy, subterfuge." In reality, Lord Grey was a little older than Ferguson, but the pastor had the upper hand, making the use of 'my boy' seem natural. "I am informed that cannon are employed in set-piece battles or in defence of strategic points."

"That is correct, sir." These last words with an element of weariness; of heard-it-all-before from non-military types who suddenly favoured themselves as generals.

"Now, tell me, Lord Grey, what will the enemy know about the little trip you've just organised?" Ferguson was enjoying his own trip into military tactics.

"He will know by now, sir, exactly why we dispatched 100 of my best cavalry to Minehead, which, incidentally, is a major part of my remaining force."

"Exactly!" Did he have to spell it out to these slow-witted soldiers? "They will think, will they not, that we aim to wait for the cannon then attack in the morning when we have them."

"I agree; that will be their assumption."

"So, they will be unprepared for our attack tonight."

It was an audacious plan of Ferguson's to gain the initiative. The element of surprise was just what they needed to even out the considerable odds against them. The royalist army was five times larger; also better equipped, and better trained, than they could claim to be.

"It's the leveller we need," said Monmouth, jumping up and waving his arms, like a man, down on his luck, who had just won a large bet on the racetrack.

And in a way, this was correct. For Monmouth had unwittingly, through Ferguson's emerging plan, bet everything on the hundred horse he had sent to Minehead.

And the stakes were as high as could be.

Richard Godfrey was their guide. He was indistinguishable in every way, especially in the gloom that was ten o'clock at night in early July. A local farmer, he had been offered the equivalent of six months' rent on his tenancy for "a couple of hours as our guide on Sedgemoor". It was easy money for he had lived on Sedgemoor all his life. He squared it away in his mind by telling himself it was for religion and freedom. But he took the money happily enough, letting the coins run through his fingers before putting them in the lockbox in his home and kissing his wife and children.

For the last time.

There was no rain now; perhaps the skies were exhausted. Tomorrow's rain, however, was in waiting; forming great big clouds that hid the moon and stars.

"A perfect night for a surprise attack." Ferguson was suddenly the expert.

But the ground underfoot was muddy and slippery. The soldiers' boots were quickly caked in mud, increasing the weight of each step enormously; slowing them down and tiring them out. Godfrey tried to warn them about the mud but it was brushed aside. Likewise, he spoke of the drainage ditches that crossed the moor in all directions, as if someone could not decide where they wanted the water to go. No sooner were a body of soldiers scrambling out of one ditch than they found themselves stumbling into another. The dark and overcast sky had the benefit of masking them from the royalist sentries but it also made it far harder for the attacking force to find their way in the rain-soaked conditions.

"For the mercy of Our Lord," said Monmouth, "how much longer can this go on?" It was a question he could have asked about his whole campaign, ever since he had landed amongst so much hope at Lyme Regis less than a month ago.

It was a five-mile stretch they had to cover but that was as the crow flies. To achieve a flanking operation in order to attack on three fronts at once and taking into account obstacles they found and had to go around, some soldiers were looking at closer to seven miles. At first, it was a simple task. They followed the winding lanes that led down to Sedgemoor; a marshy expanse that was hard to cross and there was little point, normally, in doing so, for it could be easily bypassed.

But not by an army in secret preparation for attack. The essence of their surprise was to come across the moor, where no one would choose to send an army.

Then they came to the second stage and the real problems began. They had to take off across country, across the moor towards Westonzoyland, still some two miles away. This is where they first encountered the drainage ditches; massive eight-foot-wide trenches, built in an attempt to make the land farmable. Godfrey took them past his own farm, thinking of his wife and children snug in their beds. He hoped the fee he had been paid would help him take on some extra land and, thereby, increase their income. There was even talk of the landlord selling some fields as he seemed perpetually short of cash. The idea of owning his own land appealed enormously. It would be a big step up in the world.

But was it worth the risk?

"Quiet in the ranks," the sergeants hissed as the soldiers swore. They were losing their grip on the muddy sides to the ditches; stumbling everywhere. Still a mile and a half to go.

Lord Grey wondered, as the infantry marched and he led his remaining cavalry, about the planning once they got to their destination. He estimated they had only three thousand troops. Could they split into three positions of a thousand each, and hope to make an impression on ten thousand or more? With total surprise, it was just about possible.

It all came down to the element of surprise.

Of course, the history books bulged with desperate men taking on far greater odds and, somehow, pulling through. But you had to have a strong leader; one who believed in himself and his men; one who calculated the odds coldly and then jumped.

Grey knew that Monmouth was not such a leader, but what about himself as second-in-command? Would he be forgotten in history as an irrelevance? He jerked himself out of his self-doubt and forced himself to carry out an inspection of the arrangements.

Concentrate on the Present for the Future is just the Present to come. And the Past is the Present that was.

He made a quick assessment, trying to think of every aspect of their sudden plan; sharp thinking now could make all the difference. He looked around at the shadowy shapes, all heading northwest. They were doing quite well. Grey looked again into the distance and thought he could see the royalist camp ahead; not much more than a mile to go. Soon they would split into three. He was staying in the centre but had detailed two subordinate commanders to take 200 mounted soldiers each to left and right. He glanced at his watch. It was almost a quarter past twelve. Whatever the outcome of this battle, it would be recorded as starting on July 6th and not 5th; that day was gone already.

The call to attack was to be a single note on a bugle. It was to come from a soldier staying in the centre, keeping close to Monmouth. For some reason, Monmouth had asked for the note to be F sharp. Keenly musical, Grey would be able to tell if the bugler kept to his instructions. There had to be some significance to Monmouth's strange request. He would ask him afterwards.

If there was an afterwards, that is. For the surprise attack had been suggested by Ferguson as a 'do or die in the trying' plan of action. They all hoped it would shake the remaining soldiers they commanded out of the despondency that hung about them.

Something had to change; something had to give. The hope was to change a devastating disaster into a triumphant victory.

Ferguson rode past Grey at that moment.

"Keep up, man. We've a job to do," Ferguson whispered, but loudly, so that several shadows of heads turned, seeking the target of such admonition. Grey flushed in the dark, thought of a dozen ways to provide a cutting reply but dismissed them all. This was not the time for petty squabbles to develop.

"The going is tough for the infantry, Mr Ferguson. It's a wonder no one thought of conditions underfoot in planning this exercise." He meant Ferguson, of course, and Ferguson knew he meant him.

Ferguson kicked his horse and moved ahead. He would write Grey's pernickety ways into a blistering sermon one day.

But first he was going to enjoy wielding his sword for the Lord.

For religion and liberty.

The shot came from somewhere ahead and slightly to the right. It was followed by curses and cries, then absolute silence. For several seconds, it seemed like the world had stopped. The night was heavy with humidity, as if some awful fate was pressing in on the ragbag of an army. Monmouth was riding towards the area of the noise. Lord Grey kicked his horse gently and followed him.

There was no bugle piercing through with F sharp to start the battle. Instead, it was a lonely musket shot fired into the night because of a loose trigger and a jumpy hand on it. The musket ball had found an accidental target, as Grey discovered when he rode up to the scene. Richard Godfrey, their guide, was lying in a wide and deep ditch, looking to all the world like a drowned rat. Grey dismounted and leant over, checked for a pulse, and shook his head.

"He's gone," he said.

"And so is our surprise," replied Monmouth, as if the poor dead Godfrey was responsible for how the evening had worked out.

After the moment of silence, in which the very night seemed to have stopped, it filled again with many noises. Some were distinguishable from others but most just merged to build a wall of confusing and conflicting sound.

Lord Grey spoke into the noise first. "Sire, the enemy is aroused. Speed is essential."

But Monmouth just stared at the dead body on the ground, as if all his hope had seeped into the muddy ground along with Godfrey's lifeblood.

"Sire, let me ride to attack. I have 600 cavalrymen with which to do some damage."

"Yes, of course, go now." Monmouth was slowly coming to the reality. "Go now," he called after the disappearing Grey, who was cantering through the dark and rutted marsh, trusting in his horse to find a way.

He needed to trust in something.

"All cavalry to me," Grey cried, taking no care about noise now. Within minutes, he was at the head of 600 mounted soldiers. "Draw swords and advance at the trot," he called and they left, a great clatter of metal and creak of leather against the slapping of horse hooves in the mud.

It was Ferguson who made the next move. He raised his oversized sword above his head and cried, "All true men to Monmouth, all true men to Monmouth, for religion and liberty."

"For religion and liberty," came the first patchy reply but building in confidence with each repetition.

"For religion and liberty," they cried in unison.

Ferguson had rallied the infantry and now, like Grey, thought it the time to lead them into action.

For religion and liberty. Ferguson, like Monmouth, had to find a cause to hang their baser motives on.

For religion and liberty. They charged into the night.

Chapter 30

For Ferguson, battle was a revelation. He had known joy before, but nothing quite this magnificent. The fiery sermon delivered from high in a pulpit, looking down on a spellbound audience, came close in its soaring intensity, its ability to influence the outcome of the world. But it really was nothing against the bliss of wielding a heavy sword in the name of his God.

All his life, he had eschewed violence; avoided it with some neat steps sideways. Yet now that he was plunged into it, he thought being a soldier a splendid occupation. It offered the power to make the change he wanted without deceit and cunning; rather, with clean, strong strokes and jabs.

Whoever said the pen was mightier than the sword?

Whoever it was, they certainly never compared a faded page of parchment with the magnificence of a stab up under the ribs to the heart.

Not that he wanted to cause damage to others, more that he was justifying his very existence to himself.

Kill or be killed.

They advanced in two groups. The cavalry charged ahead, trying desperately to make a gash in the royalist ranks before they became too well formed, too solid to penetrate. The infantry, effectively under Ferguson, although with Monmouth fighting bravely but despondently, advanced at a slower but gathering pace. It was after one o'clock in the morning when infantry met infantry. Everything was shrill then; sharp noises of metal on metal and cries of pain and anger rose from the moor, as if trying to pierce the heavy cloud base above. But that cloud base was not to be beaten and sent the sounds echoing straight back, causing a confusion of noise and disorder across the spreading battlefield below.

Ferguson looked around and saw their cavalry shaken, regrouping to charge again. He saw horses without riders careering over the moor, trying to find a way out of the terror but meeting ditch after ditch to rein them in. Some horses went down into the ditches and floundered in the deep water accumulated, adding their pitiful cries to the human noise everywhere around.

The cavalry charged three times without success. Each time, there were fewer who regrouped. Then, after the third charge was rebuffed, with neat volleys from ranks of redcoats, firing to order, there was little left. Scattered riders went this way and that, drifting at speed across the boggy ground.

It was time for the infantry to try their luck.

Everything about this battle was hopeless. Except for the joy Ferguson had in the act of fighting. As the foot soldiers met, he took vicious swipes at the enemy, causing more damage than anyone else. His tall, thin frame was ideally suited to the cut and thrust of swordplay, because his reach extended further than anyone else. He fired both pistols early on; one missed but the other felled a young soldier, who was then trampled underfoot by his colleagues advancing. Then Ferguson threw his pistols down; it took too long to reload them. Swinging his great sword in circles, he seemed to have set his fear, all reasonable fear, to one side while he was occupied with killing his fellow men.

He rallied men around him, drawn to the huge physical presence he made on the battlefield. He took the right side of their line while Monmouth led the left. The Duke fought with more skill but less power. Together, they advanced into the enemy, achieving what the cavalry had failed to do.

At one point in their desperate struggle, the clouds parted and both moon and stars illuminated the centre of the battle. Ferguson looked up, thinking maybe it was a sign from God that they would be victorious after all, against all the odds.

But as he looked across at Monmouth on his left, he saw the new lines of enemy forming; fresh troops advancing, with muskets levelled and bayonets fixed. It also showed how few soldiers were left of Monmouth's army; many had fallen while others were fleeing.

He had been oblivious to everything except the swing and thrust of his sword. But now there was no joy in it; just fear of death or capture. Instinctively, he turned to look behind him, for a way out of this hell. That turn saved his life, for the sword blow would have split his head open if he had remained stationary. Instead, it skimmed down the side of his shoulder, causing a superficial wound that bled profusely. He fell and the advancing troops moved over him, assuming him no danger.

And he was no danger now, for like a winded runner he had lost the power to continue. He lay with the dead as the battle moved over him and on to its final stages. He closed his eyes, his mind presenting a picture of the young, sandy-haired officer who had struck him down. If he lived through this day, he would remember that face forever. Then he remembered nothing else, for the battle moved away and he lay unconscious, seeming like the dead around him.

Thomas had been sent back with Sergeant Powell, to stand down. He had been running back and forth all day and was exhausted. He reported a final time to Hanson a little after midnight.

"Get some sleep, Thomas. Go back and see Grace and get some food into you. I don't need you again until the morning."

"Are you sure, Captain?" He liked being in the centre of things.

"Certain. I need you fit and well in the morning."

Thomas was about to salute in a cheeky way then suddenly thought it lacked respect. Instead, he nodded his assent and turned to go to the camp three quarters of a mile back towards Westonzoyland. The thought of his sister's tender concern and some hot food suddenly overwhelmed him.

That was the point at which the single shot that ended Richard Godfrey's life rang out across the otherwise peaceful night. All thoughts of food and bed vanished in an instant.

"What do you want me to do?" Thomas turned back and called to his commander.

"Find the bugler, call the alert," Hanson replied, keeping so calm he astonished himself. He had been ten years in the army but this was his first real campaign; he was untested material. "Then go forward, take Sergeant Powell with you. I want to know immediately what is going on." Thomas was the obvious choice to send out to the picket lines, for he knew where they were exactly, having spent the day running between them, exercised pointlessly by Hanson to keep him away from recognition.

"Yes, sir." Ten minutes later, while the temporary calm lay over what was to be the battlefield, a breathless Thomas and Sergeant Powell reported a sighting of the main rebel army just a mile in front of the royalist picket lines.

"It seems one of them stumbled and let off a gun, sir," Powell said.

"Sergeant, get back to camp and rouse Lord Faversham and Mr Churchill; also the Earl of Sherborne. It is evident that the rebels intend to attack and it is imperative that we present a full strength to them when they do."

"Yes, sir."

"Thomas, stay with me. I need your help to make a detailed analysis for when our commanders come up to us."

"Yes, sir.

For the next thirty minutes, Thomas saw how a good officer worked. Hanson stayed calm throughout, detailing orders to his subordinates in a controlled way so that, as they reported back, a good picture of the enemy strength and likely intentions built up. But two things impressed Thomas even more. The first was that Hanson took himself aside for a minute, before issuing the first order, and closed his eyes. He asked a couple of questions, still with his eyes firmly shut. Then opened them and took command. He had clearly used that minute to determine exactly what he needed to do in order to get the best information possible; a minute of appraisal that made all the difference between success and failure.

The second thing that impressed was that Hanson ensured others knew the exact same information he learned himself. He was at pains to ensure Thomas and others knew everything relayed to him by his runners.

"It's an insurance against me being hit," he explained to Thomas. "If I fall then at least others can pass on what I know to HQ."

The timing of those words coincided exactly with the night-time attack by the rebel cavalry, swooping down on the picket lines where some 300 men under Captain Hanson's charge made frantic attempts to form a solid defensive line while 600 mounted soldiers bore down on them.

And, whatever Hanson's original intention, Thomas was now right in the middle of it.

Thomas was dressed as a lieutenant and the fifth platoon of the first company now lacked an officer. The unfortunate platoon leader was hit by an early bullet just as the attack was sprung on them. Hanson had no choice but to give the position to Thomas, despite his lack of experience in military matters.

"Keep in a defensive position until reinforcements arrive," Hanson said. "I'm going back to meet with the commanders and then, no doubt, to organise those reinforcements."

How does the soldier find the right balance between following orders and taking the initiative? The cynical would say success justifies the initiative taken, thus condemning failed initiatives as disobeying orders. A more enlightened commander would expect his soldiers to fail from time to time and examine, instead, the methods and thinking they followed in order for them to learn for the next time.

Assuming they lived for the next time.

Thomas faced such a moment. Or, more accurately, he had it thrust upon him by the seemingly incidental matter of a change in the weather. He had been ordered by Captain Hanson to keep a defensive position until reinforcements came up. At first this was his only thought as he prepared his twenty troops to take the advancing line of infantry. It was very dark and hard to see their strength; even individual bodies were difficult to discern. All he could think was to tell his platoon to hold firm and to look out for each other.

They did hold firm, for several attacks. Thomas thought it was three advances against them but it might have been four. His twenty men were down to sixteen; three dead and one badly wounded, dragged away. Two more, plus Thomas, received minor wounds but carried on fighting. They faced a tall, thin man who fought like fury and seemed to hold the opposing ragged force together. This man thrust twice for every stroke from an ordinary soldier and cried in a great, raucous Scottish accent "For religion and liberty!" over and over again; it made a pattern to his being – cut, cry; strike, cry; thrust, cry; over and over again.

Thomas knew to get this man down would win the day; a shortcut to victory. But fighting him in all his fury was near impossible. He was cutting into Thomas' platoon and the one adjoining to the left; two more of Thomas' soldiers were down now. Soon, he would have no one left to fight. He had to do something. While parrying blows he racked his mind for ideas but nothing came; there was no experience to depend on.

And then the weather changed. It was as if God drew back the heavy clouds to take a look at the battle below. A great shimmering hole came in the sky, with light shining through from the moon and stars, sufficient to light up the night.

And the tall, thin man stopped momentarily, looking around in wonder or fear or something. Thomas saw his moment and leapt to it.

"To me," he cried. "Advance, attack, to me!" His first sword blow took a hapless soldier standing in front of the tall, thin Scot. He moved into the gap created. The Scot was still distracted, looking over the battlefield in paralysed wonder. Thomas raised his sword and brought it down heavily, noticing that the man moved his head at just the wrong moment. The blow glanced flat off his head and the sword continued downwards, hitting hard to the right shoulder before continuing down to the muddy ground with a thud. He had missed.

But no, the man was falling. He had done enough. Yes, he was on the ground, his huge sword dropped in a ditch that ran more with blood than rainwater. Then the press of soldiers behind him, the reinforcements, pushed him forwards and the tall, thin Scot was lost to him.

But the battle was won and now the slaughter began. Hanson was back with the reinforcements and in the first free moment after deploying the extra men, he sought Thomas. Thomas quickly reported what had happened, including the Scot he had felled but probably not killed.

"Withdraw your platoon, Thomas. I need you to find this mysterious Scot. He seems to be a leader and I suspect it is Robert Ferguson, the renowned trouble-maker. We need to get him." Thomas was content to pull back; killing fleeing men was not something he enjoyed.

He led his reduced platoon back a hundred yards, made sure they all had water to drink, then fanned them out to search the pile of bodies littered across the moor.

Within seconds, they came across a wounded rebel. Thomas knelt at the man's side, wondering what to do. Blood was pumping from his chest. He clearly did not have long to live.

"Rest, my friend," Thomas said, offering his water bottle then assisting the dying man to drink. "Rest, for your fight is over." He pulled the dead man's eyes closed and said a brief prayer.

May perpetual light shine upon them and may they rest in peace.

Thomas forgot then his mission to seek out the tall, thin Scot. Instead, he organised his tiny force into a makeshift hospital; pulling cloth from the dead to make bandages, straightening shattered bones and exhausting their collective water supply.

And taking the initiative for a second time that night.

"Sir, why are we doing this? These men will all be hanged anyway," his corporal asked. The corporal had a broken arm, hung in a sling made from his webbing.

"Corporal, the fighting is over for these men. It is our Christian duty to help the wounded. Now, put your doubts aside and work to alleviate suffering where we can."

Let me give without counting the cost.

Ferguson regained consciousness to see Monmouth and Grey riding at speed, heading away from the royalist army. He lay a long time in the mud, recent events coming back to him. He saw Thomas approach, recognised him, thought now was not the time.

Picking himself up, he rubbed mud from his clothes to gain some respectability. He considered going back towards Bridgewater, following Monmouth, but something made him go forwards, towards the royalist camp. He walked a hundred yards furtively then thought this is no good; looking like he was trying to melt into the background would make him stand out all the more. With a great effort he strode casually, as if he belonged on the royalist side and was just doing his duty under trying circumstances. He spotted a horse twenty yards ahead, grazing on some tufts of grass as if nothing had gone on that night. He walked towards it, trying to appear nonchalant but also speaking with his softest voice, enhanced by his Scottish accent. Two feet away, he grabbed the reins and mounted the horse before riding into the camp.

"Any chance of some breakfast?" he asked of the first sentry, careful to disguise his distinctive accent. "I've been tending to the dead and wounded all night and could certainly do with some sustenance."

"Of course, pastor. The camp kitchen is just over there."

"Thank you, my man. Go with the Lord."

With two plates of hot beef stew inside him, taken with a pint of cider, Robert Ferguson made his way out of camp without any questions being asked of a minister of God. He turned north for Bristol as soon as he was able, letting the spirited horse trot in a manner he thought was acceptable for a man of importance, not one fleeing from the executioner.

Chapter 31

Some writers of history make glory out of soldiers marching to war; banners fluttering in a gentle breeze; muskets lined to perfection.

Where is that glory when your guts are spilling on the ground that once was hard but now is muddy and bloody? What when you are faced with kill or be killed but you see the same thought in the mind of the soldier facing you? The one who would kill you; only you have got in with the fatal thrust before him? It is not easy to strike in battle; it takes nerves stronger than the steel of the blade you force on through flesh into bone and organ, to eliminate the threat before that threat eliminates you.

Your opponent slides to the ground, where his blood creates more slippery and deadly mud, like a laden painter's palette dropped to the floor, the mixed-up paints making a brown streaked with red that spreads and seeps everywhere.

You will always remember that boy's face, for now you see he is just a boy as he silently beseeches you to reverse the mortal blow; something you would willingly do but cannot. Every time you close your eyes, whether the night after the battle or fifty years later, he will come and visit you. Your features will age but not his. When you are old and grey, with lines across every part of your face and neck, he will be preserved as the day he died.

At your hands.

He will never leave you, of that you can be sure. You become the link to this world from Valhalla or Heaven, or wherever young boys-turned-soldiers while away their eternity.

Never think a death on the battlefield is over and done with. It lives on in you when the opponent has fallen.

Some argue that, in bearing this affliction, lies the true honour of the warrior. The argument goes that to kill for one's country, and then to live a full life despite it, is an equal burden to dying for one's country.

Because nobody gains from death on the battlefield.

But there are many that do well out of the confusion surrounding conflict. They seem to skim over the suffering, accumulating great riches or power yet keeping safely out of harm's way. We should not highlight Simon Taylor in this regard, for he is in a dreadful battle with himself; fighting for survival, for sense against the odds.

But we can look to Mrs Beatrice for an example of this type of body. She was bright, calculating, and a lover of the trappings of wealth. Yet she could not produce it, preferring to hang on to someone else's coat-tails while they did the hard work. Hence, she had welcomed the double opportunity that Arkwright brought her; a regular and generous payment to keep her in obscurity, then there was Arkwright's capacity for endless menial work to generate more income at the laundry.

Despite her drunken spree at the moment, Mrs Beatrice was coldly angry at her sudden misfortunes. She had a rage against those that had taken away her easy and prosperous existence. Of course, she had some savings, which her husband thankfully did not know about. She had sent Mr Beatrice out of the room on a pretext and searched the dead body of Parchman. The search revealed another bundle of cash and confirmation of who his patron was.

She had a conflict in her mind as they rode south towards the opposing armies. One part of her said to ride on, go long past the battlefield; perhaps to London, or even further. She could lose Mr Beatrice along the way and she had enough kept by to start again. It would never be the same as before but her savings were enough to get into some new venture.

But the other part of her mind, of who she was, would not let it go. She had to extract her just rewards.

And she had to get revenge.

It was that part of who she was that led her, husband in tow, into the camp of Mr John Churchill, foot commander of the loyalist army.

She knew she should not have drunk but her rage, needing sustenance, drove her on.

It was Roakes who found them.

And he was not in a generous mood. His teeth were half

gone; a mess of broken reefs and jagged rocks. His chin ached like the devil was inside him, which perhaps it was.

It was no coincidence that he found them for he was on the same mission; in search of drink. He made his way to the Earl's quarters, knowing there would always be something there to take away the pain that ran through his face from the blow with the chamber-pot.

Mr Beatrice was slumped on the ground, all thought of song gone from him as he slept in a heap.

In fact, he would never sing again; never raise a fine tune for Mrs Beatrice to add to with her towering harmony. She would sing solo in future; a harmony without a tune to hang it on.

Mrs Beatrice was sitting on a three-legged stool. Her arms were folded over her neat dress. Her hair was tidy and her back was straight, despite the pounding in her brain.

"My drunken husband did this," she said, sensing a soulmate in the Yorkshire sergeant so far from home.

"Then I am saddened to tell you that you will be a widow before the day is out," he smiled with broken teeth, sensing the same in her.

"You are hurt, Sergeant. Let me look at it. I've helped many a brave soldier in my time." She knew her part well, played it to perfection.

They settled on a credible story as she worked on his face, easing and cleansing with water and ointments she found in one corner of the tent. The lower teeth had smashed against the upper with the force of the chamber pot, making an ugly, crooked mess of his mouth. But, to Mrs Beatrice, it seemed somewhat like a battle wound and this gave Roakes his idea.

"I'm Sergeant of the Guard," he said. "I'm not supposed to be in the main fighting force but what if my instincts to follow my leader overcame me and I went anyway into battle?"

"More peculiar things have happened, sir," she replied, noting that he perked up when addressed as 'sir'. Perhaps she could work on a warrant for him, or maybe even a commission? "I must say it is brave of you, Sergeant. I am full of admiration for you." But her words really meant, *I will fib happily for you, so you gain glory and credit in abundance, but what will you say about me?*

"Did you say, Mrs Beatrice, that your husband forced you to come here?"

"Yes, sir."

"And forced you into the Earl's tent to pilfer his supplies of alcohol while others were risking their lives?"

"That is right, Sergeant Roakes." But thinking, *I would be Mrs Roakes in a twinkle if Mr Beatrice is hung in the morning.*

"Then, dare I say it Mrs Beatrice, your husband is in serious trouble."

You dare say it, sir, and you are most welcome to repeat it.

They managed to get enough movement out of Mr Beatrice to arrest him, although whether he understood what was happening was another matter. Two camp guards marched him away and Mrs Beatrice never saw her first husband again.

Roakes set four of the minor wounded to clear up the Earl's tent and make an inventory of damages.

"Come with me, Mrs Beatrice. We can go over your statement in my tent, where we will not be disturbed."

They were indeed undisturbed until the trumpets called victory several hours later.

The red coat he had borrowed was too small, making him look like an overgrown child playing at soldiers. He walked just behind Captain Hanson, a big grin on his dirty, blood-spattered face.

And the first person he saw from the camp was Grace coming hastily out of Henry's tent, fearing discovery by the Earl or one of his lackeys.

She saw him a second later and ran to him, flinging her arms around his shoulders and dancing around and around; propelling him in a circle. "Thomas!" was all she said; all she could say.

For not only was she delighted to see her brother again, safe from the battlefield, but she had another piece of news, that both reassured and explained; calmed and excited, like giving and receiving all rolled into one.

But that giving became palpable when Thomas collapsed in her arms.

"Quick," said Captain Hanson, "get him to my tent."

It was not a bad wound; more a very nasty scratch across his chest. Grace tore of the red coat, making Thomas a civilian all over again. Then she bathed it gently and bound it in the fresh bandages that Hanson provided. A sip or two of wine and he was much recovered, even joking about never becoming a regular soldier.

"Don't play games with fate," said Grace, thinking the last thing she ever wanted was the two men in her life going to be soldiers.

For there were two men back in her life right then.

There did not seem much hope right then for Monmouth's inner circle. Ferguson, central to that circle, had fought hard; a late convert to the joy that some find in battle. But to no avail, for Monmouth was completely defeated. Ferguson had seen Monmouth and Grey ride away at speed. He guessed they were aiming for the south coast, where they would hope to find a boat to take them to the continent.

Everything was naked and obvious now, their campaign exposed as the farce it pretended not to be; there had never been any hope of success.

The others of his entourage had scattered or were captured. Only Ferguson had got clean away, braving it out with style. He had his horse and chose to go north, whereas Monmouth headed south and east for the Dorset coast. It was a formal separation; the ending of an alliance.

Ferguson had cleverly thought to do the unexpected. He had also sought to divorce himself from the liability that was Monmouth in flight.

And he travelled alone, arriving in Bristol later that day to find his first visit to that city a chaotic one. He found a good but rather expensive inn and announced he was a Scot called Murray, seeking good business opportunities. He was welcomed.

But later that night, in his private room, he counted his coins and worked out he had enough for four days.

Something will turn up; it always does.

And that something turned up when a couple came down to breakfast the next day, flush with cash and seeming to like the high life. There were no spare tables in the crowded dining room.

"Good morning, sir and madam," Ferguson said, smiling at their happiness, sensing some of that good fortune spilling over to him. "I see you are without a place to sit. Please join me if you have a will to."

"Thank you, sir."

"Well, madam, I have met nothing but kindness since coming to this magnificent city and it costs me nothing but my privacy to return a little bit. Are you a native of these parts?"

"I am indeed, sir, although my husband is a stranger. He is from Yorkshire," replied Mrs Roakes, as she styled herself now.

Their story was simple and quickly declared to Ferguson. The story given was of wealthy middling sorts.

"We made our money in pigs," Roakes declared. "Big beautiful pigs and lots of them." Like the best lies, it had an element of truth to it. Roakes had been born on a Yorkshire pig farm, far from civilisation, but had left to join the army at the first opportunity.

He had never been back.

But their immediate past was glossed over, as was Ferguson's, making them an example in triplicate of superbly dishonest practice. Both parties claimed to have come from London on the coach yesterday, not realising or caring that they would have met on the coach, rather than in the inn at the end of the journey.

Roakes and Mrs Beatrice had struck lucky. She had followed Roakes to his tent but then remembered her saddlebags left in the Earl's tent.

"I'll go back for them. Which is your tent?" she said, turning and heading back in the early light of a new day.

"The far one by the hedge," he replied, wondering what could be of value in the saddlebags to make her turn back and risk discovery. He wanted to go back but had to process Mr

Beatrice's arrest and needed time to do the paperwork.

Besides, he did not want to be caught in the Earl's tent when the Earl arrived back.

She returned breathless to her new partner, slammed the heavy saddlebags down on the bed.

"The Earl gave me a leaving present," she spluttered in excitement, indicating the saddlebags. Roakes bent and looked; they were stuffed to overflowing with gold coins taken from the Earl's tent and added to her own cache.

Then Roakes proved his genius also for he went to see the Earl and came away a free man, and with the Earl's blessing, along with a smaller bag of gold but this one freely given if not honestly earned.

They left that day on the two Beatrice horses rode hard for Bristol. They planned on just a day in the town because, despite their magnificent good fortune, Mrs Beatrice wanted to pick up her remaining cash, hidden under the sink in the basement scullery that Arkwright had been chained to. They went in that evening but did not go upstairs to where Parchman lay in a pool of blood. If they had ventured onto the main floor they would, for sure, have seen the pool of blood but not Parchman, for he had staggered off after regaining consciousness and lay now in his bed at the same inn that the Roakes and Ferguson were staying at; waiting on a return visit from the doctor, who had bound his wound so expertly.

And thinking on revenge.

"Damnation," Mrs Roakes said, feeling again under the sink. "My money has gone. I bet that Arkwright woman took it. Who else would know it was there?"

"Not to worry, my dear. We have sufficient for our needs and some more to spare. We will be fine without it." But Roakes was thinking, *Why hide the money under the nose of a servant?* That seemed like asking for it to be stolen.

He liked his new partner immensely; sensed a kindred spirit, but would have to watch her carefully to ensure they continued going up in the world.

The trio travelled in style to London. Three wealthy, middling sorts; the lady had an accent from the west, while her husband was from the north. Her brother-in-law, Mr Murray, was a Scot who had married Mrs Roakes' sister some years earlier. Sadly, she had died early in their marriage and the Roakes had taken poor Mr Murray under their wing for the last two decades.

It gave Ferguson the very image he needed to slip away; nobody would suspect a widower from Scotland travelling with his in-laws. Nobody would see his tall and thin but humble frame and imagine the radical rebel, the fearsome sermon-giver, living within it.

Except Mrs Roakes, who knew exactly who he was.

It was a grey, heavy day, as if the morning was mourning the fallen in battle the night before. But there was a lightness around the royalist camp, for victory was certainly theirs. Henry mirrored that lightness by getting out of bed for the first time since his injury. He sat in a chair at the entrance to his tent, insisted the flaps were tied right back.

"But, Lord Henry, everyone will see you," his servant had objected.

"And I will see everyone," he had replied, something of the old spark back with him.

But there was only one person he wished to see.

And she came looking for him soon enough.

For he had given her extraordinary news on the night of the battle; the same news she was now passing on to Thomas.

"I must tell you, brother, of Henry." She had risen early and made polite enquiry as to Thomas' wound, which was already healing. Young bodies can swallow so much and continue as if nothing has happened. Yet a little harder strike and a young body is scarred for life, like her beloved Henry.

"Is he alright, sister?"

"Yes, healing well. But that is not my news."

She suddenly became shy, fiddling with her bonnet strings to draw them tighter around her face, as if she wanted to hide from the world, then winding the strings around her fingers. Thomas leant over and pushed her bonnet back off her face.

"You're a beauty, Grace, don't hide it. Now, tell me your news before I lose interest and cut my toenails instead." He got a shove in response but it cured Grace of her shyness.

"You know I said that Henry was betrothed to another?"

"Yes."

"Well, she came to see him with her father. It was two days ago, the day before the battle."

"And?" Thomas was thinking, *Why do you seem so happy if your rival has come to claim Henry?*

"Well," there was a sad humour in her face now, "the little vixen took one look at Henry and said she would never marry someone so disfigured. She said she liked a handsome man to hang on her arm, like the finest jewellery. And he was terribly tarnished with the gaping wound across his face."

"So, she won't marry him?"

"Exactly, brother dear. But there are two more chapters to come of this story."

The first chapter of Grace's extended tale concerned the fury of the Earl of Sherborne, stemming from his intense frustration.

"Luckily, he took it out on Sir John Withers, Penelope Withers' father, rather than Henry. He raged against the family and sent them packing back to Wiltshire. I know I should not take pleasure in such matters but the fact is that I do!"

Henry had told Grace everything during their meeting in his tent on the night of the battle. They had held hands and kissed; two people come together as they should.

"And what is the second chapter you mentioned?" Thomas asked when Grace finally finished talking about Henry.

"Just that he asked me to... well... to be his wife."

"You're forgetting one thing, Thomas," Major Hanson, his promotion confirmed by Churchill that very morning, said when Thomas was preparing to leave.

"What is that, sir?"

"Your retrial. It is a formality we must go through with."

"Really, after all this?"

"Yes, sir, even after all this." Hanson went on to explain that without a retrial, Thomas Davenport would be forever a convicted man escaping justice. The only way to square things away was to go through with a court martial all over again.

"But what if I am found guilty again?"

"You won't..."

"It is easy for you to say so, Major Hanson, but it is my life at stake."

"But you won't for two reasons. The principle witness for the prosecution has left the army quite suddenly and gone away."

"Well, that is good news. He was lying, as you know."

"And, Thomas, you have a new witness who will speak in your favour." Hanson stopped and appeared to flick through some papers, fighting to suppress a broad smile. "Ah, yes, here we have it. A new witness called Lord Henry of Sherborne."

The grin on Hanson's face was broad now. Henry had insisted on coming forward as soon as he realised there had been a miscarriage of justice. His grandfather, recognising a need to retreat, had not opposed his grandson in his desire.

The resulting retrial took six minutes. And, at the end of that six minutes, Thomas Davenport had a new lease on freedom, along with fifty pounds in recognition of his services to the royalist cause, and an honourable discharge from the army.

Chapter 32

It was Amelia's initiative and she decided to drive the buggy rather than hire a coach. It felt like she was more in control driving her and Lady Merriman.

"Are you certain about staying here, Mother?" she asked Elizabeth, getting a stamp on her foot for teasing with the term 'mother'.

"Yes," Elizabeth replied. "Much as I would like to come on your adventure, my duty is to look after your father." Elizabeth, like the others, had been raised with duty ever-present; it was an exceptionally hard cloak to take off.

But Amelia did not leave immediately, for Lady Merriman had a task of her own to perform first. Grace and Elizabeth had given her some of her mother's old clothes. These looked splendid on Grace but were still the garb of a Puritan minister's wife; not nearly splendid enough for an aristocrat.

Lady Merriman sent to Salisbury for a team of the finest seamstresses. They took up residence at Bagber Manor and worked day and night to produce a small wardrobe of exquisitely fine garments, bringing back to her what she had been. And as she imbued the air of Bagber, her family home, she found so many remaining gaps in her memory returning to her, like long-lost friends.

And on the day of her departure, she presented Amelia and Elizabeth with three beautiful dresses each. There were a further three for Grace packed in the back of the buggy.

They paraded in their dresses that morning, Elizabeth feeling self-conscious at being dressed so grandly; so unlike a minister's daughter. But they received admiration from everyone, even receiving a lop-sided grin from Simon when Amelia came to kiss both him and Elizabeth goodbye.

He could not talk, other than a slur which nobody understood, but he squeezed her hand and looked into her eyes; the eyes just like those of the wife he had once loved. Amelia smiled back, full of love and generosity for the father she had discovered when illness stripped away the materialism that had dominated.

Amelia and Elizabeth knew what they were doing. They had planned astutely and those plans had changed and honed as the dressmaking went on. At first, they had wanted Amelia and Lady Merriman to rush to the camp but were later glad that Lady Merriman had delayed them.

"It's better this way," Amelia said. "I'll write to Grace and she will organise everything at her end."

"I agree," replied Elizabeth. "Lady Merriman's memory is improving every day. That can only help matters. Let us write together for my sister is not so familiar with you."

Grace received the letter and immediately showed it to Henry.

"I'll try," he said. "You can be sure that I will try."

"Thank you, my love."

They had prepared well but even Amelia was surprised by how much memory returned to Lady Merriman as they bounced along the rutted tracks towards their destination. Amelia wished Elizabeth was there with her to consult as to further changes of plan; Lady Merriman's revelations seemed to add new scope every hour.

Henry had also prepared well. In fact, he had done a lot in the week-and-a-half since the battle. He had written on July 6th to Sir John Withers, seeking formal release from the wedding contract his grandfather had so patiently negotiated. The release came back two days later by messenger, with a neatly written postscript from Penelope:

Dear Lord H, I expect you remain devastated by my refusal to enter into marriage with someone so disfigured and I thought I should provide you with some more explanation concerning my decision. After our stormy meeting in your grandfather's tent, I considered again my options. One part of me said I should still marry you and treat your scar to all and sundry as a sign of my husband's courage in battle. I thought on this idea for much of the journey home; how it might reflect on the generosity of my spirit. I did, indeed, almost follow through with it. Yet, ultimately, I considered that I could not wake each morning to such disfigurement. The very thought of it made me shudder in apprehension. I did not, therefore, speak to Father to have him change my decision and we are not to be wed.

I know you will be greatly saddened by this decision but I feel you will find some dear soul who cares not for looks and can tolerate how you appear to others now. I would, were I in your position, take the first girl you find who feels such, for you may never find another and a solitary life without matrimony is a joy to no one.

I hope, despite what has gone on, that you and I will remain friends. It is important to have friends in high places and you remain in such a place although much tarnished by the ravages of war.

I remain, sir, your devoted servant,
Affectionately,
Penelope Withers

"Well, I suppose I might be classed as 'some dear soul' and not only am I the first to claim you, I believe I am the only one to do so!" Grace said when she had read the letter.

"Yes, I suppose I should be grateful that you came along and are so willing to marry me despite my gross disfigurement. But you do realise something, don't you, my dearest?"

"What is that?" Grace could sense the joke coming.

"Simply that I shall, for all my remaining days, pine for the lovely Penelope Withers and you will always play second fiddle to that dear lady."

He received his just reward for this joke; a sharp pinch on the arm.

The buggy was fast; perhaps Amelia drove a little recklessly. She certainly enjoyed letting the horses run and bumping along behind so that Lady Merriman had to hold onto her hat.

"We'll soon be there," Amelia said, clicking to the horses again.

"I see you are in quite a hurry," Lady Merriman replied. "I hope you will not gallop through this meeting when we get there because it will be wise to take it a jot slower. We still have a few things to work out."

Grace and Henry were waiting for them on the steps of Sherborne Hall. They had given two pennies to the first boy in the village to get news of two grand ladies driving themselves in a buggy.

For Amelia had written to both as to their mode of transport, and to expect a great deal of finery.

They were dressed for the occasion.

The ladies were welcomed with hugs from Grace, who shyly introduced her intended husband.

Neither one of them gave Henry's face a second look. But both had been warned of it and Amelia desperately wanted to stare at the huge scar that was moulding itself into his face; finding a place to settle down. She took sneak views when she was sure neither Henry or Grace were looking.

Until Grace came and whispered in her ear that it was quite alright to take a look. "I rather like it, actually. I mean that I like to look at it and see how it changes from day to day." Then she raised her voice. "Henry, come and show Amelia your scar and tell her how it came about."

"Of course, my dearest, but first I am forgetting myself as your host. What refreshments would you have, ladies?"

They both opted for wine and Grace had half a glass; she was not sure she would ever get used to the fiery temperament of alcohol. She sipped it, listening to the updates about Simon Taylor, Elizabeth's now bed-ridden husband.

When the Earl entered the room, four of the five people rose. Amelia and Grace performed deep curtsies, while Henry made a bow from the waist. Thomas stood up, politeness ingrained in him, but gave only the slightest nod of his head. This was the man behind his mock trial. The Earl of Sherborne would have seen him hung for crimes he did not commit because it suited his purpose.

Moreover, he had let Roakes get away with the rape of his sister.

It was different with Henry, however, for Grace and Thomas had shielded him from the worst of the miscarriages of justice his grandfather was responsible for. To Henry, it was a matter of confusion leading to a wrongful conviction and it was overturned as soon as the truth became apparent about Thomas saving Henry's life.

The matter of rape was a little less certain. Henry had shaken in anger when Grace told him what had happened. She had stopped short of the whole truth, telling her beloved that Roakes, the culprit, had disappeared and mentioning nothing of his grandfather's involvement. As far as Henry was concerned, the Earl had found Grace in the woods when on an extended scouting patrol and sent her with an armed escort back to camp, where she had been afforded every comfort at the Earl's expense.

There were no outright lies said but it is remarkable how the truth can be twisted this way and that.

In addition, the Earl was still livid about Henry's choice of wife; something Henry was keenly aware of and wanted to smooth over. Sir John Withers had torn up the marriage contract in front of the Earl, with a delicious smile that argued the Earl's grandson was not fit for his daughter.

Not fit now with a livid wound across his face for all to stare at.

But it was not an easy insult for the Earl to live with.

"Sir, will you partake of some of this wine?" he asked his grandfather.

"Brandy, I'll take brandy. Not that there will be any money left soon for such luxuries."

Henry ignored the barbed comment, went to the door and called for a servant, who was already carrying a flask of brandy and a single glass; he had worked for the Earl long enough to know his needs.

Lady Merriman's high-backed chair was facing away from the door where the Earl entered. She did not see him enter, nor did she hear because she was reliving the last glorious days with her father.

He made for her chair, grunted when his tired eyes saw someone in it, and stood there, clearly expecting the occupant to exit his favourite chair. But she stayed still, looking at the man who was so much older now; near the end of his life.

But he had the same features; older certainly but just the same as his son. Whereas his grandson looked so different.

"I did not know you were still alive, Lord Sherborne," she said.

"Alive and damned angry. Who on earth are..." But he had the answer before he finished the question. He felt himself sway, grabbed the arm of the chair and collapsed into it, landing on Lady Merriman, then sliding to the floor in a heap.

"You know each other?" said Henry. "What does this all mean?" He left his position in the audience and strode on stage. "Grandfather, Grandfather! Wake up."

The Earl opened his eyes, saw where he was and closed them again, not wanting to be there.

It was now that Lady Merriman stood and faced the others, while Henry helped his grandfather into the chair.

"I'll explain," she said, her voice like a fingernail tapping the best crystal glass. Henry looked at her for the first time; thought her beautiful, then went back to sit next to Grace.

"It all started almost thirty years ago," she said. "Henry, picture your grandfather thirty years younger and at the height of his powers. His son was Henry, like you all are in your family; every first-born has been named Henry since the world began. Your father was a fine man. He looked very like your grandfather but was kind, loving, generous. He was a warm man." Lady Merriman was misty-eyed now, thinking back to happy times.

"I remember when I first met him. He was twelve and I was eight, almost nine, years old. He came to Bagber Manor, my home, in 1658, bringing the news of the death of Cromwell. He came with his father and he stayed six days. My father and your grandfather seemed friends then for it was a social visit with lots of parties. Your father was an only child and so was I. We played together in the grounds. I loved your father from the first moment I saw him. He returned that love."

"We saw each other often after that. There was always some reason we could find to stay either here, or he would come to Bagber. We grew up loving each other dearly. We both expected we would marry and spend the rest of our lives together.

"The Merrimans were a poor but noble family and your grandfather was poor also. That does not make a good combination, or so the Earl decided, for as we grew through adolescence it became harder to be together. There were always reasons and excuses for why we should not meet. But we met anyway, for our love was deep." She looked at the Earl then, slumped in the chair. "I suspect, Sherborne, that you knew we still met and you were, even then, making your dreadful plans."

"We were separated when I became with child. Yes, it was out of wedlock, for we never married, although we had every intention of doing so. He was taken away somewhere and I never saw him again. I gave birth to a son at Bagber but he was taken from me right after the birth. I have not seen my son since the day we were parted; he as a new-born, me as a seventeen-year-old mother of an illegitimate child."

The next part of the story took some telling for Lady Merriman stumbled often. There had been so much change. Within two weeks of the birth of her son, her father had been murdered; slowly strangled in front of her by a large, vicious man called Parchman.

"He worked for you, did he not?" Lady Merriman asked the Earl. He saw little to be gained by denying it.

"He worked for me long ago," he said, starting with the truth but switching quickly to deceit. "I dismissed him when his cruel tendencies became apparent. I have not seen him for close to twenty years."

"That is not true," Amelia stood up. "He organised the removal of Lady Merriman from Bagber five years ago and the sale of Bagber in an uneven exchange for…"

"A pig farm," Lady Merriman concluded. "I spent many years there as a tenant. Do you say I know own the place?" Lady Merriman was being a little disingenuous for she had learned from Amelia that she had exchanged Bagber for the pig farm but it served her purpose at the moment. "God forbid that I own it for I hated the place. And I apparently willingly gave up my Bagber for it? Parchman; at your behest, Sherborne, played games with my mind. He tried to destroy my memory by screaming vile untruths at me over days and weeks and months. He reduced me to a jabbering wreck of a girl. This was all at your instruction, was it not, Sherborne?" She stopped then, looked out of the window, across the lawn to the trees beyond; another memory came to her of the treehouse that had been built for them as children. It had been their escape over the years; their secret den; their together place.

On those bare wooden boards, they had conceived their son.

"There was a kind Dr Ramsay in the village, who helped me so much. He guided my memory back to something like it had been before your vile intrusions into my mind. Parchman and Roakes; that was the name of his accomplice! And the pig farm was called Roakes Farm, I remember now."

"Not a Yorkshireman called Roakes?" Grace cried out, also standing, as if it were required of ladies entering the conversation. "He was the one who raped me in the woods."

The story digressed into the details of the rape and Roakes' arrest and subsequent release. The Earl shifted uncomfortably in his seat; everything was unravelling. It was important to him that his grandson should not know the truth about his role in releasing Roakes; in fact, he had rewarded him with a bag of coins and sent him on his way.

"Well, Parchman and Roakes cleaned my mind of memory. They played tricks on me and wore me down. Then I was taken to Roakes Farm and left there to manage a few dozen pigs until I died; or that was their intention."

Dr Ramsay had helped her regain her memory and she had returned to Bagber for a short while, until news of her return reached Sherborne Hall.

Then it was Amelia's turn to speak of her father's role in the shameful and cruel suppression of Lady Merriman's memory and very existence.

The Earl had heard enough. He rose, poured himself another glass of brandy, declared he'd had enough fairy-story recitals for one night and was going to bed. He took the decanter with

him.

He was damned if he was going to have his actions scrutinised in this way. He had certainly done some bad things but they had all been for the good of his family.

The End Justifies the Means.

He slammed the door against the wall as he strode out. Not for the first time this last month, he wished he had Maria by his side. She loved gold but she loved him too.

The others sat up long into the night, talking and examining the story from every angle.

Lady Merriman was in the thick of it, for she had a growing suspicion about something else. She would not say anything yet, for she needed to be certain. But it worked through her mind as the once fine sky turned darker and darker, until blackness descended.

Chapter 33

In the morning, Lady Merriman asked the Earl to walk with her around the garden. Henry expected him to refuse, not wanting any part of this change being forced upon him. But he accepted, even offering his arm for her to take hold of.

They were gone a long time. The others speculated as to the reason for their walk but nobody knew why two arch enemies would walk arm-in-arm around the grounds.

Lady Merriman had two stages to her attack that morning, for it was still an attack. She lulled the old Earl at first, talking of times in the past and times to come in the future; both were happy times. She chattered on any topic, except the present, but her sharp brain was ranging far ahead of the Earl, seeking the time to pounce.

"You know, there could now be a happy existence between us," she suggested as they walked around the rhododendrons and into the orchard. She knew the grounds like she had spent her whole life there; better, in fact, than the Earl knew them. "If we could find some happy accommodation such that we could live in peace as neighbours."

"You don't intend going to the law over this?" the Earl asked.

"Certainly not! That is, not if we can come to some arrangement." This was said as they left the orchard and dropped down to take the 'Wanderer's Walk' that went from the stables down to the river which swayed its gentle way through the estate.

The Earl could never remember why the walk was called so. "It's because of a female ancestor of yours. She was forced into a marriage with a cruel man who beat her and brought whores into their home. In the end, she left and came back here. It was after her father died and her brother became the Earl. He was more accommodating and allowed her to stay. Apparently, every day she came down here and wandered about all day. They started to make a path for her but she stopped the gardeners, saying she would make her own path with her footsteps chiselling out the way. It is her path we are following now. She had a sort of freedom down here along the river bank, which she never had in her real life. Forced marriages sometimes work but so often they are disasters and the woman suffer most of all."

"I see the parallel and why you led me here," the Earl replied gruffly. "I, too, had an arranged marriage thrust at me and the countess and I have never been even cordial with each other."

Do unto others as you would have done to you.

"As you forced my beloved Henry to marry another."

"We have to think of survival, of the family and its fortune."

"You gained the Redwoods lands but you lost your son. Is that a fair bargain? The Merriman lands were never quite as much as the Redwoods holdings..."

"Less than half," he replied, interrupting her.

"Yes, but you could have had a little less land and kept your son."

"Your argument has logic, I accept, but why am I being harangued by a woman on a subject exclusively for men?"

"Because, Sherborne, I want you to admit something."

He did admit it, just as they reached the river. They came to a clearing in a glade where the trees around about seemed undecided as to whether to occupy it or back away in reverence to the spot. Eliza Merriman wanted confirmation of a simple fact and willingly agreed not to prosecute the Earl in return.

Bargain struck, they walked back to the manor in silence. There was nothing more to be said.

As soon as they returned, Henry was summoned to come with her on another walk in the grounds.

"I would love to see some old haunts," she explained. "And who better to show me than the next Earl?"

Mostly, they talked about Lady Merriman's memories of the place. They could not turn a corner or enter a gate without her exclaiming in joy. It was like she was dead and rose again; everything about her had that sweetened smell; that special look; that memory re-ignited.

"We used to ride ponies here. Your father was a very good horseman. I was good too but he was especially so." Then they went from paddock through the East Copse to the rose garden. "Does Tetley still work here? He was head gardener in the old days."

"He is retired now, Lady Merriman. His son has taken over."

"Oh, I am so old. So much of my life is wasted! Does Tetley still..."

"Yes, he still lives in Bent Cottage." He read her mind. "Would you like to go there?"

Bent Cottage was actually absolutely straight, despite its age and name. The head gardener before Tetley had been Mr Bent. It had one concession to its name; a chimney rose from the single-storey parlour, in a totally crooked fashion. It seemed that there was no possible way for it to stay in place, yet it had been in place for generations, giving the cottage the look of an old man smoking his pipe. Perhaps it represented old Mr Bent, smoking as he watched over his creation forever.

"Ah, the chimney!" cried Lady Merriman, picking up her skirts and actually running along the path. Henry, following behind, got the impression of a puppy for whom everything was new and wonderful.

Yet also so familiar.

"Tetley, do you remember me?"

The old gardener looked up from his armchair, made to rise but was waved back down.

"Well, if it ain't Miss Eliza her very self. We heard you'd gone away to Yorkshire to live on a pig farm."

"That was the case but it was not my choice. But I am back now and for good."

"And your son is all grown up now, I see."

"No, Tetley, you have it wrong. I am Henry Sherborne. I am heir to the Earldom of Sherborne."

Lady Merriman changed the topic of conversation, asking about the treehouse they had played in.

"Yes, Miss Eliza. I kept it in good repair, in case you and your boy came back. I know Henry Sherborne is gone in that dreadful fire but I thought you might one day come back and now I see I was right." He chuckled to himself, made to rise again, but now his wife settled him firmly back down.

"He can't walk more than a few steps, little miss," she said, renewing Lady Merriman's memory all over again with the nickname Mrs Tetley had always used for her. "We usually get him out in the garden only it gets harder to move him with my creaking bones."

"Then you need a chair with wheels that can be pushed," Lady Merriman replied. "Pushing is a lot easier than carrying, except you can't push a stubborn pig anywhere, as I know to my cost!" She promised that the estate carpenter would attend as soon as she, through Henry, instructed him.

"Thank you, Miss Eliza," they both said.

"Now, we will go alone to visit the old treehouse."

It was a short walk across a lawn, with massive cedar trees bending down as if planning to scoop up the people below and place them high in the branches.

Which was exactly where Lady Merriman wanted to be. When they reached the treehouse, she tucked her voluminous and elegant skirts up and started to climb the tree. She fell back twice, then kicked off her shoes for better grip. In an instance, she was up on the lower branches. Henry climbed up beside her.

"We have to go much higher," she said, fighting her breathlessness.

"Of course, Lady Merriman."

"You could call me Mother," she replied and they both knew it to be the truth.

Epilogue

The bridge over the Stour at Sturminster Newton opened on Easter Day 1686. Grace, Countess of Sherborne, attended with her husband, the new Earl. He had become Earl on the death of his grandfather in January. With the old Earl had died the secret of Henry's maternity.

Or at least the risk that the secret would be exposed, for Henry and his mother had reached a pact of eternal silence in the treehouse that mid-July day. They would tell no one what the Earl had divulged to Lady Merriman that morning.

For the truth of Henry's maternity would make him illegitimate and that would bar him from inheriting the Earldom.

"It's just like Monmouth, who would be King but was illegitimate," Henry had said in the treehouse while they manufactured their pact.

"Yes, but there are two differences. You're not taking the Earldom away from anyone else. If you do not inherit, it goes into abeyance, my dear son." The use of that term of endearment sent splinters of happiness into Henry, like he belonged somewhere after a childhood of wandering.

"True. And the second reason?"

"You are a good man, born of what should have been a happy marriage, if the Earl had not insisted otherwise. And you will be a good leader, both locally and in the country at large. I feel it in my bones. We are righting a wrong done long ago, Henry my dear."

They had made their pact then, mother and son reunited but determined to hide their relationship from the rest of the world.

For if it was known, he would not come into his own.

But Henry did not feel comfortable about one aspect of his inheritance. He felt no right to the Redwoods Estate in Oxfordshire, gained for the Sherborne family by forcing Lady Merriman into extreme circumstances and ruining her happiness when on the very threshold of adulthood. The family they had married into had virtually disappeared; a mixture of plague and immigration to America. Henry discussed his ideas with Grace, although not his motive for selling.

The auction raised a considerable sum, handed over as an endowment to start a free hospital in Sherborne. It left the Sherborne family desperately poor but, as Grace said:

It is not all about money.

The executions under Judge 'Bloody' Jeffries had taken their toll. Thomas was safe, despite originally joining the rebellion, for Henry had repeatedly pronounced him to be a royalist hero, even alluding to the possibility of Thomas being a spy planted in the Monmouth camp, changing sides at the critical point. It was something that could never be proved one way or the other but it gave Thomas a cloak of immunity.

It was, quite possibly, a forerunner of things to come but not for this story.

The biggest shock of the retribution for rebellion had been Luke Davenport; held to be one of the poisonous pens behind the uprising. To be fair to the minister, he was wallowing in drink when the whole project was conceived, only making his contribution once the path had been lit by Ferguson and others. But fairness did not come into it. This was a chance to cleanse the nation of radicalism; never mind that Ferguson got clear away to live and cause trouble for another few decades to come.

Luke was arrested in the pulpit on the first Sunday in August; mid-flow into a withering criticism of the 'papists who rule our Protestant country'. He was a wise but foolish man, like many who end up on the scaffold; wise for others and foolish for himself. He shouted as he was dragged down the aisle and out into the street but they were not the cries of fear; he was simply finishing the sermon they had rudely interrupted.

Eventually, his ranting faded to nothing. Matthew looked white as milk with the sudden absence of the minister. He knew exactly why his father had been taken.

And he certainly did not have the stubborn courage that his father had. His faith was as strong but perched on unsteady legs that threatened to topple the man with fear.

The entire family planned to visit their father ten days later, in Winchester Jail. They gathered at the Davenport home. Thomas and Grace had moved back in there. Elizabeth was still at Bagber Manor; Lady Merriman would not hear of her and her family leaving.

They waited patiently in the parlour for Matthew, presuming him to be in the study. After twenty minutes, Thomas went to seek him, returning with the news that he was not there.

The letter explained everything. He knew he would be next and did not have the courage of their father; Elizabeth considered the biblical overtones of this frank statement. Jesus had had the courage to follow the path set by his father, yet Matthew did not.

He had left for Holland, taking a boat from Poole. He hoped they would not mind that he took one quarter of the cash in the house; mainly the proceeds of the sermons he had helped to write. It was to pay his passage and help him 'start again'. He would write when he got there. He concluded by commending them all to Our Lord and hoped he would see his beloved family again one day.

They travelled in grim mood to Winchester; not speaking, for they knew not what to say.

The mood coming back was grimmer still for they arrived at the jail to hear the news that Pastor Davenport had died during the night. He had several sudden convulsions and then he sat up in bed, said, "My Lord, My Lord," and fell backwards. "That was the end of a fine man," the head warden informed them. He, like humans generally, was much kinder to someone once they were on the other side of the divide.

Thomas took the two girls back home and set out for Winchester again the following day to claim the body while Grace and Elizabeth made the funeral arrangements.

They boarded up the church, not knowing what to do with it. Thomas was religious but could never be a minister. Besides, he was embarking on a career as a builder; something he loved to the core.

In the dead of January, the day before the Earl died, Amelia presented a plan to the Davenport family.

"Will you consider turning your father's church into a haven for those down on their luck? Lady Merriman will give fifty pounds to set us going. If we can raise another 100, we can ensure a bed and warming food for all those with nowhere to go."

Thomas, liking the spirit he saw now in Amelia, argued on her side and even volunteered his small inheritance towards the cash they needed. Elizabeth and Grace felt it should remain a church; waiting for a new minister to take over and steer it forwards once again. But they were persuaded by Amelia and Thomas, especially when Amelia suggested their mission be named the Luke Davenport Home.

February 1686 was its first use, with a dozen borrowed beds and a cauldron of stew in an improvised kitchen. The pulpit remained in place until one evening on visiting Elizabeth discovered several small children clambering all over it. They were in the middle of a game of conquest with the pulpit the target of their endeavours. She had it removed the next day and put into their father's old study, where it sat in command, looking down at the desk and chairs around it.

Thomas did not need to use his capital for the Luke Davenport Home as Amelia and Grace raised more than sufficient. Instead, after much reflection on his father's life, thinking of the times Luke had watched over him in his illness but also how stalwart he had been about his beliefs, Thomas commissioned a special stone to be placed above the door of the old church, now home for the less fortunate. It was inscribed with the words:

Luke Davenport in the fifth quarter of his full and varied life.

When asked what it meant he shrugged and said, "It's just something between father and son." But every so often there would be a precocious child walking past who would pronounce, "You know there cannot be five quarters. Whoever put that stone up must be a bit simple."

He did not mind being called simple for he knew there were, in actual fact, five quarters to every life; it was just that most people did not recognise the fifth.

Easter Day in 1686 was bright with a breeze; promising warm weather after a harsh winter. They set up tents in the water meadows between the bridge and the mill, making both Grace and Thomas think of their time in the army camps. The town roasted several pigs and a side of a cow on giant spits, which caused a few hushed jokes about roasting Catholics; but never too loud.

At the appointed time, the local dignitaries formed up in strict seniority order on the south side of the bridge. Mr Milligan, the builder, headed them up. The Earl and countess were in the front row, along with Lady Merriman and several others. Thomas was nowhere to be seen for he was stationed under the bridge and told to keep a keen eye out for any form of movement as several tons of man and horse made their way across for the first time.

It was a precaution typical of Mr Milligan. And it proved to be completely unnecessary. The bridge held and Thomas and the others were allowed to scrabble back to join in the celebrations.

When the meat was served and mugs of beer passed out, Henry stood to make a speech. He was on the top trestle table with three other long tables forming an irregular four-sided shape that had a mathematical name but Henry could not remember it. He had never paid much attention in lessons; preferring to think of sport and running free in the woods.

His family had paid for the bridge. His family would collect the rents. Not in person but through the good offices of Mrs Bradbury and Mrs Bryant, who accepted the two new-built cottages and the salary set aside for bridge toll collectors with great pleasure.

Henry was good at spending money he did not have. Now he declared that for every shilling raised in tolls, the Luke Davenport Home should have a penny and the town council another penny, to spend as they saw fit. It was a noble gesture for someone with a crumbling seat at Sherborne Hall, rising debts and no productive lands in Oxfordshire to help pay the way.

But it helped seal a glorious day.

Lady Merriman flourished from the first day of her new lease on freedom. She surprised in several ways. Simon Taylor had improved from his stroke sufficiently to accept the position of her land agent; not managing her existing lands but seeking out bargains on new purchases. By the Easter Day party, she had just purchased two farms adjoining her estate. And Simon, now able to talk through one side of his mouth, although with some difficulty in finding the right words, had earmarked several more properties.

Nobody knew where her capital came from. They knew that she had sold the hated pig farm in Yorkshire but that would only pay for one small farm in Bagber. Nobody saw the bag of gold coins taken from under the sink in the house on Fittle Street, taken as her just wages for five years of toil.

And then she made a remarkably good land manager; planting and improving with contagious energy; profits accumulating and reinvested. Amelia watched her in wonder. For five years, when Bagber had been her father's estate, he had made miserable returns from the land, really just benefitting from the house.

Lady Merriman was born to it, that was all. It was in her blood and she knew every inch of Bagber Manor. It was as if she was making up for lost time, now that she had a new lease on freedom.

One of the new farms had a tiny rundown farmhouse. Lady Merriman had it cleaned from top to bottom, plus a new thatched roof and well. Then she showed it herself when the Thurloes from Shaftesbury came around.

"It's the least I could do after all you've gone through," Lady Merriman declared when it sank in that Mrs Thurloe was to be the new tenant.

"Of the whole farm, Lady Merriman?"

"Of the whole farm, Mrs Thurloe."

"This is too kind but..."

"But you can't run it on your own?" Lady Merriman finished her sentence for her. "I've thought of that. Until young Alfred is old enough to manage, you will have someone to help at my expense. He can teach Alfred the ways of farming as well." To

Mrs Thurloe's protestations she replied that it was only because of association with her that Parchman had killed Mr Thurloe, her head gardener at Bagber Manor. Parchman had disappeared but he would hang for it one day.

It had been a whirlwind time for Grace. She had been an ordinary girl the previous year, until she met Henry Sherborne. It was not so much the rise to aristocracy, although that was strange enough.

They had married on Christmas Day 1685. They had waited while Grace mourned her father and while she, God save her soul, took a rushed course in catechism and became a Catholic. She knew her father would never have allowed it. She knew Matthew would disapprove strongly and would try earnestly to reverse her decision the next time they met. Even Elizabeth had been shocked and would not talk about it; in fact, Grace noted that her older sister became more extreme in her Puritanism as Grace moved away from it; resetting the balance in some bizarre way.

"I'm still your sister and love you dearly, Grace, but it is a terrible thing to turn your back on Papa's teaching. Could you not have come to an arrangement with Henry and remain true to your faith? Could you not have converted him rather than be converted yourself?" It was the only time Elizabeth ever mentioned the subject.

Only Thomas was unaffected by her conversion to Catholicism. When she told him he had said, "What ho, can you pass me that set rule, sister? I want to check something on the drawing." Later on, as the news settled on him and he became aware that she sought some reassurance from him, he said he loved her whether she was a druid or a devil worshipper and nothing would change that brotherly love he held for her.

The wedded couple, thus, found a happy accommodation. Both were devout Christians but both thought it unnecessary to follow one prescribed form of worship, while castigating the other for their particular practices. They could have been Puritans just as easily as Catholics; it mattered not what the doctrine was, just that they could worship together.

Thomas was incredibly proud. He had spent eight months working day and night on the bridge, learning at a rapid rate, soaking in practices, formulas and methods. In January, he was side-tracked to build two cottages for the two bees, right across the road from the bridge. He was the foreman with a team of skilled trades reporting to him, such was the confidence that Mr Milligan had in him. He was first on site in the morning and last away at night; often he stayed long into the evening, examining the way the house was constructed or going over the costs again as he was determined to spend no more than the allowed amount yet provide a pair of houses superior in every way. He begged a carver to work extra to put the Sherborne family coat of arms above each front door. At home, his attic bedroom became a second office, with plans and schedules strewn across an old table.

In mid-February, with the weather very harsh against builders, they were slipping behind. The old Earl had negotiated a contract that penalised Mr Milligan if he was not ready on time. Thomas did not think the new Earl, his friend and brother-in-law, would demand the penalties but he did not want to be late for the big opening.

He went around each of the building workers and asked them to work extra time in March, when they hoped the weather would be better and the nights starting to get longer. To help them see in the gloom of dusk, he rigged up a lantern system.

It was expensive on oil but it got them back on track. Big Jim worked wonders during that rushed period. Not only was he always available with his horse and cart to help move materials but he also endeared himself to the workers with his jokes and banter and songs too; these erred slightly on the wrong side of respectability but were all the funnier for that.

By the time the bridge opened, Jim and Jane were getting well established as local hauliers, with a particular specialisation in moving building materials. Grace reminded him of his promise to repay debts each time they met and both Jim and Jane neatly side-stepped the question.

Thomas showed his two sisters around the evening before the opening.

"You have definitely found your calling," said Elizabeth.

He looked from the bridge to his two sisters. Elizabeth was dressed modestly in grey and white, with a bonnet covering her hair and shading much of her face; much as Grace had used to dress. But Grace was now in a gorgeous shimmering green dress with a matching hat and white feather that seemed to reach up to pierce a hole in the sky.

We are going such different ways, he thought, *yet always stick together.* We are a family.

And then the musicians struck up in practice and the three of them danced under the new leaves until they fell exhausted onto the grass by the river.

The same river that they had followed, upstream and downstream, for most of their lives. It had taken them to Bagber Manor and from Bagber onto the wider world.

Book Two:

It Takes A Rogue

In 1688, England is on the brink of something terrible. And Dorset is in the thick of it. Will James II's dictatorial policies lead to invasion by William of Orange?

Thomas Davenport, a builder, has a diminishing workload due to national uncertainty.

Henry, the new Earl of Sherborne, has a deep secret to keep. Recently married to Grace Davenport, he walks a tightrope between loyalty and rebellion.

Matthew Davenport, exiled in Holland, jumps at the opportunity to return to Dorset as a scout for the planned invasion.

The Wiltshires are rich and aristocratic. She hungers after human warmth yet is ice-like with others. This is, until she meets Lady Roakes. Together, they learn that a rogue need not stay a rogue forever.

William gains momentum, people flocking to join him, some less salubrious than others.

Ambition, love and revenge make an intriguing tale that ranges across Dorset, causing anguish, adventure and suspense.

A must-read for those looking for an exciting story set amidst the forging of modern England.

Lightning Source UK Ltd.
Milton Keynes UK
UKHW012344050419
340551UK00001B/100/P